Our Friends in Beijing

John Simpson

JOHN MURRAY

First published in Great Britain in 2021 by John Murray (Publishers)
An Hachette UK company

1

Copyright © John Simpson 2021

'Do not go gentle into that good night' from *The Collected
Poems of Dylan Thomas: The Centenary Edition* on p. 38,
reproduced by permission of the Dylan Thomas Trust

A CIP catalogue record for this title is available from the British Library

Hardback ISBN 978-1-473-67453-0
Trade Paperback ISBN 978-1-473-67454-7
eBook ISBN 978-1-473-67455-4

Typeset in Adobe Garamond by Hewer Text UK Ltd, Edinburgh
Printed and bound in Great Britain by Clays Ltd, Elcograf S.p.A.

John Murray policy is to use papers that are natural, renewable and
recyclable products and made from wood grown in sustainable forests.
The logging and manufacturing processes are expected to conform
to the environmental regulations of the country of origin.

John Murray (Publishers)
Carmelite House
50 Victoria Embankment
London EC4Y 0DZ

www.johnmurraypress.co.uk

To Dee and Rafe, my lockdown companions

一寸相思一寸灰
'For every inch of emotion, an inch of ash'
— LI SHANGYIN, 813–858

Most of the events in these pages really happened.

But don't assume that 'I', 'we' and 'they' are the
people I, we and they actually are.

1

'*What messages?*'

Her glasses glinted in the sunlight which was shafting down through the sitting-room window.

My sitting room. My window.

I stared at her pale, spotty face. This was turning into something an awful lot deeper and nastier than I could ever have expected.

'*What messages?*'

'Fuck you!'

She didn't react, but the man standing beside her did. He took half a step forward and whacked the back of my head with the business end of his heavy metal clipboard.

The room exploded around me.

'*What messages did you send?*'

I slipped off the chair, probably a bit theatrically, and started bleeding onto my favourite Badakhshan rug. Even as I lay there, waiting for the boot to go in, I felt wryly grateful that I'd bought a carpet that was brownish-red. All that haggling with the shop-keeper in Kabul had been worth it.

Then the boot connected, and I bled some more.

'*What messages?*'

She lowered her voice.

'We will hurt you much, much more, if you don't give me an answer.'

I decided that the time had come for a tactical retreat; so I made up a couple of names and invented addresses to go with them. Clipboard man wrote them all down enthusiastically. Well, I thought, you and your friends won't be so happy when you google Princess Risborough and Ken Sington.

That made me feel a bit better.

2

Twenty-four hours earlier, I'd been standing on that same blood-coloured carpet, feet apart, staring emptily out of the window at nothing very much and trying to work out how to reboot my troubled finances.

I was beginning to get a trickle of letters starting 'Dear Sir, Unless . . .'. Except they don't call you 'Sir' any more, because the modern world has become relentlessly matey. They don't even say 'Dear Mr Swift', just 'Dear Jon'. It's important not to be taken in by this: they'll still screw you just as comprehensively as they did in the days when bankers wore shiny three-piece suits and were called things like 'H. D. Harbottle, credit manager'.

I'd just decided to cancel my subscriptions to Netflix, Sky Sports and (with rather more regret) the *New Statesman*, when the mobile rang. It was someone from my freelance agency. They're nice, friendly, warm people, but in recent times they haven't been noticeably successful at getting me work. Now, though, something unexpected had happened.

'A TV station in Hong Kong's been on, asking if you'd do an interview with them about China's position in the world.'

The female voice at the other end was comfortable and motherly.

'They're offering quite a lot for just an interview – two thousand.'

That wouldn't go anywhere near to solving the problem, but it would delay the arrival of more 'Dear Jon' letters.

'Where do I have to go?'

'They'll come to you. Whenever it suits. They're keen to film you at home.'

That was a relief: television companies tend to make a big deal about where you should turn up to be interviewed, and it's usually at some unpleasant hour of the morning. I suggested an acceptable time to the motherly woman at the other end of the line, and she said she'd pass it on.

3

The crew arrived the next day, twenty minutes too early. My big yellow tabby took against them on sight, arching his back and pumping his tail to the thickness of a toilet-brush. I call him Yorick, after the skull in *Hamlet*. He doesn't hold back about his likes and dislikes.

You probably think I'm applying human characteristics to a cat because I'm a sad old case who lives on his own since his last divorce and is desperate for a bit of company. Pinpoint accuracy, of course, but that doesn't mean Yorick isn't genuinely intelligent and protective of me.

'Just ignore him,' I said affably. 'He doesn't like strangers.'

This wasn't true: I was being polite. In fact, Yorick often takes to people he doesn't know.

The leader of the team was a young, slightly built, pale, Chinese woman with glasses and a bad complexion. She wore a boy's sand-coloured shirt and stone-coloured chinos, plus a pair of fancy white trainers with sequins on them.

They'd only brought a small tourist-type video camera, which surprised me. I supposed that, like everyone else nowadays, they were keeping costs down. The cameraman, also Chinese but tall and bulky, set it up on a tripod, equally cheap, and arranged a chair for me to sit on. He wore jeans and a T-shirt that read I'M THE BOSS though he clearly wasn't.

Another Chinese man in a suit stood around holding a large clipboard. He'd begun jotting things down on it even before I'd started speaking. Also big, I noticed.

'Oxford is very beautiful.'

'Thank you,' I said, as though it had something to do with me.

She launched into a long explanation about why they were there and what they were doing. I found it hard to follow. Her accent – mainland Chinese or Hong Kong Cantonese? I couldn't tell – was pretty impenetrable. She asked me if I'd like to do the interview in Mandarin, but I decided I didn't feel up to it. Apart from anything else, I'd have to work out what I was going to say beforehand, and that was too much effort for a couple of thousand. English it would be.

The camera started turning over. Her English improved noticeably.

'How is China seen in the world?' 'Is China regarded as a superpower?' 'Will people in Europe soon start to learn Chinese language and culture?'

It was rapid-fire stuff, and I quickly switched to autopilot. All you usually have to do in these things is make a few soothing comments, and the interviewers go away happy.

I droned on. 'The more China understands that nowadays it's in a position of responsibility, and should start to take on some of the burden of helping with the problem of international debt . . .'

I was even starting to bore myself.

At that point, through the mental fug I'd worked up around me, an entirely new tone, fierce and sharp, cut through. Her English suddenly got even better.

'I think you have had contact with many officials in mainland China.'

'Well, yes, over the years.'

'Please, you name some.'

I did.

'But I think you also know Mr Lin Lifang.'

I'd left him off the list because I knew him rather well, and didn't want to get him into trouble.

'Mr Lin is famous in China for his toughness and authority. Do you think he has an important future in Chinese politics?'

I waffled, but I could see she was determined to get something specific out of me about Lin. Alarm bells started going off in my mind.

'He is already a member of the State Council. Do you think he'll be one of China's top leaders soon?'

Hong Kong journalists were still quite outspoken in those happy days before the Chinese clampdown, but this seemed to be going beyond the call of duty.

I didn't say anything.

'There are those who think he will organise some kind of political coup in China,' she went on. 'Do you agree?'

I backed away from that as fast as I could, but she wouldn't give up.

'Mr Lin has been in Oxford recently. Did you meet him while he was here?'

You obviously know I did, I thought, so I said, 'Well, I just bumped into him by chance. His daughter is starting at my old college . . . Brasenose,' I added, thinking 'Try translating that into Chinese.'

'And did he ask you to pass on any messages?'

I started to get up, but the large man taking notes changed his grip on the clipboard and swung it round in my direction. It whacked me in the throat, over the Adam's apple, and I choked. Horribly painful. I collapsed back into the chair, unable for the moment to produce a sound. All I could do was gasp.

The thin young woman just carried on, as though things like this happened in all the television interviews she was involved in. Perhaps they did.

'What messages were they?'

I recovered my voice a little, and made a rasping noise. The clipboard changed sides and cracked me with shocking pain on the back of the neck. A reddish cloud came in front of my eyes. I stopped shouting.

'No messages,' I grunted.

'I think there was.'

'No, you should say "I think there *were*."'

She looked up at the clipboard-wielder, and he whacked me really hard again, just at the base of the skull. Brilliant colours erupted in front of my eyes, and I gave a dry retch.

Still, the grammar lesson hadn't gone entirely to waste.

'I think there were.'

That was the point when I slipped off the chair and started bleeding onto my Badakhshan carpet.

Clipboard man kicked me in the ribs, three or four times, hard enough to lift my fairly heavy body an inch or so each time.

'We will continue like this until you tell me what messages, and who you sent them to,' said the young woman, leaning over me.

I started groaning fairly convincingly. The blood was certainly genuine.

'All right, all right, I'll tell you,' I grunted, acting the part of the broken interrogatee and feeling rather clever. 'He asked me to pass on his good wishes to two of his best contacts in Britain, and to tell them he wanted to meet them in London. One' – was I overacting now? – 'is a leading socialite who works for the Queen at Buckingham Palace. Her name is Princess Risborough.'

I looked up. No flicker of anything on the pasty white face. It made me bolder.

'And the other is a hugely rich businessman who controls the reinsurance business in the City of London. His name is Sington. Ken Sington.'

I added a couple of cod addresses, which I made up on the spot. Somehow I don't imagine there actually is a Balaclava Road in Knightsbridge.

Surely I'd gone too far? But no, they seemed to swallow it. Clipboard man wrote it all down with enthusiasm. I had the impression I'd injected an element of uncertainty into their minds. So now I came out with the outraged householder bit.

'. . . How dare you come in here and attack me in my own home?'

The clipboard hit me on the side of the neck, but either because I was a more difficult target at this height, or because they were starting to think they'd got what they came for, it didn't hurt so much.

At that point the cameraman joined in with his tripod; but it was one of those feeble, spindly ones, and the camera fell off when he swung it for the second time.

I gave a laugh, not an entirely phoney one, and started to get up. The one person I could reach easily at that point was the cameraman, and I caught him with the side of my fist, right over the ear. I can't deny it felt good.

And now Yorick belatedly started yowling in a freakish kind of way, zooming round the room at speed, looking like something out of a Goya Black painting.

For some reason this really seemed to scare them. The woman shouted something wildly in a cracked voice. The cameraman and clipboard man grabbed their stuff and all three fled through the house and out through the front door.

9

'And don't fucking come back,' I yelled hoarsely as they threw themselves into their car and screeched away.

That gave the neighbours something to think about; though since most of them were students they were probably still asleep. It was only midday.

4

When I slammed the front door shut, I turned and found Yorick standing in the hall with his back arched, the heroic defender of house and home.

'Well done,' I said enthusiastically, and rubbed his head and ears. Then we went into the kitchen.

I opened a tin of smoked oysters, spooned them into a bowl and then set it in front of him. That made my head hurt horribly, so I took a swig from a nearby bottle of Jameson's. And since it seemed unreasonable to keep it all to myself, I sloshed some into his milk. Yorick likes Jameson's. I stood there, watching him slurp it up.

'Maybe, as a special reward,' I promised him grandly, 'I won't get your balls cut off.'

After that I went into the bathroom and tended my injuries, making sympathetic noises to myself in the mirror.

Later, I rang the freelance agency. The people there are busy and no doubt have problems of their own, so I didn't tell the understanding lady who'd rung before what had just happened. Instead I asked her for the name of the television station that had contacted her. She checked her notes.

'Tsim Sha Tsui Television News,' she said, pronouncing it all wrong. 'Hong Kong.'

'Let me know when they pay up, won't you?' I really meant 'if'. It didn't seem overwhelmingly likely that they would.

'Will do, dear,' she said cheerily, and rang off.

Tsim Sha Tsui is an area of southern Kowloon, just across Victoria Harbour from Central. I used to get my shirts made by a tailor in a little side street there, in the days when Hong Kong was still cheap.

Maybe there *is* a commercial TV station based in the area and I just haven't heard of it, I thought generously, but nothing of the kind showed up on Google – just a slew of restaurants and small local businesses including, inevitably, a range of massage parlours.

No happy ending then, I said out loud. I didn't laugh, because that would have made my neck hurt.

Keeping secrets isn't my thing – I'm a journalist, after all – but even so I couldn't think of anyone I could share this with. If I told my boss, he'd call corporate health and safety, and the security people, and maybe the police; and who knew where that might lead?

There wasn't really anyone else to tell. I'd been self-isolating long before Covid came along, you see. Nowadays there's just me and Yorick. I have a reasonably good relationship with my most recent ex-wife, even though I can't abide her new boyfriend, a Bentley dealer. She'd freak out if I told her, and Bentley would sneer and say, 'Well, what can you expect?'

Right now I needed a doctor. So I thought of Richard, just round the corner. He always did what he could to prepare me for difficult trips abroad, and patched me up when I got back afterwards; let's regard this as a more than usually arduous trip, I thought.

5

The receptionist said he'd see me at 6.30; which meant he'd be finished with the day's patients and would delay his journey home for my sake. Richard is funny and unshockable, and the only thing wrong with him is that he's thin and takes a lot of exercise. I prefer my doctors overweight and inclined to take a drop or two too many: that way they have less of a moral hold over me.

'Well, you've had some nasty knocks,' he said after walking round me and moving my head in directions it didn't want to go. 'But you seem to be pretty intact. Want to tell me what happened?'

I told him as much as I thought I should, so I didn't mention Hong Kong or messages from important Chinese politicians. But I did say I'd been thumped up by people posing as a Chinese camera crew. Richard tactfully didn't probe.

'If it's something about China,' he said slowly, 'I've got a patient at one of the colleges who seems to have some important connections there.'

'Such as?'

'No idea. But here's his name and email address.'

Richard is a deep old file; he wouldn't just pull something out of the air in a case like this. I took the bit of paper and said I'd make contact. Then I went home. Yorick's tail was still fluffed up, but he greeted me with enthusiasm. Perhaps he'd understood the bit about the balls.

6

I knew perfectly well what the whole thing had been about.

A week or so earlier, you see, an apparent coincidence had happened in my life. The young interviewer from the non-existent television station had been entirely correct: one of the most powerful people in the People's Republic of China had indeed turned up, together with his glamorous daughter, at my favourite Oxford watering hole. And he'd asked me to pass on a message for him.

I detest coincidences. I prefer to believe that my life is regulated by pure unadulterated chance; coincidences give the impression that something much more disturbing is going on.

Anyway, on a pleasant autumn day in Oxford, a week or so before my unpleasant introduction to the non-existent Tsim Sha Tsui TV, I headed out for a pre-lunch drink. The sun shone blindingly out of a brilliant blue sky but it was one of those days when the air develops a sharp edge, so you have to take gloves with you as well as a coat. I yanked my front door open and with a deftly placed foot blocked Yorick from escaping. He seems to think he's in the animal equivalent of Stalag Luft III.

I ambled up St Giles' and into the Banbury Road, enjoying the glow of the limestone college buildings in the sunlight. Just past the church I ducked through a stone gateway: the entrance to a pleasant old hotel. You can't miss it. It's right opposite one of the ugliest buildings known to man, housing among other things the university astrophysics department – designed in the 1970s at the time when even architects were starting to wonder if brutalism was really quite the thing after all.

And there, sitting at a courtyard table, was a character in his mid-fifties, dressed in a fur-collared, camel-haired coat which had clearly cost a bundle. He was talking to a particularly attractive Chinese woman in a dark red coat which made her look like some exotic tropical plant.

The pair of them were like the hotel and the physics building opposite: beauty in the face of ugliness. And the interesting thing was, I'd known the man in the coat for nearly thirty years, ever since he was a scrawny student in a T-shirt. Now that really was a coincidence.

7

You've probably read about Lin Lifang. He's a rich, clever, successful, deeply unscrupulous Chinese politician, and a lifelong anglophile. In my experience these things tend to go together. Don't ask me why: I'm Irish. At any rate when it suits me.

He sat there, holding a glass of nicely tinted Bollinger in a pair of light leather gloves that almost but not quite matched the champagne, looking highly intelligent and a bit saurian, with sharp, unblinking eyes and a baggy throat.

He'd had his teeth done since I'd seen him last. They used to be as irregular as a Sichuan farm fence, and almost as brown; now they were startlingly white and perfectly even. Seeing Lin's new mouth was like opening your bedroom curtains and finding it's snowed in the night. I suppose he wanted to look good on television. He was very important, and people said he would soon be more important still.

'Mister Jon Swift, as I live and breathe.'

His English was only a degree or two short of excellent, and he was deeply proud of being able to come up with expressions like this; I think he must have watched too many British films from the 1960s and 1970s. Especially the costume ones.

'I don't believe it,' I said. The difference was that I really was surprised. 'Lin – Lin Lifang. Are you following me around?'

'Oh yes, that really *is* extremely likely.'

The self-effacing yet bantering tone: he'd got the Englishness of it exactly. In fact he made a better Brit than most of those who carry the passport – though I expect he carried one anyway. He was rich enough.

'But listen, you must meet my daughter Lily. My dear, this is a very well-known Britisher indeed: Mr Jon Swift, the famous broadcaster. There's no "h" in "Jon", by the way. If you put one in when you say it, he's inclined to get annoyed.'

And he laughed the creaking khazi-door laugh he'd always had, even as a student. You can get your teeth done, but there's nothing you can do about your laugh.

Who says 'Britisher' nowadays, apart from elderly Indians and Pakistanis, and maybe the occasional Singaporean? But what struck me was the half-spiteful tone that was buried in his words, like a detonator plugged into an inert mass of plastic explosive. He must have known I'd come down in the world – that I'd had problems with my old organisation, had been lucky to grab hold of a lifeboat from a rival outfit and been hauled aboard, only to come to grief a second time. And he couldn't help rubbing it in.

Well, it had been all over the British newspapers ('TV Jon: My bosses are so ageist'), which is probably where he'd heard about it. Or maybe I was just being ultra-sensitive. When you're down on your luck you start seeing insults and sarcasm in perfectly innocent things people say.

Still, Mr Lin had never been perfectly innocent in his life. Not even, I'd wager, when he was five days old and trying to work out the route to his mother's nipple. He heard everything, computed everything, and made his moves accordingly. As I say, he was more than a touch saurian. And yet I had a real affection for him, because of our past relationship – though I didn't believe he did anything by accident.

'I imagine you're wondering why we're here,' he said smoothly; and while I was still making it-never-occurred-to-me sounds he went on: 'You see, Lily has just got a place at Brasenose. To read molecular biology.'

At least I think that's what he said she was going to read; I'm not fantastically good at differentiating between the sciences, being a classicist myself. And not a very good one.

'She gets her abilities from her mother. As you'll no doubt recall, I was a very plodding student.'

He wasn't just an expert at self-deprecation, he weaponised it. I'd often noticed that while he appeared to be mocking himself he was in fact getting at me in some obscure way.

'I don't think you've ever plodded anywhere, Lifang,' I answered, then realised not only that this was what he'd hoped I would say, but why: he wanted his daughter to see how highly he was esteemed by someone she might be impressed by.

So I decided to attach a small explosive charge of my own to the conversation. 'You just move very carefully before launching an attack.'

Get out of that one, I thought, but he decided to treat it as a compliment.

'Jon here is a descendant of the great Jonathan Swift, my dear – the Irish arch-satirist.'

I was sitting down at their table by this stage, so he leaned over and said in a faux-confidential way, 'My daughter is interested only in the sciences. The beauties of literature, English or indeed Chinese, are a closed book to her. Literally, I can say.'

'Oh, *Bà*!' said Lily in mock-exasperated fashion. *Bà* means 'daddy', by the way.

I could see she'd inherited a full supply of her father's bantering style. She smiled suddenly, like the sunshine, and her teeth, naturally or otherwise, were white and even. She hadn't inherited those from him, anyway. If only all molecular biologists looked like her, I thought, I'd have spent my entire student career in a lab.

'*I* went to Brasenose,' I said.

Actually I find all that Oxbridge college crap pretty irritating nowadays ('You must have known old So-and-so, he was up in your time – I think he was president of the Footlights') but I hoped, pathetically, that it might impress her: such is the absurd lack of self-awareness of your average sixtyish male, who hasn't yet realised that a nineteen-year-old woman is as likely to be physically attracted to him as to an unwrapped mummy in the Ashmolean.

We did the usual 'What did you read?' stuff, and droned on about how useful or otherwise classics was, and how the college had changed in forty years, and how many Chinese students there were at Oxford nowadays, and what they went on to do in life after they'd graduated.

But all the time I was thinking about something entirely different: that Lin Lifang had been expecting to bump into me. His bons mots sounded pre-prepared, like the *jus* that a cook gets ready before he turns his attention to the joint. If I was right, that meant he must have known my likely movements.

As a result, I started to feel I was playing a bit-part in some grand plan Lin had been working up. Come to think of it, he'd always made me feel a bit like that. Lin is an extremely clever man. If anyone was a plodder it was me.

A strapping young Spanish waiter came out and took our order: more coffee for Lily – I could see the poor goop was fixated on her

– another glass of Bollie for Lin, and the first G-and-slimline of the day for me.

'Make sure it's Toad, if you can,' I said, Toad being a local make of gin. The waiter said something distractedly in a Spanish accent, presumably about seeing whether they had it in the bar, and went off.

The late autumn sun came out and shone on us like Lily's smile. It made me feel unusually clear-headed.

'So why do I have the feeling that you were expecting to see me here?'

'Was I?' Lin turned to his daughter. '*Was* I?'

God, his English was good: not simply the words, but the intonation. He must have spent thousands getting it to this pitch.

'Well, you never said anything about it to me if you did.'

Her English had also cost thousands, but in her case the cash had been spent on one of those ultra-expensive British boarding schools where the girls go around in dark-blue tartan skirts, laugh too loudly and play a lot of netball. I listened carefully: to get vowel sounds like those, she must have arrived in Britain at the age of eight or nine. Money well spent, though as an old-fashioned leftie I disapproved, naturally.

Yet these two products of the People's Republic, sitting in the sunshine outside the hotel and sipping their drinks, regarded paying for an education as being utterly natural and essential. And by God they had the money; you do, if you're a senior figure in China's political hierarchy. Ever since Mao, fat, old and toothless, turned his face to the wall, riddled with the STDs he'd caught from his teenage concubines, Chinese communism has been about as Marxist as John D. Rockefeller's Standard Oil.

8

Lin had evolved from a rebellious student marching round Tiananmen Square to a faithful scion of the Chinese Communist Party. The fact that his dad was a senior Party official, an elderly mucker of Mao's and a Long Marcher from day one, wasn't unconnected with this progression. Over the years, my friend had rebelled, recanted, been rewarded with junior office, shown his quality in difficult places, been given even more difficult tasks, and excelled in them, too. Jobs don't come much more difficult in China than trying to run Xinjiang, with its huge population of maltreated, resentful Muslims.

Along the way, I'd bumped into him several times. Our first reunion happened after I saw in the Chinese press that he was making a success of being the mayor of a medium-sized city in north-eastern China. It was one of the lower rungs of political power, but he had a gift for attracting attention.

Looking at him in the autumn sunlight of Oxford, I could see how well he'd done.

'So how's the beloved party of workers and peasants, then?'

If it hadn't been for the presence of the lovely young woman in dark red, I might have added 'and corrupt bureaucrats?'.

'About as good as the admirable land of hope and glory,' said Lin equably.

You can't beat him on the insult game: he spots what you're likely to say while the thoughts are still formulating in your mind. I felt the delightful Lily was getting switched off by this exchange, though, so I brought it to a halt.

'Here for long?'

'I have to see Lily installed at Brasenose, then I've got some calls to make here in Oxford, and after that in London and Manchester. Edinburgh too. Sadly, I shan't be visiting your native heath this time.'

He meant Ireland, though I don't go there much myself nowadays: my elder brother still runs the decayed family estate in County Louth, but we don't really get on. Apart from anything else, I can't bear being freezing cold in bed at night, or having dogs sticking their noses into my crotch when I'm trying to enjoy an after-dinner glass of thirty-year-old Irish whiskey.

'Would you have got in touch with me, if I hadn't bumped into you?'

'But of course. You're the only person I know in Oxford, aside from a couple of principals of colleges.'

God, he was good. There are plenty of MPs and barristers who wouldn't have got the terminology right. Not to mention a newsroomful of sub-editors.

Oxford is classier than most bits of London, and a hell of a lot cheaper than my old stamping ground in Chelsea. And somehow it gives people the impression that you must spend most of your time studying in the Bodleian with a pile of books in front of you.

I'm loosely attached to my old college, so I go and eat and drink there rather well and remarkably cheaply, chaffing the dons. Or being chaffed by them.

'You must come and have dinner with me at high table.'

I already knew the answer he'd give, though.

'Yes, well, I'm frightfully sorry but I'm pretty much booked up this week. I've got to go to Magdalen and Trinity, and after that I have to hurry back to see our friends in Beijing.'

Of course. A Chinese government minister nearing the very top of the system isn't going to be short of a dinner or two at Oxford. Let's just say it wasn't likely he'd be hanging around alone in his suite at the Randolph, dialling room service and watching soft porn.

How things change, I thought. There had been a time when this man had looked at me as if he worshipped me. But that was in a different place, and a very different period in history. And now here he was, making me feel distinctly uneasy, as though he'd worked out plans for me that he wouldn't get round to explaining for some time to come. Not necessarily nice plans.

9

He'd filled out, he was beautifully dressed, and had a palpably good opinion of himself. Plus a daughter who'd do credit to a billionaire. When I had the chance to let my eyes wander a little, I spotted a bulky Chinese forty-year-old in a blue suit sitting at a distant table, trying to keep his eyes off us. I might have known that Lin Lifang, the grand Party boss, would take a bodyguard with him wherever he went, like a fashion accessory.

'Do you feel you're in actual danger, here in Oxford?'

I was only trying to needle him, and I succeeded. He looked down at his empty coffee cup.

'No danger,' he said quietly, though I had the impression he was saying this for Lily's benefit. 'But it's true I'd like some help from you.'

And then, as if he felt the need to be a little warmer and more personal, he added, 'Again.'

I digested that for a bit, and liked it. But I said, 'So bumping into you isn't entirely a coincidence, then.'

'I suppose not, no.'

Well, Oxford's a small place, and I have my rat runs, like everyone else. I'm not hard to find. Anyone who knew me, or followed me, would have been aware that I tended to hang out at the bar of this particular hotel fairly regularly.

'Lily,' he said brightly, 'would you just give me a moment with my old friend Jon? Nothing to trouble you with, my dear.'

She uncurled herself and made her elegant way indoors with apparent reluctance.

'I'll be frank. The gentleman sitting over there isn't really a bodyguard, though he was presented to me as such. Wished on me, shall I say? I have good reason to think that he's actually with me to keep me under observation. Things are happening back home, you see. Boiling up. And I'm not as all-powerful as I would like to be.'

I made understanding and sympathetic noises.

'There's someone I'm supposed to pass a message to, but it's proving unexpectedly difficult. I can't do it from the hotel, or from my mobile phone, and that fellow over there goes with me wherever I go. Plus I don't want to do it in front of Lily. You're really the only chap I can trust.'

I was rather moved, but before I could say anything he went on.

'No need to go into details, but it's just a phone number and a single word, plus another thing, very small. How's your memory these days? Think you can remember everything if I go through it? Without writing anything down, I mean: writing it down would definitely be a mistake.'

Like most people of my age, I'm inclined to forget things: friends' birthdays, where I parked my car, wives. But working for television means that I can keep certain things in my mind for a short period with some clarity: that's the beauty of having had to memorise thousands of pieces to camera over the years. So yes, I thought I could do that, and told him so.

'Good man,' said Lin Lifang patronisingly; the balance between us had changed greatly over the years.

I'm not going to tell you what the phone number was, naturally, but it was thirteen digits long. The idea was that I should ring it from somewhere other than my house or my mobile phone, and give the person who answered a word, plus some other stuff. The word was 'Excalibur'.

'Oh for Christ's sake, Lifang. You've got to be a bit more imaginative than that.'

He laughed, though I had the impression it was more for the benefit of the man in the blue suit than because he thought it was funny.

'Well, well, and here was me thinking you'd enjoy a reference from Monty Python.'

And, God help us, he launched into a not wholly inaccurate version of a Python song, in his creaky voice. The goon sitting a few tables away looked startled.

I laughed aloud. Presumably that was the effect he wanted. Out of the corner of my eye I saw blue suit look away, as though he was bored.

'Go over it again.'

I went over it again, and got it number-perfect. Lin sang the song again, and when he stopped I repeated the number and the word 'Excalibur' a third time. It was thoroughly lodged in my brain. As a matter of fact I could still quote it to you today.

But there was something else. With people like Lin, there always is.

'Oh yes, and I need you to play the sound from a little gizmo down the phone line. I've got it in my pocket. It's frightfully easy. You just press the green "go" button while holding it in front of the mouthpiece. It'll only last about ten seconds. When Lily comes back I'll go to the loo, and I'll leave it under the thing that holds the toilet brush. Just get rid of it somewhere carefully after you've played the sound over the phone.'

He smiled and reached out his hand to me as I stood up.

'I don't suppose we'll bump into each other again on this trip, but I hope to invite you to Beijing at some point to express my full thanks.'

Why invite me to Beijing when his power base was in Huzhang? He must have some pretty ambitious plans for the future, I thought.

Precisely on cue, Lily emerged from the hotel, and Lin went inside to the loo. Lily and I talked in a desultory way while he was gone. It was a bit awkward. Finally, Lin reappeared, and I stood up.

'It was great to bump into you both,' I said, trying to sound natural for blue-suit's sake. 'It's been a real pleasure meeting you,' I said to Lily.

And to Lin I said, 'And I look forward at some stage to coming to China and seeing you there.'

'Absolutely, old chap. It was really our good luck to meet you like this. Remarkable coincidence.'

10

I wandered into the hotel, exerting all my willpower so as not to look in blue-suit's direction. But out of the corner of my eye I could see he was standing up too, and following Lin and Lily through the gateway to the Banbury Road.

The gizmo wasn't difficult to find, tucked underneath the toilet brush holder: a little black job like an electronic car key, with one red and one green button on it and nothing else; not even the discreet name of a manufacturer. Guess why.

I headed home down St Giles'. Might as well do it straight away, I thought. Not far from my house there's a phone box, which has been liberally used over the years as a urinal by people whose sensibilities must be too great for them to be able to pee openly in the street. I pulled the door open, and waited a few seconds for the smell to subside.

Then I dialled the number. A woman's voice, with what might have been a Geordie accent, answered.

'General information.'

'I've got a message to pass on.'

'Just one moment.'

I assume she pressed a button of some kind.

'Go ahead, caller.'

Feeling awkward, I said 'Excalibur.'

I half-expected her to say something like: 'I'm sorry, no one of that name here' or 'Are you trying to be funny?'

Not a bit of it.

'Continue.'

I'd already fished the gadget out of my pocket, and now I pointed it into the mouthpiece of the phone and pressed the green button, as Lin had told me to do. It emitted a tiny screeching sound, like an old-fashioned tape deck used to when you did something wrong to it. The sound only lasted three seconds, and then it was finished. I'm no spy, and no electronic specialist either, but I assume it was a recorded voice message played at immense speed – the kind of thing someone could play back at the proper speed later. The amazing thing was how quick and easy it was.

'Message received and registered,' said the Geordie woman. 'Goodbye, caller.'

Click.

And that was it. I let the door of the phone box close, and commenced breathing through my nose again. Down the little side street I dropped the gizmo on the ground, and stamped on it. A tiny disc fell out. I picked up the various bits and distributed them among a trio of bins that some rate-payer had left outside their front garden. I tried to break the little disc in half, but I couldn't even bend it. I dropped it down a nearby drain, and then, for the second time, I let out a long breath.

I'd done my duty by old Lin. And he'd trusted me with the knowledge that he had a link to what must have been some kind of intelligence network: presumably, but not of course necessarily, British.

Maybe you think that, as a journalist, I should immediately have rung my editor and started preparing an exclusive report on Lin and his dodgy links. Well, I'm sorry, but I'm not that kind of journalist. Lin had given me the power of life and death over himself because he believed he could trust me.

And, thinking of the skinny twenty-three-year-old he'd once been, I knew he could. He might have gone up in the world since then, and become a bit superior along the way, but I wasn't going to let him down. And if you think that's betraying the sacred faith of journalism, then all I can say is you can't ever have read a newspaper or watched a bulletin on television.

11

'I always promised I'd let you know if I didn't think our arrangement was working, so I thought the time had come for us to have a chat.'

It was six days on from my Tsim Sha Tsui experience, and the wounds were healing. I could even turn my head a little. I'd put it around that I'd fallen off my bike: except that I don't have one.

We were in the room at work that I always thought of as the punishment cell; I'd had various bollockings there over the years. Sitting opposite me was my boss, looking like some self-satisfied prefect from my schooldays: too young for the job, too lucky, too inclined to ascribe the luck to his abilities.

'Oh, ah.'

It seemed the only safe response. And, surprisingly, it seemed to work: he was visibly shoved off course. He'd been steeling himself for the likelihood that I'd either rage at him or beg for mercy, and either would have made me easier to deal with. Instead he had to carry on the conversation himself.

His name was Charles, and as we used to say back in County Louth, a bigger bollix never put his arm through a coat. Before his present job he'd worked for another unfortunate outfit, before being booted out by its owner.

We were impressed by his looks and youth and quick mind, and thought he'd do great things for us. And when he didn't, we assumed it was our fault. As an organisation we always seem to behave like one of those sweet, unattractive young women who manages to land a bloke and ascribes all sorts of wonderful qualities to him before he dumps her. Usually by text message.

Charles didn't like sacking people face-to-face, so when he came to us he'd brought his own personal executioner with him. This character was pleasant enough, but started every conversation about getting rid of people or cutting back on their pay with the words 'I'm really sorry about this, but . . .' Apparently the revolutionary who oversaw the guillotining of Marie Antoinette said something similar to her as she stood there at the foot of the scaffold, with shit on her skimpy dress and her head shorn. And she, poor thing, with her habitual clumsiness, managed to step on his foot when she climbed up the steps to the guillotine. Not a good start when it's positively your final appearance.

Brian was the name of Charles's hired executioner, and we had a tenuous link in the fact that we both supported the same football club. But I didn't want to talk about football, and I didn't want to be told he was sorry, but . . . If Charles wanted to get rid of me, I told him, Charles would have to tell me to my face.

Hence this awkward meeting. Some pathetic eejit from Admin was sitting beside him, making notes on her iPad. Notes about what? I kept determinedly stumm, and she can't surely have been writing down all the meaningless stuff he launched into, about how he admired everything I had ever done for the organisation and how wonderful I'd always been.

My eyes wandered, like my attention. The organisation had spent huge amounts on building its new headquarters, but some key figure had sited the corner office where the most important meetings took place on the ground floor. That meant that every employee who'd slipped out for a crafty smoke would lean against the wall outside the windows, puffing away and staring in when there was nothing better to look at. There were a couple of them now, peering in at me.

'So your time with us will terminate in June. And of course there'll be a substantial redundancy payment. Katarzyna' – he was the only person in the entire place who could get his mouth round her name in the way they did in old Gdansk – 'can you just work it out for Jon?'

'Yes, of course, Charles,' she said with an ingratiating smile, and started piloting the iPad. It took her a moment, so I allowed myself to think what I'd spend the money on. My debts? Or a second-hand Morgan, maybe?

'Two thousand and forty-six pounds. Plus some pence.'

She looked up, smiling at me this time.

12

I was still quivering when I slipped into the George around the corner, and ordered a triple Jameson's.

'You look like you could do with it,' said the New Zealander behind the bar.

I ignored him, and put down the firewater as fast as my gullet could take it.

Two thousand quid. Wankers. Utter, utter wankers. I said it out loud, for effect.

'That's OK, mate. It's what we're here for. Look on us as a branch of the NHS.'

I grinned, but didn't say anything. What was there to say?

The door creaked open, and my producer came in: a tall, athletic-looking thirty-seven-year-old in a nicely cut outfit and running shoes. Her name was Alyssa Roberts, and she came from Lewisham. Her mum was a Nigerian princess from Kaduna, apparently. The only time I was in Kaduna, everyone I met seemed to be a prince or princess, so maybe Alyssa's mum was too. That could explain Alyssa's regal carriage and grand manner. Don't think I wasn't secretly impressed by it all, in spite of being Irish, and therefore an instinctive republican. OK, it's complicated.

'So – not good?'

We'd been in this position before, Alyssa and I, but we'd been saved by some clever footwork and an exclusive about Russia, which had got us a job with our present organisation, the outfit that was now trying to throw me off the rooftop.

'I'm sorry.'

She put her handsome, beringed hand on mine, and gave it a squeeze.

Let me say quickly that however much I would have liked it, there was nothing whatsoever between us. More's the pity. Alyssa was engaged to a tall and, now I came to think of it, tough-looking character who was some sort of broker in the City. Rich, therefore, as well as being young and in good shape.

Still, she had reason to be worried as well. She, and a vast, jovial South African cameraman called Os – 'ox' in Afrikaans – had come with me from our previous job as part of a package. Since I was being given the shove, you could bet that someone was looking to see if they couldn't be got rid of as well. And it was no good saying that Alyssa and Os should stay because they were both excellent at their jobs. The ranks had to be thinned.

Of course they preferred to cull old white Oxbridge-educated males like me, because we were expensive and unfashionable: 'Oxbridge' was a term of abuse nowadays. Os was in his fifties, and there wasn't any doubt about his whiteness and maleness, so they'd probably pinned a target on his back as well. It would be harder to chuck Alyssa out because she ticked a couple of useful boxes.

Alyssa and I had talked all this over before. Os too, though he was an uncomplicated character who didn't worry about things too much.

There was a loud door sound and he loomed over us.

I ordered some drinks, and we sat there in silence for a while after I'd passed the news on.

'Well, I can always go back and make wildlife docs in the Kruger.'

If he did, I thought, they'd be the best thing the Kruger National Park had ever seen.

The most positive sign was that Charles hadn't sent either of them his fussy little messages saying 'Please call Phoebe', Phoebe being the enviably gorgeous six-foot PA who arranged the auto-da-fés.

'I can't believe I'm still stuck in this bloody dead end,' I said, 'apologising all the time for my age and where I was educated, while they proceed to saw my balls off.'

I was on my third double, and well into the self-pitying stage. Alyssa was drinking a shandy. Os preferred to knock back a brandy and Coke.

And then I said the words which would change my whole life.

'Why don't we use my last three months to do some documentary stuff in China?'

At this time, you see, all anyone seemed to want to know about was Brexit: not my area of expertise at all, thank God. I didn't think it'd be noticed if we slipped out of the country and headed off to Beijing for a nice long time.

Suddenly I felt completely free. The guillotine blade had fallen now, so there'd be no need to be on my guard for emails entitled something fairly innocuous: 'The Future', perhaps, or 'The Way Forward' – something that wouldn't provoke me into deleting it unread, which I do with most emails likely to contain bad news.

As for everyone else, well, they behaved like GPs from the *Dr Finlay's Casebook* era – they'd say anything rather than tell you to your face you'd got terminal cancer. And they were so very relieved and grateful if you accepted your death sentence quietly and just went home.

Not me. 'Do not go gentle into that good night' was my watch-word. Not that I'm a big fan of Dylan Thomas: all that airy-fairy stream of consciousness *hwyl* irritates me. But I accept that he got some things right. And of course he used to drink, monumentally, at the George, the very pub where I was having this counsel-of-war with Alyssa and Os.

'Why China?'

'It's a long story. But I think something's going to happen there. Quite soon.'

'Something?'

'Yes. No idea what, really, but it'd probably be worth our while to be there.'

'I'll start making arrangements.'

She was a dear girl. I just wished she wouldn't explode in a shower of sparks when I told her so.

13

I opened a tin of mackerel so Yorick could dine in style. It was a messy business; not to mention the smell. I'd left him alone all day, and he needed a bit of entertainment. As I wrenched off the lid, endangering my fingers, my eye rested on a yellow Post-it note I'd stuck on the fridge. The fridge door was almost entirely covered in little squares of yellow and pink paper with my Linear B scrawl on them. Reading them is like the archaeology of my social life; most are long out of date. This one, though, had the email address of the China expert Dr Richard had written down for me.

When I'd washed the mackerel juice off my hands, I opened my laptop and wrote to ask if he'd see me. His address ended in 'magd.ox.ac.uk', so I knew it was one of the grandest colleges in the university: Magdalen, which is so big it has its own deer park and an outside stone pulpit in the main quadrangle so a preacher can address the assembled crowds. Going there makes me feel like a country bumpkin come to town.

'Tea at the SCR tomorrow? 4 p.m.?' was the China expert's terse reply, half an hour later. That stands for 'Senior Common Room', and whenever you go there someone tells you it's where Richard III sat after dinner on the night when the Princes in Tower got theirs. He stopped off at Magdalen in order to provide himself with a watertight alibi.

All those paintings, all that history, all that brain power. It scares me shitless.

One of the brains was sitting there as I came in, and waved to me pleasantly. It was the China expert.

'Whitaker – Peter Whitaker. I recognise you from the telly, naturally.'

You'd think that by now this kind of thing wouldn't affect me. Wrong. It cheers me up no end.

I told him some of what had happened, and left out the rest. I mentioned my recent encounter with Lin Lifang, but obviously said nothing whatever about the number in London and the word 'Excalibur'. But I couldn't help boasting about the length of time I'd known Lin. Whitaker grinned; maybe he thought I was making it up.

'Well, your old friend is becoming seriously interesting.'

He leaned back and sipped his Earl Grey.

'I think what he's doing is to offer himself as an alternative to the current leadership. He's built up a sizeable war chest, and he's got a great many allies – people who've been offended or slighted in some way by the top men, and want to get their own back. And I fancy the moment is coming quite soon when he'll make his challenge.'

There was a great deal more along these lines, but I won't burden you with it. For an academic who only got to China once every two years, Peter Whitaker's information was formidably good. After a couple more rounds of Darjeeling, three Marie biscuits and the refusal of a G and T before dinner (unusual for me, but I was anxious to keep all the stuff he'd been telling me in my head), he came to the point.

'The key to it all is the money. And your friend Lin's wife, Madame Jade, holds the key to that. She's a bit of a man-eater.

No, seriously. I've only met her once, but I know someone who's quite – well, close to her. Martin Prinsett. He's clever and connected, though probably not quite as clever or connected as he likes to make out. That's a common characteristic, I find.'

And he laughed at me. I couldn't help laughing back, of course.

14

Martin Prinsett was in London for a while, so I invited him to lunch at my favourite watering hole there: Malone's, off St Martin's Lane. My shout, of course; the old days of expense-account lunches have gone the way of most of the people who used to eat them.

Prinsett was already sitting in the bar, even though I was early. He was on his second glass of champagne, on my tab, and looked distinctly suave, with the pink silk scarf that seemed to be his trademark. Clever and connected, Whitaker had said, and he seemed to be all that. He was certainly keen to show me how connected he was. I started to reach Chinese political overload, so I got to the point.

'What about Madame Lin? Is it true they call her "Madame Jade"? Should I try to get a meeting with her?'

Directly the words came out I could have kicked myself for sounding so bloody eager.

He laughed. 'Jade will only see you if she wants to. And to be really frank, she tends to prefer a slightly younger model. If you see what I mean.'

I was starting to dislike him. Not just because he was young and I was old, but because it was embarrassingly clear how much he fancied himself. He was one of those people who thinks that being young has some kind of intrinsic moral value; instead of being something that happens to every one of us, and then mysteriously slips away while we're not looking.

He ran his fingers through his thick hair and grinned; under the influence of the stuff he was drinking, at my expense, his eyes were starting to match his scarf. Still, I knew I had to stick with it, so I choked down the remarks I might otherwise make.

'Maybe if we went to see her together, and ask if she'll speak to me on camera?'

'Not quite sure what would be in it for me.'

I looked down at my plate.

'Well, you could be the expert in my documentary – the person who tells us what it all means.'

He thought about that for a moment, and liked it.

'Yes, well, I can always ask her if she'll see us together. And we'll take it from there.'

I managed to make the conversation last for the length of the meal, but it wouldn't have gone on much longer: it was scarcely a meeting of minds. But it was a meeting of interests, all the same; Prinsett could see advantages for himself in the relationship, and was prepared to put up with me to get them. And it was pretty much mutual.

At the end, I thought I'd better get one thing clear.

'Are you working for the government in any way?'

If he was some sort of spook, even a part-timer, I needed to know.

He just laughed.

'Well, I do pass stuff on from time to time, because they can sometimes be helpful in terms of introductions and so forth. But basically I'm in it for myself, old mate. I want to make lots and lots of dosh, and China's the place to do it.'

'And I suppose Madame Jade gives you a hand.'

'Oh yes, she does. In every sense.'

He was still grinning offensively as we walked out and went our different ways. A swine, incontestably, but one who might be helpful. He probably thought the same about me.

15

I didn't hurry back to the office. I knew what awaited me there: a conversation with Brian, during which he'd explain to me the full details of how I was going to be made to walk the plank, while I would try to ask for one last trip. I reckoned it'd be like the condemned prisoner being allowed to draw up the menu for his last breakfast.

He'd stopped talking for a couple of seconds before I noticed.

'I know this can't have been easy for you,' Brian said soothingly, 'but if there *is* any way we can help?'

I really can't be nasty to him, I thought. And of course he's Fulham. If I leave on bad terms with him I'll have to avoid him every other Saturday down at the Cottage. So I did a bit of 'That's really nice of you'-ing, and in fact I think the good bits of the deal were genuinely down to him. Not to his smiling ratbag of a boss.

'There's so much stuff going on about Brexit, and that's not my cup of tea, as you know. Why don't I head off to China for a bit, and do some reporting there?'

The suggestion seemed to cheer him up.

'I'll see what response I can get to that,' he said. He must have rung someone, because it worked.

All the same, big organisations like the rest of the workforce to know when it carries out its personal punishments. I might not be paraded in front of the regiment and have my uniform buttons cut off, but I still had to be seen to suffer. So as I got up and moved to the door, Brian said, 'One thing. I'm afraid you won't be able to take Os.'

'I see – the beatings will continue until morale improves.'

'Oh, Jon – come on.'

'Os is part of my team.'

'Not any longer, he's not. And if I'm honest, working with you won't do him an awful lot of good in future. We've got him down to work on Brexit projects.'

I almost didn't want to ask the next question, in case it brought more punishment. But I had to know.

'Alyssa?'

'Oh yes, Alyssa can go with you.'

He said it as though nobody cared one way or the other. Well, that was their loss, not hers. I was relieved and grateful that I'd be working with her, which meant I had to keep a tight control over myself not to thank him as I walked out; that really would have been bad for business.

Alyssa met me at the George, looking very princess-like, and I told her about Os. She wasn't crazy about him anyway, so I don't think she was too upset. Even I had to admit he was an unreconstructed Afrikaner, with an embarrassing line in jokes.

'But it means you'll have to do the camera work.'

It took me a few minutes to scrape her off the walls after I said that. When I thought about it afterwards, I decided that it wasn't the threat to her status that upset her, so much as nervousness that her filming might not be up to scratch. Very much the perfectionist, our Alyssa.

'Look, this is going to be a long trip, and the only way they'll spend the cash on it is if there's just the two of us. I don't mind doing a bit of second-camera stuff, but you're going to have to do the main shooting.'

'I could kill you for agreeing to it.'

'Yes, well, China'll be a good place to do that. Quick blow to the back of the head – they all seem to be at it.'

I was still waking up with a headache in the mornings, you see.

As a way of soothing her, I told her I suspected that my old mate Lin Lifang might be heading for a big promotion, and that we could be there to report on it. I didn't tell her I suspected he was going to stage a power-grab. And of course, as with Whitaker, the Oxford prof, there was no question of telling her about Excalibur. There's an absolute rule in my business: get mixed up with the spooks as little as you possibly can. Sometimes you can't help it. This, I felt, was one of those cases. But if you do get mixed up with them, never tell anyone about it.

All the same, I was excited to have a potentially good story on my hands. It had been far too long since something like that had happened to me.

16

I first met Lin Lifang in Tiananmen Square in May 1989, during the vast demo that brought China to a complete standstill. His father was an important Party boss, but Lin had rebelled against all that and became a minor student leader.

We all know how Tiananmen ended. I managed to help Lin avoid arrest, and after we said our goodbyes he disappeared into the Chinese hinterland. A lot of the Tiananmen leaders were smuggled out to Hong Kong, and either stayed there or went to Britain, the US and Canada. Not Lin. I suppose he knew he could rely on his dad to help him.

Lin had taken a couple of long-distance buses and found his way home to the provincial capital where the old man was pretty much king. There, he did the necessary prodigal son act, grovelling and promising to be better in future. For a few months he lay low, being looked after by his loving mother and his admiring sisters. And when the hue and cry for the Tiananmen leaders faded and China's elderly, blood-spattered leader Deng Xiaoping was secure on his throne again, Lin emerged. He did two years as a postgraduate, then started work as a lowly official in the housing department of his father's empire. By that time his dad had decided that the slate had been wiped clean. Phone calls were made, and Lifang, now pretty well qualified, was sent off to somewhere entirely different in a more senior capacity.

By now – we're talking about the mid-1990s – Tiananmen had become pretty much unmentionable, which turned out to be an advantage for the young chap. After all, if no one could talk about what happened in the square, no one would talk about what Lin had done there. His natural abilities began to shine, and his seniors spotted them. China's civil service is one of the best in the world, so genuine quality is appreciated. And by now he had been thoroughly laundered.

A year or so after he'd got his new job, there was a lot of discontent in his area when some corrupt local businessman did a deal with the local mayor and pulled down an entire district composed of traditional houses, blocks of flats and shops in order to build a massive and entirely illegal shopping mall. The demo got out of hand, with cars and shops set on fire, builders beaten up and chased off, and cops shown the hard way that it was a no-go area.

Lin, as the representative of the local authority, drove down to the site in his unpretentious little car, got out, had tea with the ringleaders, agreed to their demands in almost every respect, and brought the demo to an end. And a week or so afterwards everyone he'd talked to was arrested and sentenced to five years minimum on political charges. Neat, and completely unscrupulous. A bit like the young Richard II talking down the Peasants' Revolt.

This really speeded up his promotion, as you might imagine. Most Chinese bureaucrats, like bureaucrats anywhere, are happiest sitting at their desks; going out and making contact with real people, especially angry and violent ones, isn't their thing. But they've got immense respect for anyone who has the guts to do it. As a result, Lin was promoted to mayor of a smallish city whose name I've forgotten, somewhere in the south-west. Then, by the late 1990s, he was promoted to a much larger one which I remember very well: Do-Chang.

It's a busy port on the north-eastern sea coast. Before the Japanese got there in 1938 and did their usual number on it, Do-Chang must have been rather attractive. At that stage it was a foreign enclave where French, British, German and Russian merchants traded on entirely unfair terms as a result of unconscionable pressure from their governments on the feeble Chinese authorities. The few bits of pre-war architecture that survived the attentions of the Japanese are grand and marble-fronted, with columns and the odd inscription surviving on the architraves.

Lin Lifang's biggest problem was to show the rest of China that he was there. Nothing much happened in Do-Chang except the graft that comes with being a port, and there weren't any great social problems or sources of discontent: nothing that could draw attention to Lin's toughness and negotiating abilities. So he decided to give the place a facelift, and invited journalists from all over the country to come and be impressed. He built an opera house, a very large bath complex, four shopping centres, a post office that looked like the White House, and, in a set of gardens laid out along the general lines of the Champ de Mars in Paris, the mayoral offices. They made the Elysée Palace look small and pokey.

17

So much had happened to me since Tiananmen that Lin Lifang had faded from my mind. It never occurred to me, when I started reading accounts of Do-Chang in the Chinese press, that I might know the man behind it all. I just thought that going there to report on its transformation would be a bit of a laugh. The outside world was starting to hear stories around that time about crazy Chinese opulence and ludicrous overspending, and this fitted right in with all that. I dare say the newspaper stories named Lin as the local mayor, but I didn't spot his name.

It was a genuine coincidence, of the kind that I dislike intensely.

So three of us – producer, cameraman and I – fetched up at Do-Chang's pleasant little airport one sunny morning and that afternoon we drove over to see the mayor in person. An obsequious character bowed us into the great man's presence – and there, behind a desk the size of a Wurlitzer cinema organ, sat Lin Lifang. I recognised him at once. He didn't recognise me, because he had his head down, signing documents. He wanted to make sure these *guizi* visitors realised how important and busy he was. *Guizi*, by the way, is a rude Putonghua, or 'Mandarin', term for 'foreigner'; if someone uses it about you, you've got every reason to yell at them.

For a heartbeat or two I was too stunned to say anything. I hadn't heard anything from Lin since June 1989, and knew nothing about his redemption. As for him, he put his fountain pen down – it was one of those big fat Mont Blancs – and his jaw actually dropped, in the way you read about in books but almost never see in real life. Aside from the open mouth, though, he looked sleek, well fed, relaxed and wore his thirty-five years well.

He made a couple of gargling noises which could have been an attempt to say hello. I got in with a '*nehao*' of my own, and crossed an immense green carpet to shake his hand. He seemed genuinely moved to see me, jumping up and gripping my forearm with his left hand while his right cracked the bones of mine in distinctly un-Chinese fashion.

We did our explanations in Putonghua, which impressed my colleagues. They didn't realise how basic and inaccurate my grasp of the language actually was. But Lin was proud of his English, and soon wanted to demonstrate that he'd got his money's worth.

'It's certainly a big surprise, but a very welcome one. You must come and stay in our guest house – it's very well appointed, I promise you.'

The producer got us out of that skilfully, explaining that wherever we went we had to pay our own way. He managed to make it seem like an amusing foible rather than a rule to guard against corruption. I don't suppose Lin understood what he was on about.

Whatever work Lin had done on the rest of Do-Chang, he hadn't yet managed to get a really decent international hotel group to set up there. In fact the Pleasant Golden Phoenix, where we were staying, wasn't too bad, though when I ran a bath that night the water was a dark, suggestive yellow-brown. Still, I've had worse, especially in provincial China.

The producer, whose name was Paul, explained to Lin what we'd like to do, and Lin entered into the whole business with enthusiasm. Back at the time of Tiananmen I'd told him I thought he had a talent for television, and he clearly hadn't lost it. Our biggest problem was to stop him looking into the camera and asking if he was doing everything right.

I still felt a touch paternal towards him, though less so now that the old skinniness had vanished and his bones had flesh on them. And he was pretty authoritative nowadays: the years of bossing people about and being grovelled to had had their effect, and he couldn't seem to put it aside, even for me.

Maybe that's why I started to play tricks on him. Sitting at his desk, with me a long way away, he told me how he'd fixed up coloured fountains all through the city centre, each linked to pieces of Western music. Scottish music, actually, he confided, as though he expected me to go into raptures. He looked into the camera and smiled confidingly.

'I don't believe you,' I said, scarcely able to believe my good luck.

'You'll see.'

Bob was one of the best cameramen I'd ever worked with, someone who could understand what was going on and follow the action seamlessly. Lin stood up, then I went round to join him, and Bob unshipped the camera and followed us onto the grand balcony outside the mayoral office.

'So this is your kingdom,' I said when we got outside.

Lin was too clever to be trapped like that.

'I'm just a government official,' he answered, 'but I'm lucky enough to work in this fine city of Do-Chang.'

It certainly was attractive. Lin had spent his millions well.

A large console stood at what you might call the Mussolini position on the balcony: the place to acknowledge the plaudits of a grateful citizenry. The console looked like the kind of thing you

53

find in a recording studio, with a vast number of knobs and slides on it, and lots of dials.

'What's this?'

It was the start of an unforgettable television sequence.

Lin laughed modestly, and switched the console on.

'These regulate the colours,' he said, and Bob, as intuitive as ever, panned up from Lin's fingers on the slides of the console to the grand fountains in the park below us. And, sure enough, the water gushing upwards from them turned from colourless to red as we watched.

'Try another one.'

Lin eased forward a second slide, as carefully as a Swissair pilot taking off.

The water turned blue. After that there was purple and a variety of shades of yellow and green. The people of Do-Chang got the lot.

'And I think you've got music too?'

'The Bluebells of Scotland' rang out across the city.

'Play something else.'

We had 'Loch Lomond', then 'The Skye Boat Song', and 'I Belong to Glasgow'. With his other hand, like a church organist, he gave us alternating bursts of colour.

It was gloriously funny, and only Lin didn't realise it. He thought he was providing the city with a burst of sophisticated Western son et lumière, and I suppose in a way he was. In fact, reflecting on it now, I feel embarrassed: I was behaving like one of those hard-to-watch 1930s British films where couples in white tie and tails and long silk dresses wander through Piccadilly Circus and make fun of cockney flower-sellers.

Lin, clever and observant though he was, didn't spot what I was doing. He just thought he was being classy. Some years later I explained the whole thing to him in a confessional moment, and I thought he took it rather well. He made it seem like a phase he'd gone through, before he started speaking English with a posh accent and wearing suits made by Ozwald Boateng and thousand-pound shoes from Lobb.

Back in London, my editor loved it. It summed up the *nouveau* aspect of China's sudden wealth perfectly. When you're on the slide yourself, like Britain is, it's always comforting to feel superior to the people who are starting to replace you.

I wrote my thank-you note to Lin before our report went out, so I wouldn't have to lie or apologise to him. After it had been broadcast, and whatever feedback he'd had from his political bosses in Beijing had reached him, he wrote back to me with no sign that he thought he'd been got at.

On the contrary, he invited the three of us back to Do-Chang any time we wanted, at the city's cost, and said we should bring our families as well.

Perhaps he'd forgotten our explanation about not accepting paid hospitality; but I suspect he was subtly making fun of me and my ethical pretensions.

18

I didn't contact Lin for years after that, and he didn't contact me, which made me think he'd realised that I'd turned him into a figure of fun.

It was only when Tony Blair, our esteemed prime minister – remember him? – went to China, that I thought I'd go with him and report on his talks with the Chinese government. The visit ended with Blair and the Chinese premier giving a joint but disorganised press conference in some sort of theatre.

The hacks like to shout out questions at these things, and they adore it when the prime minister calls them by their Christian name and it gets on the telly. This isn't quite my kind of thing, so I stood at the back and watched them at it.

Anyway, I was half listening to the questions and answers and half disapproving, when someone nudged me in the ribs. I don't like being touched – except of course by the kind of people I want to be touched by – so I turned round with a snarl. Then I saw it was Lin Lifang. He was grinning at me, in a way I couldn't quite work out.

The intervening years had been kind to him: he looked a million dollars, and was probably worth a hundred times that. Even in the half-light of the theatre I could see that he'd put on more weight, and that his tailor had done wonders with his figure.

I'm not particularly interested in clothes myself – you'll have spotted that if you've seen me on television – but I can recognise good tailoring as well as the next person. And this wasn't just good, it was superlative.

'Well, Mr Lin Lifang – look at you!'

'And look at you, Mr Jon Swift!'

It was like that bit in *Great Expectations* where Pip meets the pale young gentleman and says, 'The idea of its being you!'

It seemed to me I'd better do a bit of grovelling, fast.

'I do hope you didn't feel that report I did on our meeting in Do-Chang – you know, the fountains and all that, and "I Love a Lassie" and, well, all the rest of it – I do hope you didn't think . . .?'

I guessed from his expression that he did think, but that it didn't matter. Funny how the balance between us had shifted over the years: once he had been my scrawny sidekick, and now he was someone I felt it was politic to heap ashes on my head for, pre-emptively.

'Ah well. Maybe I did feel a little, how shall we say, sad about it. But then something happened.'

He went on: 'Perhaps I shouldn't say this, but you see the men who lead China don't for the most part have much sense of humour. I suppose they wouldn't have got so far if they had. Mockery, self-doubt, a sense of the ludicrous – all these things which make you and me laugh are closed off to them. They have remarkable qualities of self-belief.'

He was mocking me openly now, and I didn't know how to respond.

'And as a result they didn't understand what your film was about, in any way. They thought it was a delightful acknowledgement of Chinese cultural superiority, and they assumed this meant that I had done what I set out to do: used the opportunity you gave me to show the world how brilliant we are. I didn't have the heart to – is the word disabuse? – them.'

I nodded. 'And?'

'And they decided I deserved promotion. They looked round for a job where my mastery of the Western media could be demonstrated, and they made me what I am now: the First Minister of Foreign Trade. Surely you must have wondered why you have bumped into me here at the press conference of your delightful prime minister? It's because I was a signatory to the trade deal they've been going on about. If I'm frank, the British side didn't negotiate very well, and they could have got far more out of us. So I'm the one who's laughing now – and all as a direct result of your amusing report for television.'

I gulped a bit. But when I came to compute it all, I realised that everything had worked out to our mutual advantage. The balance between us had undoubtedly changed, though, and the cheap trick I'd played on him had put me one-down to him for ever more.

'So I owe it entirely to you that I can now look forward to a distinguished career in national politics. Not of course that we have politics in the upper levels of government in the People's Republic: we all believe the same thing, and we're all working for the same thing – the advancement of our great mother country. You should come and observe the process.'

As he said this his eyes danced amusingly. I'm sure he intended it to be a soothing poultice, after the necessary cauterising. But there was another message in this for me, too: watch me go, he was saying.

And maybe he was hinting that there'd be something in it for me, too, if and when he reached the uttermost heights.

19

Alyssa and I sat side by side in our taxi from the airport to the centre of Beijing. It's a long, long way, and there was plenty of time to talk. She told me about her mother, and how she came from Nigeria to south London and met the man who became Alyssa's father, and her difficult path through school and university.

In return, I told her what Beijing had been like when I went there first, in May 1989: simpler and more pleasant. Half the people in the big cities, and almost everyone in the rest of the country, still wore Mao suits in dark blue or grey. The streets were mostly free of cars, since for the most part only leading Party officials had them, and everyone else got about by bike.

As a result, entire rivers of cyclists flowed down both sides of every avenue, and clogged the side streets through the *hutongs* – the traditional areas in most of the central part of the city, with high grey-brick walls and elaborately decorated gateways leading to quiet courtyards where families sat and talked and ate.

People would stop in the street to stare at me. Not because of my remarkable personal attractions but because they'd never seen a European before, and couldn't work out what made me so amazingly pale. Or why I wore such weird clothes. And when I paused in the street to jot down some notes, small, giggling groups would form round me to see the strange marks I was making on the paper.

I was just getting started on the way China's politics have changed when she cut in.

'Yes, well, thanks for the history lesson, but I've always preferred to make up my own mind about these things.'

And her mouth snapped shut.

Fine, I thought – feel free to ignore the voice of experience. Actually, I didn't just think it: after a few more minutes of being jammed in Beijing's appalling traffic, like boulders in a glacier, I said it out loud.

So we started one of our arguments. These have broken out in places all over the world, from Moscow, where we were arrested for suspected black-marketeering while we were filming under-cover, to Baghdad, where we were trapped immediately after a bomb attack on an army post nearby, and carried on yelling at one another while everyone else was cowering down expecting another explosion.

Personally, I don't like rows very much. I suppose Alyssa can't bear being told what to think by some ancient character stuck in the unpalatable imperialist past. Not exactly the basis for a fruit-ful relationship. And yet it actually works. I admire her, and can put up with her bossiness, if I think it helps our endeavours. She doesn't reciprocate entirely, but she hasn't yet asked for a transfer to work with someone else, so maybe she thinks she has tamed me.

And as we arrived in the courtyard of our hotel, Mr Chang opened the door for us and greeted me with his usual effusion. I was so annoyed with Alyssa that I forgot to hand him his usual two hundred yuan, and it was only when I thought about his disappointed face that I went back and stuck a couple of bills into his white-gloved hand. He beamed again and I felt better; and I went over to Alyssa as she checked us in.

'Oh yes, very much so,' she was saying to the receptionist, who looked about fifteen, when she asked if we wanted separate rooms. That was meant for me, not the receptionist.

There seemed to be nothing, from politics to the state of the weather, which we couldn't disagree on. Even so, we needed to be on speaking terms. With the night before us, I didn't want us to go to sleep without making up after the argument.

'Don't suppose you feel like a nightcap?' I said.

But I'd misjudged it: the sparks hadn't died down sufficiently.

'What, so you can come on to me?'

It seemed unfair. I didn't always come on to her – weeks would pass without the slightest move on my part – and tonight, after eighteen hours' continuous travelling from the time I got out of my bed in Oxford that morning, was hardly the right moment.

I said nothing as we walked away from the reception desk. Usually she tried to make sure our rooms were on different floors, but this time, perhaps because I'd distracted her, our rooms were side by side.

'Let me tell you . . .'

But I'd stopped listening. I pointed with my forehead to the door to my room. It was slightly ajar. I inched closer, and put my bags down without making a sound. Then I kicked the door open.

Inside, a man as small as a child was kneeling on the floor, his bony overall-covered arse in front of me. As I started to formulate some words, another man, Hardy to his Laurel, came bursting out of the bathroom and pushed past me, disappearing down the corridor. Laurel, though, appeared trapped.

'What the fuck?' I said in crude Putonghua.

Strange how (and why, for that matter) words for coition are used as a term of abuse absolutely everywhere in the world; including, should you be interested, by the Ashaninka people of western Amazonia and the Bambenga pygmies of the Congo. The Chinese expression, in case you have occasion to use it, is *Shénme tā mā de*, but you need to get the tones right.

'Sorry – water,' said Laurel, struggling to get past me.

'If it's water, why are you in this room and not the bathroom?'

This is what I meant to say, anyway: my weak grasp of Putonghua's five different tones probably meant I was saying 'If it's shoes, why weren't you in the train?'

I grabbed him and yelled to Alyssa to ring security. There was a pause, in which Laurel wriggled some more, and Alyssa went through the contents of the box he was carrying.

'It seems to be electronic stuff,' she said.

A large man in a suit appeared in the doorway: the hotel security boss, I assumed. Behind him, mostly hidden, was someone else in a singlet and shorts, who looked as though he'd just been rousted out of bed. The large man didn't say who he was, but he grabbed Laurel where a mother cat grabs her kittens, and marched him out.

That left the guy in the singlet and shorts.

'There must have been some mistake,' he ventured.

'I'll say.'

'We'll have a report on it by tomorrow morning.'

'Good,' Alyssa put in crisply. 'But for now we'll move to another couple of rooms, if you don't mind.'

'Of course, of course.'

It took four minutes. By that time my relationship with her was thoroughly restored, and we did head down to the bar for a nightcap, after all.

'Do you think this trip is going to be tricky?' she asked as she raised her glass of red wine.

'I hope so.'

'You're a bastard, Jon. You're always trying to put the wind up me.'

But I knew her by now. She found this sort of thing funny, and even enjoyable.

'Do you think that while we've been here those two idiots will have been doing their stuff in our new rooms?'

I didn't really think so. Spooks are just civil servants: they need written instructions to do their secret work, and written instructions take time to prepare. Even in China.

There seemed to be nothing odd about my room when I finally got there, though of course there never does. To make it up to us for being disturbed, the receptionist said they had upgraded us both. That meant we got bigger but distinctly weirder suites, each with a downstairs sitting room and bathroom, and a staircase which led to a large bedroom and a vast bathroom. It occurred to me that the people who usually stayed in these rooms were more likely to need bugging than the ones who were given normal rooms, so the equipment was probably in place already; but I was too tired to care much.

'I don't suppose . . .?'

'Look, Jon, just fuck off. *Ta ma de*, wasn't it?'

She was a quick learner.

20

Breakfast was in a gloomy marble vastness the size of a Drumcondra ballroom. Gilded candlesticks as big as a basketball player stood in every corner; there was a grand piano, and (as Howard Carter said about Tutankhamun's tomb) the glint of gold everywhere. Except that here it wasn't gold, it was just gold paint.

I like my breakfasts in China to be Chinese, so I had plenty of congee and three thousand-year-old eggs (not really old at all, just preserved, with whites the colour of dark amber and the yolks a deep green). I washed it down with a rather fine oolong tea.

As for Alyssa, if her mum used to make her eat Nigerian things for breakfast like dodo and eggs, which I rather enjoy, she's given all that up. She prefers the full English washed down with a pot of black tea, heavily stewed. I could see from the way the waiter looked at me that he preferred my choices.

'Oh, yuk – look at those horrible eggs of yours. I'm sure they must be completely off. Disgusting!'

'I could say the same thing about the stuff you're eating.'

But I didn't, because things were going rather well between us this morning. In fact we were quite jolly. Part of our good mood was spent trying to work out who in the restaurant was spying on us. The out-of-town couple who switched tables to get closer to us? No – they were just nosey provincials who'd never seen a black woman with a white bloke before, and wanted to hear what strange clicks and grunts we conversed in.

There was a man in a suit by the door who looked a bit more likely, but then he folded the newspaper he'd been peering at and wandered out. Another man on his own? No – he seemed much more interested in slurping his congee. The young couple who seemed to be going past us to the buffet more often than necessary? Alyssa liked them for the spies, but I thought they were too jolly, and more likely to be honeymooners visiting the big city.

It took us a little time to notice who it really was: a weaselly man in a light-coloured jacket with a copy of that morning's *People's Daily*; throughout our entire meal he never turned a page once. Maybe he was a lip-reader, though it takes a hell of a lot of skill to read people's lips in a different language.

As far as I could see, he didn't have any means of recording our conversation. I said I suspected he was just there to see what time we walked out.

'Isn't that overkill?' Alyssa said.

'Well, State Security isn't exactly short-staffed.'

As we walked out he was sitting in the lobby outside, his newspaper in his pocket, facing the door to the breakfast room, with a phone in his hand. As we came walking out he spoke a couple of words into it and stood up.

'They're pretty useless, these Chinese spies,' Alyssa said.

'Maybe they know we're onto them, and just want to show they don't care if we are.'

She hadn't thought of that. Neither had I, till that moment. I wondered if the intention was to encourage us to be open in our movements.

'Does all this scare you?'

I thought I might as well know where we stood.

'No – well, yes, maybe a bit. I hate being watched and followed.'

There was a reason why people stared at Alyssa, and it had nothing to do with her eighteenth-dynasty looks. There's an extraordinary degree of racism among Chinese people, and although I'm extremely fond of them and their culture there's no doubt in my mind that they think Africans are a long way down the evolutionary ladder compared with the inhabitants of the Middle Kingdom.

Still, I didn't feel the need to point this out to Alyssa. If she'd thought her teachers at the London School of Economics were racist then she should see inside the minds of people here in China.

She showed no signs of suffering from jet lag. This morning she had put on a khaki jacket and trousers. All she needed was a pair of binoculars round her neck, and she could have been out for a morning's game drive in the Serengeti.

I took the lift up to my room. Just as the doors were closing, a man in a light-coloured jacket stuck his arm through and forced them open. He took no notice of me whatever, but I knew who he was: the spy from the breakfast room.

He got out at the fourth floor – my floor – and allowed me to walk ahead of him. The corridor did a little jink on the way to my room, and as I turned the corner he pushed past me. I felt a movement in the region of the side pocket of my jacket: he'd slipped something inside it. He hurried on, then pushed through the door of the emergency stairs and headed down.

I was desperate to fish whatever it was out of my pocket, but I knew there were CCTV cameras in the corridor so I waited until

I was in my room. Maybe there were cameras in there, too, but I doubted if they'd bother to put one in the lavatory.

It was an envelope with a single sheet of blue paper in it. The paper was covered with handwriting in English.

'Forgive this slightly unorthodox method of making contact...' it started.

21

Who writes like that in China? Quite a few people, actually. I can't remember the exact wording, because the note went down the lavatory pretty quick, but the message was clear: something along the lines of 'Do you remember the hiring you made, shortly after you dropped your notebook and I gave it back to you? If so, I have something which you may find of interest.'

I knew who it was. Back in our Tiananmen days, when I'd hired Lin Lifang, I'd also asked a second student to translate for me. His name was Wei Jingyi, and he was quieter and more studious than Lin, and much less obviously ambitious. Now he was a bookseller in an outer suburb of Beijing.

I knew where his shop was, because I'd visited him there several times over the years. I'd even interviewed him once, though we'd had to blur his face and cover his voice with that of an actor.

Presumably he'd sent the man in the tan jacket to give me the message. But how could Wei possibly have heard that I was back in China? And why did he want to see me?

Only one way to find out, I thought, smiling at the pathetic pun. But I wasn't going to take Alyssa. A white man was conspicuous enough in the suburbs of Beijing, but a white man with a magnificent black woman beside him would have been like Donnybrook Fair.

I didn't want to explain that to her, though: more of the habitual shower of sparks. So I didn't say anything about it when we walked out to our car: the one we'd hired from the hotel. In it sat our thick-necked driver, massive in his habitual blue suit.

I gave him the address of our bureau, and he grunted. A blue car that had been parked a little way away started up and inched after us. Two men in black were sitting in it.

'They're only doing this to intimidate us, you know,' I said as we slipped into the traffic in the direction of Tiananmen Square.

'Well, they're succeeding.'

Not that she looked intimidated. She sat upright in her seat, staring out at the ugly modern buildings.

I laughed, then slipped her the bad news.

'I've got to go somewhere. I can't tell you where, in front of Oddjob here. But I'll get out—'

'How can I make any arrangements when you just go your own way like this?' she shouted.

Oddjob gave a startled look at her in the rear-view mirror, and almost slammed into the car in front. He lurched into the next lane, and just avoided sideswiping the blue car that had been following us.

I tuned Alyssa's voice out. She seemed to be dragging in all sorts of other occasions when I'd done something like this. While she went on, I used the time to work out what I was going to do. There was a noodle bar beside the entrance to the building where our bureau was, and it had a separate exit. Oddjob and the two men in the blue car would assume I'd gone up to the bureau with Alyssa, so they wouldn't spot me leaving by the side door.

I hoped.

There was a silence now, so I told her in fairly impenetrable London argot what I was going to do. More shouting, but less volume; she'd got the point. By the time we reached the office, she almost seemed to approve of the whole thing.

'I'll mosey back to our gaff around teatime and give you the full debrief.'

Surely, even if Oddjob had taken the BBC Higher English-language course, he wouldn't understand that.

As it turned out, though, I didn't peel off when we reached the entrance to the building. When we walked through the doors together, we bumped into one of our colleagues, who'd been buying a newspaper at the kiosk in the hall.

He welcomed us warmly. Tall and thin, he dressed like a foreign correspondent ought to dress: suit, tie, and a rather snazzy hat with a tilted brim. If only I had the guts to wear one of those, I thought. Compared with him, I looked like someone who'd come to give an estimate for redecorating the office.

They'd always been nice to me in this bureau, but they really rolled out the red carpet for Alyssa. I tested my responses: was I jealous? Eventually I decided not; I chose to regard it as a compliment to us as a team.

But there was trouble here. In the past, when they'd covered human rights stories, the authorities had been indulgent: that's what Western journalists do, they'd decided. We Chinese may think it's pointless, a distraction from the function of proper journalism, which is to show how successful China is becoming and how united its people are. Yet things were changing. The top Chinese bosses were getting twitchy about everything. They were scared that their nice jobs and houses and Swiss accounts and medical care in Dubai and

Zurich might be taken away. And when people feel threatened, they turn nasty.

So all sorts of unpleasant things began happening. Our poor bureau chief was always being called in, the Beijing *Global Times* carried nasty articles about us, there were problems getting visas renewed, and we experienced the full force of automated bots on our social media.

I'd already noticed this before we left London: whenever I posted something on Twitter, there would be something unusually spiteful about me; often in an approximation of English. Originally I thought it must come from Russia, but after a while I realised it was from China.

An article in the *Global Times* even suggested that our bureau should be closed down. When that kind of thing appears, you automatically know two things: one, it's a suggestion that's going the rounds inside the Central Committee; and two, it could happen, quite soon.

Given all this, it seemed a bit look-at-me-ish to mention the incident with Laurel and Hardy the night before. I didn't raise it but Alyssa decided that she should – with the effect I'd expected. There wasn't anyone in the bureau who hadn't experienced something similar, and usually a good deal nastier. They listened politely then went on talking about something else.

After I'd talked to everyone for a while, and asked after their kids and dogs and cats, I felt honour had been satisfied and I could go. I said my goodbyes and headed downstairs and into the noodle bar.

As I sucked up my hot dry Wuhan noodles, topped with pickled radish, I risked a look out of the window. Oddjob was squatting down on his over-large haunches beside his car, and two others were sitting on the ground chatting to him: the dark-suited characters from the car that followed us.

Every time anyone came out of the revolving doors they glanced up without much interest. But the only time someone left the noodle bar by the side exit, they took no notice.

'*Niu*,' I said to myself, a bit self-consciously.

'*Niu*' actually means a cow, but for some occult reason Chinese people use it to mean 'great' or 'awesome'. I confess I've never had the balls to use it in conversation. Balls, by the way, is *dan dan* in Chinese slang. Too much information?

I emptied my glass of oolong, paid the bill, and slipped out round the side. It was a four-minute walk to the nearest subway station.

When I got there, I extracted my old Beijing travel card from my wallet, and pressed it on the pad by the barrier to the stairs. It gave a faint click and the barrier opened. I'm no subway expert, but I'd done this journey a couple of times before; so I knew where to change and which station to get out at. Beijing is so huge that it took forty-five minutes to get there.

No one seemed to be following me, though for sheer excitement's sake I did that thing you see in spy films – stepping back onto the platform at the last moment, then jumping back onto the train. I just succeeded in making myself look like an idiot.

All I need is for someone from Chaoyang to be in the carriage with me, I thought. Chaoyang is a district of Beijing famous for all the informers who ring the cops whenever they see something suspicious.

I hung around on the platform a bit self-consciously when I arrived at my station, allowing everyone else to leave the platform, in case I was being tailed, but I couldn't see anything suspicious. Even so, an old university friend of mine who went into MI5 told me you never can. But I always suspect people who come out with that sort of thing. It's like me saying journalism is an honest and honourable profession.

22

Wei Jingyi's bookshop was only five minutes' walk from the subway station. His life had taken a rather different turn from Lin Lifang's after Tiananmen. That was because his dad wasn't a big Party boss, just a quiet, gentle literature professor at Beijing Normal University who'd never recovered from the beatings he'd had during the Cultural Revolution. It was a seriously bad idea to teach eighth-century literature when the Red Guards were around.

Wei himself was less naive than most of the other Tiananmen students, and in 1989 I hired him to do things for us. He was the one who pointed out to me that security police photographers were always hanging round us; and after the massacre, when it was safe for him to send a message to me via Hong Kong, he told me that the Ministry of State Security had put out a film which, among other accusations against the foreign press, claimed that I'd handed over a brown envelope full of cash to the students so they could buy guns.

I didn't mind: it was totally ludicrous. But it showed that in China you can always get people to believe that everything bad must be linked to foreign influence: the sinister Black Hand. And so for some time after 1989 I wasn't allowed back into China. It was 1992 before the ban was lifted.

I was delighted to be allowed back in. I've been obsessed with Chinese culture ever since I first held a clay figure of a woman from the Tang dynasty in my hands, and started asking the shop-keeper questions about it. It turned out – quite a surprise, this – to be genuine: I had it tested when I got home. You'll find it in my bookcase, propped up against the George Eliots; assuming Mrs Gomulka, my Polish cleaner, hasn't smashed it while I've been away. She's a wonderful, motherly lady, and she likes Yorick, but she breaks a lot of things; it's those forearms of hers.

The outer suburb where Wei Jingyi had his bookshop is deso-late, but sharp, educated young couples come here to live because they can afford the prices. By the time they hit their early thirties, they're looking for somewhere nicer, with better air for the kids to breathe. But while they're here, they need books, so Wei had a wide clientele.

Nor was he the kind of burned-out case that so many ex-Tianan-men people turned into, obeying the rules obsequiously in case anyone brought up the little matter of what they'd been doing in June 1989. Wei Jingyi had kept an inner core of independence. Sure, he sold the usual blameless stuff any Chinese bookseller does – classical writings, the carefully vetted biographies of top politicians and plutocrats, all the ghastly stuff about how to get ahead in business, and translations of the kind of Western books that won't cause anyone any problems: Jack London, A. A. Milne – that sort of thing. Not a *1984* in sight.

But Wei Jingyi operated a top-shelf policy. He wouldn't stock the really dangerous stuff from Hong Kong or Taiwan (apart from anything else, it's getting much harder to smuggle in) but there are plenty of books which you or I might think were perfectly safe and normal, and which the Chinese authorities regard as absolute dynamite: any foreign book about Chinese politics, for instance, and any novel with a bit of sex in it, especially about gays or transsexuals.

Think of the British customs service in 1925, looking through a consignment of books arriving from the Continent, and you've got a reasonable idea of what Chinese officialdom is like in the twenty-first century. To be gay in China is to be a member of an underground resistance movement – unless, of course, your father is a leading Party member, in which case you've got all the protection you need.

Wei had a stock of books for and about gays. God knows where he kept them – it must have been somewhere pretty secure – but he sounded out his customers with care, and offered suggestions about books they might like. He preferred to cut off the covers and title-pages, because he reckoned that two-thirds of the morality police wouldn't be able to read the text.

23

I walked in to the accompaniment of a 'ping' from an old-fashioned doorbell. The shop was small and sunless, but lit by a warm, yellowish light the colour of the flame from an old-fashioned oil-lamp. The shelves went up to the ceiling on all sides, packed with paperbacks in half-a-dozen languages. Wei had even managed to fit a small sofa and armchair into the floor-space, so that three or, at a pinch, four people could sit and browse at the same time in companionable silence.

There was tea, and (for sophisticates) coffee, on the boil; and though I normally hate muzak, I always found the *pifa* sounds that were quietly pumped out in Wei's shop restful and charming. Altogether, a pleasing little book cave, where it was actually a pleasure to buy something.

But there was no sign of Wei Jingyi. The minuscule desk where he took payments and went through catalogues was empty, and the little door behind it was closed. I hung around irresolutely for a few minutes, looking through the shelves for something to read, when there was a flushing sound, and Wei came out, doing up his zip.

'Sorry, sorry,' he said quickly, at first seeing just the outline of a customer. Then he realised it was me.

'Jon, Jon, Jon, my dear friend. How are you? Welcome back to Beijing. And to my shop.'

He'd taken on a courtly way of speaking, perhaps because he thought that was how a bookseller ought to speak. It didn't wash with me, because when I looked at him all I saw was the character with beany arms and legs I'd met on my second day in the square.

I hugged him: he was still as thin as he'd been back then. He'd married a sweet wife who spoke no English and had scarcely read a book in her life, but cooked him three meals a day with pride, even though they didn't seem to have much effect on his figure.

There was a thin son, too, who read obsessively. He was around fourteen, and a smaller version of his father in 1989, except that he wore wire-framed glasses. You'll think me grossly sentimental, and you'll be right, but I loved the whole idea of this family. For me, they were the eternal China: hard-working, thoughtful, cheerful. Should I add vulnerable? I felt so then, and I especially feel so now.

We sat side by side on his leather couch and chatted in low voices. Once a customer came in, but when she saw me she muttered an apology and backed out of the door.

Things weren't good, it seemed. Wei had had links with a booksellers' outfit in Hong Kong, which had got into serious trouble with the mainland security organs when it became known that it was stocking a stupidly offensive book from Taiwan about President Xi Jinping's love life. I knew the book was stupid, because I'd read a translation of it. It contained loads of accusations, but none of them seemed to have any factual basis.

Don't get me wrong; I don't mean I necessarily think that Xi has led a pure and holy private life, utterly faithful to his formidable wife, the singer Peng Liyuan, but nothing in this book persuaded me that there was any real proof to the contrary. I thought it was a bit juvenile, like one of those programmes in

Britain where comedians who are still in their twenties think it's sophisticated to say all politicians are crooks and liars.

But the unpleasant fate which befell the partners in the Hong Kong bookshop was totally out of proportion to whatever offence they might have committed. A State Security team flew down, kidnapped them, beat them up, tortured them, questioned them for weeks, and finally let three of them go, as a warning to everyone else in Hong Kong not to do anything that China might not like. One, with remarkable courage, gave full details to the newspapers about what had happened to them. The rest stayed quiet.

Understandably, they'd given up every bit of information they had; and Wei Jingyi was one of the booksellers in mainland China they named. His shop was ransacked, and each book in it examined – mostly to destruction.

Fortunately he'd been expecting trouble, so the police weren't able to find any trace of his under-the-counter business, and eventually they let him carry on trading. It was then that he understood the quality of his customers, he said. Unobtrusively, they came in in their dozens, buying the wrecked books and the ones he gradually replaced them with, until the shop was its old, comfortable, moderately prosperous, charming self again.

It's why I love China and the Chinese.

But I knew Wei Jingyi well enough to see that something else was on his mind. The business of the Hong Kong booksellers was finished, as far as he was concerned; yet instead of relief a new anxiety seemed to have gathered round him. It was the way he frowned and wouldn't look me in the eye that convinced me.

At first he denied that anything was wrong: business was good, his customers were increasing. But something was the matter. You can always tell.

He hoisted himself out of the sofa and pulled down the blind on the street door that showed his shop was closed.

'Why did you send that weird guy to my hotel to pass me the message? And, anyway, how did you know I was staying there?'

'Lin Lifang sent that man. Name is Chang. And he's not weird. He likes American novels. Bret Easton Ellis.'

He looked up automatically at his shelves of fiction in English, in the way of booksellers everywhere. If Lin Lifang's messenger read Bret Easton Ellis, it confirmed my opinion of him; though I suppose he'd done a good job of passing on the message.

'And Lin told you I was in Beijing?'

Wei nodded.

I knew they'd kept in touch after Tiananmen, but it hadn't occurred to me they might still be talking: the Communist Party grandee and the quiet, studious bookseller, taking daily risks to keep people informed and happy.

'So why the tricks out of John Le Carré?'

Wei looked blank.

'Len Deighton? Gerald Seymour?'

My memory was starting to give way.

'John Buchan?'

'Ah, yes – "Greenjacket".'

Close enough, I suppose.

'Chang works for Lin Lifang here in Beijing. He came to see me.'

'So Lin didn't contact you personally?'

Wei gave me a look: as if.

'He had something for you, that he wanted you to see.'

'Why didn't Chang give it to me himself?'

Another look – and again he was right: if Lin was passing me stuff that was anything like as dangerous as the little black gadget he'd passed to me in Oxford, he'd need as many cut-outs as he could get.

I went quiet. Wei stood up and edged his way past the bookshelves and into the little room at the back. After a tussle that I could hear every move of, he came out with something in a hand towel. It was a thin, A4-sized packet, wrapped up in waterproof plastic, and he was drying it off.

I put my hand out for it, and opened it. Inside were a dozen or so pages of Chinese typescript.

'Please don't tell me you've been keeping that in the toilet cistern.'

He nodded, a bit sheepishly.

I gestured towards the section where he kept English-language crime fiction, mostly Agatha Christie. Chinese people learning English are always advised to read her in order to learn colloquial English; which is why so many educated Chinese sound as though they're ordering afternoon tea in Fortnum's: far too many 'pleases' and 'would you minds'.

'I promise you, in those books the villains keep their secrets in the cistern. It's the first place every policeman looks. What you've got to do is use the camera on your phone to make copies of a document like this. Then you burn the originals and put the little memory card with the copies on it somewhere where no one will think of looking. Have you got a copy of the Chinese constitution here?'

Wei shook his head.

'Glad to hear it. I bet you've got Zhou Enlai's memoirs, though.'

'Right up at the top there.'

'That's all the feeble old wanker's worth. You should have stuck it in one of the volumes. No one who's interested in life or truth will possibly ever want it. Too late now, though. I'll have to do it myself.'

I looked at him: he looked like a scolded kid.

'Never mind,' I said brightly. 'All's well that ends well.'

His eyes stole towards the Chinese translation section.

'Do you know what this is? Have you read it?'

He shook his head. 'No, of course not.'

He looked down at the floor.

'You have, haven't you?'

After a moment he nodded, still looking down.

'All right – just give me a rough idea of what it's about. Like you used to in Tiananmen, when people handed us documents. You were very good at telling me what they were about, I remember. Even the long ones.'

He looked me in the eyes now.

'OK. It's a kind of manifesto for when Lin gets rid of Xi and takes over. A complete justification for doing that. He wants you to keep it, for safety. And maybe because he wants you to know what he's doing.'

I wanted time to work all this out, so I turned and peered at the bookcases, while Wei hung around, awkward and worried.

I thought I could see what had happened. Lin must have thought it was too dangerous to keep something as explosive as this in his office in Huzhang. And by directing me to it, here in Wei's bookshop, he was trusting his liberty and maybe his life to me again.

'What were you going to do about it before I turned up?'

'I was thinking of destroying it. But for one thing it's quite interesting, and for another, I think Lin could well take over and I'd be in real trouble if it wasn't here when he wanted it.'

'You poor old bookseller,' I said, laughing. 'Heads you lose, tails I win.'

He hadn't heard that expression, and it took me a while to

reassure him that no one was going to come and decapitate him. And while I calmed him down, I knew what I'd have to do.

'Look – I'll take it off your hands and send it to someone in London who'll keep it safely. And if Lin asks you for it back, I can send it to you straightaway.'

He gave me the kind of look a bear might give to someone who pulls his leg out of a mantrap.

'Thank you, Jon. You've always been very kind to me.'

'Yeah, right,' I said.

But I was quite affected, all the same.

I took the manuscript out of its wet plastic wrapping and shoved it down the waistband of my trousers, at the back. Then I hung my shirt over it. Not comfortable, but fairly effective. OK, I know I'd just ticked off poor old Wei for not being more up to date in the way he kept Lin's document, but it was more secure with me. A Brit, especially a Brit working for a well-known international organisation, was far safer than a Chinese bookseller. The Party thinks it can do anything it likes with its own people.

Outside, when I left, a dark-blue Mercedes was waiting with the engine running. It was parked sufficiently far away for me to wonder whether I was supposed to see it.

I headed off towards the subway station. The Mercedes eased out and started following me as I walked to the station. I didn't see any reason why I shouldn't look round at it, so I did, various times. Every now and then it would stop, so as not to be forced by the traffic to overtake me.

Then I did something stupid: I turned round and walked quickly towards it. The driver started up and tried to drive away, but I stood in its path and he'd have had to knock me over to get away. Just like the tank-man of Tiananmen Square, I thought irrelevantly. Except I didn't have any shopping bags.

It stopped. I nipped to the rear door and yanked it open.

'Who the fuck are you, and why are you following me?' I barked.

A thin man in a dark-blue suit was sitting in the back, with a phone on his knee.

'*Hundan*,' I added for good measure. 'Arsehole.' I gave it my best accent.

He answered in polite, rather halting English. 'Perhaps we can drive you somewhere?'

'Back to my hotel, then. But you're going to have to tell me who you are.'

'I'm just someone who's interested in your safety.'

'And who are you working for?'

'For a friend.'

'Is his name Lin?'

'You can guess, but I'm not going to tell you.'

That seemed to be that. We sat side by side in total silence for the entire journey – quite a long one, in Beijing's benighted traffic. China is still full of drivers who've only just got behind the steering wheel of a car. It took us an hour and a half to get back to the hotel.

'Don't follow me again,' I said as I got out.

'I obey my instructions,' said blue suit.

And that was that. I told Alyssa about the book in the toilet cistern, but not about my ride home.

24

The next morning we didn't have anything pressing to do, so I offered to show her Tiananmen Square.

'Not too many lectures, though,' she said, 'you're supposed to be a journalist, not a tour guide.'

I pretended not to hear.

For me, that vast expanse opposite the Gate of Heavenly Peace, with the Great Hall of the People on one side, the museum on the other, and the mausoleum where they keep whatever's genuinely left of Mao's embalmed body, only means one thing: 1989. Fortunately, Alyssa was interested in that. I did mention the monument in the middle of the square, but only because it was where the leaders gathered during the demo, and where the crowd was corralled when the shooting started, late on the night of 3 June. Even when I was allowed back, three years later, there were still bullet-marks on the steps.

I gave Alyssa a much shortened version of what happened in the square, but just standing there brought it all back to me. And I remembered clearly the day I first bumped into Lin Lifang. So I told her about that, too.

It was hot, and the sweat was starting to soak through the armpits of my tropical suit. Aside from me, there was another dominant smell: the brackish combination of the little brown pancakes the local stallholders were cooking and selling, together with the portable toilets which some city bureaucrat had decided that twenty thousand campers would require. And there was a dominant sound: the crunching of glass underfoot. That, and the voices of young people sitting on the ground singing, laughing, or occasionally chanting slogans.

Tiananmen Square is the biggest open space in any city I've ever been to, and until the big demos started in May 1989 the police always made sure that no crowds gathered there. 'The empty space at the heart of Chinese communism,' I'd called it in one of my poncier television scripts; I was inclined to repeat it a bit too often.

The reason for the broken glass everywhere was that the demonstration was against the boss of China's Communist Party, Deng Xiaoping; and 'Xiaoping', if said in a particular way, meant 'little bottle'. So when you turned up in the square you brought a bottle of Coke with you, or one of the sugary rip-offs that factories were starting to produce. And after you'd downed the contents you held the empty bottle up in the air with one hand, and then let go. The crash of glass on paving stone invariably brought a laugh and a cheer, no matter how many times it was repeated, because it was a political statement: Deng Xiaoping was finished.

If only it had been as easy as that.

I found all the broken glass irritating. It meant you couldn't sit down with the students outside their tents (three weeks or so later I watched as dozens of military vehicles drove over them) without brushing the ground where you wanted to sit. That way you always seemed to get a sliver of Coke bottle in the palm of your hand. I took to bringing a packet of Elastoplast with me when I left my hotel room every morning, for this very contingency.

Sweaty though I was, and despite the painful little gash on the heel of my left hand, I felt I had been born for this moment. My Chinese was pretty rudimentary, only good enough for simple expressions of fact and opinion, but it was adequate for the earnest discussions I had hour after hour, day after day, with these students. God, they were naive: sometimes I felt like yelling at them. But they were sweet and decent and charming as well, so I didn't.

'You can't just take over an entire country and bring it to a halt,' I would say, as best as my limited Putonghua would allow, 'and not have some idea what you're going to do next.'

'Ah,' they would reply, 'that's for our leaders to decide.'

They were still the children of Maoism, you see: order-obeyers by instinct.

'But who are your leaders? And how were they chosen?'

The fact was, of course, that the leaders of the Tiananmen protest were mostly self-selecting. The great Chinese democracy movement was about as democratic as David Cameron and Boris Johnson standing for the leadership of the Oxford Union, or Donald Trump becoming President of the United States on the basis of getting fewer votes than Hillary Clinton. Periclean Athens it wasn't. But then neither was Periclean Athens, as I understand it.

I liked some of the leaders, and disliked others. There was a distinct tendency, among many of these rebels against communist directionism, to order you around and stop you doing whatever it was you were trying to do; in my case, reporting.

I had wandered over to the monument in the centre of the square. It was decorated with Zhou Enlai's own calligraphy, Zhou being Mao's utterly, not to say creepily, faithful premier, the one who's supposed to have said, when asked about the effects of the French Revolution, that it was too soon to tell.

Typical. Though actually it seems to have been a bit of a bad translation, since the old codger thought he was being asked about the student riots of 1968.

The area round the monument was ringed with police tape – the students must have nicked a supply of it when they'd taken over the square, five days earlier – and at the gap serving as an entrance a student was blocking the way. He was training to be a jobsworth.

'Your pass.'

'Here's my press pass. Look – hanging round my neck.'

'That's no good. You need a special pass to enter this part of the square. Orders.'

'*Húshuo*,' I said. Being able to use a few rude words in Mandarin has always been a source of pride to me. *Húshuo* means 'bollocks', though it isn't really anatomical. More like 'bullshit', I suppose. It's got a dismissive, arrogant, put-down sound to it.

'You can't come in.'

'Go and tell Chai Ling that Jon Swift wants to see her.'

Actually, I had no great confidence that she'd remember who I was, but I thought she'd probably tell him to let me in anyway, and there was a good chance that while he was off searching for her I could just ease my way through.

Which is what happened. I found Chai Ling before the jobsworth did, and although she didn't seem to have any recollection of me, she was certainly happy to talk to me. The jobsworth slunk away.

Chai Ling looked gentle and delicate, but there was steel inside that slender frame and behind those wide eyes. I had the impression that she, like the other leaders, had zero idea about what the students should do next. I had no idea either, but it wasn't my function to provide these thousands of kids with leadership.

The trouble was, there were lots of leaders, all self-appointed, and despite all their discussions they couldn't agree on anything. Eight or nine of them were sitting round a table covered with half-empty plastic water bottles, shouting, laughing, doodling, or looking bored. This was the first time I'd seen them together, and the only thing they seemed able to do was contradict each other. Some were dopey and opinionated. The rest were clever and opinionated.

The only other leader I knew was Wuer Kaishi, an intelligent, domineering character with dark, pudgy features, definitely not Han Chinese; he was a Uighur from the north-west, and his dad was a senior Party official.

A week or so later, he pissed off the Premier, Li Peng, to the point where Li decided the time had come to send the troops in to clear the square. Then the inevitable rumour went round that Wuer had been a plant whose orders were to provide the regime with an excuse to mow the students down.

I didn't believe it at the time, and I don't believe it now; I think he was just one of those people who has to have a barney with someone; and if that someone is the Premier of China with the power of life and death at his fingertips, so be it.

'Hey, Wuer!' I called out cheerily.

He looked at me as though I was a parking meter attendant, and turned away.

25

'Can I help?' asked a voice.

I turned my head. A youngish, slightly built student was standing there, not doing much but keeping an eye on everything that was going on. Funny: the very first thing I remember about him was the way he kept watch. There was nothing remotely saurian about him at that time: he was young, willing, eager to help and definitely impressed by a large, linen-suited Western journalist.

I explained that I was on the lookout for a story, and wanted to get some idea what the students' long-term plans were going to be. Even though my Chinese wasn't really up to the job of explaining this, he seemed to grasp it perfectly.

'I don't think any of us really have any plans.'

'But for Christ's sake, surely you must have some idea what to do.'

'I sometimes think we just know what we don't want, not what we do want.'

It sounded even better in Putonghua. Something about his quick agreement charmed me, after Wuer's rudeness.

'So tell me what you don't want.'

I knew it all already, but the way he put it had a particular precision. He told me about the frightening uniformity of the Cultural Revolution, and the things that had happened to his parents' generation during the course of it: the teachers they'd abused and sometimes beaten up, the scholars whose houses they'd ransacked, the books they'd destroyed, the paintings and objects they'd burned, the elderly people they'd screamed at for fun. A friend of his had taken part in the lynching of some local academic, and could never get rid of the guilt for what he'd done.

'And my own father – he was so frightened he soiled himself when the Red Guards came to our door. I was just newborn at the time, but my brother told me.'

His father had never recovered from this, even though his career had been rescued by Deng Xiaoping.

'What does your dad do now?'

'He's the Party Secretary of Xiewan.'

'And what does he think about what you're doing?'

'He thinks we're exactly the same as the Red Guards in the Cultural Revolution. He's afraid we'll come and get him. Every day he writes to me and tells me to leave the square. The other guys here think it's funny when they read his letters.'

'Do you?'

'No, I quite like my dad. But I think I'm right to be here.'

And that was it. Someone banged on a plate with a spoon, and he told me that yet another meeting was about to start.

'What is your name?'

'Jon Swift.'

It's not easy to pronounce if you're Chinese, but he made a pretty fair job of it, repeating it after me.

'Zhon Ser-wiff. I see. My name is Lin Lifang.'

Funny – even at that moment it seemed to me that this name, which was later to become one of the most famous in China, had a sort of ring to it. Or maybe I'm imagining it, all these years later. Anyway, we shook hands awkwardly, and he turned away.

As I looked round for someone else to talk to, a slightly older character came over and spoke to me.

'Be careful of him. He's not necessarily one of us, you know.'

'So what else could he be?'

'He's the son of a Party official.'

'So's Wuer Kaishi.'

'Yes, but Wuer's not Chinese, he's a Uighur. He's got a reason to be against the system.'

'You seem to be very certain about everything.'

'I'm young and Chinese and a student, so of course I'm certain.'

It was intended to be funny, so I should have laughed. I didn't. Even though he was making fun of himself and his type, I didn't want to hear anything against the odd, confessional character I'd just met.

I went back to our makeshift office in the Beijing Hotel nearby, and wrote a rather jaundiced report about students who were strong enough to hold China to ransom, but too feeble to make up their minds about anything. It didn't go down well in London: the outside world thought the students were a mixture of Mahatma Gandhi, Nelson Mandela and Greta Thunberg.

The following day I bumped into Lin again, just a few yards from the monument. I was talking to groups of students, as ever, partly to improve my Chinese, and partly to get a better understanding of what they were planning to do. In the background I could see Lin's slight figure threading his way through the packed crowd. He didn't look in my direction, yet I was sure he knew exactly where I was. He stopped and talked to a couple of people along the way, but after that he kept on pushing towards me. Still without looking at me.

'Hello, Mr Jon.'

'Well, fancy seeing you here.'

We talked about the weather and the situation for short while. Then he said, 'I think people have been telling you that I'm working for the government.'

'Not people – one person. Is it true?'

'No, of course not. My father hates it that I'm here. He's always sending me messages telling me to come home.'

'How do you know someone's been talking to me?'

He didn't answer. But he was one of those people who always seem to know about things that mattered.

By the way, I'm probably giving you the impression that my Chinese was fluent, from the way I've recorded all these conversations. I'm only too happy for you to think that, but it isn't true. It's perfectly possible that quite a lot of what I've recorded here has been inaccurate or misunderstood – I don't know. But I'm sure I've got the gist of it right. Just don't take my word for everything, one hundred per cent, that's all.

26

That night I decided to sleep in the square, so as to share the student experience. Naturally, turning on the hard stone surface, I kept wishing I was in my comfortable bed in the Beijing Hotel. The bodily smells around me, the grunts and snores and occasional mutterings kept me from proper sleep, and there always seemed to be someone picking his or her way between the prone bodies to get to the portable toilets, and more often than not treading on an arm or a leg as they went.

The next day was going to be a big one. Many of the top Party politicians had decided that the students were winning, that the tipping-point was getting very close now, and that the old boy, Deng Xiaoping, would be forced to resign. So most of them, in the way of politicians and bureaucrats the world over, started edging away from him. It reminded me of my own beloved organisation, back in London. In his place, the plotters assumed, would come Jiang Zemin, Deng's deputy, a lot less authoritarian and rather more open to the West. People nowadays think that the Tiananmen demonstrations were all about brave young students wanting democracy. Well, there was plenty of that, but the hard, uncompromising fact just below the surface was that this was an old-fashioned power struggle between a couple of elderly communist leaders who were prepared to use any weapon against each other that came to hand.

The morning was magical. I may be crabby and old, but the bright sun shining out of a lapis lazuli sky on thousands of young, self-sacrificing, idealistic students as they opened their eyes to another day impressed itself on my consciousness. It must have been a bit like that during the Children's Crusade, before they all got massacred. In Tiananmen Square the massacre was still three weeks away, and nobody thought such a thing was possible.

Suddenly, there was Lin Lifang, standing beside me with a plastic mug full to the brim with *pu-er* tea. Just the way I like it.

'I thought this might help you wake up.'

'But how did you know I was here?'

'I saw you come last night.'

Well, I thought with a twinge of admiration, I didn't spot you. The *pu-er* tasted superb after the odours of the night, and helped me get up and pull myself together.

'I'm just going back to my hotel to find my team and get a wash and shave.'

'Don't forget the first trucks will be here by around ten.'

'Trucks?'

'All the main ministries and public organisations are going to be parading through the square this morning in support of the students. They think Deng is finished.'

There was a certain something in his voice.

'You don't?'

'Deng Xiaoping is tough and old and very brave. It's taken him a lot of suffering to get to the top, and I don't think he'll give up easily.'

'Is that what your dad says?'

He laughed. 'The last time I spoke to him, yes.'

'Well, we'll see . . .'

'I've got a friend here called Wei Jingyi. Can we stay with you and translate?'

I knew how much my camera crew would appreciate that. They needed someone to keep the police off their backs and show them what to do and which rules they could ignore. All this requires intelligence, and intelligence shone out of Lin's crafty eyes.

Wei Jingyi was gentler, and a lot less manipulative. Lin called him over and introduced us. I liked him more than I liked Lin, but I knew which one I wanted to hire for the camera crew and which I wanted working with me.

27

Uncountable numbers of lorries covered with banners and jam-packed with officials chanting slogans around the general theme of 'Deng must go!' passed through the packed crowds and wound their way around the square: flatbeds, with all sorts of unlikely people hanging off them, each vehicle associated with a particular state group or government ministry.

There were trucks representing taxmen and government advertising agents, trucks for the food-processing industry, trucks for railwaymen, trucks for street-cleaners, trucks for the people who built social housing. Local government officials had at least a dozen. The police had loads of them, one for each main police station in Beijing and plenty from the provinces. The People's Liberation Army was particularly well represented. One truck was restricted to two-star generals. Colonels were the lowest ranks that I could see on the other PLA trucks. Different kinds of surgeons and physicians had their trucks, and so did nurses and hospital porters. There was one for supreme court judges, several for prosecutors, one for defenders, and plenty for the clerks and ushers. Lin told me later he'd been told that the prisoners had tried to get their gaolers to let them go too, but apparently someone reflected that after the festivities were over they'd probably just keep driving.

Each truck had its own sound system, blaring away, so the racket was indescribable. And perched on the back, waving flags and chanting slogans, was everyone who wanted to be able to say afterwards that they had been part of the great political change they were certain was coming.

Every newspaper in the country seemed to be represented, and there were big trucks for television and radio, with a couple of popular soap operas represented too. The stars, leaning off and blowing kisses, got the biggest cheer of the day. If you want to know which was my favourite, it was the three trucks from the Ministry of State Security. Yes, the spooks were out in force, including representatives of the thugs whose job it was to smash your teeth if the interrogators told them to. They were smiling and waving too. Even torturers like a carnival.

Lin translated every banner (I can only recognise a few dozen characters, so I'm functionally illiterate in Chinese), explaining the nuances. For instance, that while the top levels of the civil service were there, most senior politicians had stayed away. It took all day for the demonstration to unfold, and a few of the less interesting trucks were still going through the rapidly emptying square at six o'clock that night.

And then this vast nation paused to sit back and see what was going to happen. Lin and I sat watching state television until it was time for us to start editing our report for that night's news. The television news was a model of political balance. If Deng resigned, they'd be able to say they'd told people all about the opposition to him. And if he survived they'd say they'd been careful not to report the accusations against him. Western news organisations often pride themselves on their balance, but in China reporting the news was always a high-wire act.

I bullied Lin into ringing his dad to ask him what he thought. He was really unwilling, but I was implacable – and after an awkward conversation Lin put the phone down and said, 'He doesn't think it's going to happen.'

'What isn't going to happen?'

'Deng isn't going to resign.'

'But he's got to, hasn't he?'

'My dad says the old man has got balls of steel. The only hope was to break his nerve, and if he hasn't resigned by now he'll never go.'

It made one of my best stories ever, thanks to Lin Lifang. They splashed it in London that night – 'China's leader, Deng Xiaoping, defies the biggest protest the country has ever seen and hangs on to power' – while everyone else was still reporting the extraordinary turnout and saying it wasn't clear what would happen. No one else spotted the truck representing State Security, either; another exclusive which Lin notched up for me. I loved the shot of the plug-uglies grinning and waving their massive fists in the air. 'Even the thugs of State Security enjoyed their moment in the sun,' I wrote. Well, I thought, they'll be too busy trying to save their jobs to come round and sort me out.

28

Days passed, and May gave way to June. The deadlock in the square continued. Deng Xiaoping didn't cave in, as everyone thought he would, but he couldn't do anything because he couldn't find a general prepared to clear the students out. Apparently most of the generals had children in the square, and those who didn't refused to contemplate the murderous business.

Lots of foreign journalists, bored with waiting for something to happen, decided that the story was pretty much over. I didn't agree: not because I was so amazingly clear-sighted, but because I had Lin Lifang's advice to rely on; and his advice came direct from his dad.

Then, on the stuffy night of 3 June, as I was in the room in the Beijing Hotel we used as an office, sitting with my feet on the desk fanning myself with an old copy of the *Spectator*, Lin came running to the room. He was in a real panic.

'They're coming! They're coming!'

It took me some time to work out who he meant. Deng Xiaoping had managed to find his general at long last. The troops were on their way.

'And you know this how?'

He was so used to being treated as the fount of all knowledge that I think he was annoyed by the question.

'You said you wouldn't ask me about my sources.'

'No, but if I'm going to report it, I need to know how strong it is.'

'All right, my dad got it from a general who's a friend of the one whose troops are being ordered in.'

'And how strong is it?'

'Very strong.'

I did report it that night, and it made the lead. But by the time our report went out, the whole massacre had started up anyway.

We were just getting ready to go out and film when our female translator burst in.

'They're at Wukesong!' she yelled. Wukesong is in the west of Beijing. 'Hundreds of army trucks! And tanks! There are hundreds of tanks with them too.'

The tanks I doubted – much more likely to be armoured personnel carriers, I thought, though in fact it turned out she was right. But there was no doubt that everything was kicking off.

Sean and I looked at each other. He came from Derry, and I'd worked with him as my cameraman before. I knew how tough he was, and how quietly amusing. Just the kind of character you need alongside you when the shit is flying.

I'm not going to go into detail about that dreadful night: everyone knows what happened and I've told my part of the story again and again. Except the bit about how I saw the crowd attacking three weedy-looking, terrified soldiers who climbed out of an APC which had been set on fire.

Not being able to hold back, I waded in and bashed a couple of demonstrators with a half-brick I spotted on the ground. It was already wet with blood, so someone else must have been using it before me. The soldiers all survived – rescued by a group of students. But I was sick of the violence; and when Sean said he was running out of batteries and cassettes I suggested we go back to the hotel and replenish our stocks.

Lin looked drained and exhausted, but he perked up when I said that.

'Only for half an hour or so,' I said, but I knew how hard it would be to get everybody back on the streets again afterwards.

And so it proved: not because we were too scared, but because soon after we reached the hotel the army turned Chang'an Avenue, which ran past it, into a field of fire, shooting down everyone who came out onto it. We had a grandstand view from our hotel balcony on the seventh floor.

Don't imagine we were safe, even there; the soldiers squirted off burst after burst at us if they saw movement, and on the next balcony to ours a jolly Korean news photographer, who was always winking and smiling, took a round in the chest and died.

We got all the famous pictures, from the massacre in the avenue below us to the toppling of the statue of the Goddess of Democracy and the unfurling of a huge canvas barrier which stopped us, and everyone else, from seeing what went on in the square. But we could hear the long bursts of gunfire that followed.

During the early hours we were raided by the security police. There was a loud hammering on the door to the room we were filming from.

'Don't open it!'

Too late: Lin was standing near the door and pulled it open. Five burly plain-clothes security men were standing outside, and they grabbed him.

I screamed insults in Chinese. The security guys looked shocked that a *guizi* would know words like that, and for a heartbeat they paused. In that moment I got hold of Lin's other arm, and a tug of war started, with a human being instead of a rope. Sean ran over and held me round the shoulders, and together we pulled Lin back into the room.

'Now fuck off, or I'll report you to the Committee for State Security!' I yelled, not thinking about what I was saying; after all, it must have been the committee that had sent them.

They mumbled something apologetic-sounding, and went off to bang on another door further down the corridor. I suspect what swung the whole incident was my frenzied Mandarin: they simply hadn't been prepared for a large Westerner screaming obscenities at them in terms they could more or less understand.

I leant against an armchair, sweating with the violence and the heat – we'd switched the air-con off, so as not to affect the sound-track for filming – and grinned at Sean. He grinned back, and I saw he was holding his little camera (his big one was still on the tripod, on the balcony). He began looking through the eye-piece.

'You didn't get that, did you?'

'Bits of it. Enough.'

He was panting like me, but he'd had the coolness of mind to grab his gear on his way to helping me block a raid by the secret police. The Brits make great cameramen, and so do the Aussies, the Saffers, the Italians and the French; but always pick an Irishman if you think there's going to be trouble.

I looked round for Lin. He was sitting on the floor beside me, and (I still feel embarrassed to recall it) took my hand in his and kissed it.

Sean looked away, tactfully, and I pulled Lin to his feet: not difficult, since he was so light.

'You saved me.'

I made the kind of non-verbal sounds you make when some-one says something you can't entirely compute emotionally.

'Anyone would have done it' was what I finally came up with. Pretty feeble.

'They would have killed me, I know.'

'Well, they haven't.' I looked round. 'Have a glass of Jameson's. That'll sort you out.'

Offering a tot of Ireland's best is my equivalent of an Englishman suggesting a nice cup of tea.

Lin drank down a *taoscan* – the Irish equivalent of a dram – and I watched a flush pass across his pale face.

'There now, see how it's doing you good,' I said, just like my grandma.

'I'm very grateful.'

'No, well, time for everyone to get back to work. There's a lot of shooting going on out there still.'

29

At last it was day. The sun shone on the blood in the roadway beneath us, some of it dry and brown, some wet and reflecting the colours of the morning. There was the sound of gunfire, long bursts of it, and the occasional sound of screaming to show that the soldiers were still finding targets down there.

I'd lost all track of time as a result of watching so much horror, and I was shocked to see it was after nine o'clock. We'd been filming here for thirteen hours. Now came the difficult business of getting the pictures back to our base – another hotel, the Great Wall, about a quarter of a mile away.

I knew I could trust Lin to come with me, whatever the danger. We talked it over for a bit, but this wasn't something we could plan for; we'd just have to hope for a bit of luck. We copied the best of our material onto two cassettes, and I downed a quick Jameson's and forced Lin to drink one too. Amazing how it cheers you up.

In those days the cassettes we used were the size of a paperback, and were inclined to clank when you moved them around. It would be no good carrying them in a bag; the hotel lobby was full of secret policemen, like the ones who'd tried to snatch Lin during the night. They would search us, find the cassettes, and beat the bejaysus out of us.

Yet if we were to get to the Great Wall before noon, when we'd need to send the cassettes by courier to Hong Kong and Tokyo, we'd have to leave now. They were more likely to attack Lin than me, so I strapped one cassette to my left leg with gaffer tape and the other to my right, and pulled my socks up over them. If they stopped me and ripped the tape off, it was going to be a pain-fest. I shook hands with Sean, and we moved out.

We took the lift to the mezzanine floor, so we could see what was happening below us in the lobby. As I'd expected, it was full of spooks – maybe twenty of them. But by now they'd spotted our nervous faces looking down at them, and all we could do was walk down with as much confidence as we could muster.

The staircase was long, marble and very wide, and the cassettes made a horrible noise somewhere around my lower legs. There was no turning back. If we tried to run upstairs again, it would just be an invitation to the spooks to come and get us.

So, trying to keep calm and relaxed, we walked side by side towards the glass front of the hotel, and the revolving doors in the middle of it. A couple of besuited characters, large of build and aggressive of manner, came striding over.

God bless those wasteful Chinese architects, who designed their buildings as though square-metres didn't count and supplies of marble were eternal. The lobby was as big as the Taj Mahal, and the distance from the bottom of the staircase to the spooks must have been a good twenty yards.

While we were still too far away for them to hear the cassettes clanking, there was a wild burst of firing right outside. It went on for six seconds, at least: that's a lot of bullets from an automatic weapon. After that there was another burst, even longer, and the two spooks turned and ran over to the window to see what was going on.

Lin and I looked at each other and ran towards a huge hole in a window at the side of the hotel, where a tank round must have come in during the night. The hole was big enough for us to jump through side by side, and although there were yells at us to stop, I could hear from the voices that they did not have much conviction.

Even when we'd got away from the hotel and run across the forecourt to Chang'an Avenue, we still weren't safe. For a good half-hour we had to lie in the gutter, with my head close to Lin's feet, while the bullets cracked and whined through the air just over our heads. By this stage I don't think the soldiers cared what they were firing at, it was just a way of keeping the streets clear.

Lin said afterwards that a bullet had chipped off a bit of paving-stone not far from his right arm. I didn't notice. When I wasn't trying to bury myself into the roadway, I was congratulating myself that we'd chosen to come down the hotel staircase at the moment we did.

The rest of the story is a bit anticlimactic. When, finally, the shooting let up, we got to our feet and made our way to our base with no further trouble. We got the pictures there in time, and a couple of faithful airline passengers took them to Hong Kong and Tokyo for us, so all the pictures we'd filmed reached their destination.

I've forgotten to mention the man with the shopping-bags who stood in front of a line of tanks and actually climbed up and gave the crew a piece of his mind, shouting into the lead tank's cockpit, but I'm sure you remember him. I'd had a grandstand view of the entire thing. In the days and weeks that followed, we got lots of awards and official pats on the back, if that sort of thing matters. I pretend it doesn't, but of course it does. It was worth another £20,000 on my contract.

Later that day our office in London decreed that I should go to Hong Kong and edit a long documentary about it all, and for once I didn't resist. I needed a bath and a decent meal, and an absence of gunfire.

I told Lin. To my surprise, he burst into floods of tears.

'What's going to happen to me?'

I felt really sorry, and more than a little guilty. All I'd been thinking about was the story, not the people like him who'd got caught up in it.

What could I do to protect him, though? I'd have been delighted to take him to Hong Kong with me, but that was completely impossible. Soldiers or secret police would simply march him off when we got to the airport.

'Look – you'll have to head off home to your dad and get him to look after you. You'll be a lot safer that way.'

He nodded, and wiped the tears away with a loud sniff. I imagine he'd worked that out already.

'But I'm not leaving you till you go, Jon.'

That made me feel even more paternal towards him. He was only ten years younger than me, but he seemed impossibly vulnerable.

In the evening he drove me through the streets of Beijing to the airport. The main highway was blocked, so we had to take a long, circuitous route through the suburbs. I was shocked to see the after-effects of the violence everywhere: local Communist Party headquarters smashed and looted, police stations burned out, offices of the Ministry of State Security wrecked. It was starting to dawn on me that this hadn't just been a clear-out of the students in Tiananmen Square, it had been a revolution that almost succeeded – an anti-communist revolution. Amazing.

'Look at that,' said Lin, slowing down to a halt outside a police station.

It wasn't nice: the mob had poured petrol over a policeman and set fire to him; and afterwards someone had propped up his body against a wall and stuck a cigarette between his cracked and blackened lips. You've got to hate people an awful lot, as well as the system they work for, to do that to them.

We reached the airport at last. China might have come close to collapse, but my flight to Hong Kong was only delayed by ten minutes.

'Don't come in,' I said, turning to Lin as he sat behind the steering wheel.

'I must,' he said simply.

He carried my bag to the check-in desk, and stood there for an instant, looking more than ever like a kid in his T-shirt and shorts. Then he threw his arms round my neck and hugged me, while everyone watched.

'I'll never forget how you've helped me,' said Lin.

He turned away and walked out of the airport building with dignity.

30

And now it was nearly thirty years later: thirty years during which China had survived a shortish period of being cold-shouldered around the world, then spent a decade or so keeping its head down and making itself immensely rich. And then, when Xi Jinping became leader in 2012, it really started to flex its muscles. Some of us who remembered Tiananmen Square and the uprising against the Communist Party which followed the massacre wondered whether the Party could hang on to power indefinitely.

But thirty years is a long time, and two generations had grown up knowing nothing but the extraordinary prosperity the system had brought. If you stayed quiet, paid lip-service to a system which had no other ideology than to demand obedience, and concentrated on making money, you could live quite a rewarding life.

It didn't make sense to put that increasing prosperity in danger by challenging the system, just for the sake of some foreign ideal which no longer seemed quite so impressive. If democracy could make Donald Trump President of the United States, was it such a fantastic thing after all?

31

In her room at our hotel, Alyssa was working away, making arrangements. That gave me an hour or so to myself.

I made a discreet phone call to a contact of mine.

'Why don't we go to our usual place?' I said.

Our usual place was Ritan Park, a pleasant little area near the hotel, with a lake and several artistic boulders and a couple of traditional teahouses where you can get a bowl of noodles.

The contact and I had been to Ritan a couple of times in the past, once for me to see if a particular theory of mine about China's military strategy was right (it wasn't, apparently) and once for him to pump me about a series of demonstrations that had broken out near Xian.

Talking to him was like dancing with your sister: it felt slightly dodgy, and neither of us ever seemed to get what we really wanted from it. He had one of those flimsy cover jobs at the British embassy: deputy information officer, or third commercial attaché, or something. If you want to see who's in the British intelligence game, look at their titles. They're always a couple of steps below the level you'd expect for their age and seniority. The Foreign Office, which they pretend to work for, tends to disapprove and won't let them have any of the plum jobs; and since they're paid the usual rate for their diplomatic job but are getting a Secret

Intelligence Service salary as well, they don't much care what their title is. But it does make them easier to spot; and not just to journalists.

I watched Raj Harish walking towards me across the park. You certainly wouldn't think he was a spook by looking at him: third generation from India, with parents and grandparents running a travel agency in Hounslow. Raj was modestly built, and didn't dress anything like a diplomat.

Today he was in a Chelsea shirt with shorts and flip-flops. My great-uncle, who was a spook in the First World War and afterwards, would have been appalled – though come to think of it, he was brought up on Kipling's *Kim*, like all his generation, and that's full of unlikely Indians who are spooks; so perhaps he wouldn't have been so upset, after all.

I liked Raj a great deal. He had a vinegary approach to everything, and especially to the Chinese. He seemed to feel that in the twenty-first century it was an offence against reason for Marxism–Leninism to exist, let alone be the ruling ideology in one of the world's great bastions of capitalistic endeavour. He didn't think much of journalism, either, as he was always happy to let me know.

'It's just a way of earning a crust, Raj. Like being a spook.'

I always found it funny that Raj would never admit that's what he was. But accusing him of spying was my way of deflecting the criticisms of my own calling. He was right, of course: journalism *is* a crap way of life. I'm exhibit A where that's concerned.

We talked about nothing much for a while, and ate our noodles. It was only when we pushed the plates away that we got down to business.

'Why do I have the impression that you've got something you want me to look at?'

His accent was flat, no-nonsense London. He was one of the most perceptive characters I've come across. Whoever recruited him for SIS knew what they were doing.

I pulled Wei Jingyi's manuscript out of my shirt and handed it to him; it was distastefully warm, but I'm sure he'd had worse. He flicked his way through it for a few minutes, while I made sure no one was watching us. No one was, not even the waiter. He was too busy resting his feet on a stool in the kitchen. I could see him every time the breeze shifted the curtain. Good place, this.

'Yes, well, it looks fairly genuine. But I can't be certain.'

His caution was another thing I liked about him: you knew, when he did finally commit himself to something, that you could bank on it.

'We're interested in Mr Lin Lifang – very interested.'

'We?'

'The embassy.'

'Ah.'

'You know him, don't you?'

I gave him the potted history of my links with Lin. Then I thought I'd bring him up to date.

'There's this character Prinsett – Martin Prinsett, who seems to be pretty close to Lin's wife. British businessman. Do you know him?'

'I might do.'

'Well, I'll tell you what I think: I think you're in this together, and you want to get Lin Lifang working for you. If he doesn't already, which I'm inclined to suspect.'

Raj laughed.

'Journalism – I love it. Dig out a couple of diverse bits of information, stick them together, hype them up, and bingo! You've got yourself a story.'

'Well, have I?'

'Lin's an interesting character, and you'd do well to stick to him.'

'And I assume he's working for you.'

He put his head down close to mine and took hold of my wrist.

'Listen, Jon, we're mates and I really like you. But my advice would be to forget all this stuff and back off. This is serious, and it's for the professionals. If you get mixed up in it, you could end up in a bad situation. We've got protection, you see – we're in the business, just like the Chinese are, and that gives us enough of an edge to stay safe. You haven't got any protection at all, except the feeling that it'd cause too much of a fuss if they did something to you. But they can perfectly well pick you up and charge you with something nasty, and you could find yourself in jail for twenty years. Twenty years of having to watch yourself day and night, of never knowing if someone was going to poison you or shank you.'

'And no bending down in the shower, I suppose.'

'That'd be the good bit,' Raj said.

We both laughed.

'I can see you won't be warned off.'

He was right. I needed this trip to be a success, if I was to have any chance of avoiding the axe which was being sharpened for me even now, back in London. Shrugging and looking around for a story about pandas wouldn't do the business.

I didn't feel this had anything to do with Raj, though, so I didn't mention it to him. Maybe with hindsight I should have – it was the kind of thing he'd have understood immediately.

'And this manuscript?'

'I'd get rid of it as fast as you can.'

'What, chuck it away?'

'Up to you. But that'd be the safest thing.'

Funnily enough, I didn't feel like doing the safest thing.

Then, as offhandedly as if he was telling me he'd call for the bill, he said, 'I don't suppose you'd let me copy it?'

'So it *is* worth something to you, is it?'

'Oh, I wouldn't go as far as that. But if you're going to dump it, we might as well know what it's all about. I've only just flicked through it, after all.'

I laughed.

'So I get to do all the work for you, and you get the OBE.'

Usually his expression was serious and thoughtful, but now he cracked a grin.

'That sounds like a pretty good division of labour to me.'

I thought about it for a moment or two. I'd broken the unwritten code in a couple of ways, first by showing Raj I knew that Lin Lifang was working for British intelligence, and then by letting him see Lin's manuscript. I could put up reasonably strong arguments for doing both of those things, because they would help me get a better story. But that was it.

'Sorry,' I said. 'Thus far and no farther.'

'I had a feeling that's what you'd say.'

I slipped the manuscript back inside my shirt as nonchalantly as I could. We paid up, shook hands, and walked off in opposite directions.

On the way back to the hotel I decided what I was going to do with it.

32

Alyssa was sitting in the lobby when I got back. From the moment I stepped through the doors I could see she was furious; something about the way her shoulders were hunched. She must have been waiting a long time, and she didn't like to be kept waiting.

'Why don't we head down to the shopping mall? We can be more private there.'

She nodded, though it obviously irritated her to have to follow my lead in anything. We scarcely spoke on the way. In the mall we went straight to a teahouse and ordered some *pu-er*. Then I waited for her to let loose.

Actually, her annoyance at having to wait was mild compared with her fury when I explained about Wei Jingyi and the manuscript. For a moment I thought she was going to hit me.

'You fucking, fucking idiot, you're really putting our lives at risk. They'll find out what you've done and they'll come and get us – both of us.'

She didn't bother keeping her voice down. Not that it mattered: even if she'd been whispering, the look on her face would have shown anybody nearby what was going on. As it happened, though, we were in a quiet corner and no one seemed to be around.

I had a lot of admiration for Alyssa. She was formidable, and I'd never seen her really scared before. Perhaps she wasn't, even now. I was starting to get the impression that what really annoyed her was that I'd made a move without consulting her.

'Well, I'm sorry I didn't ask you about it first, I really am. But I couldn't have done that, because the man I spoke to in the park wouldn't have agreed to see you.'

She calmed down a bit; I don't think she'd been expecting me to apologise or explain. Alyssa was always thinking about the move after next, and she must have assumed I'd carry on blustering. I suppose that's what I usually do.

'Well, all right. But what's going to happen now? Have you got this thing on you?'

Discreetly, so that only she could see, I pointed to my shirt. The manuscript was tucked in there, quite securely, and didn't seem to be showing. I'd already decided to carry it round with me everywhere, until I could get rid of it. That meant either posting it or handing it to someone who was leaving the country. Someone reliable, who wouldn't get into trouble as a result of doing it. Even while Alyssa's voice was going on and on at me, I was trying to work out the best way of doing this.

'Yes,' I said a couple of times, more or less at random. It seemed like a good way of calming her down.

Giving the manuscript to a journalist was absolutely out. At a time like this, when the authorities seemed to be gearing up for a clampdown, journalists would get special attention. That left business people, though they could be damaged by smuggling something like this. And tourists. There were a few small groups of tourists staying in our hotel, going out for their daily doses of the Great Wall and the Forbidden City. Maybe I should . . .

'So who do you think?'

'The tourists, I suppose.'

'The *what*?'

It brought back the full force of her fury.

'You haven't been listening to a single thing I've been saying, have you? I'm asking you about who we should interview and you say "The tourists" for fuck's sake. What tourists?'

'Sorry – I was still thinking about how to get rid of the manuscript. I think we should try to get one of the tourists in our hotel to do it.'

There were more aftershocks, but she was obviously attracted by the idea. I let her subside before raising the subject again.

'If we disguise it in some way, then I could address the envelope to Jenny, and give her a ring in a day or so and tell her to expect it.'

Jenny was my PA, back in London. She was quick-witted and rather adventurous, and I was sure she would enjoy this kind of thing. All that was needed was to find the kind of pigeon I could rely on. Maybe the bunch of tourists in our hotel would provide one.

'I suppose so,' said Alyssa grudgingly.

The key thing, I realised, was to avoid the closed-circuit TV cameras in the hotel lobby. There was no shortage of them, except in the passageway leading to the lifts. Presumably they weren't needed there, since there were cameras outside the lifts and in the lobby. If I could find a likely tourist and steer them into the camera-free zone, we were in business.

Alyssa and I sat in the lobby for a while and waited. Now the storm was past, she was being rather nice to me, as compensation.

Groups of people from various parts of the world drifted past, but no Brits. And then, while I was deep in conversation with Alyssa, the answer to our problem appeared.

'Excuse me, Sir David.'

It's a bit late to explain this, but when I hit my sixties I started to look like David Attenborough. The resemblance wasn't there in earlier years, but as my hair has grown whiter it's become hard to avoid.

It annoys me for two reasons: first, because it means that I don't get recognised for who I actually am, and second, because he's ninety-something and I'm three decades younger. I also suspect he's a lot nicer and more sane than me. Not to mention better at his job. For once, though, it was a godsend that someone should mistake me for him.

I made my voice a bit throatier and older.

'Hello, yes?'

Alyssa, who knows my feelings about this, turned her head away and was struggling not to grin.

'I'm really sorry to interrupt you – I hope you forgive me – but are you here filming a programme? I just wondered if I could have a quick photo with you.'

She was in her forties, I suppose, dark-haired and dark-eyed; a bit on the large side but not unattractively so.

'But of course, dear lady.'

I was trying to think myself into the role, you see.

She went through the usual business of fiddling about with her phone, then asking Alyssa if she'd mind taking the shot. I put my arm round her, gripped her shoulder and grinned suitably. She was rather delightful, I decided.

'Er, *Sir David* . . .'

I'd obviously been holding on with a bit too much enthusiasm, and Alyssa was calling me to heel.

'Maybe I could ask you to do me a real favour in return,' I said, still trying to keep it throaty. And, steering her into the

CCTV-free zone with the skill of a ballroom dancer, I asked if she'd mind taking a letter back home for me.

Half an hour earlier, I should explain, Alyssa had asked the girl behind the reception desk for an envelope, and I'd written Jenny's name and London address on it. With a flash of improvisational brilliance I'd added the words NATURAL HISTORY UNIT.

I put it into the dark-haired woman's hands.

'Oh, I thought your Natural History Unit was in Bristol.'

'Ah well, you know how it is – they're always changing everything around.'

I realised that my real voice was starting to come through, so I tried to make it older and more crackly.

'You know, you're starting to remind me very much of that other man on TV – the one who does the news. All those wars.'

'Ah yes, dear lady – I know the one you mean. Brilliant fellow. He's actually a distant relative. Broadcasters tend to keep it in the family. We're a nepotistic lot, I'm afraid.'

She looked at me for a moment, then nodded: doubtfully, I thought.

Alyssa clearly thought so too.

'*Sir David*,' she said with an emphasis that was much too heavy, 'don't forget you've got to take that phone call from New York. We really ought to be—'

'Oh yes – absolutely,' said the dark-haired woman.

She was obviously still trying to work out who I reminded her of.

I ran through a few basic instructions about posting it when she got back to London, and gave her a fiver to pay for the stamps. She put the envelope into her backpack with a flourish, as though she was on important business for the nation, and politely refused the note I was holding out. I had the feeling that there was something in her glance that said, 'If you weren't in your nineties . . .'

But I was probably just imagining it.

33

That evening I said goodnight to Alyssa, and walked down the corridor to my room. You never see or hear anyone else in this place, I thought: either the rooms are remarkably well insulated, or the hotel's empty.

I reached my door and started fiddling around with the key – which wasn't really a key, but a kind of credit card – and saw that the door was slightly open, a quarter of an inch or so. I pushed it very gently and slipped through.

The downstairs part was dark and the curtains were closed but on the upper floor a light was on. Just a small one: the flexible kind on a stalk which is the last thing you turn out at night when you go to sleep.

Someone was hanging around in my bedroom, waiting for me.

There are three things you can do at a time like this: tiptoe out and go and have a drink in the bar and hope the bastard goes away; shout for help; or creep in and take him by surprise. In this case, all three had their drawbacks. Heading back down to the bar seemed attractive, but would leave the basic problem unsolved. Shouting, in the thick-walled, mausoleum-like silence of this hotel, wasn't guaranteed to work. That left creeping in.

Of course, I didn't think through the options in this way, rationally and carefully. I'm more of the bull-in-the-china-shop type, inclined to rush in and create a loud noise. 'Must learn not to give way to mindless aggression' my old rugby master once wrote on my school report.

But I have learned the value of sneakiness. I crept across the downstairs floor, which was thickly carpeted, and made my way soundlessly to the foot of the open staircase. I still couldn't see the interloper, but I heard the bed give a little creak as he – or was it she? – shifted position.

The stairs were concrete, and covered with carpet. I reckoned I could get almost to the top before I needed to start roaring and frightening whoever it was. So I went up on my hands and knees, and lifted my head just enough to get a look.

I know what you're thinking. If this was a Bond film, some gorgeous girl would be lying there in a see-through negligée, saying, 'What kept you, James?' And I'd reply with some carefully crafted double entendre which people would still be quoting as they filed out of the cinema at the end. But this was real life; girls like that are in short supply, and women don't seem to wear negligées in bed much nowadays.

No. As I raised my head above the last couple of stairs I could see who it was: not Pussy Galore, but the suited, black-shoed form of the man I'd last seen outside Malone's restaurant in London.

Martin Prinsett, the good friend of the Lins.

I'd brought my walking stick with me. Ever since I was injured in a bombing attack – the US Air Force, naturally – I take it everywhere. My shrapnel-weakened leg sometimes needs a bit of support, and it's a useful way or reminding my bosses that they still owe me. Now I whacked it down on the top step, which made Prinsett jump a bit.

'You total arsehole,' I said.

Not much of a James Bond one-liner, I grant you.

'Look, I'm really, really sorry, but I was scared,' he bleated. 'Someone's been following me, and I thought I'd be safe here. Then I came up and watched a bit of TV to calm my nerves.'

He pointed to the screen. It was on, and someone was telling us in dumb-show what new levels the pound had dropped to.

'Why isn't the sound on?'

Not the most urgent question, I suppose, but it needed to be asked.

'Because I didn't want anyone to know I was here.'

This was all getting too much for me.

'OK, so who's after you?'

And since it seemed likely to be a long story I encouraged him to come down the stairs to my sitting room and go through the contents of the minibar with me.

He settled himself on a sofa, under a large picture of a Tang dynasty horse, with a double whisky in his hand and the door shut and bolted.

'You should see that woman. She's a killer.'

I assumed he was talking about Madame Lin, so I didn't break the flow.

'I went to Huzhang because it's big and heavily industrialised, and most Western businessmen haven't even heard of it. And since the Lins run it, I made sure I got to know them. One thing led to another.'

'You were sleeping with her.'

'Well, I . . . Yes.'

'And Lin Lifang found out.'

It wasn't a question. Lin Lifang was the kind of man who'd know if you'd forgotten to return a library book.

'Lin confronted her, and they had a screaming row – really violent. Right in front of me. But she's the dangerous one, believe me. When I said I'd better get out of Huzhang, I thought she was going to kill me there and then.'

'But you did anyway.'

'If I hadn't, Lin's thugs would have taken me out.'

I could see the problem.

'I hired a car and drove to another city. The Lins had Huzhang airport completely under their control, so it was too dangerous to fly from there.'

'But there's something else you want to tell me, isn't there?'

'Yes.'

He sat there, sipping his whisky and trying to work out how to phrase it. And, presumably, what to leave out. I suddenly felt sorry for this character who'd previously seemed so pleased with himself. And, anyway, showing sympathy for someone who's badly scared is a useful way of getting them to tell you everything.

'You poor bastard. It must have been pretty scary.'

It wasn't just a tactic: he was almost quivering with fear.

My words did the trick, and the confession started to flow. Altogether, it was a seedy business. Prinsett had gone to Huzhang in the hope of representing a variety of high-level luxury concerns – perfumes, watches, clothes, cars – but he'd ended up as Madame Jade's man of business. The watches and cars started to appear all right, but so did some vicious stuff: lion bones, tiger bones, ivory, pangolins, abalone. Anything there was a market for, regardless of ethics.

She'd set up a couple of factories which turned out fake antiquities for the Hong Kong, Singapore and Taiwan markets, and for the wealthy Chinese collectors in Vancouver, San Francisco and London. They were starting to sell to European and American museums too.

According to Prinsett, Madame Jade was behind some of China's biggest and most profitable scams, and Lin Lifang protected her. Prinsett himself wasn't, he claimed, involved in every aspect of what she did, but he knew what was going on, because she told him about it.

'In bed.'

'Well, yes, sometimes.'

I tried to see him through her eyes. Prinsett wasn't necessarily good-looking by Western standards, but he had delicate features, clear blue eyes, and a small silky beard. And he was tall and willowy; too bony, I'd have said, but then I'm not a middle-aged Chinese cougar looking for someone to spend the night with.

'She liked it when I spoke Welsh to her,' he added, for no reason I could see. 'And sang.'

He grinned, a bit foolishly.

'In Welsh?'

'Not only in Welsh.'

'So you think she's followed you to Beijing.'

'I booked myself onto my usual flight to Geneva yesterday, and I assume they'll know about that. I'm just hoping they won't find out that I didn't get on board.'

'Surely they can find that out, though?'

'Yes, probably, but for the time being I think they'll just have checked with the airline and seen that I was booked to Geneva. I don't think it would have occurred to them that I might stay an extra night or two here in Beijing.'

'And why would you want to do that?'

'Because I knew you'd be here. You told me this was the hotel you always stayed at.'

I remembered. It was when we'd just decided to have another dozen oysters. Suddenly, Malone's seemed enviably safe, and an awfully long way away.

'I rang the switchboard from the taxi as I came in, and asked the hotel operator which room you were in. Security's useless here – she told me straight out. Then when I arrived I explained to the man on the desk that I'd left my key card in my room: 547. I guessed they wouldn't ask for any ID, and he didn't. He just handed me a new one. So I came here and waited.'

'What do you think they'd do if they found you?'

He didn't say anything. He didn't really need to.

'And it's worth running this risk, just to tell me what you've been up to with her?'

'I needed to let someone know what has been going on; someone who could tell the world. After that I'd be happy to take my chances.'

He sounded genuine, and I actually felt some admiration for him. And pity.

After that, as we sat there, he showed me a variety of documents to back up his story. I'd need to get them professionally translated, I thought, as we went over the fine details: dates, names of organisations, exact consignments. There was obviously a tremendous story here, and an important one.

The only problem was, if we did a big reveal about Madame Jade, my good friend Lin Lifang would be brought down too. Did I want that? Well, no. I liked Lin, and if he became the next leader of China I'd be in a fantastic position. I might even make a bit of cash, for a change.

And yet on the other hand, I'm a newsman from way back. I've spent my entire life searching for stories, and now this hugely important one had landed in my lap. Could I simply dump it in the bin and walk away? I knew I couldn't. Look, I've tried to be honest with you. So I'm asking you now to believe me when I say that reporting a story has always been more important to me than my safety, my happiness, my future, and (clearly) my sanity. If I ignored all this stuff about Madame Jade's evil dealings, I'd be a worse shit than ever.

What a position to be in. I pulled out a plastic travelling-bottle of Jameson's and poured us both a big slug.

Sorry about this, Lin old son, I thought, as I downed the stuff in one go: I'm going to pull your wife down, and you'll go down with her. But I couldn't keep out of my mind the image of him from thirty years before: skinny and vulnerable, and a bit inclined to hero-worship.

Of course, I had plenty of stuff on Lin already – the Excalibur phone call, and the document he'd written, which I hoped was on its way to London. But these things had been handed to me as a direct result of our friendship, and I regarded them as some-thing to maintain a permanent silence about, as a matter of honour.

I know, I know – I'm beginning to sound like something out of *The Prisoner of Zenda*. But if Lin was secretly a traitor to China, if he was planning to overthrow the unsavoury leadership of his own country, well, that seemed to me to be his business. As long as he could square it with his own conscience, I didn't feel it was my job to betray him.

The depredations and crimes of Lin's wife were totally different. Assuming Prinsett was correct, they were serious stuff. And since all this had come my way, I knew I'd have to report on it.

I banged my glass down hard on the table. Maybe, subcon-sciously, I felt like a judge hammering his gavel.

Prinsett jumped.

'Listen to me,' I said.

His blue eyes locked onto mine.

'You're in real trouble. These people won't give up on you – they'll follow you, and catch you. And I don't think anyone will help you. Forget all the stuff about witness protection programmes. For one thing, no government is going to help you that way. And, anyway, for someone like you to go and live in Woolloomooloo or Medicine Hat for the rest of your life would be much worse than getting a bullet in the back of the neck. There's only one way out: you'll have to bring Madame Jade to justice. That's the sole way she won't be able to get you.'

I might be sounding more than usually pompous, but it was true. And it was important for me, too. Now he'd told me the whole story, I was on Madame Jade's hit list at number two, just behind him.

'The two of us will do it together. That's why you came to see me, isn't it?'

He nodded. 'I suppose so.'

'Good. Now you've got to do the hardest thing you've ever done: you've got to head back to Huzhang and try to make it up with her.'

He shook his head, but I knew I had to be relentless. And I thought I stood a chance of convincing him.

'Get her to let me come there and see them. I'll gather together the materials for a report that will be so bad the Chinese authorities will have to arrest her and put her on trial. It's the only way either of us is going to survive.'

He sat there for a bit, breathing heavily.

'But . . .' he said once, then went quiet while he thought about it again.

I thought I'd take one last shot at it.

'You're a dead man unless you can destroy her. It's her or you.'
More silence. Then, 'OK, I'll do it.'
I shook his hand.

After that we had to work out a brief history for him, in case they checked up. He mustn't stay here at the hotel: that would make it look as though we were plotting something together. So we rang the Four Seasons (it's the new name of the Beijing Hotel, where I'd taken refuge during the Tiananmen massacre) and got him a room there.

The plan was that he'd ring Madame Jade in the morning and see if he could talk her round – and persuade her husband to accept him back in Huzhang. Preferably without killing him.

I didn't go down to the lobby with him, in case there might be some character sitting behind a copy of the *People's Daily* there. We shook hands again at the door of my room, and he walked off down the silent corridor with a grace and litheness I'd only just started to notice. At the point where the corridor turned, he looked back and waved to me. He'll do it, I thought.

34

Over breakfast the next morning, Alyssa listened without interruption to my story. She felt, as I did, that we had to uncover a good story here in China, in order to cover our backs in London; and while I'm certain she'd have preferred one which was a bit less laden with risk, she could see that a report about the wife of a top Chinese leader being involved in importing tiger bones and selling phony antiquities would make a pretty fair splash around the world.

We hung around for a long time, ordering pots of tea and the occasional Tsingtao beer and going over the story again and again, working out what material we'd need and who we should confide in. I had some ideas about that.

'There's a couple of people here who'd be really useful. One is my friend Raj, who works for the British embassy and is almost certainly a spook. And the other is a rough, tough dissident I know called Terry Ho. You'll like Raj, but my guess is you won't like Terry much. He doesn't seem to clean his teeth all that often. Or change his clothes.'

'Yuk,' she said; but it annoyed her that I'd made up my mind who she'd like and who she wouldn't, so we had a mild barney about that for a while.

The other thing we discussed at some length was who we should talk to in our organisation about the story. Alyssa was keen that we should get onto someone senior and give them the full details before we started.

I resisted. I'd had so many fights over the years with my editors, trying to keep control of the way I covered stories, while they tried to take them off me and give me my instructions from thousands of miles away. Now I wanted to keep this one in Alyssa's hands and my own.

In the end we compromised: not a word I often associate with her. My argument was that the office would immediately start to put security all over us, and I was afraid that would wreck the story. Alyssa didn't have such a hostile view of our employers as I did, but I was absolutely certain that the best way was for us to run the story as we saw fit.

'How about I ring Os and give him a general idea of what we're doing, and what the problems might be? We could make an arrangement to call him every three or four days, and if for some reason we don't, he should go to the management and let them know.'

Alyssa liked that – and rightly, because even though she wasn't particularly fond of Os, she knew we could rely on him.

I went up to my room to phone him. It was a delight to hear his gruff voice and detect his genuine enthusiasm.

Of course he hadn't been doing anything of interest about Brexit; stopping him from coming to China was just a way of heaping extra punishment on me. He'd been sent to film the comings and goings in Downing Street, and there's nothing more boring than that.

I switched to Afrikaans, another language I don't speak well, because I assumed it would confuse anyone who was listening.

'We've got a story here, Os, and it's quite a tricky one. I'd feel a lot happier if I thought you knew about it. I can't give you the details, but if you don't hear from us for a few days – three, say – then get on to the management and let them know. Otherwise assume everything is going reasonably well.'

'OK, *baasjie*,' Os rumbled. I could tell he was happy just being in the loop. He seemed to put up with my mangling of the *moedertaal* with remarkable patience.

I'd just ended the call when my phone rang.

'It's Martin,' said the excited voice at the other end. 'Martin Prinsett. I really need you to come round as quick as you can. Something's come up.'

I asked him for his room number, and said I'd be round as quick as possible; the Four Seasons was only about twenty minutes away. I tried calling Alyssa, but her phone was busy the whole time and I didn't leave her a message.

I'll call her as I walk along, I thought.

But I'm a careless sod, and I'd forgotten to charge up my phone. So as I hurried down the avenue and pressed her number again, I saw the screen fade to black. My grandmother back in County Louth used to quote the old adage, when she saw I hadn't done my shoelaces up, about 'for the want of a nail, the shoe was lost'. You know the one – it ends up with the kingdom being lost.

Well, I suppose she was right. Anyway, I wasn't able to tell Alyssa where I was going. I'll do it when I get to the Four Seasons, I thought.

Only I didn't get to the Four Seasons. A big blacked-out four-by-four drew up beside me as I hurried along Chang'an Avenue. And a couple of men I hadn't noticed rushed up behind me, grabbed me and got me into the back of the car before I even had a chance to yell.

35

Because I'd stupidly broken rule number one in the 'operating in difficult areas' manual, it was a couple of hours before Alyssa decided that something must have happened to me. She rang our local bureau, but didn't feel that anyone there had grasped the disturbing possibilities. No one at our office in London was remotely interested. I'd show up, they said. She didn't want to explain to them why she was worried, so she just left it. That left her with only two other people to contact: Raj Harish and Terry Ho who I'd mentioned to her earlier.

Raj was immediately worried. I'd vanished just before eleven in the morning and the timing of my disappearance seemed to disturb him the most.

'Not to worry, I'll get some enquiries going. We'll find him. All that stuff you hear from the Yanks about white hats and black hats you can forget,' Raj told her. 'You know, Deng Xiaoping once said that in the evening everyone's hat was grey.'

'Did he really?' Alyssa asked, doubtfully.

'No, I made it up. But it was just the kind of thing he always said.'

Alyssa liked him better after that. And she liked him even more when he promised to speak to one or two of his Chinese security contacts. But she was worried, sitting in her room by the phone, too worried to be able to read or look at the internet.

It was 7.30 when Raj came round to the hotel. They sat in the bar with a couple of untasted Tsingtaos in front of them.

'I've been talking it over with someone in Chinese military intelligence.'

Alyssa noticed that every time he used words like 'intelligence' or 'secret' he dropped his voice. It was more noticeable, she thought, than if he'd just said them normally.

'The military people here don't get on with the civilian ones so he was prepared to be a bit more open.'

He took a swig of his Tsingtao like a full stop, before opening up a new line of thought.

'We've got to consider the possibility that Jon has disappeared because of the document he got from the bookseller.'

I'd rather covered up the details of what I'd told Raj, so this was awkward. Alyssa had given me her views at some length about journalists who got too close to government officials. I'll cultivate anyone, I had said.

'Would you have cultivated Heinrich Himmler?'

'Well, I'd definitely have gone to meet him. I mean, I used to see Saddam Hussein quite a bit. And Colonel Gaddafi. And I got reasonably close to Osama bin Laden.'

Anyway, since she needed Raj's help, she was willing to stay quiet about the whole complicated question.

Raj went on, 'I think it'd be an amazing coincidence if Jon had got hold of a document like the one the bookseller gave him, and then disappeared for a different reason.'

'All right, so who does your military intelligence buddy' – she found herself dropping her voice like he did – 'think is behind this non-coincidence?'

'I didn't ask him that, because he obviously doesn't know anything about the document. His assumption is that State

Security has picked him up and is giving him a going-over to get information out of him.'

Alyssa didn't like the sound of that.

'But according to my friend, it isn't likely they'll do anything really bad to him, because that would lead to all sorts of international problems. Of course they do nasty things to journalists all the time, but those are Chinese journalists; or they're usually from Xinjiang or Hong Kong – people the government can get away with beating up and killing. The Chinese leadership doesn't like being made to feel uncomfortable, and State Security knows that very well. That's my friend's view, anyway.'

'And you – what do you think?'

Raj looked away.

'Well, we know a little more about it, don't we? I think the document's what it's all about. That means it's either State Security trying to find out what Lin Lifang is planning to do, or it's Lin who's had second thoughts and wants to make sure Jon doesn't say anything. And that'd be a lot more serious than State Security asking him a few questions.'

'And you think it's Lin's lot, don't you?'

'I'm afraid it could be.'

'So what do I do?'

'Nothing. You'll just have to wait till we hear something.'

'Wait,' Alyssa repeated dully.

'I'll keep the contacts going, and let you know the moment I hear anything.'

He drained his beer and walked out.

Alyssa sat there for a bit, while the barman watched her. Barmen can always spot a crisis when they see one. Then she made her mind up and signed the bill.

Outside in the street she dialled Terry Ho's number.

'I'm a colleague of your friend Jon. He gave me your number. Can I see you? It's rather urgent. I'm in the place he always stays.'

Terry had a long-suffering wife, who knew she came right at the back of a long queue of political dissidents, work contacts, and a couple of girlfriends. It sounded to Alyssa as though he was in the middle of dinner.

'I'll be there in half an hour,' he said through a mouthful.

Alyssa waited for him in the hotel forecourt. When he arrived she was a little put off by his teeth, and by the impression he always gave that he'd been sleeping rough for a couple of nights. But she could see he was clever, and she was rather touched by his obvious concern.

She told him everything, except Raj's name and job: she just said he was a diplomat. As he listened, Terry banged his fist against his head a couple of times in frustration.

'He told me yesterday that the two of you were onto a good story, but he didn't say what. I meant to tell him to be careful and not go out alone. But I didn't do it.'

They talked it over. Alyssa could see that Terry was formulating some plan, but he didn't tell her what it was.

36

Let me be frank. After my seventh round of waterboarding I would have told them anything. I even tried to, but they were so busy hurting me they didn't give me a chance. One of them got a hard-on while he was doing things to me. A guy I interviewed in Argentina in the early 1980s, a young Jewish psychiatrist, said that when he'd been tortured at the dreadful ESMA complex in Buenos Aires the men doing it were out of their minds with the pleasure they were getting, and scarcely even bothered to ask him any questions. I remember wondering at the time how I would hold up under torture, and hoping I'd never find out. Well, I have now.

You long for it to end. If that means dying, you pray you'll be drowned this time, and you even try to help the process along. Except that they're too clever for that. They've got ways of prolonging it. If only it was just a matter of physical harm, like being kicked or beaten, I could have dealt with that. After all, that's what happened to me in Oxford at the start of all this.

But what happened in that bathroom in the house on the outskirts of Beijing was infinitely worse. And looking at the torturers' faces while they did these things was a major part of it.

I have to confess it: I told my captors everything I knew about Wei Jingyi, the bookseller. More than I knew, in fact: I invented things, hoping they wouldn't believe me, and not even caring whether they did or not.

It was the worst thing that has ever happened to me and I behaved badly. All I would say, before you judge me, is that I'm pretty sure you'd behave the same way.

It was a lot easier when they started asking me about the document. For a start, it was in Chinese, so I could say with some hope of being believed that I had no idea what it was about. Secondly, it was safely in London by now, and so was the woman who thought I was David Attenborough.

She was in the clear. I had no memory of her name, nor any idea where she lived. She'd told me, of course, and given me her email address too. I wrote it all down at the time but after I'd heard from Jenny that she'd received the document I destroyed the bit of paper I'd written everything down on.

Jenny was safe, too. When they asked me who I'd sent the document to in London, I gave them the details of my awful boss, Charles: full name, email address, office address, phone number. Go round and tie him to a plank, I thought.

I'm not a bad poker player, and I know how to disguise my thoughts reasonably well. But when you're lying naked, waiting to be drowned again, and they tell you that this time they're going to put a live electric wire into the water, and they're doing things to your body at the same time, I suppose it's not difficult for them to tell the genuine from the made-up.

So when they asked for the details of the pigeon who'd taken it to London, 'sally.stevens@gmail.com' didn't impress them; maybe I paused a moment too long as I tried to remember what I'd invented earlier. I actually told them the truth at first, that I'd forgotten her name and email almost as soon as she walked out of the hotel. But they didn't think anyone in my job could be so stupid.

It was no good pretending to be unconscious. I did quite a bit of that, naturally, but they were thoroughly experienced at this, especially the bastard in charge, who was always smiling. He was the one with the hard-on. They just continued, whether they thought I was conscious or not. I suppose it didn't really matter to them.

Horrible, horrible stuff, and I'm sorry I've dwelt on it so much. But it came to an end, as even the worst things always do; and just to be left on my own, throbbing with pain and bleeding from places you don't want to bleed from, was a kind of relief I'd never previously experienced. In the end they took me out of that filthy bathroom and dumped me down.

'Fuck this dirty pig,' said the smiley one, and the words had a kind of final sound to them.

Thank God, I thought, they're going to kill me now.

But they didn't. The floor had those grey marble tiles shot through with red streaks that I'd noticed when I was brought in. I could hear noises downstairs for a while, then a car engine, then nothing. I've no idea how long I lay there, not doing anything, just trying to carry on existing. They'd broken me down to the point where I was an organism, not a person. I didn't even want to survive.

I must have wandered off into unconsciousness for a while, and when I woke up and realised that no one was going to do anything else to me I started feeling better. I was alive, and no part of me seemed to have been actually lost, though my nasal passages and throat felt as though they'd been hosting the Rugby World Cup. And my forehead and my knees and shins were bloody. Blood had flowed from my ears, as far as I could judge, and from other places. They'd shoved things into me.

They'd stolen my watch, but when I woke the light was different so I assumed that quite a few hours had gone past. I tried moving but it was too painful, so I lay there for a long time, neither fully asleep nor fully awake.

When I came back to full consciousness, and saw the light coming through the far window, I decided that I'd had enough of lying down. Yet when I tried turning over and getting up I yelled out and sank back again.

After a long time I managed to get to my feet and tried out a few steps, leaning heavily on the wall, and that felt good. I navigated around the wall to the door and peered out. All dark, all silent. I got myself out onto the landing. On the far side was the bathroom; I had no desire to go in there. Three other doors were open and one was closed. What is it about closed doors? I eased my way round by using the balustrade and tried the handle.

It wasn't quite as empty as the rest of the house, and it was a lot more sinister. In the middle stood one of those huge padded mahogany armchairs. There were plastic-coated wires dangling from the arms, and twisted as though they'd been used to tie someone up. I took one glance at the upholstered seat of the chair and looked away quickly. Gobs of blood had been sprayed onto the marble tiles in various directions. Judging from the state of the blood it must have been a day or so earlier. Mr Smiley and his friends had been busy boys.

I turned away and limped back to the landing.

Getting out of the house was a long process. I realised I was on one of those big estates in the hills overlooking Beijing, which the young and wealthy like because they think the air there won't kill them.

The estate was quiet and not designed for walking around. I reasoned – correctly, as it turned out – that a place like this would have a guard on the gate.

Two blokes were sitting there, chatting and listening to the radio. One was drinking out of a small thermos. I must have looked pretty bad judging by their reactions.

I launched into inaccurate Chinese, but they seemed to get the point. I'd been brought in by some gangsters and tortured, I said. They fell over each other to call a taxi.

When the taxi arrived I told the driver to take me to the hotel, and fell fast asleep.

When I woke up, Mr Chang the doorman was shaking me.

'Mr Jon, Mr Jon – this hotel. Get out, please.'

He dug the money out of his own pocket to pay the driver. Then he helped me in, very gently, and set me down in a chair in the lobby. I was so glad to be back in the safety of the hotel that I cried a bit, which was embarrassing. But the little group of hotel people and passing guests who had gathered round me clucked sympathetically. One patted my head. That shot violent pains down my neck and shoulders, but it was kindly meant.

And then Alyssa was there, and she was crying too, and a couple of porters held me under the arms and pretty much carried me to the fourth floor.

'Well, so I got in here at last,' I croaked, after the porters and Mr Chang had been paid. I was lying on her double bed, looking out of the window.

'Yes, well, don't try your luck,' she said, but she was beaming at me. 'I was so worried about you.'

'*You* were worried,' I croaked.

But the business of lying on a really comfortable bed got in the way of the banter, and I found myself drifting off to sleep. Faintly, in the background, I heard her say, 'Yes, isn't it great? He's basically all right, but he's looking a bit roughed up.'

Before I dropped off I remembered to tell her that she must ring Os. Was there anything else to tell her? I was still trying to work it out when I slipped off into unconsciousness.

37

As soon as I woke up, I knew what it was. Maybe my unconscious mind had been turning it over while I slept.

It was Martin Prinsett who'd called me, and led me into the ambush on the avenue. Had he done it voluntarily, or had someone forced him? I didn't feel up to interrogating him for a bit, but Alyssa needed to know about it.

There was a ring at the door.

A middle-aged character in a white jacket, the hotel doctor, I suppose, was standing there. He came over and started prodding me with a rubber-gloved finger. The examination took twenty minutes, and he asked Alyssa to leave the room for most of that time.

The verdict was that I'd suffered a good deal of trauma but nothing was actually broken – I could have told him that – and a few days' rest would sort me out. I could have told him that too. He murmured something to Alyssa about psychiatric help – I distinctly heard the words – but I didn't find that so interesting. She smiled at me as he left, and got on the phone some more.

It all seemed distinctly positive, and the best bit of all was that I was in Alyssa's bed, and she seemed all set to look after me.

'And no funny business,' she said, looking at me as she put the phone down on another call.

'How could you say that to an injured man, at a time like this?' I muttered plaintively.

'Because I know you too well. You'll still be trying it on when you're on your deathbed.'

'If you don't treat me nicely, maybe this will be my deathbed.'

She laughed, and I laughed, and we both felt quite good as a result. Normal service was being resumed.

Later, as my appetite came back and I sat there looking through the room service menu, sipping Johnnie Walker from her mini-bar, she told me what had happened while I'd been away.

We invited Raj and Terry Ho to come and hear my story. Raj's advice had been bang on the nail: don't make a big fuss for the first couple of days, in case London ordered me home. After all, he worked for a big dysfunctional outfit too. That way, although the key people all knew, it hadn't got into the papers back home.

I was glad about that. The thought of all those hacks misspelling my name and getting my age and general circumstances wrong and wanting to interview me so they could write up their own ideas of what happened had been worrying me. Instead, Alyssa was able to sort everything out with a few phone calls: our desk in London, the foreign ministry, the British embassy, the Irish embassy. None of them wanted any trouble, and they were all delighted to shut the file. I expect plenty of them thought I'd made it all up anyway.

For the first time, I told her about Prinsett's call and how it had lured me into the ambush on Chang'an Avenue.

'Do you think he knew what he was doing?' she asked.

'I can't work it out. Would you mind speaking to him?' I asked. 'I don't feel up to it.'

She snorted, and I let myself drift back to sleep.

In the evening the other two came, and Alyssa did that encouraging business of plumping the pillows and making me sit up in bed, and she organised a glass of hot whisky and lemon and some hot soup from room service. Somehow, she had also got hold of a big bottle of Jameson's. Plus she'd bought me a pair of silk pyjamas so that I could hold court in style. A couple of golden dragons chased each other round on a royal-blue background: very fetching.

Raj and Terry had different ideas about who might be responsible; they got on moderately well, though each was wary of the other. Raj took notes, which I found obscurely satisfying. Usually I'm the one who takes notes about what other people say.

'Definitely State Security,' Terry said; but he thought State Security was behind just about everything in China. 'The use of a big private house argues money, and that looks like Lin's people,' Raj countered.

Alyssa had spoken to Martin Prinsett by this stage, and he'd denied having anything to do with the kidnap plot. The reason he'd called me was that he'd just heard from Madame Jade, and she seemed to be open to the idea that we should go to Huzhang with him. That's why he was worked up when he spoke to me, he said.

They talked it over for a while, without reaching any agreement.

I half listened, but an unpleasant realisation was coming over me. I'd been so focused on my own problems I'd utterly forgotten about the room with the bloodstained armchair in it. I'm told that when you've had a big shock you get lapses like these; though in my case I think it was because I was trying to offload the memory of what I'd done. Now I was safe and comfortable I felt even more ashamed of myself.

So I told them everything I'd seen.

'Wei Jingyi,' Terry said quietly.

They all looked at me.

'Wei disappeared four days ago,' Terry went on. 'They told his wife not to tell anyone, but after a couple of days she got in touch with me.'

I was trying to come to terms with all this. Wei must have been taken to the house before I arrived. And judging from the evidence of the armchair, he must have been lugged out of it a day or so before I got there. I was appalled, but a faint glimmer of something like relief started to creep over me. Maybe my betrayal of him hadn't done him any damage after all, because the damage had already been done.

The others were arguing over whether Wei's disappearance was part of the same pattern as mine.

'It has to be,' Alyssa said. 'Otherwise we've got to consider a major coincidence. And I personally don't believe in coincidences, big or small.'

She looked at me meaningfully: it was a direct quote.

I began to talk about the questions the interrogators had put to me about Wei, but gave the impression I'd held out and hadn't admitted anything of importance. I decided not to go into detail about the methods they'd used on me, except to say I'd been waterboarded. It probably wasn't necessary anyway; I suspect the doctor will have given them an outline of what had happened.

I couldn't tell whether they believed my line about not giving in to questioning about Wei. Probably not. I wouldn't have believed it, if someone had told me a story like that.

When I'd finished, they talked as though I wasn't there; perhaps they found the things I'd said a bit difficult to process. I watched them: the British spy whose dad was an Indian travel agent, the

Chinese dissident who was always looking for a fight with authority, and the half-south Londoner, half-Nigerian princess. Alyssa was the one who summed it all up, naturally.

'It looks to me as though it's all part of a scheme to flush out Lin Lifang and make him take action prematurely, so they can stop him and put him away.'

I grinned.

'The real question is, what do we do?'

I thought it was time to remind them I was still a player.

'Let me just say I'm not leaving China. I know that's what the office will want me to do' – I looked at Alyssa, who nodded – 'and I dare say the embassy would much prefer not to have me hanging round and being a nuisance. But I'm not going.'

I looked from Raj to Terry Ho.

Terry nodded.

'But this isn't just something that happened to me by chance. It happened because we were on a story, and I don't believe in leaving a story until it's finished.'

Having delivered my credo, a little self-consciously, I felt tired, and lay back on the pillows. Looking back, I hope the whole performance wasn't too dramatic.

Everything now depended on Alyssa, since it would be hard for me to stay in Beijing on my own.

'It's obviously pretty dangerous, getting involved like this,' she said.

Fuck, I thought, but she went on. 'We *are* involved, though, and it might not even help us if we left and went back to London. So I agree with Jon – I think we should carry on here and try to finish our story.'

I was really pleased. If we got a really top-class story out of all this, that ineffable so-and-so Charles might be forced to rescind my redundancy when we got back to London. That was a big element in my decision to stay. And it would save Alyssa's job as well.

'I think you're both a bit bonkers,' Raj said with his lop-sided smile, 'but in your position I'd probably do the same. Presumably, if you're following a news story, you don't want someone else to get it first.'

I suddenly felt I couldn't take any more of this positivity and understanding.

'Now bugger off, the lot of you, and let me sleep.'

Before they went, Terry Ho said, 'I don't think I ought to tell Wei's wife about what you saw in the house. It could have been someone else, after all.'

Everyone nodded, but I think we were all pretty certain who the person in the bloodstained armchair had been.

'I'll pass the message on to my government contacts,' Raj said. 'The police ought to examine the house and close it down, anyway.'

And that was that. I'm not sure I even remember seeing them leave.

Eleven hours later Alyssa woke me up with a breakfast tray.

'I didn't order you congee,' she said cheerfully. 'This is much more healthy and nourishing.'

I laid into the omelette and poured large amounts of tea and orange juice down my still unpleasantly painful throat. The best thing was, I kept everything down. The world was starting to feel like an altogether better place.

'What did you tell London?'

'I just said you'd been following up a story and had come back safe and sound.'

'They must have thought I've been on a bender. Or off with some woman.'

'I hope so. It'll be good for your reputation. The key thing is, they aren't worried. In fact I don't think they ever were. And that means they won't be sending out someone from security to clomp around after us.'

Nowadays just about all news organisations have security departments. Our security detail in London usually included three or four ex-SAS or SBS characters, plus the odd Royal Marine and military policeman: tough, clever, funny, inclined to be indulgent towards old hacks like me, but not necessarily the kind of person you'd want for a complicated political operation like this.

What they're best at is warning you when the incoming is getting too close, schmoozing hostile military commanders who love the idea of meeting someone from the British special services, and giving you a decent excuse for getting out when things are becoming scary: after all, if a tough character who runs ten miles before breakfast and has done twenty-five years with the world's toughest regiment thinks it's time to go, there's nothing remotely shameful in heading off with him.

Yet I couldn't see how any of them could help us here. If Chinese State Security wanted to rub out Alyssa and me, they'd do it whether or not we had a security man with us. And they'd include him too, no matter how many medals he'd got for Afghanistan and Iraq.

38

I had a great time recovering. I did a lot of groaning and got plenty of sympathy, and was allowed to eat and drink more or less what I wanted. Alyssa actually shaved me once, and did it surprisingly well. She could get a job in one of those expensive men's barbers in the area around Jermyn Street, I told her, thinking she'd be irritated.

She took it as a compliment. And asked me for a tip.

It wasn't too long before I got up and staggered groggily round the room in my silk pyjamas; Alyssa had bought me three pairs on expenses. She'd also bought me a silk dressing-gown. I fancied myself in it no end, and did Noël Coward impersonations while she sat in an armchair and laughed.

Those were happy days.

One morning she announced she had to go to the bureau to talk things over. I lolled round on the bed for a while, then watched a bit of cricket on television and listened to some idiot going on about Russia's political aims as though he knew what he was talking about. After that I fussed around and made myself a cup of tea. I was halfway through it when there was a knock at the door: rather deferential, I thought. I padded over and opened it.

A couple of Chinese doctors stood there, smiling politely. The larger and older one, who stood slightly in front, actually had a

Gladstone bag, like doctors in the 1920s, and he raised it up to show me; as if to say 'I come in peace'. Blast Alyssa, I thought – she should have told me to expect them.

The older one made little hissing noises at me, as if he was calming a savage animal. The younger one did all the speaking. His English was impressive.

'Our colleague, who you saw the other day, asked us to look in and check on your condition. I'm glad to see you're able to move around now. How is the pain?'

By this time I was sitting on an upright chair, and the older doctor was running his fingers over my head and neck and pressing various muscles. I told them where it still hurt, and what my bowel movements were like – Chinese doctors are always interested in that – and how I was sleeping, and whether I had had any fever.

'Do you mind if we examine you further?'

I wasn't enthusiastic, but who is when they see a doctor? I took off my top, and they examined the bruises on my arms and back. Then I took off my pyjama bottoms. At first they examined my knees, which were healing quite well. Then they asked me to lie facedown on the bed.

'Is this really necessary?' I was starting to say.

At that moment the younger one grabbed my feet, while the older one pulled my hands together pretty roughly, and they started tying me up. Stark naked.

'You fuckers! Get off me!' I yelled, but the hotel walls and doors were too thick for the sound to carry.

'Now listen to me,' said the younger doctor, putting his mouth close to my ear. 'We can do anything we want to you now. We can kill you, or we can hurt you very much. But this is just a warning. You should leave Beijing and not return. And if you talk about this when you go back to London, you must remember that we have plenty of people there in UK, and we can get you any time we want. You will never be free of us unless you agree to keep quiet.'

The older one, who wasn't old at all – it was just the manner he'd assumed – pulled a hammer out of his bag. I froze with fear. I honestly can't say whether I would have told them what they wanted to know. The thought that I might have to undergo even a small part of what had already been done to me was a paralysing one, so maybe I would have.

I was still spluttering when a noise came from the door: an electronic whirr and the sound of a lock opening, and Alyssa came in.

'Come on, mad dog and Englishman,' she called out jokily. 'It's midday.'

And then she moved further along the little corridor and saw the three of us, with me lying on the bed.

'These bastards . . .' I started to croak, but she was way ahead of me.

She was carrying a leather thing that was half a handbag and half a briefcase, and without pausing for a fraction of a second she swung it like a weapon at the head of the English-speaking doctor. It took him hard, just above the stethoscope, and for a moment I thought he was going down. But after dropping his head he raised it again. By this time Alyssa had started on the older one, and he was raising his arms and shouting at her, '*Gun kai!*' – 'Get off!'

If I hadn't been quite so much at a disadvantage, I'd have laughed out loud.

She went on belabouring them with her bag, whacking their white-coated backs, and trying to get a serious blow in at their heads but not quite managing it. They ran to the door, wrenched it open, and headed off down the corridor.

Which just left the two of us. Alyssa's fury turned to tears almost immediately: tears of rage, not tears of pity for her poor, trussed-up colleague lying stark naked on the bed.

'Those swine,' she hissed.

'Errm.'

I tried to jerk my head round to indicate my bonds.

'I'm such an idiot to have left you on your own. And look what you get into immediately I do. You must have let them in. Why didn't you take more care? I can't believe you could be so stupid.'

She went on for quite a while like this. I waggled my bound hands and feet around, in the hope that eventually she would come down to earth and do the necessary.

And then the mood swung.

'Did they hurt you?'

Well, I wasn't going to say no at a time like that. I invented a bit of violence and pain, but I suppose she could see I was more or less intact so I soon gave up.

'Actually,' I said, 'what I'd really like is for you to untie me.'

She apologised, and had me free in a moment.

'Don't turn over,' she commanded, so I just lay there.

'I'll bring your pyjamas, then you must get back into bed.'

And while I was obeying orders I could hear her in the next room, giving a great deal of grief to the people on the desk downstairs and demanding to speak to the manager.

She was still bristling when she came back in.

'The reception desk says they must have come straight up here without asking for you. That means they knew which room you were in. Mine.'

If you recall, we'd switched rooms when I returned from my ordeal. We hadn't bothered to tell the hotel management.

'I imagine they know lots of things.'

I gradually talked her down, and made her a cup of tea, and had a good stiff Jameson's. It felt like bumping into an old friend.

I told her everything the doctors had said to me, and at the end I said, 'I'm sticking on here,' meaning Beijing, 'because I'd find it hard to live with myself if I went home now. But you must do whatever you think is right.'

That stirred her up again.

'I can't believe you'd just sit there in bed and say something like that to me, after everything that's happened.'

'So . . .'

I still wasn't entirely clear.

'So of course I'm staying, and I'm really upset that you'd think I'd want to go.'

'But I—'

'Don't start pretending you didn't mean it.'

And so on. You can't work with Alyssa if you're not prepared to endure this kind of thing from time to time.

It didn't last, though, and soon she was telling me what the bureau people had said to her. They thought we should get out of Beijing for a while, and do some reporting in provincial China. It would put clear water between us and this whole incident, they said.

It felt good to be discussing work again, and we went over a range of stories which the bureau had suggested to her. Some were pretty run-of-the-mill – the construction of the biggest dam in the history of the world, an apparently successful drug which supposedly stopped malaria, and the world's first fully operational driverless bus.

But there were edgier stories as well. We discussed them at length, interrupted only by room service with some soothing food, and eventually settled on something which would look good if we could do it: a piece about the Uighurs in Xinjiang. Alyssa said she'd go back to the bureau and get the necessary permissions and contacts.

'If I leave you alone, though, maybe you'll get yourself into trouble again.'

'Go away, woman, and inflict your presence on someone else. I need shut-eye.'

This time I double-locked the door, and set a chair in front of it in case anybody managed to undo it. On the chair was the tray with the remains of our room-service meal. I reckoned if it went over, I'd have plenty of time to ring for help.

39

Everything for our trip to Xinjiang had been sorted out. Terry Ho would go with us. He had (among various others) a Uighur girl-friend and was active in supporting their cause. The plan was to go in two days' time. Alyssa had decided that I'd be OK to fly by then.

On the afternoon before we were to leave, there was a phone call. It was someone whose English was moderately good. She wanted to tell me that Wu Sen, the deputy mayor of Huzhang, was inviting Alyssa and me to a banquet in Beijing that evening. She told us where and when to come: the Golden Duck restaurant near Tiananmen Square, at 7.45.

Alyssa was in her room at the time, so it was left to me to explain that this was out of the question. I'd been ill, I said, and we were flying to the north-west quite early the following morning.

'Please tell Wu Sen that, much as we would like to meet him this evening, it's quite impossible.'

She wouldn't accept that. Wu Sen was clearly the kind of person you didn't say no to, especially when he was inviting you to a banquet. Some other day would be impossible. It had to be tonight; the restaurant was already booked. Mr Wu was even sending a limousine to take us there. Refusal was not, as people like to say nowadays, an option.

I suppose I was still a bit feeble; I'd never have agreed to a set-up like this in the normal way. Now, though, I caved in, expecting a volcanic eruption from Alyssa when I told her. But *la donna è mobile*: she'd heard about the Golden Duck and was quite keen to go there, especially at someone else's expense. And when I pleaded tiredness and the aftermath of my injuries she just snorted.

So that was all right.

The Golden Duck restaurant looks as though it was designed by someone whose usual job was creating video games. Every imaginable cliché was there, from the lions outside the door to the portraits of Xing dynasty emperors and the scarlet silk gowns of the waitresses. The maître d' was dressed like Confucius, and a bit inclined to talk like him too. Alyssa loved it.

Wu Sen was already there when we arrived. So were his personal assistant, a smarmy young man; his secretary, dressed in a skirt slit up to her right hip and looking as though she took down a lot more than shorthand; and a man in his forties who smiled a lot and had a clammy handshake but was never quite introduced to us by name or function. Coming from the provinces, they did a lot of staring at Alyssa's skin colour. She took absolutely no notice. I may tease her about her taste, but she's got a lot of class.

At the Golden Duck, don't bother asking for steak. Duck is all they do, but they give you absolutely every imaginable part of it from the beak to the feet, and taking in the skin, the tongue, the heart, the liver, the broth, and – thank God – the actual meat, sliced as thin as a postage stamp. Each of these things comes as a separate course, so a duck banquet takes for ever. In the meantime, the waitresses kept on pouring Maotai into your glass.

I happen to like Maotai, but I can't deny that it tastes like an infusion of motor oil and ancient, unwashed pants. It's just that, after you've mastered the taste, there's a punch to it which is, if not actually attractive, then at least tempting and interesting. You keep on drinking it, anyway.

It was obvious to me that Wu Sen wanted to tell me something: or, more probably, to give me a warning. After all, everyone else in Beijing seemed to be doing that. The difference was, Wu Sen was spending quite a lot of money to do something that other people had so far used violence for. Not his own money, presumably, but the local government's.

Even so, it seemed like a positive approach.

We had reached the liver stage when I realised that something had changed. Wu's personal assistant took over the delivery of the Maotai, topping up my glass almost every time I took a sip. And though he gave Wu Sen glass for glass, I couldn't help noticing that he produced a tiny medicine bottle each time and put a droplet in it whenever he poured the Maotai: some kind of antidote, presumably, to stop him getting drunk.

By now we were heavily into an argument about where China was going. I produced my old and much-honed argument that in the long run Marxism–Leninism and capitalism were incompatible, and that the Party would either have to give up the ghost, like the one in the USSR, or crush the life out of all the independent-minded intellectuals Chinese capitalism had created.

I'm not sure I believed it entirely, but when I felt myself faltering I'd withdraw to another argument: the old Trotskyist one that when the living standards of the working class start to fall sharply, a revolution is on its way. I'm not sure how true that was, either, not being an economist, but it usually wipes the smile off the faces of Chinese bureaucrats when you tell them.

It did now. Wu Sen started getting surprisingly rude, criticising Britain and its education system. None of it was new to me, of course, or even completely unwelcome; being Irish, I could attack the Brits a great deal more effectively than he could, and often do. Soon, though, he seemed to be verging on the distinctly personal. He talked about people who came to other countries in order to seek out damaging information, and had a general crack about Western journalists who wanted to destroy the good relationships between nations.

I let him rave on. The Maotai, and to a lesser extent the duck, were starting to take over an even bigger part of my attention, and Mr Wu's secretary and her dress took the rest. I must have shown it, because I felt a sharp kick under the table. I switched my gaze. Alyssa was frowning at me angrily, and nodding her head in Wu Sen's direction.

'I asked you what your purpose was in coming to China?'

I produced some sort of bland answer about this being an interesting time in China's relations with the West.

'You see, we think you have come here to cause difficulties for Mr Lin Lifang. We think you are hoping to provoke some kind of political upheaval.'

All sorts of alarm bells were starting to ring in my Maotai-befuddled brain. Was Lin getting nervous about the dirt I had on him – the Excalibur business, and now the manuscript in Wei Jingyi's cistern – and wanting to warn me off? Thank God they hadn't asked me anything about Lin when they were waterboarding me: I'd have told them everything about him, too.

Or had they been working for Lin? I sat up and thought about that, with the clarity that a shocking new idea can have.

I turned back to Wu Sen. Nothing was further from my mind, I said; I had no idea how he could have come to such a conclusion.

Alyssa did rather better than that.

'But you see we're off to Xinjiang tomorrow morning to do some reporting on the Uighur crisis. We'd scarcely be doing that if we were planning to report on Mr Lin, would we?'

Wu Sen went quiet. The anonymous, smiling character sitting opposite him started some new line of discussion which seemed intended to calm things down. The secretary smiled, and more Maotai was poured. Even so, I stayed reasonably alert. The purpose behind this unpleasant little gathering, I could now see, was to act as a warning to us.

Alyssa took charge.

'Mr Wu, we're sorry if you've got the wrong impression about our mission here in China, but I can assure you it has nothing to do with Mr Lin. Perhaps we should continue our discussion when we return from Xinjiang in a week or so's time? Can I invite you to be our guest?'

Wu bowed until his chin nearly touched his cup of duck broth. Alyssa had struck precisely the right note.

After that my awareness of things became a lot more vague, though I seem to remember seeing Wu Sen waving his assistant away when he wanted to pour another drop of the antidote into his Maotai. We appeared destined to drink each other under the table.

40

I woke up with Alyssa shaking me. It was eight o'clock the following morning. I had appalling pains under my armpits, which must have happened as a result of being dragged out of the restaurant, loaded into the limo and dragged upstairs to sleep it off. I felt deeply ashamed, and it was obvious that Alyssa disapproved. But she paused at the door when she went to order me a pot of coffee.

'That horrible Wu Sen was in a worse state afterwards than you were. And when I said sorry to the head waiter, he said every good Chinese banquet should end up with the two main guests being carried out. So maybe it wasn't that bad after all.'

'I knew that,' I said weakly, though I didn't.

As it turned out, though, we didn't leave for Xinjiang that morning. Just before we left the hotel, I got a call from Terry Ho. He'd heard from Wei Jingyi's wife: the police had called her to say that Wei's body had been found on a building site in north Beijing. He was seriously injured, but apparently what had killed him was a massive heart attack. The police knew who he was, because someone had written his name and the address of his bookshop on a piece of paper and left it in his pocket. It wasn't done to be helpful: the men who had tortured him wanted everyone to know what happened to people like him.

It took us an hour to get to the police mortuary where his body was being held, and we didn't talk much on the way. Alyssa cried from time to time. I thought about that charming little family scene, with Wei and his wife and their scrawny, bespectacled kid; and I couldn't get the bloodstained armchair in the house of horrors out of my mind.

Terry was waiting for us when we drove up to the main entrance, his face more haggard than ever. None of us said anything. As we followed Terry across the entrance hall and into the lift, I felt a real sense of dread. Maybe Alyssa spotted the signs. She put her arm through mine and gave it a companionable squeeze.

Wei's wife and son were sitting miserably on a couple of hard, official chairs in a waiting room. Some character in a white coat took charge of the two of them, and guided them into the next room. We followed. It was like every official mortuary I've ever been in, except that the notices on the walls were in Chinese.

The man in the white coat pulled the handle of a large drawer with a rasping, metallic sound. A figure lay in it, wrapped from head to foot in a stained white sheet.

His wife looked at us questioningly. I nodded, and she pulled the sheet back. Poor Wei – I wouldn't have recognised him. The violence he'd suffered and the effects of the heart attack had turned him into something else altogether. She made a faint noise, and her face was covered with tears.

I looked away. The little son stood behind us, his eyes on the floor. He didn't seem to be crying. Everything in his life that meant anything had been taken from him. I put my hand out and gripped the boy's shoulder. It was hard and bony and unresponsive. I don't suppose he noticed I was touching him.

I thought up conventional expressions like 'If there's anything I can do . . .' but I scarcely even began to utter them. There was nothing I could do, and when there had been – when they were beating the shit out of me – I'd betrayed Wei utterly, in order to stop them hurting me any more. The fact that it wouldn't have mattered to him by that stage was beside the point.

Terry jerked his head awkwardly to show it was time for us to go, and Alyssa and I moved away. Neither of us said anything to the woman and the little boy. We walked out of the room, and now I was the one who put my arm round Alyssa as we made our way along the corridor.

'That poor kid – did you see his face?'

'Don't,' I said.

41

The light was going, and empty desert lay below us, with a line of purple mountains in the distance. I wasn't feeling too good after the previous night's Maotai and the morning's visit to the mortuary, and I certainly couldn't face the unmentionable plastic tray of noodles and compulsory fizzy drink that the smiling flight attendant brought me. Alyssa nudged me sympathetically and asked how I was feeling.

'Rough,' I said shortly, and looked out of the window again.

The two of us were sitting side by side near the front of the plane. At least three of our fellow-passengers were taking more interest in us than was justified. Alyssa was sure I was exaggerating, but even she agreed that at least one person was watching us.

Behind us somewhere, betraying no sign of recognition, sat Terry Ho and his Uighur girlfriend. He'd wanted to stay for Wei Jingyi's funeral, but in the end he'd decided he would only attract extra police attention. Wei's widow and son had enough to worry about without that.

We'd spotted Terry and his friend in the Departures lounge before we left. But we didn't say anything to them and kept well apart. These flights had plenty of official narks on them. Several times, people got up out of their seats to wander down the aisle and take a look at us; though this could simply have been because they'd never seen a black woman before.

Xinjiang from this height looked waterless and poor, yet with the kind of glamour that mountainous deserts always have. It's the air, I think: chilly and thin and invigorating. It cut into us as we walked down the aircraft steps and across the tarmac.

'Very welcome to Kashgar', said a big, cheery notice in three languages over the terminal building. It didn't reflect the reception we got. A plain-clothes Uighur man and a couple of uniformed Chinese policemen were waiting just inside. They stepped forward the moment we set foot inside the entrance, and grabbed our arms. I was still arguing the toss when Terry and the Uighur girl walked past us hand in hand, without looking in our direction. That at least was something.

The uniformed cops marched us down a corridor to an anonymous door and knocked on it. Inside sat two senior-looking Chinese men and a younger Uighur woman, all in uniform. From their attitudes, it looked as though they'd been waiting for us.

There was a member of our family, an empire-builder called Sir Charles Napier. It isn't fashionable to talk about people like him any longer, but he was the one who grabbed Sindh for the British in the 1840s. Another Irish Prod, naturally: without us and the Scots the British empire would have consisted of the Channel Islands.

Anyway, Sir Charles was wandering through the jungle near his camp, unarmed, when he saw a tiger crouched down ready to spring. He directed such a stare at the poor tiger that it shrank back into the undergrowth and headed off. I've no idea whether the story is true – there weren't any witnesses, after all, and Charles Napier was one of the world's premier bullshitters – but my father used to tell me about him because, he said, it showed you could assert the power of command.

'Make them feel they're the ones who are in the wrong place, with egg-stains on their lapels and their flies undone,' he used to say.

It helped now.

The panel of cops were still settling in their chairs and giving us the once-over, when I had a go.

'What do you think you're doing, delaying us like this? Ms Roberts and I are here on official business with the full knowledge and agreement of the ministry of information in Beijing. This is absolutely outrageous.'

And so on and on for a while, until I ran out of breath.

It had a gratifying effect. The head man – beribboned, with a bald head – had clearly been intending to read us a lecture on the duties of a good journalist (something about the true purpose of journalism being to strengthen friendly relations between peoples, no doubt) and to browbeat us into submission.

He tried. We were in danger of being charged with espionage, he said, since our passports (which they were going through, page by page) contained no specific permission to come to Xinjiang. By this time I'd spotted that Alyssa had set down her mobile phone carelessly on the table in front of her. From the way she didn't give it even a glance I could see she was recording the whole scene. That emboldened me.

'Congratulations, captain' – I was probably downgrading him by a couple of ranks – 'because you'll soon be the most famous policeman in the whole of China. I'll send a report to London on the way you've treated two well-known international broadcasters, and how you've made it clear that your own rules operate here, and not Beijing's. I imagine your superiors will find it deeply embarrassing.'

All tosh, of course. The world's news outlets don't usually care about incidents like this. The most I could hope for was three lines in 'Other News' somewhere in the back of the *Independent* website.

The policeman with the bald head didn't understand any of that. For all he knew, he'd be getting awkward phone calls from Beijing. He looked at his colleague with a query in his expression, and the colleague closed his eyes in silent assent. The bald chief told us we would be watched wherever we went, and that if we attempted to speak to anyone who didn't have permission to speak to the foreign media we would be asked to leave Xinjiang.

But he hoped we would enjoy our visit; and at that very moment the door opened and a battered trolley appeared, covered with cups and a large teapot, and pushed by a Uighur who looked as though he'd seen everything and never said anything about it to anyone.

'Our city is very beautiful,' said the bald cop.

He started pouring the tea.

After you've yelled at them and threatened them with terrible consequences you must then soothe them and win them over to your side.

'To be honest,' I said, 'my real reason for wanting to come here was to see the famous house of my great-uncle, Sir George Macartney.'

Macartney was the British consul in Kashgar between 1890 and 1918, and from this vantage point ('where three empires meet', a late Victorian author called it, and the name stuck) he successfully kept watch on a huge range of Russian imperial adventurers and Chinese officials, and then the agents of the Chinese republic and, finally, an assortment of Soviet spies. He was, naturally, Anglo-Irish, but he and I were only related very distantly.

Macartney's wife Catherine served lunch and tea to everyone who called, grew roses, scandalised everyone by riding alone in the mountains wearing jodhpurs, and eventually wrote an insightful memoir of their years in Xinjiang.

But what the Chinese were really interested in was the fact that Sir George was half-Chinese; his mum was the daughter of some top mandarin Macartney senior had courted and married during the latter years of the Qing dynasty. It's fascinating to Chinese people to think that some British imperial bigwig should have been a bit like them. Fair enough; imagine how interested we would have been if some half-Brit had been a sidekick of Mao's on the Great March.

The bald policeman promised me a personally escorted tour of the one-time British consulate the following morning.

'And tonight', he said jovially, looking round the table, 'you must be our guests at a banquet.'

My stomach turned over at the thought, but I knew there was no refusing.

'And because we are in Xinjiang, you must sample our wonderful local food.'

I was a bit vague what the local food was. I just hoped I'd only see it once.

A police car took us to our hotel, an ugly four-storey box that pre-dated China's opening up to the world. It was the place we'd arranged for Terry and his girlfriend to stay in, so that was good. Alyssa and I unpacked, then met downstairs for a beer; I couldn't face spirits of any kind.

Various characters who might have been spooks were scattered around the lobby, and I spotted Terry and the girl – I really must find out her name, I thought – sitting in a far corner of the bar. I wandered over to the barman and ordered our Tsingtaos; and in a voice intended to carry to Terry's table I asked the barman to put it on the bill for room 319. In both English and Chinese, so he'd be sure to get it. It was hard not to look at Terry when I took the beers back to Alyssa, but I managed it.

I won't go into detail about our meal that night. All I can say is if you like your horse-meat chewy, underdone, covered with pungent sauce and in appallingly large portions, then Xinjiang is the place for you. Everything on the menu seemed to be horse-related; I was relieved to see that the drinks weren't made of fermented horse urine. The Uighurs rode with the Golden Horde, and no one is allowed to forget it.

Alyssa made her way through all four courses with relish; or maybe she just put on a better show than me. The others loved her for it, and the charming little Uighur policewoman put her arms round her at the end and kissed her on both cheeks. Which made me wish I'd made more of an effort myself.

At the end we drank some pretty potent local stuff, and the two male policemen started to get very merry. After my experience of the evening before, I did plenty of apparent sipping, but managed not to ingest too much of the fiery stuff. All three of the cops were too far gone to notice.

'We knew all about you days ago,' the bald one said.

Which was strange, given that we'd kept it very much between the two of us. Maybe he was making it up, of course. Or maybe not.

I thought this would be a good moment to see if they knew anything about Terry.

'In fact we just decided to come here on the spur of the moment,' I said, rather proud of my Chinese idiom. 'We don't know anyone here.'

Either they were too far gone to pick up on the reference, or they believed me.

'But now you know us,' the junior policeman said. 'We'll get people to show you round.'

Yes, I bet you will, I thought.

'Especially Macartney's house.'

'Oh yes, especially Paul McCartney's house!' the senior policeman shouted, and started singing 'Penny Lane'. It took me a while to recognise it, but when I did I joined in. Alyssa beamed, and the little policewoman laughed aloud. The Uighur waiter came into the room and did a dance in the corner.

'That', said Alyssa as we walked back to our hotel in the dark – since it was only just round the corner, like everything else in Kashgar – 'was a big success.'

A couple of dogged spooks were sitting in the lobby reading old editions of the local newspaper. Alyssa and I picked up our keys and headed for the lift.

'I expect Terry will come to my room tonight,' I said when we got in. 'Want to wait there for him?'

'Good try, buddy boy.'

She said it with a fetching grin, and headed off to her own room. She wasn't walking very straight.

42

I'd taken one or two basic precautions before I left my hotel room, mostly for the sake of curiosity; I wanted to see whether the local security people would check through my stuff while I was away. So I'd threaded a small piece of black cotton loosely through the zip on my suitcase, and lined up a couple of scratch marks on my laptop cover with a scarcely visible mark on the desk.

When I struggled back to my room I found that the thread had disappeared and the marks were out of alignment, so someone had gone through my bag and looked at my laptop. It appeared as though they hadn't done anything more than riffle through the contents of the suitcase. The fact is, if I've brought something with me that I want to keep secret, I keep it with me.

I was still messing around with my suitcase when there was a faint scratching at the door. It was Terry, with his girlfriend following behind him. He smiled at me. A good dentist could devote the rest of his or her career to sorting Terry's teeth out. In dumbshow, he asked me to come out into the corridor, so I let the door rest on the latch and walked a few steps with them.

Terry put his mouth close to my ear: 'I've fixed a meeting in the town for an hour's time. Pretend you're going to bed, and meet us out here in thirty minutes from now.'

I squeezed his arm to show I'd understood; though I couldn't see how we were going to get out of the hotel without passing the spooks in the lobby.

I went back to my bed and made undressing noises, hoping they'd only put microphones and not cameras in the room. Then I went and cleaned my teeth. No point in skimping on the detail, I felt, so I put on a good show for anyone who might be listening. The question was, should I get Alyssa to come too? I argued it over with myself, but decided not to.

It was just Terry and me. He'd reconnoitred the hotel and found a back door which we could easily slip out of. It was dark outside, and Kashgar's streets are dimly lit at night. I'd put on a dark sweater and black trousers and covered my white hair with a beanie.

Terry approved.

We headed through a couple of back alleys into an unpaved side street. There was no one around. Getting to the rendezvous took a good fifteen minutes, but that was because Terry led us on a roundabout journey.

We came to the front of a single-storeyed house between a car repair workshop and what smelled like a butcher's.

Terry knocked softly on the front door.

Three rough-looking characters sat there, illuminated by an oil lamp on an upturned box. A page from a Chinese newspaper was pinned on the wall; otherwise the room was empty of decoration. The three stood up politely, and we shook hands. Terry explained that they could speak Chinese to us, and that I would understand. I only hoped I would. The main one grinned suddenly, and flashed an incomplete set of dark-brown teeth. He and Terry could have a competition, I thought.

'We'd like to know about your group, and the way the Chinese authorities control people here in Kashgar,' Terry said succinctly.

The man with the teeth nodded in a stately way, while I pulled out my mobile phone, switched on the video camera and started to film. He began talking.

It was a depressing story. I'd heard its equivalent all over the world: Kachins in Burma, Muslims in Kashmir and parts of the Philippines, Zoroastrians in Iran, Yazidis in Iraq, Shi'ites in Bahrain, Christians in a dozen countries. Not to mention Muslim refugees in Austria and Mexicans in Texas: people who just wanted to use their own language and teach their religion to their children, and had suffered as a result.

I listened with a mixture of anger and familiarity. He described conditions for the prisoners: not as bad as for Bosnian Muslims in Serbian camps, maybe, or Yazidis at the hands of ISIS, but pretty savage all the same. Threats, beatings for refusing to accept the rules, constant fear.

'So what are you going to do about this?' I asked in my halting Chinese; it took him a while to understand what I was saying, and Terry had to repeat the question.

He had just begun to speak when a faint creaking sound in the next room silenced him. Apparently one of their lookouts was in there, and there were supposedly others out in the street and at the back of the house.

The man with the teeth carried on talking in a quieter voice, while one of the others tiptoed round to the interconnecting door and threw it open.

The scene was almost comical. Three policemen were holding the lookout down on the floor, and all four faces were turned up towards us, like a freeze-frame.

Then the door slammed, and the man I'd been interviewing pointed to a hatch in the low ceiling and made a back for me to stand on and then for Terry to climb up. As we heaved ourselves up into the small space above the room, I could hear the three Uighurs below us charge through the front door and out into the street.

I spotted a square lighter than the surrounding darkness at the end of the loft, and forced my way through it onto the roof of the shop next door, turning to pull Terry up after me.

A punch-up had started down in the street below us, and there was a good deal of shouting, but we carried on across the butcher's shop roof and the flat-topped building beyond that.

I'd got us out of the loft, but Terry took over now, waving his long arm to show me which direction we should take. Then, when we reached the end of the low building, he held on to the gutter with both hands and dropped himself down.

As I moved up to where he'd been, I heard the sound of his feet hitting the ground, then a door opening and light streaming out, and a voice shouting in a language I didn't understand.

I was too committed by this stage to stop, so I jumped down and hit somebody hard with my feet. It wasn't Terry. He was already standing up, hopping awkwardly as though he'd hurt himself, and signalling the way down a little back street.

God knows how he worked it out, but after five or six minutes' running and fast walking we saw our hotel looming up ahead of us against the sky. A long way behind us in the darkness there was shouting and a pistol shot. Then the predictable sound of police sirens.

The little side door was still unlocked. We slipped in gratefully and charged, now completely out of breath, up the emergency stairs to the third floor. Within seconds I opened the door to my room and slipped as quietly as possible into bed, fully clothed. I hoped the sobbing sound of my breathing wouldn't be audible over the microphones.

Five minutes later there was a loud hammering on my door. I jumped out of bed, aghast, then remembered the towelling dressing-gown on the back of the bathroom door. I wrapped it round me and went over to the door, remembering at the last moment to slip my shoes off.

'Yes?' I said, and 'What the fuck is it?' for good measure.

I hoped that the way I was gripping the neck of the dressing-gown meant that my clothes were covered. These small Chinese sizes, I thought – they made me feel like Jack Lemmon in *Some Like it Hot.*

The bald policeman stood outside in the hall, with a couple of uniformed men behind him.

'Oh,' he said when he saw me.

'Look, I'm trying to get some sleep,' I said, and then good manners made me add, 'After that very good dinner you gave us.'

He peered past me into the room, in the suspicious way policemen have.

'Are you looking for someone? You can come in if you like.'

Maybe he thought I might have Alyssa in the bed. He shook his head.

'Very sorry, Mr Jon,' he said slowly. 'There's been some trouble in the town, and I am checking that you are all right.'

Good effort, I thought, but it seemed better if I kept the irritated tone going.

'Well, please don't bother any more. I'm fine, and I'd like to get back to sleep.'

We said our good nights and I shut the door.

And I dropped back onto the bed with tiredness and relief.

Alyssa was incandescent when I told her the next morning.

'This is starting to be a habit with you.'

I suggested a walk before breakfast, so I could tell her everything that had happened. It was hard to work out what upset her most: leaving her in the hotel without telling her, or nearly getting caught, or going on a fool's errand like that in the first place.

'I've never heard of anything so fucking irresponsible and unprofessional. Especially after the last time. And I suppose you thought I wouldn't be capable of something like that. Well, times have changed, you bloody old antediluvian, and technically I'm superior to you anyway. If you'd had the courtesy to let me know what you were planning, I'd have stopped you. This was obviously going to be the kind of thing that would go badly wrong.'

And quite a lot more of the same. She looked up and shook her head as though some greater power was looking on, watching the whole business and, naturally, sympathising with her.

'Well, I got away with it. And I've got a video of the interview on my phone.'

'You haven't done anything to get rid of it yet?'

Another shake of the head at my total incompetence.

'No. But we can do it right away.'

That gave her something to think about. We sat down in a bright, modern cafe with WiFi, and sent the video as an attachment to a South African email address which I used for dodgy material. The video didn't look too bad at all. It was dimly lit, but that added to the sense of fear and menace.

And since I hadn't had the presence of mind to switch off my recorder when we were interrupted, it had picked up everything – the ruckus in the next room, our escape over the rooftops, lots of muted swearing, and everything else that happened back to the moment I got into bed and realised the recorder was still running.

Alyssa snorted, as though all this proved everything she'd suspected. But she could see it was good material, and by the time we walked back to our hotel she was even starting to joke about what had happened.

'Anyway,' I said, characteristically pushing it too far, 'you couldn't have come – you had far too much of that awful horse-piss we had to drink.'

It annoyed her, but made her laugh at the same time. So that was all right.

Terry and his girlfriend were sitting in the hotel breakfast room when we arrived. We sat down at a table some way away. But when I saw Terry get up and help himself to some congee I went and stood beside him, spooning a couple of preserved eggs, bruise-green and purple, onto my plate. Years of talking surreptitiously in live studios have taught me to speak out of the corner of my mouth. His time in prison had done the same for Terry.

'OK?'

'No probs.'

'Did they knock on your door?'

'We asleep.'

'See you in town.'

'He's fine,' I told Alyssa.

'I think he's a liability.'

She often had a down on the people I'd known before I started working with her.

'No, no.'

But I confess I was beginning to wonder.

We headed out to take a look at Sir George Macartney's consulate. A depressing pseudo-antique hotel had been built bang in front of the old consulate, where the gateway and drive would once have been. It gave the original building the air of a stage set.

Still, it was in good condition, and there were plenty of curled-up, fading photos and exhibits connected to Macartney's years there. The inscriptions were heavily Maoist, with lots of 'imperialists' and 'brutal colonialists' thrown in, but I couldn't help noticing that there were at least three mentions of the fact that this grand British aristo had had a Chinese mother. Even Maoists can be snobs.

Terry and the girl were wandering round the place when we arrived. I hoped it would look like pure chance.

Leaning over one of the glass-fronted cabinets I muttered, 'We're leaving tomorrow.'

'Us too,' Terry replied.

That afternoon, as Alyssa and I were wandering back in the direction of the hotel, a large black Chinese-made car stopped beside us and a familiar bald head poked out of the back window. He wasn't smiling.

'Get in, please.'

Alyssa got in the back seat, beside him, and I crammed in as well. It was an awkward place to have an official conversation.

'I know where you were last night, Mr Jon, and who you were speaking to. You escaped, which was clever, but we have two witnesses to your meeting.'

I wondered which one of the three had managed to hold out against the questioning. The one with the teeth, I imagined: a tough character, who couldn't be easily broken.

'I know about your friends too.'

He meant Terry and his girlfriend.

'You have made yourselves liable to arrest and imprisonment here.'

At least, I think that's what he meant: we talked in an inadequate mixture of Chinese and English.

But he didn't seem to be saying he was going to arrest us. I was just formulating my response in Chinese when Alyssa's voice, sharp and metallic, broke in.

'I think you should tell your colleagues to get out of the car,' she told him.

To my surprise, he ordered them out at once.

'I'm only going to say this once . . .' she said.

I don't know if he understood the words she used, but no one could mistake the tone.

'At dinner last night, when you'd been drinking, you said many unwise things about the government in Beijing and about your superior officers.'

Had he? I hadn't noticed. But then I'd been as far gone as he was.

She pulled out her mobile phone.

'This has a very good recording device on it. I recorded everything you said. I've sent the tape to my colleagues in London, with instructions that if anything happens to us, they should broadcast it on our Chinese language service. That means it'll be heard all over China by tonight.'

She paused. The poor man just sat there, looking straight ahead of him through the windscreen.

'I suggest that, in order to avoid any complications like this, you should allow us and our two friends to leave on the next flight to Beijing. And let the three men you've arrested go.'

Her mouth shut like one of those spring-charged letterboxes that postmen hate. It was as neat and as brutal a piece of blackmail as I've ever heard.

We got out of the car without asking his permission and walked back to the hotel.

'I didn't hear him say anything like that last night,' I said.

'Well, he couldn't be sure he didn't, could he, given the condition he was in?'

'And I didn't see you recording him on your phone.'

'Same answer.'

I was careful not to laugh too loud.

I'd always admired her, but I think this was when I started properly falling in love with her.

43

In the end, though, our trip to Kashgar turned out to be just an interlude, a sideshow. We turned up some interesting and important material, but not the killer story we'd been hoping for. That's the thing about the news business: you never know if the story you're covering is going to be the most talked about issue of the year, or if people will say 'Oh, have you been away?' when you get home. And your brilliant story can sometimes be overtaken by something altogether different, so they'll go, 'Yes, that thing you've been working on is very interesting but what about the such-and-such story? That's the one we're really keen on.'

I've always admired the way the editor of *The Times* in 1915 changed the story and decided to give the nation a rest from the latest war news and lead with Sir Ernest Shackleton's adventures in rescuing his men in the Antarctic. I'm sure there must have been plenty of head-shaking at the paper's editorial conference the next day. Still, the editor was right in the long run: *sub specie aeternitatis*, as my old history teacher in Dublin would have put it. Under the gaze of eternity.

There was no farewell committee when we left Kashgar, and no attempt to stop us. Clearly the bald-headed policeman had taken Alyssa's advice and decided it was safer to let us go without a fuss.

Terry and his girlfriend were sitting there in the Departures lounge, and as before we blanked them.

When we landed in Beijing no one was waiting to arrest us.

So there we were, back in the bar at the hotel, sipping pungent black *pu-er* tea and trying to decide what to do next. And then two things happened that changed everything. The first was that I spotted someone I knew well: tall, with spiky greying hair and a relaxed, easy-going look, walking across the lobby. I bounded out of my chair and hurried over to cut him off.

'Gary!'

He stopped and turned, the smile already gathering on his face. I really loved the man. He'd saved my life twice, and rescued my professional reputation far more often than that. Gary Sung was Singaporean and a cameraman from a famous clan. I'd worked everywhere with him: Afghanistan, Iraq, Iran, Burma, Russia, and countless times in China and Hong Kong. He was gentle and funny and disturbingly brave, with a detailed knowledge of the English Premier League. The only failing I ever found in him was that he supported Liverpool.

He came over and said hello to Alyssa. Alyssa, as ever, was a bit standoffish. She doesn't like accepting anyone else's assessment of people; she treats them as though they're on probation. Gary wasn't offended.

He had been working on a documentary in central China, and had a few more days to go before returning home. But he could hang on after that, he said, if we had something we wanted him to do.

Alyssa asked him if he'd like something to drink.

'Coffee?' he said, with that questioning intonation which shows he's worked with Australians over the years.

At that moment my mobile rang. The name 'Martin Prinsett' flashed up.

'The last time I took a call from you, something really unpleasant happened.'

He obviously wasn't listening.

'Things are getting quite *interesting* here,' he said, without mentioning where 'here' was. I suppose that was his way of being secure.

He sounded nervous. I was tempted to make him more so by asking about 'our mutual friend', but I thought that would be getting too Dickensian, as well as being deeply obvious.

'So we should come there?'

'Oh yes, I would say so. As soon as you can.'

'OK, fine. Would you mind booking us a couple of rooms?'

He rang off without saying goodbye. Perhaps he didn't like being treated like a travel agent.

Alyssa seemed a bit limp.

'All this flying backwards and forwards. Are we really achieving anything?'

'It's how you get stories.'

'Right, well, let's do it then,' she said, with the clipped voice and snap of the jaw she'd shown the bald police chief.

She went up to pack, while I carried on talking to Gary. I'd already decided I was going to tell him absolutely everything.

'Can you hang around till we get back from Huzhang?' I asked him when I'd finished the story.

'Sure. But listen, Jon, you're getting into this pretty deep. Are you sure it's OK?'

He looked at me in his wise old way, and I was quite affected.

'God knows. But when you and I went over the mountains into Afghanistan, did we know it was going to work out?'

He grinned at me, and leaned over and squeezed my shoulder.

44

Alyssa and I were jammed in, side by side, on yet another plane. The food was marginally different: processed cheese in the sandwich instead of processed meat, and the drink seemed to be distantly related to the guava.

It was already dark when we arrived in Huzhang. We were tired. The ride to the centre of the city was interminable, and the business of checking in at the hotel seemed endless.

'Your passports, please.'

'Oh, have we crossed an international frontier?'

'Come on, Jon.'

She was right. Being snotty to an eighteen-year-old trainee behind a hotel desk wasn't going to change China's national security policy.

'Sorry – here it is.'

The trainee coughed a couple of times into a balled-up paper handkerchief.

'You should be at home with a cold like that,' I said.

She smiled ruefully and gave us our room keys.

When there was a view, which there wasn't at this time of night, my room was probably quite pleasant. Otherwise it just looked like every other modern hotel room throughout the entire People's Republic: a bit of framed calligraphy on one wall, a crappy picture of some rural activity on another. Lots of heavy furniture made of teak, which would have been better left standing in the forests of Burma, and some electronics already out of date; Chinese Central TV, the country's sole home-grown channel on the television across from the bed; a room service menu with hamburgers and Coke on it, and, to add a bit of cosmopolitan interest, fish and chips.

All right, I was tired and ratty, but you might hope that your hotel would reflect something of the region you found yourself in.

Things seemed better the following morning. The sun was actually shining – an increasing rarity in Chinese cities, whatever the season – and Alyssa looked sharp and efficient at the breakfast table.

We headed out into the city centre. It was immediately obvious that something weird was going on. Lin Lifang, for all his smoothness and his Western ways, seemed to be turning the place into an old-style Maoist stronghold. There were loudspeakers on most of the lamp posts, playing songs from the days of the Cultural Revolution, extolling the Great Helmsman. Perhaps Lin remembered his days as mayor of Do-Chang. Only this wasn't 'Scotland the Brave'.

Chairman Mao loves the people,
He is our guide
to building a new China.
Hurrah, lead us forward!

The Communist Party is like the sun,
Wherever it shines, it is bright.
Wherever the Communist Party is,
Hurrah, the people are liberated!

I know: and it could do with a few lines about the millions who died of hunger thanks to the Great Helmsman's utter inability to run the country properly. The tunes were rotten and derivative too. 'The sound of Kool-Aid', an American friend of mine used to call this kind of thing, and he was absolutely right. It's the type of music to commit mass suicide to.

'I think it's rather catchy,' Alyssa said.

But I knew that was because I'd bored her by sounding off about Mao. One of my exes once said I'd make a great preacher. She didn't mean it to be flattering.

Some of the slogans on the big state-owned buildings were in English, but they were straight out of the Cultural Revolution too, all about working hard and producing more and following the leadership of the Party.

I'm sure my old friend Lin Lifang didn't really see himself as the new Mao; he must have thought this was a useful way of doing down the semi-capitalistic leadership in Beijing, by remembering the good old days. Actually, of course, those were the days when screaming teenagers kicked their way into the houses of elderly, dignified professors, burned their books, and dragged them out to be beaten and humiliated in front of huge crowds.

As we walked, we worked out a plan. Alyssa would ring the Party Secretary's office and tell them we'd arrived, and suggest that we should pay a visit the following day. Still, it was clear that everyone knew we were here already. We counted four men and a woman following us on foot. When we spotted a white Nissan rolling along behind us at 3 mph, we turned sharply to our left and into a large shopping mall.

Alyssa made the call, and fixed the appointment. That left us a lot of time with nothing to do except wander round the city and enjoy ourselves. Alyssa was glowing with health and good looks. I had the impression that a lot of the stares she got in the street were to do with that, rather than the fact that she was black. She's impossible to miss: slim, statuesque, with that air of physical and mental confidence that would have been arrogance if she'd allowed it to be; though I suspect it actually came from a feeling that she's got to fight her corner in a world that doesn't necessarily welcome her.

And even I didn't look too bad, I thought, as I glimpsed myself in a window. Overweight, certainly, though less than I had been before I was gone over by the Gestapo. My pink shirt and linen jacket gave me a raffish air. I looked like what I unmistakably was: an old-fashioned gent going slightly to seed. Every club in the area of St James's and Covent Garden can show you loads of comparable specimens.

A purist might have said I was a touch bandy-legged, too. I've often noticed, though, that a man who walks down the street with an attractive woman tends to look better than when he's walking alone – there's a sort of transmission effect.

'I've been reading about the Thousand Steps. We should go there.'

My heart sank.

'Don't look like that, you lazy man. "A thousand" is just a Chinese expression meaning "a lot", my guide-book says.'

I knew that, but it didn't make me feel better.

By the time you read this, the Thousand Steps will have ceased to exist. Lin Lifang had a nice little project to pull down the traditional shops on either side of the steps, which meandered down from the cliff top on which the original city had been built to the river below, and turn it into the world's biggest shopping mall on a variety of levels.

Just what mankind needs – the world's biggest shopping mall. So the little jewellers' shops and cookery stalls and barbers' and fortune-tellers' stalls were all scheduled for bulldozing, to be replaced by Dior and Watches of Switzerland and Uniqlo. Quite a few of the shopkeepers were complaining about it as we wandered down the steps.

'I'll just have to go and live with my daughter in the village,' an ancient character in a stringy white beard, T-shirt and shorts muttered gloomily to his neighbour, as he cooked delicious little balls of sweet dough over a fire. 'She and her husband won't be happy to see me.'

He coughed and spat elaborately onto the step beside him; not, I saw, for the first time that day.

'I think we can guess why,' said another ancient, and everyone fell about laughing.

So did I, though it occurred to me that these two old boys were probably younger than me. Alyssa was looking sideways at me; maybe she was thinking the same thing.

We stopped at another stall, and I bought a cardboard cup of soup with some sort of meat swimming in it.

'Delicious,' I said, though in fact it was pretty revolting.

I watched her as she leaned over the counter at a little shop that sold carved earrings in wood and bone, and asked how much one particular set was.

'Thirty yuan,' said the woman, smiling back.

Good humour seemed to be catching, this fine morning.

She held the earrings up to her earlobes.

'What do you think?'

Don't gush, I warned myself, though I felt like it.

'Yeah, they look OK. Why don't I get them for you?'

'No, I'll get them, thanks.'

I went quiet.

We followed the steps as they turned sharply round on themselves, like a chicane. There, in a corner formed by the steps and the wall of a tatty old house made of wattle and daub, was a table at which another old man sat, fiddling with bits of grubby stick. He was a fortune-teller.

A slightly younger man sat opposite him, waiting eagerly for him to speak.

When he did, although it was in Putonghua I could scarcely understand a word. It seemed to be about buying something, but for all I know it could have been a cow or a life insurance policy. The client didn't seem enthusiastic with the verdict, and slapped down a few discoloured notes on the table as he stood up and stalked off. He coughed and spat as he went.

'Your turn,' said Alyssa, and pushed me down into the client's chair.

'What do you want to know?' asked the fortune-teller.

He stretched out his palms, and I realised I was supposed to put my hands in his. His grip was firm and dry and warm.

All right, I thought – you got me into this, woman, and you must take the consequences.

'Will I find love?'

He turned my hands over and looked at the palms. Utter load of nonsense, I thought.

'For some reason that I can't understand, you are known in many parts of the world. Not for who you are, but for what you say. Maybe you write books; I cannot understand the reason. You will live many, many years yet, and you will soon have a son even though you are an old man. Your son will be your pride and joy, and he will close your eyes with many tears, but only when everything you have known and worked for has faded away and been forgotten. As for finding love, my answer is not yet, and not here in Huzhang. Maybe somewhere else. That will be a hundred yuan,' he said, without altering his tone in any way.

Alyssa fell about laughing when I told her what he'd said. 'So you can finally lay off trying to hit on me.'

'Listen, I've had women begging me to hit on them.'

'Well, I'm begging you to stop. And I don't believe you anyway.'

I wasn't sure she meant it. Or is that what men always think?

'Time to get back,' she said, and we geared ourselves up for the effort that five hundred steps represented.

45

Back at the hotel I lay on my bed for a while, distinctly unsettled. I don't believe people can see into the future – how can that be possible? – yet this felt as though someone had peered through the curtains of my life and seen who I was and what I was doing. And although the fortune-teller must surely be a charlatan, how could he have known that I was a broadcaster whose reports were seen around the world? If that was a lucky shot, it was a good one. So might all this mean that, at my great age, someone was going to give me a son? And who might that be?

Beside me, the phone rang. It was Alyssa.

'Can I come round? We need to talk.'

Usually when women use expressions like that, you know it's time to head for the hills. Now, though, I was grateful to get away from my own thoughts.

When I opened the door, she was standing there with a piece of paper in her hand. I ushered her in and looked at it.

Since they're definitely listening in on us . . . it started.

We'd already established this. The previous day I'd shouted out loud, in Chinese, that you couldn't get any answer from room service in this benighted hotel and within three minutes a waiter arrived at the door with an order pad, apologising.

. . . we should use it to our advantage. Let's say how Lin has brought peace to this city, then say that London could benefit from this. Then you can say, 'If only he would give us an interview.'

Much too clunky and obvious, I thought, reading it in silence. But I reflected that it wouldn't be subtle old Lin who'd hear this, it'd be one of his toadying officials. So maybe it was worth a try.

'Amazing how Mr Lin has dealt with crime here in Huzhang, isn't it?'

My voice was much too loud, but it was a good start.

Alyssa nodded encouragingly. 'Yes – they should follow some of his methods back home in London. It's such a pity Lin doesn't seem to want to do an interview with us. It would definitely raise his profile in the UK.'

'And in other countries round the world. Don't forget we have a total audience of 350 million.'

I've gone too far now, I thought, but Alyssa was still grinning approvingly.

I ploughed on. 'Maybe we should let Mr Lin know that if he did an interview with us, it'd make him a figure of international significance.'

Alyssa squeezed my arm in a way she'd never done before. Could she be the type who likes kids? I wondered.

'Don't go getting ideas,' she hissed.

After all this time working together she could tell what I was thinking.

'See you later,' she said, and smiled.

I was reminded of Lauren Bacall in *To Have and Have Not*: 'You know how to whistle, don't you, Steve? You just put your lips together and . . . blow.'

I lay on my bed for a while, and thought about my life. Then, when that got too depressing, I picked up a novel by Anthony

Trollope I'd brought with me. Usually I like those big triple-decker Victorian things about florid grandees who gamble too much and beautiful young women, but this one didn't seem to do it for me.

I was still only on page fifteen when the phone by my bed rang again.

The voice was Martin Prinsett's. Sharp and nervous.

'I've got to see you.'

I wanted to say I was relaxing and wanted an early night. Listening to his voice, though, I knew I couldn't.

'Where?'

'I'll come round to your hotel. They know me there.'

I rang Alyssa.

'Oh, for Christ's sake – I've just got ready for bed.'

'But the other night you were furious when I didn't ring you.'

'Well, now I'm furious because you have.' She paused. 'I'd better get dressed and come down.'

We met in the lobby. Prinsett was flustered and wouldn't look either of us in the eye. Then he downed two Japanese whiskies and looked round at the main door of the hotel several times.

'You expecting someone?'

'No, no, it's just that I'm – well, I suppose I'm a bit overwrought.'

Alyssa surprised me by resting her hand on his knee and saying, 'Well, you're with us now. You can tell us the whole thing, you know.'

Really, I thought, this woman's range is extraordinary. It certainly had an effect on Prinsett.

'Thank you. It'd be good to talk to someone.'

At that point two men, burly and wearing casual clothes, walked in through the entrance.

'Jesus Christ, it's them. They must have worked out where I was going.'

He put his glass down so hard I thought it would crack. That helped the two men spot where he was. They sat down a little way off, positioned so they'd be able to stop him if he made a run for the door.

'Mingdu and Rong,' he said. He made them sound like a comedy duo. 'They're her enforcers.'

Madame Jade's, clearly. He must be in serious trouble.

'Why not just tell us all about it?' Alyssa said.

The gentleness in her voice masked the ease with which she got out her mobile phone and set it down in front of him.

'No recording.'

'But that's the only way we can help you.'

'Oh . . . maybe leave it on, then.'

He sat there and tried to collect himself. Mingdu and Rong – despite their tough appearance, I found it hard to take them seriously – watched us openly.

'There's something going on. Something big, and I'm worried about it.'

I consciously put on a kind of 'Yes, I really appreciate the importance of what you're saying' expression.

I'd changed my view of Prinsett. Now I thought he was a bit of a wally, who'd been comprehensively spooked by being forced to make love on a regular basis to one of China's most voracious women: a passion-stopper if ever there was one.

'It started quite soon after I arrived here, two years ago. My relationship with Jade, I mean. First I helped her daughter Lily prepare for the Oxford exams, then I started getting involved in the, well, businesses the Lins were running. She trusted me. I was the go-between, travelling to Beijing and Hong Kong and so on. And after that I suppose she thought I was reliable.'

I nodded.

'But there's something she's been doing . . . She and Lifang are planning something. I'm not quite certain what it is, because she wouldn't go into details. But she did say it'd have a huge effect on the country.'

Mingdu and Rong can't have understood what Prinsett was saying, but at that moment they looked at each other meaningfully and got up.

He couldn't see them from where he was sitting, so he carried on talking.

Before I could do anything, one of them punched him hard in the side of the head, and he went down, gasping for air and retching. The other one punched me in the stomach and kicked me on the kneecap as I went down too. Nice.

Alyssa screamed loudly, but to no effect. The night staff at the hotel knew who the two men were, and they were going to keep their heads down.

As Alyssa was trying to hold on to Prinsett, the larger of the two thugs – let's assume it was Rong – kicked her savagely. She yelped and let go. Rong turned and started hammering Prinsett with his fists. Then he dragged him towards the hotel entrance. The other one, Mingdu, picked up Prinsett's phone from the table, threw it onto the floor, and stamped on it.

I don't like seeing private property messed with. So although I was suffering pain in a number of places, I launched myself at Mingdu with the aggression that once got me a trial for Leinster. He went down across a glass-topped table and a sofa with me on top of him, and the glass fractured and went everywhere. Somehow a shard of it rammed into his leg.

He screamed as he lay underneath me, and blood started spurting out of him like a fountain. Who'd have thought the old man would have so much blood in him?

I rolled off him, and he lay there holding his leg and not looking angry any more but rather disappointed, and I started feeling sorry for him. Not sorry enough to do anything to staunch the blood, though.

'That's what you get,' I explained to him as I picked myself up.

His mate ran through the hotel's front door, so it was just the three of us now.

'You can't leave him like that.'

'All right,' I told her, 'if you're so worried about him, you sort him out.'

She grabbed a cloth from the bar and tied it round his leg, between the knee and the place where the blood was coming from. I went over to look at Prinsett.

'You've got me into a whole lot more trouble now,' he said from the floor.

That's Prinsett for you: you couldn't even save his neck without being complained at.

'You're welcome.'

'And my phone's been smashed.' He looked as though that was my fault, too.

'You'd better stay the night here,' I said, becoming suddenly practical despite the grogginess which had come over me, big time.

He nodded.

I looked back at Mingdu. He was gazing at Alyssa with puppy-like worship as she finished tying up his leg. I remember thinking this is all getting a bit complicated.

Belatedly, the manager appeared.

'You fighting here. No good,' he complained.

'Well, don't let thugs like him in.'

My Chinese was probably just as bad as his English, and since I couldn't think of a suitable translation for 'thug' I just said 'bad men'. If I'd been back in Dublin I'd have said 'gurrier', though people don't seem to use that expression so much nowadays. My dad might have said 'corner-boys', and funnily enough there's a Chinese expression which is rather like it. I suppose they constitute a worldwide phenomenon.

The manager had summoned a couple of porters, and they were doing something about the blood and the shards of glass, hissing disapprovingly under their breath.

Alyssa was saying severely, 'You did deserve it, you know', and Mingdu, lying back in his armchair, was looking contrite even though he didn't speak a word of English.

She organised a cab to take him back to whatever lair he'd emerged from, and was arranging to pay Prinsett's hotel bill for the night.

That just left me.

'I suppose I ought to be grateful to you,' she said, looking at the blood down her front.

'Well, a bit of hero worship wouldn't come amiss.'

'God, you're just like an overgrown teenager. As a result, we're in even worse trouble than we were before you did your Sir Galahad bit.'

I felt it was time to head to my room.

In the morning, I came down to breakfast as though that's what everyone does after nearly killing a hired assassin the night before. Alyssa and Prinsett were deep in conversation.

'He says we ought to go and see Madame Jade as soon as possible,' Alyssa said, without taking the trouble to greet me.

'Fine by me.'

My stomach gave a nervous lurch, all the same.

'And explain.'

'Explain about what?'

'About what happened last night, and why we're here, and what we want.'

Prinsett was still frightened, I could see, but he decided to act tough.

'I'll say I didn't know who those two were working for, so I can ask if we can come and see her.'

That sounded particularly screwy to me, but Alyssa was all for it. She liked the face-to-face, confrontational stuff.

Prinsett had borrowed Alyssa's phone; he dialled Madame Jade's private number. For some reason he'd perked up.

'It's Martin here.'

His Chinese, even in a few brief words, was infinitely better than mine.

'Yes, well, thank you. Lord knows who they were, but fortunately Jon Swift was here and he attacked one of them and chased the other away.'

He was looking at me as he said it.

I glanced at Alyssa with a God-help-us kind of expression, but she frowned and nodded towards him, to tell me he was doing exactly the right thing.

There was a burst of Chinese from the other end, and Prinsett made pacifying faces. As though Madame Jade could see him.

'We're to go round right now,' he said, as though he'd negotiated something really useful.

Alyssa, true to type, nodded and said, 'Great.'

My instinct was to make a run for the afternoon flight to London. But you've got to act the part, haven't you? Funny how, even when your life is in jeopardy, you still find yourself trying to make a good impression. Not on Prinsett, of course – I didn't much care what he thought. Just on Alyssa.

46

'No need to be nervous,' I told Prinsett, though I was nervous myself.

'Have you noticed we're being followed?'

I hadn't, but I nodded anyway. When your job is observing things, it's bad for business to admit you haven't spotted something so predictable.

'There was a black saloon parked outside the hotel. It's behind us.'

'Oh yes,' I said, as though that settled anything.

My neck still ached. Yet here I was, cruising for yet another bruising.

It was after ten-thirty when our taxi arrived at the gateway to the Lins' mansion. It was only a little less well guarded than Downing Street. We were expected, which helped, but we still had to go through a metal-detecting machine and allow ourselves to be patted down by a couple of goons. A tough-looking female guard was on hand for Alyssa.

The taxi driver wasn't allowed any closer than the roadway, so we had to walk from the gatehouse up the curving drive to the mansion. It was, naturally, very grand: a slice of white-painted, pillared Georgian architecture. It looked as though it had been bodily transplanted from the edges of Regent's Park.

There were even flower-baskets hanging by the double front door.

This opened silently at the precise moment we stepped onto the portico, and a couple of doormen in some kind of uniform greeted us.

I'm assuming that Lin himself designed the house when he got the job here some years earlier. Most top Chinese bureaucrats prefer a traditional *siheyuan*, complete with vermilion-painted entrance gate, copper door-knocker and hanging lanterns. Not Lifang. As an anglophile, he was confident enough not to worry about the image he was projecting. He must have designed the doormen's uniforms, too: dark blue and buttoned up to the chin. Very smart, but scarcely Mao Zedong Thought.

One of the uniforms went ahead of us across the vast entrance hall, while the other one brought up the rear. There were some magnificent ancestor-paintings on the walls of the grand drawing room, and those vast comfortable sofas and armchairs the British upper class equip their country houses with, and which the rest of us never seem to find when we go to John Lewis.

Fresh flowers stood in vases on little tables all round the room, and there was a grand piano in one corner with actual sheet music on it. Maybe Lily played, when she was home. Someone did, anyway.

The man who had led us into the room asked if we would like something to drink. Alyssa opted for tea and I followed suit. The time passed with some ritual involving a pot and some delicate little china cups. It all made me feel increasingly nervous.

Then there were rustling sounds on the stairs, and Madame Jade came in. There must have been a time when she, like her daughter Lily, was stunningly beautiful, but that time had passed.

Even so, John Donne's snippet about Lady Magdalen Herbert still applied:

> No spring nor summer beauty hath such grace
> As I have seen in one autumnal face.

Yet the bad temper of thirty years had left its marks on Jade. She looked pretty fierce as she shook hands with me, and then with Alyssa. As for poor old Prinsett, she cut him dead – didn't even look in his direction.

'I don't understand why you're here?'

Prinsett should have translated, but he was distracted. I decided to do it, for Alyssa's benefit.

Alyssa began talking as Jade seemed to understand her English.

'We are very keen to speak to you and your husband about the successes you have achieved here in Huzhang – culturally, politically and in terms of controlling crime.'

'My husband must decide for himself. I have no interest in speaking to you at all.'

She now spoke in English. Her accent was strong and the words were halting.

'Perhaps if I told you the areas of questioning—?'

'You don't seem to understand. I will not speak to you under any circumstances. That is the message I wanted to give you by allowing you to come here.'

Alyssa persisted gamely, but it was like shooting a tank with a BB gun. We were still standing in the middle of the room when Jade called out 'Wen!' and one of the uniformed men came in. She barked out an instruction.

Wen grunted, and moved slowly towards us with his arms out. It was the bum's rush.

'Ah, my dear,' came a familiar voice from the hallway. 'I see you've met my friend Mr Swift, and his charming associate. Ah yes – and Mr Prinsett too.'

Lin Lifang walked into the room, wearing a Mao suit in some kind of black shimmery material. It fitted him superbly. Wen lurched out of the firing line, and I shook hands with Lin. He bowed to Alyssa with an approving look in his eye.

'Jonathan has sung your praises to me,' he purred, though I'd never mentioned her to him.

Alyssa liked that. Not so Madame Jade.

'I have told Wen to show them out.'

'Oh, that seems a shame. They've only just arrived.'

She gave him a look, but he carried on smiling as though he hadn't noticed.

'I propose we have tea. "High tea",' he added, using those invisible quotation marks which were intended to make fun of me.

It was a weird experience: the Party boss, his dragon-lady wife, her erstwhile and very nervous lover, plus Alyssa and me, all behaving as though we were at Fortnum and Mason's, smiling and balancing cups, saucers and little plates. Wen even brought in some cakes on a stand, and passed them round. I suppose it made a change from kneeing people in the groin.

I'm writing this as though it was all a big joke. I promise you, it wasn't.

After a few minutes Lin said smoothly, 'Would you mind looking after our guests for a moment, my dear? I'd just like to show Mr Swift my collection.'

He held his hand out courteously to me; it was an order, not an invitation. Her eyes narrowed, but she didn't say anything. Prinsett stayed where he was. As we walked out of the room, I heard Alyssa still doing her best.

'Did you design this lovely house yourself?'

No reply.

'My wife is a little – well, stirred up,' said Lin to me in a quiet voice. 'I know you'll forgive her.'

I nodded, not being able to think of a reply. We wandered through three interconnecting rooms, then turned into a gallery like something out of a museum. There were glass cases all along the walls, with clay tomb-figures and vases and textiles in them. On the wall at the far end, under glass, was a breathtaking gown in imperial yellow.

'That belonged to the Chongzhen emperor, from the end of the Ming period. Approximately 1630, in Western terms.'

'Great. How much of all this is genuine?'

He laughed. 'I can see Mr Prinsett has been speaking out of turn.'

'He said your wife runs an antiquities factory in the city. They grind up old, broken figures and mould the clay into brilliant Tang dynasty figures worth millions. Because the clay itself is genuinely old, the figures pass the thermo-luminescence tests.'

'I don't know anything about that. If anything illegal is going on, I'm sure the relevant authorities will deal with it.'

'But you are the relevant authorities.'

He smiled his brilliant-white orthodontic smile. 'What I can assure you is that everything in this room is one hundred per cent genuine. Two hundred per cent, actually.'

His creaky laugh followed me as I went to look in the glass cases. I wouldn't know a genuine Tang dynasty tomb figure from something out of a Christmas cracker, but these things were certainly great to look at.

The laughter stopped.

'My message,' he said in a different and much quieter tone of voice. 'Were you able to pass it along after I saw you that day in Oxford?'

'Absolutely. Someone at the other end said it had been accepted and registered.'

'Wonderful. All we need now is a sign from those people that they're supporting us.'

'Well, I don't think you should wait for them to send a gunboat.'

'Ha ha,' he said, but without actually laughing. 'This is the twenty-first century. Governments register their support in other ways.'

'I imagine they'll wait to see how successful you are before they do anything.'

'Of course. Of course. Well, as you've probably guessed, the moment is coming. I do hope you'll remain in China to report on what happens. In your usual inimitable fashion.'

I nodded. But there was something boiling up inside me, which I couldn't keep down any more. Especially since he was asking me for favours.

'You probably know I was kidnapped and tortured, and that Wei Jingyi was also held in the same house and died as a result of the way he was treated.'

Lin frowned and nodded.

I went on: 'Well, there are people who say that you were behind it. Because you wanted to find out how much we knew, and whether we'd told anyone.'

It's quite draining to have things like this out with people, and after I'd finished my little speech I felt empty and exhausted. I suppose I'd been bottling it all up.

The effect on Lin was amazing. He dropped down onto some expensive Ming chair and looked at me. All the usual banter seemed to have drained out of him.

'Never – never,' he said. 'I may be tough, but I swear to you on my child's life that I would never do this to you or poor Jingyi. Please.'

He reached up and gripped my hands, and there were tears in his eyes.

And I believed him. Was I a sap for doing that? I didn't think so at the time, and I don't think so now.

When we rejoined the happy tea party, it was clear no one had said anything for a while. Three pairs of eyes – four, if you include Wen's – turned to look at us.

'Mr Swift has been explaining to me that he and his very charming associate' – I noticed he always avoided saying Alyssa's name; presumably he found the 's's too hard to navigate – 'haven't yet decided whether to stay in our rather boring provincial city, or return to Beijing. If they leave, will you go with them, Mr, ah, Prinsett?'

'No – yes,' said Prinsett. He looked as though he'd been hypnotised.

'No doubt you'll require time to tidy up your affairs here.'

'I suppose so.'

'Well, it has been a great pleasure to see you.'

'So we can't persuade you to do an interview with us?' Alyssa's voice sounded genuinely pleading.

Madame Jade shook her head and frowned crossly. It made it hard to imagine I'd ever thought she was beautiful.

'I feel this isn't quite the moment,' Lin put in calmly. 'But the time will come quite soon, I suspect. Perhaps it would be better to stay here in Huzhang if it's to happen.'

Alyssa misunderstood him.

'So you think something's going to happen?'

Madame Jade stood up and made a sign of her own to Wen.

'Our guests are leaving now,' she said to Wen in Chinese.

He came over to us, his arms out as before, as though he was herding a gaggle of geese. Lin smiled blandly.

'We'll be in touch, dear friends,' he said.

Madame Jade sniffed audibly.

47

Something strange was happening in Huzhang.

People who don't know China often assume it's a country where everyone obeys orders and behaves like an automaton. But the West's views of China were formed during the Cultural Revolution, when you had to do what you were told, or else be beaten to a pulp. We saw all those news pictures of millions of people chanting official slogans and marching in step, and we assumed that was what they wanted to do.

Huzhang seemed to be going back to those days. I'd already noticed the Maoist music from the loudspeakers, and the posters everywhere carrying slogans about the revolutionary will of the people. There were the Mao suits too. Generally speaking, people in China have mostly given them up. You do see them, especially in rural areas, but they're a rarity, like old men wearing shepherds' smocks in Edwardian England.

In Huzhang, though, there were quite a lot of Mao suits, even in the city centre: new and often well tailored. And when you drove round, you could see groups of people – quite big groups – marching backwards and forwards on areas of open land that the developers hadn't yet reached. There was singing, too: 'The East is Red' and other songs the tunes of which I vaguely remembered but whose words I'd forgotten. It was like a trip to the past.

The only thing that was missing was swarms of Red Guards beating up anyone they didn't like the look of. Maybe they'd be along soon.

Lin Lifang, the Party Secretary of the city, was turning the place into a Maoist throwback. Why? Well, Maoism was an easy, ready-made doctrine to recruit people, and keep them disciplined. But to what end? Presumably Lin needed something more than a bunch of discontented politicos to help him in his bid for the leadership.

That made him a throwback to an older time, before communism: the period of the warlords who weakened China disastrously in the 1920s and 1930s, and allowed the Japanese to invade. You can't be a warlord if you don't have an army, and that's exactly what Lin was creating on the empty fields and building-sites. What wasn't clear to me was whether, if he staged a bid for power, he would keep it in Huzhang or take it with him to Beijing.

But there were more immediate things to consider. Martin Prinsett's state of mind, for instance. He was badly scared, and wanted to get out as quickly as he could. Yet something was clearly on his mind other than his desperation to leave.

We met up with him in the hotel lobby. You couldn't see the bloodstains any longer, and they'd replaced the chairs and table that had been broken. The staff treated us with kid gloves, as though they thought we might start another donnybrook at any moment.

Prinsett came up and began speaking without any preliminaries.

'I think she was planning to do something to me there in the mansion, but Lin stopped her. He told me to get out soon, though – you heard him. I'd like to go to Beijing with you, if you don't mind.'

From being the prince consort he'd become apologetic and rather feeble.

I nodded.

'And you don't mind if I stay here in the hotel? I'd feel a bit safer than I would in my flat.'

He gave an anxious glance round the lobby.

Alyssa and I went to our rooms. I did a bit of reading, and drank a couple of beers.

Half an hour later there was a tentative knock at the door. I peered through the spy hole, and saw an unnaturally bulbous image of Prinsett looming up.

'I've been thinking,' he said, and I noticed that a strange calmness had come over him. 'I don't think I'm going to get away from here, and I'd like to tell you about some of the things that are going on.'

'What do you mean, you're not going to get away? I'll be with you. No one will do anything to you with me around.'

I actually think I meant it.

He took no notice. He didn't even seem to be listening. His thick fair hair wasn't combed as carefully as it had been in the past, and his pink scarf was untied and flapped about when he moved. It made me feel that one of the complex programmes keeping him going had been switched off.

He dropped down into the armchair beside me.

'It'd make me feel better if someone else knew what I've been mixed up in.'

Again, that weird sense of calm.

'All right,' I said, 'but let's not forget . . .'

I made a circular gesture with my forefinger. The rooms in the hotel were probably fitted with microphones or cameras. I told him in dumb-show that we should head downstairs. There was a cavernous restaurant on the ground floor that was usually empty; most people seemed to prefer the one at the top of the building. On our way down I knocked on Alyssa's door and did some more dumb-show.

In the restaurant a couple of listless waiters hung around at the far end. Otherwise the place was empty. We sat opposite Prinsett and listened to his story.

In a quiet, expressionless voice he explained that the factory making Han and Tang dynasty antiquities was just a sideshow. Lin Lifang and Madame Jade made serious money by importing live and dead animals from Africa. I'd noticed a delegation of people who looked as though they came from South Africa in the hotel earlier: jolly, well dressed and speaking English loudly.

'It's all a huge scam. They send live giraffes, lions and elephants over here to Huzhang Zoo. Except that there isn't a zoo in Huzhang. No problem – the animals are slaughtered soon after they arrive, and the bones and teeth are sold in South-East Asia for traditional medicines. There's some rhino horn too, though it's getting harder to kill rhinos in southern Africa nowadays.

'The profits are unbelievable. They grind up the horn and the lion bones and mix them with ground-up giraffe bones – a bit like cutting cocaine with talcum powder. It bulks it out, and since the stuff doesn't work anyway, nobody knows.'

'How much cash does this bring in?'

'I don't know – huge amounts. You'll never believe how much this crap goes for. Huzhang has become the big centre for it, and pretty much the whole trade is run by the Lins. Not just the parents, but the daughter as well.'

'I don't follow,' Alyssa said. 'If it's all phoney, why do they bother with real lions and giraffes? Surely they could just use bones from cows and sheep.'

'You're forgetting how precise Chinese people are. There are all sorts of independent experts whose job it is to verify the process and put seals on the pots of powder.'

'And they can't be bought?'

'Well, you see, the Lins' operation guarantees the quality. If a single inspector rejected just one pot, the trust in the operation would collapse. The Lins' USP is that their stuff is a hundred-per-cent perfect.'

Alyssa made a face that said 'you surprise me, but I believe you'.

'And what do you do?' I asked. 'I can't see you cutting animals up with a bone-saw.'

He winced.

'I'm the one who negotiates with the various African governments and organises the movement of the animals.'

'Which governments?'

It took a bit of pressure, but in the end he told me. They were all sub-Saharan, and none of the names would surprise you.

'There's a South African delegation staying in this hotel at the moment. We're negotiating for a consignment of fifteen elephants, all for the wonderful Huzhang City Zoo. Which doesn't actually exist.'

This would make a brilliant story, I thought. Not quite up there with Lin Lifang staging a coup against the central Party leadership, but pretty good, and full of the kind of stuff viewers want to see. Certainly a job-saver.

'I'm going to need you to say all this on camera. And I'm afraid you'll have to be a bit more specific than you've been so far.'

Alyssa sat back in her chair and gave a little whistle.

'Well, you wanted something good to take back to London with us. Looks like you've found it.'

We talked it through with Prinsett. He'd have to give us his story on camera, which was easy enough, but we'd need several other, much more difficult elements as well: an interview with someone involved in killing the animals, or maybe in cutting up the bones and turning them into traditional 'medicine'; some video of the process; and ideally some audio of one of Prinsett's African contacts, talking about the deal. And we'd need to get a pot or two of the powder, to take back to London for analysis.

'Tricky, that,' Alyssa said. 'Suppose we get caught with the stuff.'

'There are ways and means,' said Prinsett.

At that precise moment, as if he'd been summoned up for the purpose, a large, suited black man came out of the lift and started walking across the lobby, past the restaurant.

'That's the head of the delegation.'

'Go and grab him, then bring him over here and introduce me.'

Prinsett jumped up, went out into the lobby and intercepted the bulky figure before he could get to the concierge's desk.

'Minister!' he said in something of a return to his usual manner. 'I wonder if you'd have time to talk to a friend of mine?'

The minister didn't look enthusiastic, but he came over all the same.

'Hello, sir,' I said, with something of Prinsett's gushing tone. 'My name is Swift. I'm in the transport business. This is my associate, Ms Roberts.'

He'd clocked her already, and preened a little, for her benefit. It was clear I meant nothing at all to him.

Prinsett then started to play a blinder.

'Swift here knows a little about our business arrangement, supplying zoos all over China with animals, and he's offering us an interesting deal if he can take over the shipping.'

'Interesting' obviously meant a better cut. The minister started to look at me as though I existed after all.

Alyssa had sat down again, and was messing around in her handbag. I knew what that meant: she was switching on the camera on her phone. Looking bored, she fished it out and answered it. I was pretty sure there wasn't anyone at the other end, but she acted out the part pretty well. The minister seemed to be taken in by the display.

'OK, well, thanks so much for thinking of me, and stay safe. Lots of love.'

She made a kissing sound. That kept his attention.

Alyssa pressed the 'off' button, then casually set the phone down on her handbag as it lay on the table. The camera lens pointed at the minister's face.

Prinsett and I talked about our proposal, though I was careful not to get into specifics. I hadn't had a great deal of experience of shipping wild animals around the globe.

Instead, I hit on a useful dodge.

'We won't talk precise figures now, minister, but I can assure you that I will pay you a minimum of twenty per cent more than you're receiving at the moment, as long as you can give me an assurance that you can provide us with animals in the same quantities you have been providing my friend Mr Prinsett with: in particular, elephant, lion, cheetah and leopard.'

'Oh yes, I can assure you of that,' rumbled the minister, smiling.

'All live? After all, we'll need to supply them to zoos here and around China, won't we?'

'All live, I promise.'

The minister smiled a brilliant smile.

'And rhinos?'

The smile faded slightly.

'Rhinos are, you know, a little harder nowadays. We cannot promise live rhinos.'

'But you can give us body parts of rhinos? For scientific research, naturally?'

'Oh yes, I can undertake to do that.'

The smile came back, full version.

'Horns and all?'

'Yes, yes, yes, horns and all.'

Bingo. I leant over to shake his hand, then risked a quick glance at Alyssa. From the way she was smiling brilliantly in the minister's direction, I could tell she'd got it all.

By the time I'd come back from bowing to the minister on his way out Alyssa had sent the material to London.

48

'Yes, it's all fine so far,' Alyssa was saying, 'but we still need two major things.'

I leaned forward, my elbows on the table. Our orders had finally arrived.

She was taking over the story, and that was fine by me. Reporting it would be the easy part; fixing everything was much more difficult.

'We'll have to put all this in its context – China's attitudes towards animals, especially. Then we'll need an interview with someone who's involved in the business of slaughtering the animals. And finally we'll have to have clear, unequivocal pictures of the animals being cut up for body parts.'

She went quiet for a moment. Her clarity of thought had run quite a long way ahead of her sense of what these things would mean in practical terms. But it was clear she had something in mind.

'Apparently there's a big wet market here. I thought that just meant seafood, but it seems it's animals as well.'

This all happened before the outbreak of Covid-19, by the way. After that, the entire world knew about China's wet markets; especially the one in Wuhan.

'We can do a bit of surreptitious filming there.'

I nodded obediently. You can't have two bosses on a story, and Alyssa was now quite clearly in pole position.

She explained it all in greater detail to Prinsett, who was chewing on his unappetising hamburger. He nodded, his mouth full. Then he raised his hand to show he wanted to say something.

'As it happens, we've been using a wildlife biologist who's from here, but Jade took against him when she saw he didn't like what we were doing, and she sacked him. I know how to contact him, if you want.'

'Oh yes,' I said, 'we want him. We want him really badly.'

Alyssa frowned, so I shut up. Prinsett went through the contacts list on a new phone he had bought.

'Shall I fix a meeting with him?'

He looked at Alyssa, not me. She nodded.

Within fifteen minutes it was all arranged: we'd meet the biologist in a small restaurant well known for its noodles, down a narrow alley in the city centre, not far from our hotel. We agreed Alyssa should leave the hotel first, and head there on her own.

Prinsett and I would set out fifteen minutes later, and we'd all meet up twenty minutes after that at a stall outside the New World department store that sold fried crickets and prawns on sticks.

The usual tail made an appearance behind us, but since I could only detect one spook I suggested to Prinsett that we should split up.

'Whoever gets followed should try hard to shake him. Then we should meet in twenty minutes at the easternmost entrance to the New World department store.'

He nodded.

The tail decided to follow me. I crossed the street and let Prinsett forge ahead for a while, so I could check that no one else was on his tail. Then I thought I'd have a bit of fun.

I dodged into a shop which sold art supplies, and which, I could see, had another entrance/exit in the parallel street behind. A free-standing rack of pens gave me cover as I ducked down and watched the spook wandering around, looking for me. There were enough displays for me to be able to move over to the far exit, make a play of opening the door then duck down again. It worked. The spook went rushing out of the exit, and I hurried back to the door I'd originally entered by and got out into the street. Then I crossed the street and went into a dark little teahouse nearly opposite to watch.

The spook, in a serious flap by this time, came running back out of the art shop, and stood looking in all directions. I almost felt sorry for him.

I ordered a pot of *pu-er* and waited for him to make up his mind. Eventually he did, heading off in the wrong direction. One person can't possibly follow two who've decided to split up, so he didn't really deserve to get into trouble when he finally went back to report. The fault lay with his bosses, who hadn't put more people on the job.

I downed my tea and headed for the eastern entrance to the New World, by the cricket-and-prawn stall. Alyssa already had a prawn in her hand, so I ordered a couple of crickets, just to freak her out. In fact they're surprisingly tasty, if you don't mind picking out the occasional angular, crackly leg from between your teeth.

Prinsett came puffing up, tense and nervous.

'No problem,' I said soothingly. 'Let's head back into the store, then split up when we're inside and meet outside the far entrance in five.'

Alyssa meticulously wrapped her prawn in a bit of tissue, and followed us inside the main entrance to the store. Five minutes later we all met up again on the other side of the building. There were plenty of people around, but I couldn't spot any followers. You shouldn't be able to, of course, but the standards of surveillance didn't seem very high.

Alyssa signalled for a taxi, and we got into it.

'Don't tell him the address of the restaurant,' she said sharply. 'Ask him to drop us somewhere nearby, and we can walk to it.'

It all seemed like a game, and we were winning.

49

The biologist was there already: tall, thin, anxious, and probably short of sleep. His name was Dr Ma.

Dr Ma was definitely worried about talking to Prinsett; he'd only seen him in the past with Madame Jade, and it took a bit of persuading to convince him that Prinsett had switched sides. What did it, was when Alyssa leaned across the melamine table with her phone and showed him the interview we'd filmed surreptitiously with the African minister. After that, Dr Ma positively smiled.

He went into an explanation of what was going on. There was quite a lot of noise around us, with friends greeting each other and arguing about who was going to pay, and I lost him after the first few sentences. But I could see from Prinsett's reactions and short, interjected questions that he knew exactly what had been happening.

Dr Ma paused when the food arrived, and he launched into his five types of vegetable soup and his pork slices and rice with real enthusiasm. It looked as though he hadn't been eating much recently.

When Prinsett realised that neither Alyssa nor I could keep up, he started asking short questions, switching from Chinese to English with great fluency, so that we could follow.

'Do you know how many lions were brought in during your time at the zoo?'

He looked at us. 'Forty-seven.'

'What happened to them?'

'They were all slaughtered here.'

The details kept coming. He pulled out a little notebook in which he'd jotted down the figures. Thirty-six giraffes. Twelve chimpanzees. Two hundred pangolins. A small but unknown number of hippopotamuses, brought in simply so their bones could be added to the mix. There were tigers and orang-utans too. He saw them, but because the African animals were his speciality he didn't know how many.

We were silent when he stopped talking. I suppose Alyssa and I were stunned by what he'd said.

She asked him if he'd be prepared to let me interview him on camera, but before he could answer Prinsett broke in.

'Listen, it's important to make sure you know I wasn't involved in this. It's true I helped Jade with selling fake antiquities, but that was all.'

Our disbelief must have shown on our faces.

'OK, well, yes, I did know about it. Jade told me some of it. But I didn't have any part in it. My job was organising the fake antiquities.'

I could see he wanted us to tell him it was all right, that we believed him. Neither of us did. I didn't feel like patting his shoulder and saying, 'Don't worry, I understand.'

Dr Ma broke in and said he had to go.

'What about our interview?'

'No, no.'

'Look, we'll just film your hands and your notes, without sound. Would that be all right?'

Dr Ma looked at Prinsett, and Prinsett nodded encouragingly.

'OK, I trust you,' said Dr Ma in English.

It would have been impossible to interview him there openly anyway, with all the other diners yelling at each other across the tables. And Dr Ma's hands and the notes, if used properly, could tell the story just as well.

Alyssa did a good, discreet, speedy job of it, and you'd have had to sit very close to realise she was filming him. Anyone watching would have thought she was making gestures while holding her phone in her hand: just a little slowly, perhaps.

50

She and I had already worked out that we had to get some pictures from the big wet market in the old centre of the city. It wasn't necessarily going to be relevant to the business of importing animals from Africa, but Alyssa felt it would help us talk about the Chinese attitude to wildlife: essentially, that it was there to be exploited.

I'm squeamish where animals are concerned – more, illogically, than I am about humans – so I wasn't looking forward to seeing the wet market. I'd been to places like it in South-East Asia, and knew what we'd be in for.

We decided we should split up before we even left the restaurant. If there was anyone waiting outside to follow us, then Alyssa and I should try to draw them off. Prinsett and Dr Ma would wait for half an hour, then Prinsett would go out alone; and Dr Ma would order some more tea and wait until he felt comfortable about leaving.

'Not that there'll be anyone outside,' I said in my usual over-confident way. 'We threw the only spook off the trail a couple of hours ago.'

Seriously wrong. As we left the restaurant, at least four different men in suits threw cigarettes away and got into their cars. As I say, out here in the sticks the level of sophistication wasn't high.

We hailed a cab, and three cars eased out and followed us. Once, just for entertainment's sake, I told the driver to stop in a lay-by. Two of the three cars couldn't stop, and were carried along in the flow of traffic. The one that was left stopped on the other side of the road and waited.

'I suppose someone in the restaurant clocked us and rang the cops.'

I nodded.

'As long as they don't try to stop us in the wet market, we'll be OK.'

She was right about that, too. We were just tourists now, filling in time before we left, so visiting the wet market was a perfectly reasonable thing to do. And if we took some pictures, we wouldn't be doing anything wrong.

I motioned to the driver, and we edged out into the traffic again.

It took us a while to get there. Sophisticated spooks drive ahead of you as well as behind, and you're hardly aware of them. These spooks weren't sophisticated; they followed our taxi.

The wet market is a huge place, covering acres of ground. If you're a cook or a sociologist or a Chinese bon viveur, it must be a treasure house of wonders; but if you like animals, it's an extermination camp.

There's a powerful smell in the place that's hard to define: fish guts, excrement, generator fuel, wet oilskins – all those, and many more. And it's heaving with people, buying, selling, sampling, and just wandering around, often smoking and coughing and spitting.

I spotted one of the secret cops standing at another stall, watching us. No point in telling Alyssa, I thought: what was happening in the market was worrying enough.

'I'm not looking forward to seeing what they do to animals here,' she said.

She was right. I've seen a lot of nasty things, but the sheer uncaring brutality all round got me, even worse than the stench of shit and spilt guts. A stallholder pulled a snake out of a basket, held it by the head with the tail hanging down, and ripped it open with a knife from tail to head as it wriggled. Another sliced the head off a large furry rat, presumably fattened up for weeks. Its body lay twitching on the block for several seconds. And we watched as a large civet cat was yanked out of a cage that was far too small, and beaten over the head with a wooden mallet until it lay still.

Civet cats have two uses in China: their glands are used in traditional medicine and their flesh is used in hugely expensive dishes, especially in Guangdong province, where it's flavoured with chrysanthemum flowers and called 'dragon-tiger-phoenix soup'. Nothing as crude as 'eviscerated wildcat'.

While an enthusiastic buyer stood and watched, the stallholder cut the civet open. It was only cowed and injured, not dead, so it gave a despairing yowl. He let its guts tumble out onto the table, before reaching in with ungloved hands and pulling the glands out with professional ease. They lay on the block, steaming and running with blood.

As I say, I pride myself on an iron stomach, but when I thought of Yorick at home I felt really angry. Still, I suppose executioners in Britain did something similar to human beings until less than three hundred years ago, so none of us has any right to feel too superior.

Two of the secret cops were hanging round while all this was going on, keeping an eye on our movements. As I looked, one of them took a call and stood there nodding and staring at me, forgetting he was supposed to be undercover. He nodded one last time and ended the call.

The civet dealer had no objection to our watching him. There was nothing illegal about anything he was doing, and a couple of other bystanders had gathered round too. So when Alyssa held up her iPhone and looked at him questioningly, he nodded and smiled as he scooped the glands into a plastic bag, and put the furry, headless body into another one. The smashed head lay on the floor for a little longer, until he reached down and dropped it in a bucket. It made a dull sound: the bucket wasn't empty.

We moved on, taking with us our little group of watchers. They didn't show any signs of stopping us.

At the far end of the huge and cavernous market, away from the animals and snakes, there were sections for shellfish and crustaceans and live fish; big ones, one or two the size of a small man. Watching them being held up and eviscerated felt pretty bad too, though the stench down this end of the market was easier to take.

In the months that followed, there were plenty of stories about bats, and how Covid-19 had crossed the species barrier to human beings from them. That was in Wuhan, where there are a lot of bats for sale in the wet market. Here in Huzhang I spotted a few bats, some alive and fluttering around noisily in cages, and others dead with their wings nailed to a board, but no one seemed to be buying them. According to Prinsett, they weren't a delicacy in Huzhang, though maybe dealers bought them here and transported them to areas where people relished them.

By now I could see all four secret cops. One of them was filming our every move on his phone. I still didn't say anything about it to Alyssa. She was nearly at the end of her tether after looking at so much butchery and blood. At this point I said that I thought we should go.

In spite of everything, she put up a fight. I suppose she felt she should be the one to say when we'd got enough material, and she was right. But if we hung around much longer I thought the policemen might make a move on us.

They didn't. We were free to wander out and find our car.

A tear or two appeared in Alyssa's eyes on the journey back, and when we got to the hotel she took the lift upstairs without saying anything. I went and lay on my bed. It had affected me too: more than just the smell, it was the weakness and inability of the animals to resist the hammer and the chopper and the gutting knife which made me feel bad.

At seven that evening I rang her room and suggested going downstairs for a drink. She agreed. I rang Martin's room too, but he didn't answer.

Alyssa looked more together when she came into the bar. We ordered G and Ts, and got proper British gin. But instead of real tonic it was laced with some local concoction made in Shenzhen, which tasted like washing-up liquid. Alyssa laughed aloud when I said that, so I could see she was getting back to her old self.

51

Martin Prinsett spotted us, and walked quickly over. I could see something was up, but I insisted on getting him a drink before letting him speak.

'Don't have the tonic,' I warned.

Someone had pushed something under the door of his hotel room. He pulled it out of his pocket and unfolded it. Alyssa looked at it, then handed it to me. It was a copy of a photograph. I peered at it. It showed the door of a fridge – not the kind you have in your kitchen, but an industrial one. There were several notices in Chinese pasted on the door, and one in English: 'Danger', with a skull and crossbones in red above it. Someone in a white coat was reaching into it and either putting in or pulling out a tray of little capsules.

'So?' I said.

Martin didn't reply for a while. He was reading the Chinese notices.

Then he straightened up and looked at me.

'This must be some kind of fridge where they keep traditional medicines. Look – you can see the characters "*Shīzi*", meaning "lion", on the fridge door. There are several other notices I'm finding it harder to read.'

'And what's the bloke with the tray of capsules doing? Assuming it is a bloke.'

'Take a look at a second photo that was put under the door.'

It was about the size of the other one. Alyssa looked at it carefully.

'No, this is a woman.'

She handed it to me. It certainly looked like a woman; and for some reason I thought she was faintly familiar. The camera angle was an acute one, and the picture had been taken close to her right ear, from the back. You could see her whole ear, quite a lot of the side of her face and the corner of her right eye. Not much to go on – and yet I couldn't shake off the idea that I'd seen her somewhere.

'Whoever it is, she can't be up to any good, can she?' I said. 'I mean, why would someone slip a couple of pictures under the door if she isn't doing anything wrong?'

'Oh, you journalists, always adding two and two and making twenty-two.'

Raj Harish, the spook, had said almost exactly the same thing to me, when I sat with him in Ritan Park soon after we arrived on this particular trip. It irritated me just as much now.

Alyssa leaned in and picked up the two pictures.

'I don't think we've got twenty-two here, I think we've got a story someone wants us to know about. All we have to do is decide what the person was so keen to tell you.'

That shut him up.

'Something important is happening here. Now – who's the woman in the white coat, and what are the little gizmos she's taking out? Or maybe putting in?' I said.

I sat back and took a slug of gin and tonic-water substitute. All this Sherlockery was tiring.

Alyssa looked at me and said, 'So if she's taking them out, what's she going to do with them?'

'As you say' – Martin looked at me – 'the fact that someone has given me these two photos makes me think it must be something significant.'

There was a self-regard about him I found irritating. I began to wonder whether it had something to do with Jade sending her two heavies to sort him out, in this bar; maybe she'd decided he knew too much, and wanted to silence him. And perhaps she'd agreed to let him come back to Huzhang in order to do just that.

I didn't say that to him, though. He was much too flaky. He wasn't listening anyway, but peering at one of the pictures, holding it at a slight angle.

'Look at this,' he said, and pointed to a notice on the wall.

To be honest, it meant nothing to me: just a line of Chinese characters I couldn't read.

'It looks like the name of a state institution of some kind.'

He peered at it again, then straightened up in triumph.

'The something something of Molecular Biology.'

He held it closer.

'That could be "State".' He thought for a moment. 'It could be the Institute of Molecular Biology.'

Instead of looking triumphant and preening, he went quiet.

Alyssa asked, 'Where is it?'

Martin shifted uncomfortably.

'The labs are out on the main road north – there's a turn-off which is always guarded, but you can see the buildings from the highway. I suppose it's possible that's the one.'

I kept stumm, but I was thinking hard. I was back in the courtyard of the Old Parsonage Hotel in Oxford, with a glass of Bollinger in front of me, and Lin Lifang saying, '*You see, Lily has just got a place at Brasenose. To read molecular biology.*'

'And do you know anyone who's worked there?'

My voice took on a harsh, metallic ring, like a prosecutor's at a murder trial.

'No.'

He looked away.

'I think you do, Martin. I think Lily, the Lins' daughter, spent some time there. The one you helped to get into Oxford.'

There was a silence.

'Well, she didn't work there or study there; she did all that in England. But it's true she spent a few weeks at the institute, just before she went off to Oxford. I can't believe, though, that—'

'Well, I'm beginning to.'

I knew now who the woman in the photos reminded me of.

Alyssa nodded.

'I think you're being a bit too protective of her,' she told Martin.

He gnawed the side of his finger.

'Well, I do know the editor of the main newspaper here, the *Daily Banner*. He might have some idea what those photos are all about. And he owes me – I persuaded Lin to let him keep his job, when he got into trouble for making fun of the songs about Mao.'

'Could he have sent them to you?'

'It's possible. Though I don't know why.'

Alyssa started another line of questioning.

'Is the lab lit up at night?'

'Let me think – well, it's certainly not floodlit, but there are always people working there at night-time, often really late. I've seen the lights on at three or four in the morning, when I've driven past.'

Alyssa looked at me.

'OK, well, I think we've all got a long night ahead of us.'

Martin looked at her questioningly.

'Look – we're here to make a film for television. It's not impossible that something bad is going on at this lab, and we'll need pictures of it if our film is going to be any good.'

I nodded. God, I thought, I've worked with plenty of people who, at a time like this, would start remembering they had to make urgent calls to their families, or have an early night.

52

We worked out a plan of action. Martin would go round to the *Daily Banner*'s offices, where his mate would still be overseeing the next day's edition. No phone calls, no text messages: those would probably be monitored.

Alyssa and I, meanwhile, would find a way of getting to the institute. It could only be by taxi, and we'd have to think how we were going to summon one without raising suspicions.

Not easy.

The only place that Martin could think of where we could be dropped off near the institute was a roadhouse about a mile from it. I'd better get my walking shoes on, I thought, and I headed upstairs while Martin looked up the address on Baidu, the Chinese equivalent of Google.

He'd left by the time I got back. Alyssa was looking at a sketch map he'd drawn for her.

'It needn't take us much time,' she said, as though our conversation had gone on uninterrupted.

According to Martin, the roadhouse stayed open till midnight. It was unusual for a Western couple to go to a restaurant on the outskirts of the city at ten o'clock at night, yet not so amazingly weird that the taxi driver would feel he'd have to report us.

Our biggest problem was getting out of the hotel.

It wasn't as hard as you might think. Alyssa and I paid the bill, and went to the lift.'

I pressed the button for my floor and we got out together. We wandered along the passage then went down the emergency stairs to the basement car park. There were CCTV cameras there, of course, but with luck no one would be watching the screens at this time of the evening. By the time the security people checked the tapes, hopefully we'd have left Huzhang. That was my theory, anyway.

We hurried through the car park and stumbled up the ramp into the main street. Nobody showed their face or shouted at us. A hundred yards or so down the street one of the city's orange cabs was passing, and we hailed it.

The driver was inclined to be chatty, but only about local things. I let him yack on while we looked out of the windows. An occasional 'dui', 'yes, right', kept him happy, even when I hadn't the faintest idea what he was talking about. When we reached the roadhouse I gave him a decent tip.

The place was about a quarter full, and usefully dark. Red lampshades hung low over the tables. We sat on stools at the bar and ordered a couple of Pearl River beers, and after a reasonable amount of time we paid up and left. The night was cold, and there was a sharp wind.

'Just a few shots of the front of the building plus the sign,' Alyssa said; once again, she'd be doing the filming on her phone. 'Then a quick piece to camera. Do you know what you'll be saying?'

'As little as possible.'

I wasn't joking. At the moment we knew hardly anything about the story, yet we had to have a piece to camera, because it would prove we'd actually been there. But what should I say?

As we trudged along, with cars occasionally flashing past us and throwing up leaves and little bits of gravel, I worked it out in my mind. Keep it vague and general, I told myself.

'Of course, all this is based on the assumption that Martin's photos are of real interest,' Alyssa said, 'and that this is the building where they were taken.'

She always liked to inject a bit of scepticism into what we were doing. And to be honest, I was starting to lose faith in the project myself; maybe it was the cold, and the effect of the Pearl River beer wearing off.

But Alyssa was composed of tougher stuff. 'Actually, I've got a good feeling about this.'

'Great,' I muttered.

After about twelve or fifteen minutes' walking we caught sight of the institute between the trees on the right-hand side, just before the turn-off. As Martin had said, there were lots of lights on inside. The high gate was closed, and it looked to me as though the guard hut just inside was empty; no light was on anyway.

Alyssa took some arty stuff of the gate at a bit of an angle, then some more just straight on in case the angle stuff didn't work. After that she moved closer to the gate and filmed the building itself, about a hundred yards away: wide, close, zoom in to lighted window, wide, zoom in again, pan across the front of the building. The full monty. And she got various shots of the sign that said in Chinese, and English, that this was the Huzhang Institute of Molecular Biology, who its director was, and what the opening hours were.

Alyssa got me to stand by the sign.

'Turning over,' she said.

'This is the Huzhang Institute of Molecular Biology,' I declaimed. 'It's ten o'clock at night, yet the lights are still blazing on every floor of the building. The assumption is that there's some important work being done here. But we don't yet know what that work is.'

I couldn't think of anything else to say. Maybe, by the time we came to edit the report, we'd have found out what was happening there. If so, we could always chop those last few words out.

Now we'd got that in the can, Alyssa suggested we should take a quiet turn round the buildings in the dark. That sounded a good idea.

There were bushes of some kind on the outer edge of the lawn in front of the main building. We bent down and, using the bushes as cover, shuffled our way towards the main building.

The downstairs rooms seemed to be administrative ones, which was disappointing. One or two people in white coats were wandering around, or looking at computer screens. Alyssa took a few shots through the window. Not very inspiring.

We backed away. The bushes had come to an end, but there was a courtyard at the back of the main building, so we made our way across it to the more modern building behind.

A glimpse through one of the windows was more promising. It was some kind of laboratory area, and there were various fridges, the upright and chest variety, dotted around the room. Some looked very much like the fridge that Lily Lin – assuming it was her – had been standing in front of in the photos.

Alyssa looked at me excitedly, and got closer to the window, holding her phone on the windowsill to steady it, while keeping her head down. No one inside seemed to notice.

We moved on. There were more buildings behind: big prefabricated barns of corrugated iron, three storeys high. No windows now: we had to creep along the outer wall, hoping for a chance to get a look inside.

I started to notice a sharp animal stench. A couple of big flat-bed trucks were parked at the back of the building. They had high sides, but these had been lowered, as though something big had been transported here, then taken into the barn.

At that moment a high-pitched scream made us both leap up. I could feel my hands trembling. But it wasn't anything living: there was a sharp mechanical edge to it.

Alyssa, who was ahead of me, reached back and grabbed my arm.

'Look!' she breathed in my ear, over the racket.

The big doors of the barn were slightly open, and the noise was coming through them. This was the really dangerous bit. Something was going on in there, and we had to get across the forecourt to see what it was.

The screaming took on a new intensity, then changed to a horrible grating sound. We edged our way closer.

When we were still a good ten feet from the gates we could see clearly.

Alyssa gasped, and I grabbed her arm: partly to tell her to keep quiet, and partly because I was horrified.

Inside was a man, guiding something the size of a piece of furniture towards the big circular saw that stood fixed to the floor. Two or three other men were watching, all in clothes that looked like oilskins, dark and shining with blood.

The furniture-sized object was covered with a familiar orange and white mottling. It was unmistakably the legs and back end of a giraffe.

Under the cover of the screaming I hissed in Alyssa's ear, 'Let's get closer.'

She nodded, and switched her phone camera on so she could get a walking shot, going as close to the open doors as she dared.

I came to a halt behind her. Thank God we were both wearing dark clothes, I thought.

'It's got to be me who does the filming,' she'd said earlier. 'No one will see me in the dark.'

And she'd laughed that laugh of hers.

Here, the noise of the big bone-saw was overwhelming. I saw a pile of giraffe limbs waiting to be sawn up. Further on was a heap of animal carcasses that were the colour, I thought, of lions. Judging from the stench, the animals must have been slaughtered somewhere else, some time ago, and brought here to be cut into small pieces. This was a real industry.

At that moment Alyssa's view was blocked. One of the men in oilskins was coming through the narrow gap between the open doors. We stood close to one of the trucks, and dodged down behind the rear wheel. The man came straight towards us.

Two things were in our favour: the screaming noise of the saw, and the fact that he was walking out from the bright light into the dark. I hunched down, my face close to the ground, with Alyssa just behind me. I could feel her knee on my foot, but I had to take the pain. I didn't dare move.

The man came closer and closer, until I could smell the oilskins and the blood that covered him. Then he stopped, a yard away from us, and opened his clothes. A jet of liquid landed just in front of me, and continued to spread a pool of foul-smelling urine until it almost reached my knees.

Then he gave a grunt, fiddled around with his clothes, and went back in. The saw stopped screaming.

'We've really got to get out of here,' I whispered.

Alyssa nodded.

'I've got loads of this,' she whispered back.

'Enough?'

'Oh God, yes. Much more than enough.'

I could see the disgust in her face. The giraffe leg and the heap of lion carcasses were the evidence we needed, and she'd got it all.

At this point I managed to screw everything up. My knee locked, and I fell over and hit my head on the wheel arch of the truck. If only the saw had still been screaming, there wouldn't have been a problem. Now, though, a head stuck out through the opening of the doors and stared into the darkness. If I'd still been hunched down, it probably wouldn't have mattered. But the man caught a glimpse of my pallid face in the darkness, and yelled out to the others.

They came pouring out through the doors. But our eyes were used to the darkness, and theirs weren't. I grabbed Alyssa's arm and we headed back the way we'd come, sticking close to the wall, while the workers were shouting and running round the yard.

There was no going back to the front of the building, where we'd filmed our piece to camera earlier: by the time we got there, all the other workers in the place would be rushing out. I looked at the concrete wall. It was only an inch or so higher than my head, with barbed wire on the top.

I pulled off my coat, threw it over the wire, and grabbed Alyssa's leg to hoist her onto the wall. She did it in one easy movement, and knelt on my coat to hold out her hand for me. I grabbed it and pulled myself up. It was agonising, but I managed to get one knee on top of the wall. She dropped down on the far side, which meant I could rest on the coat as it lay on the barbed wire. Then I flopped over, and landed on my side next to her. She pulled at my coat and it came away with a ripping sound.

There were some empty huts on this side of the wall. We ran over to them and lay down beside one of them. I knew I'd cut my leg on the barbed wire, but I wasn't bleeding badly.

Alyssa was grinning.

'Fantastic bit of work!'

I was less enthusiastic, and whispered some complaint about my leg and my torn coat. But her eyes were shining in the faint light of the stars. We'd got what we needed, and we'd managed to escape.

So far, anyway.

53

The hut we were sheltering beside smelled of pigs: a lot better than decaying giraffe or lion.

'I'm going to switch on the Hotspot on my phone to give us a signal,' I whispered to Alyssa. 'You can use it to send the pics and my stand-up to someone in London. Then, when we know it's there, we can delete everything from your phone, in case we get caught.'

'I'll send it to Simon Williams,' she said, Simon being the producer in London who usually took in our reports. 'I'll say it's urgent, and ask him to hang on to it till we get back.'

The lights of the roadhouse were getting closer. We'd been walking for a good fifteen minutes. My leg hurt, and I could feel the wind flapping the tears in my trouser-leg.

To take my mind off it, I concentrated on the spicy *xiao mian* noodles I was going to order, and the beer I was going to wash it down with. After that we could ring for a taxi to take us back to the hotel.

We reached the car park of the roadhouse, and I started to say 'I could really do with some . . .'

That was as far as I got. Three men in dark coats, each wearing a white shirt and a black tie, detached themselves from the darkness and walked slowly towards us. I saw how they blocked off our escape routes; and when I turned round to see if we could run back the way we'd come, there was another dark coat behind us; we must have walked past him without noticing.

This was serious. If we were going to get away from them, it wouldn't be by running. And, given that there were four of them, it wouldn't be by violent resistance either. It would only be by guile.

'*Ni hao*,' I said, in a chatty kind of way.

No one replied. One of the four, smaller but a bit older than the others, pointed to a people-carrier that was parked near the entrance to the roadhouse.

'No, thank you,' I said with faux-politeness. 'We're going to have something to eat first, then we'll get a cab back to our hotel. We're flying to Beijing tomorrow morning. If it's any business of yours,' I added in English.

'Yes, it is,' said the head honcho, also in English.

'Look, we're cold and tired, and we'd like something to eat before we go back to our hotel.'

I assumed I'd get a punch in the face.

Instead, the older guy said, 'Well, I don't see why not.'

54

There were five of us sitting scrunched up in a big booth with seats of imitation dark leather. The man who'd been behind us stayed by the door, in case we tried to do a runner.

There was something nightmarish about the whole business. It felt like one of those dreams where the everyday and the disturbing are mixed up together. All five of us ordered Tsingtaos, and Alyssa, on my advice, joined me in ordering *xiao mian*. The suits said they didn't want anything to eat.

By now I'd forgotten all about the pain in my left leg where the barbed wire had sliced it, but I was conscious of my ripped trouser leg. Fortunately no one could see it under the table.

The waitress headed off, and that just left the five of us.

'Suppose you tell me what this is all about,' I said to the older man. Which sounds like every thriller you've ever seen. Now, I thought, he'll say, 'I ask the questions around here.'

But no. He smiled and said, 'Mr Ser-wiff, we have been told that you came here to break into the Institute for Molecular Biology. Please assure me this is not true.'

'I'm happy to, because it isn't. We came here because we had a quiet evening before we leave first thing tomorrow, and I wanted to get some pictures of the building for a friend of mine who studied there.'

'This is quite difficult to believe,' he said, but at that moment our noodles arrived.

Noodles, and particularly *xiao mian* noodles, take a lot of eating. You have to get your head down close to the bowl. The dish is particularly spicy, so talking is difficult.

'Do you mind?' I said, pointing with my spoon towards the *xiao mian*.

Alyssa gave me a faint, encouraging smile.

Eventually, I couldn't put it off any longer. But I had my story ready.

'So, we've just been to see the institute. We wanted to take some pictures of it for Lily Lin, a friend of ours. She's the daughter of Lin Lifang, and she's studying in Oxford, where I live.'

Then I added, 'I recorded a little message for her outside the institute. If my colleague Alyssa would be kind enough to show it to you . . .'

Alyssa smiled and produced her phone. She switched it on.

'Oh God, Jon, I don't seem to have it any more. I must have deleted it all. I'm so sorry.'

She was a pretty good actress, and of course such things happen every day, especially to the non-technically minded. But I could see that he felt this was all too convenient.

'Do you mind?' he said urbanely, and looked through her phone. Even before we left the disused pigsty she'd sent everything incriminating to London. All that was left were a few harmless tourist videos of Beijing. Before he had even glanced at them she knew, and I knew, and he knew, that we'd won this round. What the others thought, I didn't care.

'I thought she'd like to see her alma mater,' I said. 'I'm sorry it seems to have disappeared. Maybe we could go back now and shoot the pictures again?'

That was probably a request too far. He smiled and shook his head.

Alyssa nudged me under the table with her knee: high non-verbal praise indeed.

'We can offer you a ride to your hotel?' he said.

On the way back we got positively matey. He was from Yunfu, in Guangdong province, which I had visited. I scarcely remembered it, because it's got absolutely nothing of interest except some high modern buildings; but I said something nice about its climate, which is warm and tropical all year round, so honour was satisfied. Then I complimented him on his English, which was reasonably good. It's a great way of ingratiating yourself with someone difficult.

He beamed, and quoted Lewis Carroll at me:

Twinkle, twinkle, little bat!
How I wonder what you're at!

I let loose a few more compliments after that, some of which I actually meant. By the time we reached our hotel, even the other suits were smiling.

'You were fantastic,' Alyssa said as we walked through the door.

'Well, you were the one who did the filming. And deleted everything afterwards.'

We glowed in mutual appreciation.

'Maybe we should check on Martin before we turn in,' she said.

The night receptionist looked at the key rack and said he'd gone up to his room. She thought it must have been a couple of hours earlier.

'I'll give him a ring,' said Alyssa.

He didn't answer the phone.

We retreated across the vast lobby, and I suggested trying his mobile. After all, there can be a hundred reasons why someone doesn't answer their room phone.

There was no answer on the mobile either.

'OK, let's not get too worked up,' Alyssa said, though I could see she was as anxious as I was. 'Let's sit down here for a few minutes, get a drink, and call him again. He could be having a shower. Or maybe he's in a deep sleep.'

I didn't think so, but I agreed. I downed my whisky without even noticing it.

When I tried his number once more, there was still no reply.

55

'I'm not getting any answer from my friend in Room 354,' I told the receptionist. 'Could one of your security people go with us to the room?'

Did she looked worried? I thought so, as she picked up the house phone.

A couple of minutes passed before a sloppy-looking character in an open-necked shirt and baggy trousers came out of a side office, wiping his mouth on his sleeve.

She explained to him and gave him the master key. He didn't seem enthusiastic, and fussed about for a while before following us over to the lift.

Outside Martin's room there was no answer to my knocking or calling. The security man pressed his card key against the pad. It made an electronic sound, and he pushed the door open.

The place was empty of people, but that's all it was empty of. It stank like an explosion in a barber's shop. And there was stuff everywhere: the insides of the mattress, the foam from the pillows, Martin's books split apart and the pages pulled out and thrown everywhere, his clothes ripped up and lying all over the floor. It was the contents of his washbag that made the smell. Whoever had ripped everything out of his suitcase had cut out the lining and flung the bits around the room in a rage.

But there was no sign of Martin. With a feeling of some dread I went over to the bathroom and opened the door. That's where the bodies always are in the movies. Usually in the shower, or lying in the bath.

No body. The shower was pristine and the bath empty.

'Maybe he slipped out,' Alyssa started to say.

But I'd already spotted the mirrored door of the big built-in wardrobe. It was slightly open. As I looked I could see there were a couple of scrape marks on the carpet leading up to it: the kind of marks someone's heels make when they're dragged.

'In there,' I said, in a harsh voice.

Alyssa put her hand over her mouth. I gestured to the security man to open the wardrobe door.

'Check it out.'

His face was a putty colour, and his mouth hung open. He shook his head.

It always seems to come down to me, I thought. I pulled the door open. The result was horrifying.

Martin came half-swinging out, held up by his neck, so I had to hold him up. He seemed absurdly heavy.

His face was slate-grey and bulging; his eyes were open, though they hadn't looked at anything for a good hour. Now they never would.

Alyssa walked quickly into the bathroom and threw up. I knew how she felt, though I've seen many other dead bodies, plenty of them more unsightly than nervous Martin Prinsett. That's what you get for messing around with other people's wives, Marty, I thought.

The security man was still hanging around uselessly, so I called him over to help me. Together we pulled Martin off the rack where his killer or killers had carefully hung him. His body lurched out and ended up lying on the floor.

Even now the security man was useless. I had to hit him on the shoulder to make him call for help on his radio. As for Alyssa, I thought I'd persuade her to go to her room, but now she'd cleaned herself up she decided to take charge. I flopped down in an armchair while Alyssa went downstairs with the security man.

As soon as they were out of the room I realised that this was my chance to go through Martin's stuff – starting with him.

It wasn't very pleasant, but I found it just about bearable as long as I didn't look him in the face. There was nothing whatever in his jacket pockets, which seemed odd, and his phone, the new one, which he kept in his inside right-hand pocket like an old-fashioned wallet, was missing.

Now I had a nastier job: going through his trouser-pockets. I slipped my hands into them, one after the other, feeling his thighs against the backs of my hands. Why does a dead body always feel as though it's already been in the freezer?

Nothing there anyway.

I got up, went over to the bed and looked at the wreckage of his suitcase.

Again, nothing.

Just for the sake of it, I gritted my teeth and decided to check through everything, all over again; with the same result.

I flopped down into the armchair, doing my best to keep my eyes off his face, and waited for the police to arrive. And since there was nothing else to think about, I tried to work out in my own mind what might have happened.

While we'd headed off to the institute, Martin said he was going to see his friend the newspaper editor, on the assumption that it had been this editor who had put the pictures of Lily Lin standing beside the fridge under the door.

But why weren't these pictures on him still? Could the murderer have taken them?

As I sat there I thought it through as best I could. The key seemed to be where the pictures had originally come from.

OK, I thought, if it had been the newspaper editor, he'd have explained to Martin what the pictures meant, and why he'd sent them to him. The answer to that, presumably, was that they linked Lily Lin, and by extension her parents as well, to the trade in animal bones. So whoever killed him, here in this room, must have stolen the pictures, together with his phone, on which there must have been lots of sensitive stuff – not least the odd lover's message to Madame Jade.

Was Martin killed in order to get the pictures or his phone? Lin Lifang seemed to have a good idea what had gone on between them, and I didn't think of him as the volcanic, abandoned lover type, so it didn't seem likely that Martin had been killed out of pure jealousy. If ever there was someone who liked his vengeance cold, it was my old friend Lin.

That left the photos. If they were the reason Martin was killed, someone must have decided it was essential to stop him taking them to Beijing. But did the murderer actually find the photos? Surely the frenzy of destruction in the room was an indication that the murderer had failed?

I tried to imagine the scene: 'Tell me where the picture is, or I'll throttle you.'

But Martin, for some reason, didn't tell him. Maybe he couldn't. Maybe he didn't think the threat was serious. Maybe it didn't start off by being that serious. And – the final maybe – perhaps the killer, having got his hands round Martin's throat, couldn't stop.

All this thinking took six or seven minutes: time spent not looking Martin in the face. Now, though, I found I couldn't keep my eyes off him. He lay on the floor still wearing his black loafers. And for some reason my mind wandered off to a time when I'd escaped from a very nasty group of mercenaries in Angola with my notes tucked into my shoes. Rather smelly they were, when I finally took them out after three days of walking through the bush.

It didn't seem very likely. If they'd gone through Martin's clothes so carefully, they must surely have checked his shoes. But it was worth a look.

I bent over the lower part of the body, shielding what I was doing in case there were cameras in the room. Lifting his legs and easing the shoes off his feet, which were starting to swell, was the nastiest bit of all.

Worth it, though. There was a wad of paper folded up in the front of his right shoe.

I unfolded it. It was the second picture – the one that showed Lily Lin more identifiably. I could see that Martin had written notes on the edges of the picture – notes which he must have made during the conversation with his editor friend, since they hadn't been there when I'd last seen the picture.

At that point I heard voices in the corridor. I jammed the shoes back on his feet – nasty job, that – stuck the folded picture down the front of my shirt, and threw myself back into the armchair.

Three uniforms and a suit came in. I recognised the suit.

'Whatever kept you?' I asked.

'This is terrible, Mr Ser-wiff,' said the man from Yunfu. 'I'm very sorry for your loss.'

That's what everyone says nowadays. Yet something inside me said it didn't come as enough of a shock to him. Or was it simply that nothing comes as much of a shock to a senior policeman whose job is dealing with political crimes?

'I'll say.'

The uniforms were fanning out around the room, doing every-thing I'd done except for checking poor old Martin's footwear. The most senior uniform looked at the chief, then nodded towards me. He shook his head, which was a relief; if they'd searched me, they'd have got what they wanted.

I gave the man from Yunfu a statement, in which I said that Alyssa and I had left Martin to go to the institute. I assumed he'd stayed in the hotel when we left. At the end, a uniformed cop closed his notebook and the chief thanked me politely. I had no idea whether he believed me.

All I wanted to do was examine the notes Martin had scrawled on the photo, but I had to let the latest scene play out first. Other people arrived, some in uniform and some not. Martin's body was taken off to the police mortuary.

And then, at last, the man from Yunfu said his polite goodbyes and apologies, and I was on my own.

I decided not to take out Martin's piece of paper and look at it, in case there were cameras in the room. So I sat there with my head in my hands for a few minutes after the police left. Then I texted Alyssa to say I was coming up to see her.

Nothing more than that, because they were probably reading our messages. How, after all, did the man from Yunfu know he should turn up at the roadhouse to find us? Because Martin had messaged me to go there, that's how.

Alyssa was tearful, and when she greeted me in the doorway of her room with a comradely hug I whispered in her ear, 'Let's get out of the hotel.'

She nodded, grabbed her bag and pulled the door to behind her. We'd found a late-night place nearby, which we both liked: cheerful, noisy, and brightly lit. We headed for it.

Sure enough, as we came through the hotel door a couple of men got out of a car, separated and hung back about twenty yards from us, one directly behind and one on the right.

The greasy spoon was a good choice. Even at close to midnight, it was still buzzing. Tables were hard to get, and that made it even better. Encouraged by a couple of hundred yuan, the waiter found a place for us, tucked in between two big round tables packed with noisy people. He turned the two trackers away. Very gratifying.

Would they pull out their IDs and insist? I caught a glimpse of them in a big gilt-framed mirror: no, they went back out into the street. No one seemed to take any notice of us, apart from directing the odd admiring glance at Alyssa and speculating on what attraction I might hold for her. I could have told them: zero.

56

Neither of us wanted to look at a plate of food but we thought we'd better order something for form's sake. It was only when the food arrived that I took out the piece of paper to show her.

'This is definitely Lin Lifang's daughter – the one I met in Oxford.'

'What do the words on it say?'

Martin's writing was bad. There were some dates, which were readable, and several words, which mostly weren't.

'I can't make it out,' Alyssa said. 'Is that "City"?'

I took a duck pancake, and as I chewed it I realised what the word was.

'Not "City",' I said. 'It must be "Lily".'

'I don't know what you're talking about, with your mouth full.'

I swallowed. Then I took a gulp of tea, to steady myself.

'Lily.'

'Fuck,' said Alyssa, who didn't usually swear. 'What else does it say?'

It was hard to work it out: Martin should have been a doctor. His figures were easier to understand, especially the dates, and even more especially '28 Jan.', though at first I thought it said '2B Jer'. After that came 'CC'. That could mean all sorts of things, but one possibility was 'Central Committee'. The assembly of the

Chinese Communist Party. Beside that, he had scribbled Chinese characters which were way beyond my understanding: 打击.

The next time the waitress came past, I asked her for some more tea, and waited until she came back with a full pot. Then I asked her what the characters meant. She peered at them while I held my hand as artlessly as I could over the face in the photo.

'Ah,' she said offhandedly, and whacked the back of her right hand in the palm of her left.

'Dǎjí,' she said, and wafted off.

I didn't know what that meant, though it clearly had an aggressive feel to it; so I tapped it into the translation app on my phone. 'Strike, hit', my phone told me.

'Lin must be planning some sort of attack on 28 January,' I said, half to myself. 'But does it mean a physical or metaphorical attack? And does it mean here or in Beijing?'

'And could it have been Martin's newspaper friend who told him that Lin was planning to stage something on 28 January?'

'Surely not. The newspaper editor was in trouble with the Lins; he'd never know a thing like that.'

'Newspaper editors know things.'

'Yes, but this must be hugely secret. I mean, if you were going to stage some big challenge to the power of the Communist Party, you wouldn't tell all and sundry about it beforehand, would you?'

'Well, I think—'

'Ring him,' she said.

'But it's after midnight.'

'He'll be there. Putting the paper to bed.'

I wished someone would put me to bed, given that we'd had a 6 a.m. start. But I decided that I'd go round and see him in person.

'You can pack and get some rest,' I said.

The office of the *Daily Banner* was within easy walking distance, and when I got there the editor was in. It wasn't a problem getting to see him.

'Martin Prinsett is dead,' I said, without any preliminaries. The editor sat down abruptly in his swivel chair.

'But I only saw him two days ago,' he said.

My Chinese, never good, was unlikely to take me much further. Fortunately, he spoke my language better.

'He told me he was coming to see you this evening, with some photographs.'

The editor shook his head. 'I've been busy here all evening. No one came to see me.'

'Do you know anything about a strike, an attack, on 28 January?'

He shook his head again.

'But there is something brewing here, isn't there?'

'Brewing?'

'Don't worry.'

I recognised a man scared for himself and his job. I gave him the barest outline of Martin's murder, and he was just picking up the phone to check it with the police as I closed his door and headed back to the hotel.

Outside, the air was chilly. There seemed to be a few people in uniform hanging around. Maybe, I thought, it had something to do with 28 January. I turned a corner, and there was the man from Yunfu and a couple of plain-clothes policemen.

'You're out very late, Mr Ser-wiff.'

I made the obvious retort.

'Ah yes, but I have a job to do. The Party Secretary wants to see you.'

'He can see me in the morning.'

'No, I'm afraid not. You are leaving for the airport at six a.m., I think.'

He made a slight movement of his head, and the heavies came and stood round me. Obediently I got into his car; there didn't seem much alternative.

57

'My dear Jon,' said Lin Lifang. 'A thousand apologies for disturbing your rest.'

I grunted, and he put a whisky into my hand. He poured another one for himself.

'What the fuck is going on here? Martin Prinsett has been murdered in his room, and you kidnap me and bring me here.'

Martin's death clearly wasn't news to him. On the spur of the moment I decided to put such cards as I had on the table.

'Look, Martin knew something. He had photos of your daughter at the Institute of Molecular Biology, and someone told him about the 28th of January.'

I couldn't tell whether I'd been really clever, or unbelievably stupid.

'Those are two big accusations, Jon.'

'I haven't made any accusations yet.'

His clever eyes ranged over my face.

'You know you're safe with me, don't you, Jon? I owe you so much.'

I won't do anything violent to you, was what he meant.

'But I have to make sure you won't betray my secrets to anyone.'

'Look, I'm a journalist, and I'm making a film about you and what's happening here. I'm not a police nark.'

'Nark?'

I explained, and he smiled.

'Well, I'll offer you a devil's pact. I won't tell you any details about what's going on, but I will let you know where to be at the right moment. If you agree to keep quiet about everything.'

I couldn't decide what to say for the moment, so I opened up a second front.

'Look, my friend Martin has been murdered. Did you have him killed? Out of jealousy, maybe?'

He looked mildly alarmed.

'Prinsett committed suicide this evening,' he said.

'Sorry. I examined the body. Someone strangled him. There were thumb-marks on the throat.'

Funny how we instinctively avoid using the possessive when we talk about a dead person – 'the throat' not 'his throat'.

There was a pause. Now it was Lin who was trying to work out how much to say.

'This is all very strange,' I went on. 'Your wife and daughter are heavily involved in the illegal importation of African animals, dead or alive, into China, to be turned into traditional medicine. Which is also illegal. I can only assume that the murder of Martin Prinsett is in some way connected with this, and that you're involved too.'

Lin actually smiled: the last reaction I would have expected.

'You were always hot-headed, my dear Jon, even in Tiananmen Square. Maybe I owe my life, or at least my liberty, to that; so I shall not take offence at what you say.'

There was a moment or two of silence, while he fiddled with his empty whisky glass. Then he got up and poured us another slug.

'My wife was having an affair with Prinsett. I think you should ask her what happened to him.'

'All right. Call her down.'

Lin shook his head. 'Not until you've assured me you'll accept my devil's pact.'

I was starting to wonder if there was any way out of all this that might not end with me lying on a slab in the mortuary.

'If you cooperate with me, I'll make sure you benefit from it. Not necessarily financially, because I know you've got scruples about that. But in terms of your reporting. I can promise to give you "a story". But for my safety, as well as yours, I won't answer any questions about what is going to happen. You must wait for my . . .'

He paused. 'Is the word "tip"?'

I nodded, and polished off my whisky.

'I assume you mean "tip-off".'

'Of course. Of course. Well, you must wait for that. And then, assuming you do, you will have an excellent story: the inside story of a political revolution.'

He said the last seven words as though they were the subtitle of a book.

God knows how I was going to explain this to Alyssa, I thought. Agreeing to a deal like this goes against everything she holds dear, and which I ought to believe in.

Lin tapped three buttons on the phone on his desk; I was reminded of the way he changed the Scottish music on his balcony, all those years before. Then he barked an instruction. A couple of minutes later, Madame Jade came into the room and sat down. Her eyes were red.

'Jon here wants to know if you killed your lover.'

That, at least, is what I assume he barked at her. I made out the word '*ji*'; Chinese has rather a lot of words for 'kill'; but then so does English.

She said nothing, but drew herself up in her chair. A little of her old grandeur came back, in spite of the red eyes.

'Well, if you won't tell us—'

'Yes, I'll tell you. I would never do something like that. I loved him.'

She shut her mouth obstinately.

'Well, you'll have to make up your own mind,' Lin said to me. 'In the meantime, will you accept my conditions?'

'I don't suppose I have any alternative.'

'No – exactly. But I know that I can trust you, and I give you my assurance that you can trust me.'

I said my goodbyes to the two of them, and was ushered out by one of the servants.

As I walked across the grand hall, I still couldn't decide which of them had been responsible for Martin's death. Or how I was going to break the news of the deal I'd made to Alyssa.

58

A few hours later, the policeman and a couple of his sidekicks escorted us to the plane. As we waited in the queue I talked to him.

'You and Comrade Lin Lifang both speak such good English, and you both tend to quote things from English books. Do you know him well?'

'Yes, I have that privilege,' he said, without any apparent irony.

'How?'

'We were postgraduate students together, here at the university. Students of English. There was a British professor who taught us – Dr Jenkinson. He particularly liked Lewis Carroll and Monty Python, and made us learn passages from them. "No one expects the Spanish Inquisition."'

'Yes, yes, very droll, thank you. And do you see him much? Comrade Lin, I mean.'

'Well, I'm the chief of his personal security detail.'

We shook hands, and Alyssa and I boarded the plane.

Once again, no one was waiting to arrest us when we arrived in Beijing. We got a taxi back to our hotel, and were received with the usual greetings.

'We should meet down here in half an hour,' Alyssa said, as we were handed our keys. It didn't sound negotiable.

I switched on my television set, more out of habit than anything else. China Central TV came on, but at that moment the phone rang. It was a friend of mine on the foreign desk at home: a witty, shrewd character called Daniel.

'Thought you'd like to know,' he said. 'Reuter's have just flashed up the death of a top journo in Huzhang. That's where you've been, isn't it?'

'Yes,' I said, but my voice was just a croak.

'Someone called Xu Weide.'

He didn't pronounce it very well, but I knew who he meant.

'Apparently he was the editor of the *Daily Banner*. Anyway, coming directly after the death of your chum Prinsett, I thought I'd better let you know.'

I was still thanking him when I saw the characters for 'Huzhang' flash up on the television set, beside the smooth-faced CCTV announcer. I turned the sound up.

'It is with sadness that the authorities in Huzhang report the death of a leading journalist there. Xu Weide was the editor of the *Daily Banner* newspaper. The police report that he was involved in an accident near his office.'

I'll bet he was, I thought, as I switched off: an accident involving a cut throat or a bullet in the brain. Xu Weide was the one whose words Martin had jotted down on the photocopy of Lin's daughter, which I still had in the inside pocket of my jacket.

When I went downstairs, Alyssa was already sitting there. She'd heard about the death of Xu.

'Scary, eh?'

I nodded.

'That's two people who knew about all this. It only leaves us,' she said.

'Well, yes – but whoever did the killings must surely be getting their orders from Lin and/or his wife, and it was Lin's own security chief who put us on the plane.'

Alyssa looked at me pityingly.

'Suppose they only wanted to get us out of Huzhang because they thought the killing of foreigners there would attract far too much attention? Suppose they're planning to kill us here in Beijing?'

This hadn't actually occurred to me.

'I'll give Gary a call and let him know we're back.'

Gary Sung, my cameraman friend, was our secret weapon: as far as our various enemies were concerned, he was not obviously associated with us. He'd finished his filming assignment in Beijing, and was only waiting for us to come back before heading home to Singapore.

'Fancy a wander?' I said when he appeared.

We shook hands formally. Odd, for people who'd done and shared so much together, but Gary is almost as old-fashioned as I am. Just younger, that's all.

It was a long walk. I'd broached the whole subject to him before, but things had moved on since then and I wanted him to know everything. He knew all about what had happened to Martin – it had been big news for a couple of days – but he hadn't yet heard about the murder of Xu Weide. He shook his head when I told him.

'I still think you're getting into this a bit too deep, Jon.'

'Yes, well, you know how it is – when the spoon's in your hand, you've got to keep stirring.'

He didn't reply, but he shook his head.

After a few seconds, he patted me on the shoulder and said, 'Just tell me what I can do.'

It felt good to hear him say that.

'There's quite a lot, though not at the moment. For now, the most important thing is that you know everything about it, and you've got copies of the various things that are connected to the story in some way – the photos of Lin's daughter at the lab, for instance.'

As we walked, I gave him Raj's name and mobile number.

'This man is SIS, you know – British intelligence. Don't be put off by that. He's actually helpful and sympathetic. It's clear to me from what he's said that SIS knows more or less everything that's going on with Lin Lifang. Martin Prinsett was definitely working for them, and maybe Madame Jade too.

'So if Lin really is thinking about carrying out a political coup, they might even give him their backing. My impression is that Raj can be trusted. But I could be wrong. Nowadays I don't know who anybody is working for. I mean, *you* could be SIS. Or State Security, for that matter.'

Gary Sung is as straight dealing as it gets, and he's not always certain when I'm joking. It took him a moment or two before he laughed.

'You can be a real bastard at times, Jon.'

By this time we were heading back to the hotel, and as we went I coached him through the details of my story, to make sure he knew exactly what had happened.

'And what about that producer of yours – Alyssa?'

'She's all right.'

He looked at me shrewdly.

'That all?'

'Well, she's got quite a temper, but she's clever.'

'And attractive.'

'I suppose – but it'd be like dating an unexploded mortar round.'

Gary laughed again. He got the reference: outside Jalalabad in eastern Afghanistan, some years ago, the Taliban fired a mortar round at us but it failed to go off.

We walked along in silence for a while. Then Gary said, 'Look, Jon, I don't think it's safe for you to hang around the hotel. Everyone knows you're staying there. Suppose the guys who came for your friend Martin and the newspaper man want to get you and Alyssa? It'd be the easiest thing in the world. There's no proper security there.'

I knew he was right. I'd have to find somewhere else for us to stay.

'You will keep in touch with me?' Gary asked.

'You're now the only person I *can* keep in touch with. Do you mind staying on in Beijing for a few more days?'

'Sure. Just don't get into any more trouble.'

I gripped his arm.

'Listen – will you take care of the photo for me? It'd probably be better to send it to London, but you'll know what to do with it.'

I slipped it into his hand in much the same way I slipped two hundred yuan to Mr Chang, the hotel door-keeper.

We said our goodbyes some way from the hotel, because I didn't like people to see that we were working together. He wandered off to the shops, and I went back to see Alyssa.

59

As ever, Mr Chang was at the hotel door.

'Mr Zhon,' he said, with a surprising amount of diffidence. 'I thought I should tell you: two men are asking about you.'

'Do you think they're a problem?'

He looked me in the eye for a moment or two.

'For you, yes.'

All those hundred-yuan notes hadn't gone to waste, I thought.

'I'll go and get my colleague – you know, the lady – and then we'll leave by another exit. Is there one?'

His eyes swivelled to his left, but he didn't move his head.

'Down there is a door to the street.'

'Thank you, Mr Chang. You're a good friend.'

'Knowing you long time, Mr Zhon.'

He ushered me through into the lobby, and I turned and looked back. Two men in black coats were standing outside. There was just time to fish out another couple of notes and put them in his hand.

Fortunately, Alyssa was sitting in the lobby, waiting.

'Hi,' I said shortly. 'We're going to go out through the side door. Sharpish.'

We headed across the lobby, trying not to give the impression that anything was amiss.

*   *   *

There was a shout behind us. I'm not sure if it came from the heavies or from someone they'd collided with. Looking back, I could see a commotion on the pavement behind us. They were catching up with us.

My mind was racing trying to think of somewhere we could go.

Terry Ho, I thought – the dissident who'd come with us to Xinjiang, together with his Uighur girlfriend. I guessed Alyssa wouldn't be enthusiastic, but Terry would find us a place to hang out. We needed to get to the mall to buy a cheap phone. Then I could ring him.

We were getting close to a tailor's shop I knew. In my palmier days I used to get my suits made there; they were reasonably good, and not too expensive. Madame Gao, who ran the place, kept a big blown-up photo on her wall of the Prince of Wales, which gave the impression that he dropped in from time to time to get some clothes knocked up. Madame Gao was fragrant, in her late forties, and rather other-worldly, except in the matter of invoices.

'Mr Ser-wiff! Wonderful to see you!'

She was less effusive towards Alyssa. This was a men's tailors shop, after all.

There wasn't anyone else in the front of the shop, though I could hear the overworked Mr Gao hard at it in the back room.

'We've got a problem. There are two very unpleasant men chasing us. As you know I'm a journalist, and so is Alyssa here, and we've done something to annoy them.'

Madame Gao looked out and spotted the pair as they hovered outside.

'Can we use your door at the back?'

The situation appealed to her romantic instincts. She started measuring my arms and shoulders, and pulled out a book of cloth

269

samples to show Alyssa. Then she made signs for us to go into the workroom where Mr Gao was.

She didn't explain anything to him, but pushed us past him to a rear exit. Before I had a chance to thank her, we were in an alley that ran parallel to the main avenue.

'The Silk Road shopping mall is just a hundred yards or so from here,' I told Alyssa. It was a big, raucous and rather enjoyable building on umpteen floors. We could easily get a phone and a SIM card there, and since it had untold numbers of entrances and exits we'd be really unlucky if the two thugs found us there.

The alley we were in was used more or less as a dump, and there were cardboard boxes, heaps of rubbish and at least one pool of blood leaking from a dead animal or bird. We navigated our way through it, and found ourselves out in the road that ran along the side of the Silk Road shopping mall.

Excellent – but the lights were against us, so it was impossible to cross; and while we hovered there our two pursuers came running up to the pedestrian crossing fifty yards away and spotted us.

But they made a strategic error. Instead of crossing the road against the lights, which is something plenty of people do in Beijing, they came running down our side of the avenue towards us. And we simply dodged out into the traffic. By and large, Chinese drivers are patient towards foreigners, even jaywalking ones, so although there was a bit of hooting we managed to get through the six lanes of traffic safely.

The heavies were less lucky. Drivers shouted and blasted them with their horns, and one large red Toyota seemed to drive directly at them. Stupidly, that meant they got into a shouting match with the driver. By the time it was over, we'd dodged into one of the side doors of the Silk Road and found the nearest escalator. I bent down as though to tie up my shoelace and Alyssa did too. It was the first time since the hotel lobby that we'd had a chance to say anything very much.

'Who the hell are they?'

I thought it over as we reached the top of the escalator and launched ourselves into the shoving, laughing crowd of shoppers. I like the Silk Road shopping mall: it swarms with buyers and sellers, and though some of them are Westerners, most are Chinese; so a lot of good-natured pushing and shoving goes on. Women and girls do most of the selling, which adds to the enjoyment.

'Here, darling, you love this!'

'Come over here and take a look at my fabulous fabrics!'

'You'll never find tea like this anywhere else in China! Why not try a cup?'

'Hey, handsome, want your feet rubbed?'

'You look tired – have some broth. Best in Beijing!'

And so on. Alyssa, used to the street markets of Lagos and Brixton, entered into the spirit of it too, and for a while I think we both forgot we were being hunted. There was certainly no sign of the two heavies in the crowd behind us.

We reached the far end of the huge building, and had to turn a corner. A girl of no more than fourteen was swinging a big yellow imitation leather suitcase backwards and forwards, to show us how little it weighed. In normal times I'd have perhaps tried to get the suitcase for a tenner.

But these weren't normal times. I spotted a bullet-head and a dark suit in the distance. Even though the head wasn't pointing in my direction, it was clear we had to do something fast.

Down this end of the building, on just about every floor, the masseuses did their stuff in little curtained-off sections, wrestling with the necks, shoulders and bodies of their clients. Do more dodgy things go on there? Quite possibly; but I've never experienced anything more erotic in these massage rooms than a foot-rub. After all, there's no privacy – just a flimsy curtain between the beds.

'How about it?' I asked Alyssa, and she nodded.

'Two massages,' I said in Chinese.

The women seemed to understand. We were led to the back of the section, where the beds were. They pulled the curtains round us, and we took off our clothes.

I lay on the bed with my face pointing downwards in a towel-covered hole so I could breathe, and I'd just pulled a covering over myself when a giggling woman came in and asked how hard I wanted the massage.

'Not too hard,' I said. I know how strong even the skinniest and feeblest-looking Chinese masseuse can be.

Then there was an outburst of male shouting and female squealing from the front of the section. I couldn't understand a word of it.

'Cover us both up,' I whispered to the woman who was working on me, and thank God she understood.

She pulled the towels right up over my head, and told the masseuse with Alyssa to do the same. I lay absolutely still, trying not to breathe, and listened to the crunching of rubber-soled footsteps coming closer, and curtains being ripped aside.

And then it was Alyssa's curtains and mine being jerked. Through the open slot I could see a pair of basic black shoes by the head of the bed. In spite of the situation, I noticed that they showed signs of greater wear on the inner side than the outer. Being a cop is hard on the feet.

Both masseuses put up an angry fuss, and the curtains were whisked together again. The rubber soles retreated into the distance.

Probably best to let the massage take its course, I thought, and Alyssa must have thought the same. God knows, I needed a bit of relaxation after all that; imagine the ignominy of being arrested in your underpants. It was a good fifteen minutes before I asked Alyssa, in the quietest voice I could manage, how it was going.

'For Christ's sake shut up,' she hissed, and the sound made both masseuses giggle.

'What, are you at the good bit?'

To do her credit, she giggled herself.

'No, I just think we should keep quiet.'

When I stood up, I couldn't decide whether it was fear or relaxation that made my legs wobble; maybe it was a combination of the two. I dished out a couple of good tips to the women, and thanked them in my old-fashioned Putonghua.

They giggled again – it seemed to be their main form of communication – and they said '*Xie xie*' together, in chorus. 'Thanks'. Very charming.

60

The police seemed to have gone, so we headed to a little teahouse at the far end of the shopping mall. We drank little cups of monkey-picked oolong and ate little biscuits tasting of mint and aniseed. For some reason that might have had something to do with the massage, I felt too embarrassed to say much. But after a bit Alyssa let out a laugh.

Her voice was ever soft, gentle, and low, an excellent thing in women.

'What's the matter? You've gone all quiet.'

'I was just thinking of the two us lying there,' I said.

'Did you see his boots?'

'Yes I bloody did. Much too close.'

'I could smell him,' she said with a grimace.

'Perhaps it was me.'

'No, you've got a different smell. Just as bad.'

And she laughed again.

There's a poem by poor, awkward old Thomas Hardy about being stuck in a hansom cab in a rainstorm with a girl in a new 'terracotta' dress. He finds her really attractive; but by the time he's worked himself up to the point where he's actually going to do something about it, the rain stops and she hops out. And he says sadly,

I should have kissed her if the rain
Had lasted a minute more.

That's how I felt now, as Alyssa stood up. Maybe she'd spotted the signs.

'Come on, you've got to ring your friend Terry and get him to find us a place to spend the night. Make sure he gets us separate rooms,' she said firmly.

I bought a cheap phone from one stall in the market, and a SIM card from another. I probably didn't need to be so careful, but you never know; and when I got through to Terry, I restricted myself to the absolute minimum.

'*Ni hao ma?*', which just means 'How are you?'

There was a pause.

'Fine.'

I could hear from his tone that he recognised my voice.

'Can we meet up? Where we did last time?'

'OK. Forty minutes?'

'See you there.'

When I'd seen him last, it had been in the street, on the far side of the Gate of Heavenly Peace, where a painting of old Mao's vast moon-face stares out across Tiananmen Square. It was a short bus ride for us: less conspicuous than a cab.

Terry, as ever, was sharp and to the point.

'You look as though someone's following you.'

He didn't, I notice, make a move to kiss Alyssa, and she didn't seem to invite it.

'Well, they have been.'

We sat down on a wall. I remembered taking shelter here during the Tiananmen massacre, but I didn't think it would interest either of them.

'We need somewhere to stay for a bit. As you say, someone's after us, but it's not clear who.'

I explained what had been happening, and Terry thought about it for a while.

'You're right – it doesn't sound like Lin's people. It could be State Security, I suppose. Did they have lapel badges?'

'All I saw was a pair of shoes. Otherwise they were too far away to tell.'

'That'd be my guess.'

'So can you get us somewhere to stay?' Alyssa said.

'Oh sure. Though you may not like it much.'

'If it's safe, we'll like it.'

I had another call I needed to make, so I wandered away and dialled Raj's number at the British embassy.

'Hi,' he said when I spoke to him.

Again, no names. And I used the procedure I'd used with Terry.

'Same place?'

'I can't leave the office for a couple of hours, but I'll see you there at four, if that's OK.'

It seemed to me that Alyssa and I would be safer if we kept on the move, so when I rejoined them I suggested we go and check out the place Terry had in mind for us.

It was a longish trip by bus. My knowledge of Beijing geography outside the central area is limited, so I wasn't even sure which direction we went in. When we got there, it was utterly characterless: not the kind of area you'd want to wake up in.

Neither was the flat. It was on the fifth floor of a shoddily built block, no lift, facing out over an ugly stretch of common ground covered in rubbish. Terry went in first, and started yelling at the people who were in there.

'Get out, you dirty fuckers! Who said you could come and

squat here? I never said you could. Come on, take your junk and get out!'

They shambled around, picking up their stuff obediently. Now I could see that there were actually four of them, sad-looking characters with the pallor and listlessness of opium addicts; when I thought about it, I could detect the smell of the smoke over and above the stench of dirty clothes and decaying food.

'Where will they go?'

'I don't care. This is a place for people who are in trouble with the police to hide in, and these idiots are just taking advantage of it. They'll have to find somewhere to go and do their shit. Go on!' he shouted, 'get out of here before I turn nasty!'

I was the only wet liberal round here, I could see. Alyssa was hissing in disapproval at the dirt and smell.

'You go off and see your friend,' she said, meaning Raj. She didn't turn to look at me. 'I've got my hands full sorting this place out.'

She looked at Terry. 'You'll have to help me. I'll need cleaning stuff and some decent bedding.'

Terry nodded obediently. He even seemed a bit apologetic. As for me, I slithered out. I'm reasonably good at looking after myself and my cat, but I'm not exactly Mr Kleen. Besides, opium addicts often have problems holding their water in, and the smell was getting to me.

61

In little more than half an hour I was back at the teahouse in Ritan Park, watching a solitary pair of ducks cruise up and down the lake, and trying to work out from the occasional sudden splashes how many fish there were in the dark green depths.

'Hands up,' said a voice behind me, in rather good Chinese.

'Oh fuck off, Raj.'

'How did you know it was me?'

'Because only spooks suss out the rendezvous five minutes beforehand, then slither off and come back dead on time. It's the way they train you.'

He grinned. 'Whoever said I was a spook? I'll sue them.'

I went and ordered the inevitable pot of tea, and the aged man behind the bar undertook to bring it out.

'All right, I've got a bit of an idea what's happening to you.'

And he proceeded to run through an account of it all. Up until that morning, anyway.

'I assume Martin Prinsett was working for SIS?' I ventured.

'You can assume all you like, but the fact remains that he's dead now, so he isn't working for anyone. Not even himself.'

'Why?'

'*Cherchez la femme?*'

'Believe me, I do my best. But don't you think my mate Lin was responsible for killing him?'

'Who knows? The Lins are a weird couple. Let's put it this way: if I was a swinger, I wouldn't accept an invitation from them.'

I told him how the older policeman, Lin's enforcer, had ushered us onto the plane.

'Sounds like classic State Security.'

'Yes, but surely this guy's loyalties are with the Lins now?'

'In this kind of business, you can never tell.'

'So when Alyssa and I get followed by a couple of heavyweights today, here in Beijing, who would they be working for?'

'Not the Lins, I wouldn't have thought.'

He coughed, and that reminded me.

'Take a look at this.'

I turned on my phone and showed him the shots I'd taken of the picture of Lily in the institute. He looked at it from a couple of different angles.

'This is Martin's handwriting on this one.'

'So he *was* working for you.'

'Well, he used to give us a head's-up on the Lins and what they were doing, that's all.'

'And what do you think the picture shows?'

'I'd say it's a scientist holding a tray of some kind of medicine.'

'And if I told you that the scientist is the Lins' daughter Lily, who's now in Oxford studying molecular biology?'

For the first time, I'd succeeded in telling him something he hadn't expected.

'Something else. When my colleague and I went poking round at the Institute of Molecular Biology in Huzhang, we filmed the bodies of African wild animals being cut up into small pieces.'

'Listen, Jon,' he said with a new urgency. 'Something serious is going on. Everyone we're in contact with is getting really nervous. I think you know what I'm talking about. Not the juju stuff with lion and tiger bones – that's just a major fiddle, which has earned the Lin family a lot of money. What I'm talking about is a political coup that will change the entire future of China.'

It was tempting to say I knew all this, but although that might make me feel good, it would probably mean I wouldn't get anything else out of him. He'd shut up immediately.

'I saw Lin yesterday. He didn't seem to me to be like Mussolini about to march on Rome.'

'In this society, you don't need to march anywhere. You just have to force a vote at the Party Congress, and if you win it you've got your revolution.'

'Has Lin got that kind of influence?'

'I've no idea, frankly. But I do know that the leadership group are going bananas about it. Haven't you noticed the extra police everywhere?'

Embarrassingly, I hadn't.

'How do you know they're going bananas?'

'We have our methods.'

I bet you have, I thought. But I decided, on the spur of the moment, to put a more important question to him. I still can't decide whether I was right to do it.

'When I saw Lin in Oxford, he got me to send a message to your lot. I had to play some stuff down a phone line. Well, I assume it was your lot. Was it about all this?'

I had to admire Raj's ability to control his reactions.

'You know I can't comment on anything like that.'

'OK, well then, you can't expect me to comment about anything either,' I said. 'Or consult you about the way I'm going to report this.' I looked at my watch. 'Hmm. Good timing for tonight's news.'

He must have known I was bluffing, but the mechanics of television news are probably just as labyrinthine as the mechanics of espionage, so maybe he couldn't be sure.

He raised a hand, as if to stop me doing anything impulsive.

'I'm only asking you to put one or two cards on the table,' I said. 'I shan't ask you why Lin wanted to contact you, or what he wanted you to do to help him. That's your business. But did he give you an outline of his plans?'

'Maybe.'

I went quiet for a bit. Lin must have been in touch with SIS for a long time. Not bad, having someone so senior feeding them information. Well, to my certain knowledge, they had someone close to Putin in Russia over the years, not to mention three of Saddam Hussein's ministers, so why shouldn't they have someone on the payroll who was high up in the Chinese leadership, and who picked up lots of nice Savile Row suits and a box at the opera every time he came to town?

Lin didn't need money: as a government minister, and then the Party boss in a city like Huzhang, he had that in industrial quantities – especially given his involvement in the traditional medicine business. What he wanted was status: the respect and affection of high-up Brits. And Martin Prinsett had been his main go-between with SIS. Until Martin began sleeping with Madame Jade.

Sitting there, watching the big greedy fish launch themselves out of the dark water at the afternoon parade of insects, I started to see a little sense in it all.

'So do you think he'll do the business? Stage some kind of coup?'

Raj's eyes glistened. Christ, I thought, you're that close to having the new President of China on your payroll, open to every blackmail call the British government chose to make. Sensational. And I know about it.

The trouble is, everyone's going to be against me: not just Lin, not just the Party leadership and the Ministry of State Security, but SIS and the British embassy too. As they used to say in 1940s Hollywood *noir* films, I knew too much. I could just disappear, and no one would know or care what had happened to me. And whatever compensation might come as a result, my two ex-wives would get it. Plus an obnoxious Bentley salesman.

That's what made me decide what to say next.

'Listen, Raj. As soon as I get back to my safe house' – I thought I'd use the kind of language he'd understand – 'I'm going to start recording the details of my experiences with Lin, and send it for safekeeping to someone in London who'll look after it carefully, and decide what to do with it. You have my word of honour that I won't go out of my way to stir things up for your outfit, or the British government. And as long as they play right by me, that's a firm undertaking. But I will tell the truth. After all, with so much trouble flying around, I feel I need to get something in the bank, just in case.'

'I'm sorry, but my boss isn't going to like this.'

I hadn't had much sleep recently and I lost my rag.

'Well, tell him that if he does anything to damage me the stuff will hit the fan so hard they'll be cleaning it up all over Vauxhall Cross for years.'

I sat back, and tried to calm down.

'I dunno, Jon – maybe you're doing the right thing, from your point of view. I might even do something like this myself, if it was me. But I'll have to tell my boss that I advised you not to.'

'Listen,' I said, and I felt a sudden wave of affection for this clever blend of south London and southern India, 'you've got to do what you think is right for you. But if you help me, I'll make sure you'll never regret it.'

He reached out and gripped my hand. I'd always assumed that people who worked for the secret service had their personal emotions surgically removed; but it looked as though some had been left in Raj, by mistake.

I didn't have the foggiest idea what I should do now.

I shook hands with Raj and said goodbye. I thought I'd better work on the principle that he might have back-up, and that someone would follow me. So I spent a bit of time wandering in the wrong direction, then when I got bored with that I sat down on a park bench, took a long look round for a few minutes, and headed off to the bus stop. Nobody seemed to be taking any interest in me. Still, although being a journalist trains you for a lot of things, it doesn't necessarily help you to act like a spook. Anyway I knew perfectly well that nowadays there were lots of ways to keep an eye on someone that didn't include having somebody following twenty paces behind them.

I spotted a 156 bus and hopped on it. The other passengers looked at me casually, but no one called the police or did a citizen's arrest on me.

I pressed the buzzer when I we got close to ground zero, thanked the driver (a mistake, but it's something we do in Oxford – half a world away) and jumped off. No one got off with me.

God, it was dreary here. In central Beijing the architecture was bad but at least everything reeked of wealth. Here, the architecture was bad and everything reeked of poverty: the poverty of ideas as well as the pocket. Don't let anyone kid you Chinese communism has created a higher form of civilisation. I'd rather have Las Vegas any day, and that's just about the most depressing place I can think of in the entire Western world; except possibly for Benidorm.

I banged on the door for quite a while before Alyssa opened it.

'Well, look who's here, now the hard work's all finished.'

When I went in and looked round, I could see she'd done a pretty impressive job. With Terry's help, no doubt. I could see just by looking at him that he'd had a rough time. Or, to borrow my grandfather's expression when speaking of his ferocious second wife – that she'd passed him under the harrow.

The place no longer stank of dream-stick smokers and their urine. It was bright and clean, and there were a couple of inviting-looking camp beds and folding chairs. Someone had cleaned the windows, too.

'God, you've done a fantastic job.'

And I meant it. That brought a little softening in the expression.

'Yes, well, I've been at it for four hours now, and a lot of it wasn't very nice. So while you were poncing about meeting contacts, I was cleaning out the toilet for the first time in months.'

I said nothing for a few beats of time, to show this had sunk in. Then: 'Anything I can do?'

That sparked off quite a long response, which I won't trouble you with. A lot of it seemed to turn on my upbringing and the fact that I'd been to a private school. She was unfair, though; I was forced to do some nasty tasks at my alma mater in County Wicklow. And then there'd been the time in Mozambique when my cameraman and I had been forced to clean the latrines of the crowded prison we were being held in. Using just a couple of old cloths.

Still, much safer not to point this out; and anyway Alyssa was slowly coming down from the ceiling and starting to take pride in what she'd done.

'No pictures on the walls, though,' I said when I thought the moment was right.

She started smiling after that.

Terry looked on awkwardly. He still hadn't been forgiven.

'I'll come by in the morning and see how things are going. And don't worry – no one knows about this place, so you'll be safe here.'

Alyssa had even bought us a bottle of Qingdao wine, purple-red and viscous; China's lesser-known wineries still have a long way to go. Still, it can get you drunk, and I think we both needed that.

We didn't have any of our stuff, of course, but Alyssa had sent Terry out to buy us toothbrushes, soap and combs.

The camp beds were in different rooms. Alyssa said I could choose which one I wanted. By now the wine had started to work its spell, so I said, 'The one you're going to sleep in?'

'Oh, give it a rest, you old sod.'

But there are many different ways of saying something like that, and this way seemed moderately jovial. And anyway at my age, after a day like I'd had, I was actually rather relieved.

62

My room faced east, and since there were no curtains I got the sun early on. The Qingdao wine still affected my head and throat, but I felt a lot more chipper. I pottered round a bit, and dug out my notebook to jot down a structure for what I was going to say. I'd just settled down in the folding chair Alyssa had bought when she came in.

I explained that I was recording an account of our dealings with the Lins, in case something happened to us. That shocked her a little, but after thinking about it for a moment, she said, 'Why don't we do it like an interview? I could ask you questions about the whole thing, and if there are points that are not clear I can get you to go over them again.'

It took us the best part of an hour to get it done. Alyssa made a good forensic interviewer.

'What now?'

The edge was off her voice, now that we'd achieved what we'd set out to do.

'Send it to Sarah.'

'What, Sarah McIntosh? Why her?'

I detected a professional rivalry. Sarah and I had worked for several years on the road, and I'd always found her sensible and level-headed. Emailing the recording to her took a bit of time, because the WiFi signal in this area was feeble. The separate message of explanation, warning her not to tell anyone about this unless something happened to us, went much faster.

Once it had gone, I could sit back in the folding chair and relax.

And at that very moment, the door was flung open.

There was a lot of shouting, and two men in black windcheaters and black jeans burst into the room. They were armed with night sticks, and they were both screaming at the tops of their voices. I suppose they teach them that at riot school.

Alyssa stayed calm, and I tried to give the impression that I was too. The shouting died away.

'Who are you, and where did you get the authority to behave like this?'

That was what I tried to say, though my vocabulary and tones probably let me down. Even so, it had the effect that speaking Chinese often does in China: it was such a surprise, they went quiet.

But then there was a second wave, which appeared in the doorway now. Two more men, also in black windcheaters, were pulling a third man with them. Blood was running freely down his face, and some of his hair had been pulled out in bunches, leaving his scalp horribly bloody. His legs didn't seem to be working.

His eyes raised to meet mine, but I'd recognised him already.

'I'm very sorry,' Terry Ho muttered, through teeth that seemed to be broken. Those bad teeth of his.

He'd always been so bold, so keen to take on the police and the rest of the state system; and they'd broken him, like they'd broken his teeth.

'I couldn't—' he started to say, but one of the policemen hit him over his battered head with a night stick.

287

I was frozen with shock, but Alyssa was magnificent. She sprang over and grabbed the night stick, and brandished it in his face.

'Don't touch him again or I'll fucking kill you!' she screamed, and the two men who'd brought Terry into the room reared back like frightened animals. It was wonderful to see.

Terry dropped in a heap on the floor, and Alyssa knelt over him, whispering little sympathetic words and stroking his damaged head. It seemed to crack the last of Terry's self-control, and he started weeping silently, shaking his head from side to side.

At long last, I did something. I walked over to the biggest and possibly most senior of the cops and grabbed him by the windcheater.

'Listen, arsehole' (I used the word *hundan*, which is more anatomical than sweary, but I couldn't think of anything worse on the spur of the moment), 'I'm ordering you to get out of this place at once. And leave this poor man here. Go on, get out.'

For a moment I thought it was going to work. He certainly wavered, but then I suppose he thought about what his bosses would say if he abandoned the place. He wasn't aggressive, which I suppose was a small victory. In fact he was almost placatory. But he still stayed where he was.

'You must come with me.'

God, they'd sent an English-speaker to arrest us.

I was worried that if I gave in too easily, Alyssa would think I was being feeble. But when I glanced at her, she looked up from where she was caring for Terry and gave a little nod.

'We'll only come on one condition,' I said. 'That you call an ambulance right now and have this man taken to hospital. We'll wait here until they take him. Then we'll go with you.'

He nodded, and made a quick call to the emergency services, giving the address of this ill-omened place. I joined Alyssa on the floor beside Terry, and ignored the oafs standing around in their identical clothes.

Terry started to mutter that he was sorry again, so I hushed him.

'They'll patch you up in hospital, and maybe we can get you sent home,' I told him.

He nodded and lay back quietly.

The ambulance took nearly half an hour, during which time scarcely a single word was spoken by any of the seven of us. My guess was that the senior policeman didn't want to check with his base, in case he got the order to bring Terry back. He knew that if he obeyed, Alyssa and I would be difficult again.

The ambulance team brought in a stretcher for Terry, and loaded him onto it quite gently. I touched the back of his hand – even that had suffered – and told him once again that he had no reason to feel bad.

He tried to answer, but the ambulance crew were impatient to get going. The head policeman signed to one of the others to go with Terry to the hospital, and they left.

I felt we still had the moral high ground, or at least a bit of it, so I turned away and rang Gary Sung, the cameraman. I rattled out a quick message: 'Alyssa and I have been arrested by some policemen wearing strange uniforms,' I said, turning so the head policeman could hear me, 'and they brought with them that local freelance journalist friend of mine called Terry Ho – you remember. He's in a very bad way and has obviously been beaten up. He's now on his way to hospital, and we've agreed to go with the policemen.'

I turned to the head policeman. 'Where are you taking us?'

He turned his head away, and it looked as though whatever rope I'd had had reached its limit. I spoke to Gary again.

'He won't say where we're going, but please tell Raj at the British embassy, and let the Western media in Beijing know what's happened.'

'Got all that, Jon. I'm really sorry. I'll make sure you get out, though. And the best of luck.'

His calm, steady voice made me feel a great deal better.

'That was a colleague of mine,' I said grandly. 'He's ringing the British embassy right now, and after that he'll tell the international press.' And then I used my favourite line, 'You'll soon be the most famous policeman in China.'

I could see that it worried him; which, naturally, I enjoyed. I started on a long riff about what had happened to policemen in other countries who'd arrested me. I made most of it up. It worked, all the same. He began making calming noises, as though we were badly behaved dogs, and waved his men out of the door while he escorted us to the waiting car himself: no cuffs, no hands on elbows, and no pushing our heads down as we got into the car. When they do that, it means they've watched too many rubbish television shows about the New York police.

63

I couldn't identify the large, ugly building where we ended up. It presumably belonged to some arm of the government, though it didn't have any obvious sign outside: just the state's equivalent of a coat of arms, scarlet with a rising sun. There was a reception desk, which we didn't go near, and a security check, which we went round. Our policeman's black wind-cheater and his badge got him in, and he waved us in with him. Refusing to look either of us in the eye or to speak to us, he pressed the button for the fourteenth floor, and we whizzed up soundlessly. I kept my mind blank: we were going to have to play this by ear.

We walked into an outer office with lots of uniformed women sitting in front of desktops, then into an inner office with three younger uniformed women sitting at slightly newer desktops. None of them looked up. Our policeman went over to the door at the far end, and knocked on it. There was a noise from inside, and he turned the handle with reverent care and put his head round the door. Then he straightened up and signed for us to walk in.

There were books on the wall in English as well as Chinese, and all the frippery you get in senior Chinese people's offices: a discreet portrait of the Party leader looking unconvincingly jovial, a variety of framed certificates, a couple of old class photos in which everyone looks as though a broomstick had been shoved up their arse, and a couple of ornaments in crystal glass. Behind all this sat a small woman in her fifties, wearing a neat dark-blue Mao jacket and a pair of rimless glasses. She reminded me of Rosa Klebb, with Chinese characteristics.

'Watch out for her shoes,' I muttered to Alyssa.

Gratifyingly, this produced a grin.

'Mr Ser-wiff, Miss Roberts. Please sit down. Tea?' Her English was good.

I decided I wasn't going to be matey-matey, just because she was offering me a thimbleful of warm water.

'I rather expected you'd start off by beating us up, like our poor friend Terry Ho.'

She waved her hand dismissively, as though someone had introduced a nasty smell into the room.

'That man refused to cooperate.'

'What, like we're going to do?'

'I hope not. I very much hope not.'

Well, at least you're not screaming at us, I thought. And just in case she hadn't heard the news, I told her that I'd asked a colleague of mine to ring the British embassy and pass the word round that we'd been abducted.

She didn't look bothered, unlike the policeman now sitting meekly in the corner of the room, staring at the carpet. In fact she didn't look anything very detectable. She reached for a box of tissues and dabbed her nose.

'You see, we need your help.'

'Don't ask me,' I said. 'My solution to everything nowadays is to take aspirin.'

She smiled, a bit painfully. 'I was told you make jokes.'

The anger suddenly welled up inside me.

'I'm not making jokes about my friend Terry Ho being tortured.'

'We had to find out where you were. He was obstructive.'

Alyssa broke in. 'My colleague and I can't agree to talk any more unless you undertake to see that Terry Ho gets proper hospital treatment for the injuries he's suffered, and is allowed to go home a free man when he's recovered.'

'Yes.'

'What do you mean, yes?' Alyssa said. 'Yes, you agree?'

'Yes, I agree.'

It was a bit deflating.

'In that case,' Alyssa went on, thinking fast, 'make a phone call now to ensure that it happens.'

The woman in the Mao jacket picked up the phone and barked into it. From the words I could understand, she was doing what Alyssa had demanded.

'I have given the necessary instructions. Now, can we talk about the reason I wanted you to come here?'

Alyssa nodded.

'We believe that Comrade Lin Lifang, who you know well, is coming to Beijing to stage a political coup d'état. And we think you know his plans.'

'Oh, come on,' I said, 'this all sounds far too James Bond.'

'Well, you were the one who thought I was like Rosa Klebb. Oh yes – please don't think that because I'm Chinese I don't understand your cultural references. Perhaps you imagine I'm a barbarian. I spent five years in London in the 1990s. That taught me quite a lot, I can promise you.'

I grinned. Alyssa looked annoyed; then she started to smile too.

I couldn't work out what Rosa Klebb's expression was, because she was looking down at her hands, folded on the desk in front of her. When she looked up again, though, I thought there was a twinkle in her eye. Or maybe that's just what I wanted her to have.

'What did you do in London?'

'I was attached to the School of Oriental and African Studies, SOAS, but I also did courses at New Scotland Yard and other places.'

Probably, I imagined, including MI5 and MI6. In the 1990s the Brits still dreamed of forming a strategic partnership with China. Those were the days.

I looked with greater interest now at the framed certificates on the walls. Most of them were from China, but there were three or four that could have been from Britain: they had that best-of-breed look.

'Well, it doesn't seem to have done your career any harm.'

'No. I am the most senior female official in the Chinese security service.'

I went quiet. I thought about how big China's security service must be, if it has to cope with 1.4 billion people? And how good you've got to be as a woman to work your way up to the very top of it, in one of the world's most sexist societies?

'But we need your help,' she added.

'Look, we're journalists. It's not our job to get involved in politics. We just stand on the sidelines and report what's happening.'

'Well, I'm sorry to say that if you don't cooperate with us, I won't be able to stand in the way of the various people who want to charge you with a number of criminal activities since you have been in China. At New Scotland Yard, I remember, the expression they used was "throwing the book at you". It's quite a heavy book, Mr Ser-wiff. I imagine you and the charming Miss Roberts would have to serve quite a few years in prison.'

Beside me, Alyssa stirred. She gave me a grin.

'So what is it you're asking us to do?'

I was glad she was the one who asked the question.

'Mr Lin seems to trust you. Get in touch with him – he's still in Huzhang, but we have reason to think he's coming to Beijing in the next day or so – and keep close to him. Find out what his plans are, and tell us. And then, perhaps, we won't find it necessary to charge you.'

'I don't think you'd dare to go through with putting the two of us on trial. It'd create a stink all round the world.'

'Yes, quite probably, Mr Ser-wiff; and you may well be correct. But we could certainly throw you out ignominiously – is that the correct word? – and you'd never be allowed back into China. I imagine that even in your profession, being thrown out of a country as important as this would be a disadvantage to you. And just think of all the nasty things the *Global Times* would say about you.'

She actually smiled.

The *Global Times* is an unpleasant rag, tabloid in attitude if not in actual shape, and it says precisely what the Chinese leadership wants it to say. It doesn't hold back when it's annoyed about something. 'Traitor', liar', 'wretch', 'criminal', 'spy' are the nicer terms it uses for people it doesn't like.

I felt sure that if I started to be identified as a spy, my bosses in London would be only too happy to dump me. I looked at Alyssa again.

'Not much option,' she said.

'All right,' I muttered.

But I guessed she felt like I did: that there must be some way of wriggling out of this, without destroying what principles we had left.

Our meeting with Rosa Klebb (her name was actually Wu Xiangli) lasted another half-hour. She spent part of it trying to persuade us that Lin Lifang was a genuinely bad character. She even promised that if the coup failed, the central government would wind up the Lins' trade in animal body parts. The rest of the time was spent telling us how to work with the go-betweens she'd give us. They would, she said, speak English at least as well as she did.

We stood up at the end, and Madame Wu shook hands with both of us, quite long and with seeming warmth. Perhaps MI5 taught her to do that.

Yet all this was dreadful, I reflected. I'd given my word to Lin Lifang that I wouldn't betray him – even though I accepted that he was a bad character.

Alyssa and I were quiet as we walked out of the office, accompanied by our tame policeman, and headed over to the unmarked car which, Madame Wu had decreed, was to be our means of getting around for the next few days. The driver spoke English, so we said nothing of any significance until we got back to the hotel. It felt like coming home.

I guessed it might be hard to make direct contact with Lin. But there was always his security sidekick, the man from Yunfu. I still had his card. A call to him might just do the trick – though we would need to work out what to say beforehand. It would be our best and probably last shot.

The big thing in our favour was Lin's tremendous self-belief. If he really was going to stage a coup, it could only be because he thought he'd succeed; and he'd have his dedicated foreign correspondent to cover what he was doing. We'd have to play each side off against the other, I thought. That's all that stands between us and a major shit-shower.

64

'Hello, Mr Ser-wiff,' said Mr Chang the doorman. 'I hope there were no problems?'

Inside, there was the comforting face of Gary Sung. He put his arms round me and hugged me. Then he did the same to Alyssa, and she let him.

'I could do with a decent dinner,' I said.

They both nodded. I imagine Alyssa felt like I did: depressed, manipulated and lacking in confidence about what to do.

And then a thought occurred to me.

'Maybe there's a way out of this,' I said as we reached our floor.

'I very much doubt it.'

'No, let me explain over dinner. Christ, I'm hungry.'

'Me too.'

I mustn't drink too much tonight, I thought, as I walked towards my room. After all, you never know what's just around the corner.

Gary took us to a restaurant where a Chinese bloke, a black woman and a white man wouldn't attract attention. He knows his Beijing.

'So what's your idea?' Alyssa said.

The dishes were coming thick and fast; as always, I'd over-ordered.

Nobody was sitting near us, and everyone else in the restaurant, staff and customers, was yelling at each other and putting down the food and drink at a rate that made earwigging an impossibility. It was one of those classy joints that people have opened in converted courtyard houses in *hutongs*, and it was done up with loads of Mao posters and porcelain figures of Red Guards from the Cultural Revolution, plus the kind of heavy, dark furniture wealthy Beijingers used to go in for during the 1930s.

'To be absolutely open with Lin. Tell him what happened, and what we're doing.'

'But that's crazy. And that woman will know immediately.'

'No, you see, I don't think so. We'll have to be extremely careful. But if we play Lin off against the government, and vice versa, we might just come out of this OK.'

'I think you're just worried about stabbing your old friend in the back.'

'All right, there's an element of that. But if we level with Lin we can just let them fight it out between them, and report on whoever wins.'

'You may be more of a slimy bastard than I realised.'

'But a nice slimy bastard?'

'All slimy bastards are slimy. And bastards.'

Gary had been sitting quietly, listening to all this.

'I don't think we've got any alternative,' he said now.

The quieter you are, I've noticed, the more force your judgement has when you declare it. And of course his use of 'we' was reassuring.

Alyssa looked at him seriously.

'I suppose you're right.' She looked at me. 'How are you going to present it to the Lins?'

'My granddad – the dubious one who was a spy in the First World War, not the decent one who died at Passchendaele – he always used to say that whatever lie you told, it should be as close to the truth as you can possibly make it.'

'And in this case—?'

'I'll just explain that we were arrested, taken to Rosa Klebb's lair, and told to make contact with Lin so that we'd be able to tell Rosa what he was doing.'

She thought about it. 'And why would you do a thing like that?'

'For old times' sake.'

'So you're a sentimental slimy bastard.'

Gary didn't seem entirely comfortable with all this banter, but I didn't mind.

The food was really good, and so for a change was the Chinese wine. Stick to the whites and forget the reds, is my advice.

I finished with a large Chinese brandy, which bore no great likeness to real brandy but was full of fire and alcohol and flavour of a kind.

We headed back to the hotel on foot. I'd drunk a bit more than I'd meant to, but not too much. A pair of young lovers wandered along the avenue behind us and always managed to keep pace with us, in spite of the effort they were putting into kissing.

We said goodnight to Gary, whose room was in a different part of the hotel, and went up in the lift together.

'I think that couple wanted us to see them out there,' I said, not caring about microphones or cameras. 'They must be Madame Wu's people. She's tweaking our lead.'

65

Back in the room, I dug out the man from Yunfu's card and thought about what I should say to him. It was complicated. Madame Wu's lot would be listening in, so I'd have to give him a coded message while convincing her that I was doing what she wanted me to do.

In the end, I stopped trying to work everything out. Another thing my granddad used to say was, 'Keep it natural. That's what I always did with the Boche.'

'Hello. This is your friend here – the one you took to the airport. My people back in London think what you're doing is very interesting, and want me to report on it. Could you ask the boss if he'd be prepared to see me when he gets here?'

There was a silence, while he digested that. 'I'll be in contact.'

'I'm staying at—'

'I know where you're staying. I'll call you in the morning.'

In fact, though, he didn't call: he texted the single word 'yes'.

As I'd hoped, Lin's desire for the limelight and his amazing confidence in himself had conquered any fears he might have about being tricked. Maybe, too, he still had some residual affection for me, just as I had for him.

I suppose I'm a chancer and a bullshitter, but if you grow up with all that Anglo-Irish gentility stuff, some of it's bound to stick to you permanently. And even if it doesn't govern the way you live your life, it'll leave you with a residue you can't ever quite get rid of. Fundamentally it's just another form of guilt-trip, the equivalent I suppose of being Catholic. Or an accountant.

After breakfast, Alyssa went upstairs to sort herself out, while I stayed down in the bar with Gary and ordered a pot of tea. Something would happen, I felt. It was unnerving not knowing what was coming or how it would come. And I'd just started convincing myself that it was probably a bit too soon to expect some sort of contact, when Mr Chang the doorman loomed up beside me with something in his hand.

'Someone gave me this for you, Mr Ser-wiff.'

'You're a good man, Mr Chang,' I said.

It was an envelope, of the old-fashioned airmail kind, with red and blue markings round the edges. Someone's been hoarding this for a long time, I thought. There was a single half-sheet of thin paper inside, with a single printed line on it. If they'd thought that would be a protection, they were wrong. It's easier to identify a printer nowadays than to identify handwriting.

Black Toyota wait outside. Go aboard. Be alone.

The English was of the 'I-speak-your-weight' variety. That's what Google Translate does for you. I asked Gary to stay behind and tell Alyssa I was going out to meet someone. It took me a moment or two to persuade him he didn't need to come with me.

Behind the wheel of the black Toyota sat someone who looked like a character out of *The Lord of the Rings*. Not one of the nicer ones. He was squat and had no discernible neck and very big hands which gripped the steering wheel even though we weren't going anywhere yet.

There was a lot of stuff on the back seat, so I got in the front.

'*Ni hao,*' I said, more out of habit than anything else.

He moved his head round as though it was on a clockwork mechanism and looked at me with entirely dead eyes. Then his head went back. That made me feel more like Sam Gamgee than ever.

Until he spoke.

'Good morning, Mr Ser-wiff.'

It looked as though he'd come in peace. That was a relief.

He apologised politely, before reaching over to put a loose-fitting black bandana over my eyes. It smelled fusty, and I panicked for an instant. Then I relaxed. I might not be able to see, but I could hear perfectly well.

He steered his way through the traffic as though he was more used to riding a motorbike. I could feel the movement, and hear the horns blowing. Now I was more worried about being in a crash than I was about what was going to happen when we got there.

I really must work out the geography of this city, I thought for the hundredth time. Even so, the violent movement of the Toyota had shaken my bandana and I could see just a little over the top of it. We'd left the traffic by this time, and were clearly going up at a slight incline. From what I could see, we were in one of those grand areas in the surrounding hills, where the wealthy people of Beijing tell themselves the air won't give them lung problems. Or cancer.

The houses got bigger and bigger and further and further apart, and the gardens were starting to be spectacular. The orc seemed to choose one at random, and roared up the slope to the porte-cochère. Directly we stopped, I pulled off the bandana. No one tried to put it on me again.

An attentive character was already standing there. In China you can usually distinguish the heavies from the functionaries, even though they all tend to wear dark suits. This was a functionary.

'Welcome,' he said as he opened the car door.

My legs still felt a bit shaky, but I followed him into the house. Every room I could see into was full of people on phones or screens. There was a constant bustle, and secretaries scurried around with files in their hands or under their arms.

Something was up.

Lin Lifang was sitting at a desk, with papers heaped up on it and a small thermos to one side. Television screens flashed and flickered: Chinese Central TV, CNN, the BBC, and a couple of Hong Kong channels. He seemed to keep an eye on them all, while greeting me effusively.

'Welcome, welcome, my dear Jon. I trust I find you well?'

'As well as anyone can be, after being transported too fast through a Beijing traffic jam.'

'Perhaps I shouldn't have told him to hurry. People can be so literal.'

As ever, I felt vaguely got at: Lin's stock in trade.

'Now, what I need to know first is whether you're planning to betray me.'

He smiled as though he was talking about the weather.

This was where all my soul-searching stood me in good stead. I was Macbeth, he was King Duncan, and he was asking me if I was going to knife him. So I started to explain what had happened since I'd seen him last: how Madame Wu had threatened me, how I felt I had to go along with what she wanted, and how all I really wanted was to report honestly on the outcome.

It was all true, and I could tell by his pleasant smile that it wasn't going down too badly.

'So you want to play the referee, while people like Madame Wu and myself get muddy and exhausted in the game?'

'Not the referee, no. I want to be the sports reporter, in the commentary box.'

'But that doesn't now seem possible. You're working for Madame Wu.'

'Well, not really. Listen, Lifang, I've put all my cards, such as they are, on the table. Both here and with Madame Wu. I'm not hiding anything, especially from you. I'll tell her what's happening, because I've got to. But the only way I'll be able to find out what's going on is if you tell me.'

What I was saying was that he could use me as a conduit for any misinformation he chose to give me. Both he and Madame Wu would know what I was doing.

'What's going on here is high politics,' Lin said. 'I'm in contact with virtually every member of the Central Committee, asking them if they would be prepared to vote for a motion of no confidence.'

'And make you General Secretary in Xi Jinping's place.'

'Oh well, my dear fellow, I haven't really thought that part of it through.' He smiled in that funny lopsided way of his. 'And, anyway, that's up to them, not me.'

I didn't smile back, because I didn't want to seem smarmy. If I was going to be neutral, I was going to take my position seriously.

'What have you got to lose, from letting me stay here? If you come out on top, our material will be part of your legend for ever.'

'I may not come out on top.'

'In that case my producer and I will probably be shot as spies.'

'No, I really don't think that will happen. But I imagine you'll be persona non grata in China, assuming you survive the – what's that French word? – the dénouement.'

'So you think there might be a shoot-out?'

'Who knows, my dear Jon. They are capable of doing anything if their power is challenged.'

'And what might you be capable of?'

It was a risky thing to say, but I wanted to show him I was nothing more than an onlooker.

'You'll have to wait and see.'

At that moment a young man in a suit came in and began whispering to him.

'Well, that's really excellent,' Lin said in English, rubbing his hands together.

No doubt whose benefit that was for.

I'd noticed a couple of cars arriving, one after the other. Now a little line of people, mostly men, started coming through the door to greet Lin and shake his hand.

'I wonder if you'd mind . . .' he said to me.

You can always tell members of the Central Committee when they come to town for a big gathering. For a start, they all wear the same clothes. Entire outfitters' stores open up to them, dishing out dark suits, black shoes, white shirts and red ties, all for free. They just have to provide their own pants and socks.

Out in the hallway there were more of them, all waiting to shake the great man's hand and offer him their vote. Maybe he's starting to get somewhere, I thought.

After a while, when a couple of minibuses had taken the delegates away, and no new ones had arrived, I got Lin's tough-looking secretary to allow me another audience.

'All right – do you want me to tell Madame Wu what I've seen here?'

He grinned mischievously.

'I wouldn't dream of instructing a famous international journalist what to report. You must do what you see fit. Oh, by the way, we're expecting four more busloads of delegates in the next couple of hours. You can wait and check, if you like.'

'But I'm free to go if I want? Your goons won't stop me?'

'My dear fellow!'

They didn't. In fact, one of them drove me back to the centre of town and dropped me at the hotel. Alyssa seemed relieved to see me, and asked me loads of questions about Lin's place and the people round him.

'It sounds as though you think he's starting to get somewhere.'

'Well, I only spoke to a tiny number of delegates, I suppose – fewer than twenty altogether. But yes, he seems pretty confident.'

'Or so he wants you to think. Are you going to tell all this to Rosa Klebb?'

I was gratified that she chose to use one of the nicknames I'd thought up. Usually she kept a certain distance from my ideas.

'I've got that phone number she gave me somewhere. I'll just give it a quick call.'

'And say what?'

'Well, just what I saw. That'll keep her off our backs, and it'll be what Lin wants too. Bingo. I don't think I've ever been able to keep two opposite sides happy with my reporting before.'

'No, I'm sure you haven't,' Alyssa said.

I went upstairs and made the call. It felt weird, not having to worry what the various listeners-in thought of what I was saying. A dull Chinese voice suddenly got sharp and interested at the other end of the line. Male, young-sounding.

'You'll make sure to tell Madame Wu all this?'

'Oh yes, sir.'

'You know what,' Alyssa said when I joined her downstairs, 'you ought to tell your mate at the embassy. Raj.'

'I suppose so.'

I couldn't quite work out why I was reluctant. Maybe I thought that dealing with three lots of agents would be a bit too much. And then there was the problem of how to contact him. Every phone call I made would be listened to, and that might put Raj in a difficult position.

'I didn't just sit here knitting while you were gone. I've been out and bought four different phones and four SIM cards, just in case.'

She beamed. I beamed.

I thought I'd meet Raj at the Silk Road shopping mall: it had served us well before, with its seething crowds and its variety of entrances and exits. The problem was telling him over the phone where to meet. I didn't want to be followed around by a gang of earwiggers equipped with directional microphones. Alyssa and I thought about it for a bit.

'You told me you used to do the crossword in *The Times*. Whenever I've looked at it, which isn't very often, they always seem to find cryptic ways of saying things that are pretty simple.'

She was right, though of course I had no idea whether Raj did *The Times'* crossword. But since he was approximately five times cleverer than me, it might have attracted him. T. S. Eliot used to finish *The Times'* crossword on his twenty-five-minute ride to Piccadilly on the number 19 bus in the mornings; me, it was a red-letter day if I finished it at all – and even then it took me until night-time.

But I could surely think up some description which he would work out, and anyone listening would find baffling. I thought about it for a bit. Silkworms ate mulberry leaves. Shakespeare had a famous mulberry tree in his garden at New Place, Stratford. I tried it out on Alyssa, but she thought it was much too public school. Raj probably would too; but it was worth a try. I dialled his number.

'You're going to think this is pretty crazy, but can you remember what kind of tree the Swan of Avon had in his garden?'

'Yes, he had—'

'OK, good. Well, you know the street of the stuff produced by the things that feed on that tree?'

'Yes, I can guess what you mean. What time?'

'An hour later than the last time we met. As you go in from my direction.'

'For fuck's sake, Jon.'

'Do you do *The Times*' crossword, by the way?'

'We used to have a boss who said it was the easiest way to keep your mind sharp.'

'Maybe that's where I've been going wrong,' I said, and rang off.

Alyssa was giving me a familiar look.

'That was the stupidest phone call I've heard in a long time.'

'I didn't want anyone listening in to know where we were going to meet.'

'You've got to hope that no one in State Security does *The Times* crossword. Or knows anything about Shakespeare.'

'Well,' said Gary, 'I'm a lot more used to the Brits than they are, and I've never heard of any of this.'

66

A young girl who should have been in school screamed at us from a fabrics stall, so I chose a silk scarf with that beautiful watered pattern you find in Central Asia, and wrapped it round my neck. It seemed a lucky thing to do, and Alyssa liked it. Raj stood and watched.

It had taken us forever to get there. All three of us had left the hotel, but separately and at different times, and Alyssa and I had played a variety of games, splitting up and meeting again. Gary had hung back and kept watch for followers. Sometimes there'd be several of them, but after much ducking and diving he texted us to say that we seemed to be clean.

'So tell me what's going on,' I said, after a slender waitress in a tight-fitting *qipao* had poured us each a cup of keemun.

'Well, you seem to be playing both sides against the middle,' Raj said.

'And you know this how?' Alyssa asked.

'Partly what Jon's told me. Partly from my own sources.'

'So what do you think?'

'I think you could be in serious trouble. Both of you. No matter who wins this battle.'

Some people sat down at a table near us, so he moved his stool closer to mine and turned his back to them.

'And don't come running to me if it happens. HMG can't be seen to support anyone here at a time like this, and you being on the wrong side means we'll just wash our hands of you. Sorry,' he added.

'Well, actually, I don't feel too comfortable having my embassy stepping in to help, if I get into trouble.'

It happened to me during the Angolan civil war, and I was nearly shot as a spy as a result. I swore I'd never ask a British embassy for help again.

There was a silence. Alyssa sipped her tea. The man at the next table reached down and shifted his briefcase. The edge of it had been pointing at Raj, but now it was pointed straight at me.

'Raj, those bastards are recording us.'

'Ignore them.'

'No.'

I stood up angrily and went over to the other table.

'*Ni hao.* Can I help you?'

'Jon!' Raj called, but I took no notice.

'If you want to hear us talk, come and sit at our table.'

The smartly dressed woman stood up as if she was going to leave, but the man stayed sitting. Oh fuck, I thought, have I made a dreadful mistake?

'I'm only doing what I was told to do,' he said.

'Well, bugger off and go and spy on someone else.'

I felt thoroughly vindicated. The man got up, and the two of them left.

I grinned. 'That got rid of them.'

Alyssa didn't seem impressed, and Raj was frowning.

'For Christ's sake, Jon, it's just part of the job. It happens to me every day. That's why I'm careful what I say. You think you've scored an important point, but you haven't: you've just got some poor idiot into trouble with his boss. Look, you're a lot older and more experienced in many ways than I am, but maybe not with this sort of thing. This is how we play the game. So forgive me if I say, just accept it.'

That put me in my place. Alyssa looked away, as though it wasn't her concern, but under the table, she nudged my foot with hers. That made the whole humiliation almost worthwhile. Until a day or so before, Alyssa would have been right up there with the leaders of the lynch mob.

As for Raj, he obviously felt guilty about the way he'd reacted. He began to be more open. Of course, it was easier now the spooks had gone.

'How did they know we'd be meeting here?'

Asking that was another mistake on my part.

'Oh, they'll have followed me from the embassy after listening in to your phone call.'

All that stuff about Shakespeare's mulberry tree, and our hour and a half of dodging around now seemed stupid.

Perhaps because I felt foolish, I went onto the attack. 'It's obvious that Lin has been in contact with you. That's why he sent you that message through me, back in Oxford. I suspect that he was telling you that he was planning to launch an attempt to overthrow Xi Jinping.'

I paused to let Raj say something in reply. He fiddled with his cup instead, and didn't raise his eyes from the table.

I went on: 'Well, that's my conclusion, and at some point I'll report it: that Lin Lifang is a British agent.'

Raj stayed remarkably calm.

'You must report what you want – there's nothing I can do to stop you. All I'd say is that you'll be doing everyone a lot of damage if you do. And that includes yourself.'

'So what'll you do – get someone to kill me?'

'That's not our style. No, I was going to appeal to your sense of patriotism.'

'I don't need lectures on patriotism from you, thank you very much. I lost four members of my family in the two world wars.'

It sounded pompous and mean, and I honestly hadn't meant to suggest that I was somehow more of a Brit than he was. And anyway Raj had actually been born in the UK, which was more than I had.

He coughed politely, then said, 'You know, all sorts of relatives of mine volunteered to fight in 1914 and in 1939, and my grand-father got a medal from the king for storming a trench full of Japs in Burma on his own. No one's giving anyone lectures. I just want you to consider whether you're serving the national interest if you say publicly that Lin is working for us.'

I found him quite intimidating now. Not at all the kind of person you'd want to be despised by – though perhaps it was too late for that.

Alyssa sat there, enduring all this. God knows how much lower I must have sunk in her estimation. She cut in:

'Jon and I won't report anything about that side of things for the moment. We'll wait and see what happens. But at some point we'll ask you for a proper briefing. And we'll expect you to tell us as much of the truth as you're able to.'

Raj took another sip of tea.

'Let's see what happens.'

I had the feeling he'd taken what she'd said on board.

But he obviously thought we'd stay quiet for the time being. And he was right. If the coup succeeded, Lin would have Alyssa and me killed if he thought we were going to report something like this; he was more than capable of it, and he might do it

313

anyway, just to be on the safe side. And if Xi beat off Lin's challenge, and we reported that Lin had been working for the British, the Chinese would use it in their propaganda forever more. They'd probably accuse me of being a British agent. And given all the trouble I was in back home, I'd get the boot in the most public and humiliating way possible; they'd have to do that, for the sake of their own reputation.

Altogether, I didn't feel all that great about myself as we threaded our way out of the Silk Road shopping mall and said our good-byes. Until, that is, Alyssa put her arm through mine and pulled me close.

'That was a bit rough back there,' she said, grinning. 'Never mind. You may be a pompous old prat, but there are moments when I'm almost fond of you.'

67

All the same, there was something wrong. Not just with me, but with the others too. When we got back to the hotel, at around six o'clock, Gary was sprawled in an armchair in the lobby, looking pale. There was sweat on his forehead.

After he'd gone upstairs I realised that my stomach was feeling unsettled; and before I could tell her, Alyssa said she wasn't well.

'How bad are you feeling?'

'Not that great,' she answered.

'You know what I think?' I said.

She shook her head, with a touch of her old asperity.

'They've got a full-time nurse here. Let me call her and she can give you the once-over.'

She agreed, not very graciously.

The nurse looked harassed, but agreed to see Alyssa at once.

I stood in the outer office while the temperature business was done. The nurse produced a long white plastic thing and pointed it at Alyssa's forehead. Then she pulled the trigger. It was like watching an execution out of some gangster series.

'*Bié dān xīn!*' said the nurse – 'Don't worry!' – and we all grinned.

'She should spend time in bed,' the nurse went on in Chinese. 'She has a slight fever, but I think it may be food poisoning. Drink lots, don't eat much, sleep as much as possible.'

There always seems to be some bug going around in Beijing.

I translated all this for Alyssa. She was quite nervous. It's funny how people who are strong in other ways can be scared of illness. I suppose it invades you in a way that the prospect of physical danger doesn't. I was philosophical. My attitude is, if I catch something, I catch it; and if it kills me, only Yorick will mind.

The next thirty-six hours weren't great. Gary recovered quite quickly, and I didn't seem to be badly affected. But Alyssa was really sick, and drifted in and out of consciousness. I couldn't get anyone else to nurse her, so I had to do it myself. That meant taking her to the loo, cleaning her up when she was sick or had diarrhoea, and sleeping on the floor at the end of her bed. She wasn't a good patient, and I was a rotten nurse, so we often yelled at each other.

She was embarrassed by everything that went on, which I fully understood, and she hated the fact that I was there to witness it. I didn't exactly enjoy cleaning the toilet and the bathroom floor after her, but what was the alternative?

Eventually, she stopped needing my help and started to improve, so I was able to tidy up, change my clothes and slip out of the hotel. I hopped in a cab and went to see Lin Lifang at his head-quarters in the outer suburbs. After that, with Lin's knowledge, I headed back to the centre of town to see Madame Wu – and told her what was happening at Lin's place.

It was a weird threesome, like having two girlfriends who each knew I was seeing the other. Madame Wu was clever enough to encourage it, and Lin went along with it; so they must have both felt they were getting something out of the relationship.

'I'm beginning to think you're using me as a go-between in case Lin Lifang wins,' I said to Madame Wu.

From the way she laughed, I think I'd hit the nail on the head. She probably meant to sound scornful, but it didn't come out that way. And she took a quick look at the far corner of the ceiling, which I assumed was where someone had planted a microphone. In the dear old People's Republic, the watchers are watched as carefully as the people they're watching. After all, if you're in power you've got to be especially certain about the loyalty of the people who are shoring you up.

Lin, meanwhile, appeared even smoother and more confident when I went to see him.

'We now have the support of three hundred and ninety delegates. Maybe you saw one or two of them as you came in?'

Well, I'd seen a bunch of guys with dark suits, red ties and low foreheads in the hallway.

'How about telling me where they come from?'

'Is that something you want to know, or is it at Madame Wu's urging?'

'God, Lifang, if you fail and they shoot you, the world's going to lose a great English-speaker.'

He loved that, of course.

'Firstly, I'm not going to lose. And secondly, shooting politicians went out with Chairman Mao. If something goes wrong, I shall spend the rest of my life in a well-equipped house in Zhongnanhai, like Zhao Ziyang did.'

Zhongnanhai is the vast leadership compound near the Forbidden City, and Zhao Ziyang was the Party general secretary who sided with the students in Tiananmen Square in 1989 and was purged. He died in Zhongnanhai years later, after writing his memoirs. They were excruciatingly boring, and managed to say almost nothing about what had really happened.

*   *   *

By this stage poor Alyssa was sitting up in a chair beside her bed, looking weak and uncharacteristically gentle.

Finally, I managed to get hold of a doctor: one who specialised in looking after people in the foreign embassies, and made a lot of money as a result.

'I don't think it's a virus,' he said. 'It was probably something you ate.'

'Do you really think we might all have eaten something that made us ill?'

He nodded judiciously.

'Yes, fairly sure.'

It was a bit of a mystery.

'If she gets worse, call this number and I'll make sure she's admitted to my clinic at once.'

But she didn't get worse.

'I think I could manage some soup,' she said.

I chose one from the room service menu that had lots of vegetables and egg-white, together with chicken.

'And tea?'

'Oh, for Christ's sake, Jon – what do you think?'

So I ordered a beer for her, and a bottle of hot saki for me.

She lay back, looking weak. But also beautiful.

'Stop staring at me in that pervy way, Swift. Mr Ser-wiff, that is. I know what you're thinking. You're just an animal.'

'The word is "zoonotic".'

'Yes, well, if you're thinking of jumping the species barrier, find someone else to do it with.'

Not bad for someone in her condition.

'Well, given that I've wiped your arse and cleaned up your sick, that's fine by me.'

'You horrible, disgusting bastard.'

Still, she laughed. At that moment the room service waiter appeared with the food, and started laying it out.

I helped her sit up in bed with lots of pillow-punching, and put a tray on her lap.

'You're looking weak,' I said out loud. 'If I promise not to say anything else rude, will you let me feed you?'

'No, no – go away. I don't need you.'

But she did.

I plied the soup spoon with care. I had fallen for a woman twenty years younger, and a great deal sharper and more intuitive.

'Look, just because I've been ill and you helped me, don't imagine that gives you any rights over me. We're just workmates, that's all. Got it?'

I ladled a bit more chicken and egg-white into her and nodded humbly. I didn't mean it, though.

68

The next morning Alyssa seemed a lot better. Her temperature was almost normal.

'All I want to do is sleep.' Then she brightened up a bit. 'I'm sorry I'm not being any help to you. And I am grateful, you know.'

This time I didn't make any wisecracks.

Gary was also in bed when I banged on his door, but that was a matter of choice. He'd bought a box of pirated videos of old Liverpool matches, and was going through them one by one.

'I suppose you ought to go home.'

He looked at me.

'I want to see that you're all right.'

'Well, if something happens, you'll be able to film it. Then you'll get Cameraman of the Year.'

'It's all I think about,' he said mockingly, and watched Liverpool score another goal.

I'd arranged to go round to Lin's headquarters. He couldn't see me immediately, so I kicked my heels in a side room and read an ancient copy of the *Economist*. It seemed that Donald Trump's chances of becoming President were improving, and *The Economist* wasn't sure this was a good thing.

*   *   *

'My dear Jon. I am so sorry to have kept you waiting. How is your colleague?'

I told him.

'And your spying activities?'

I told him that too.

'And how's the coup d'état coming along?' I said.

He laughed, and repeated it a couple of times, grinning.

'The coup d'état. Very amusing. Well, the answer is, we are making great strides – great strides. In three weeks' time I think we'll be getting somewhere.'

He burbled on in his confident, amusing way, while I sat and thought it over. Three weeks: he must be saying that for Madame Wu's benefit. She'll believe he's told me this in order to pass it on to her, and think he'll actually make his move sooner than that. It could make her take action against him prematurely. These fucking politicians. I was having real trouble keeping up with it all.

'You seem preoccupied.'

'Sorry – not been getting much sleep lately. Can I ask you something?'

He made an assenting face. There didn't seem to be any trace of the person I knew thirty years ago. Now he was well filled-out and, yes, handsome. Wealth and authority had done wonders for him.

'It seemed a bit odd that my two colleagues and I should have become ill at the same time. It's true that we ate dinner together at a restaurant, but we remembered afterwards that we'd had different things, and didn't share dishes.'

I paused.

'I mean, I know I've spent too much time reporting on Russian poisonings. But it does seem a bit strange.'

'If you're asking whether I've had you poisoned, I can assure you I didn't. If it was anyone, it was probably your close friend Madame Wu.'

Some oppositional instinct came over me.

'Why was Martin Prinsett murdered?'

Lin seemed to swell up, and his face suffused with blood. I thought he was going to slam his hand down on the bell in front of him. But he calmed himself, and smiled unconvincingly.

'I keep forgetting you're a journalist. Of course you must be faced with such suggestions all the time. But I've always assumed you would have sufficient sense to discriminate between the ones that are true and the ones manufactured by State Security.'

'And you're saying the one about Martin Prinsett isn't true.'

'Got it in one. Did I say that right?'

This time his smile was genuine. But I took the risk of pushing the idea a little further.

'The expression's right, but what about the story? Martin knew all about your traditional medicine scam. He gave me the photos of your daughter Lily at the institute. And he was matey enough with your wife to know that you were planning this whole political shebang.'

'Really, Jon, I always enjoy hearing you talk: it's like a master class in English slang. But I assure you I had no more to do with Prinsett's death than I had with you and your friends being ill.'

Macbeth again, I thought: 'Faith, here's an equivocator, that could swear in both the scales against either scale . . .'

Lin put out his hand.

'By the way, do you have that photograph?'

'Sure. I've got plenty more.'

'Ah. Of course.'

Our leave-taking was awkward. In spite of everything, I still liked him, and from time to time I thought it was mutual. But he had a government to overthrow, and someone from his past like me couldn't be allowed to get in the way.

'By the way,' he said as I was walking out, 'you might like to see how far our political campaign is progressing.'

He pressed a button on his console and rattled off something I couldn't catch.

'My colleague Danny will show you.'

He turned away, and I closed the door behind me. Danny came into the anteroom, smiling and holding out his hand. He was young, smartly dressed and an obvious Hong Konger. We went over to his desk.

'Mr Lin said I should show you everything. These are the lists of members of the Central Committee who have agreed to support him. You'll see I have categorised them according to their enthusiasm: red for the ones we can rely on completely, pink for the moderately reliable, light blue for the ones we think we can sway, and dark blue and black for the ones we think will stay loyal to the regime.'

Since everything was in Chinese characters I only had Danny's word for it. For all I knew it could be Lin Lifang's Christmas present list. But assuming I was being told the truth, there must have been around a hundred reds and maybe twice as many pinks. And although there were more blacks and dark blues, the gap between them wasn't great. And if you threw in the light blues, the ones they thought were persuadable, then it was probably just about fifty–fifty.

That'll give Madame Wu something to think about, I thought; which is presumably what Lin and Danny wanted.

'Can I have a printout of this?' Well, you never know, do you, and trying my luck has been a habit all my life.

Danny smiled politely and muttered something about not being authorised.

'I could always take a shot of it with my phone.'

But even polite, well-dressed Danny with his Hong Kong manners wasn't having any of that. He waved to the thick-necked driver who'd brought me, and said his goodbyes.

It didn't seem right to ask to be driven straight to the Ministry of State Security, so we went back to the hotel and I picked up a cab from there. The taxi driver was nervous about going to the ministry, so I had to promise him a big tip.

As ever, I waited a long time before the great lady was ready to see me. That gave me a chance to go over everything in my mind. Why wasn't she taking action against Lin Lifang right away, even though he was starting to be a real threat to the regime she supported? Four possibilities, I thought.

One, she needed to gather more evidence against him. Two, she didn't actually rate him as a threat, and wanted to wait until he'd flushed out all his potential supporters; at which time she could move in and arrest the lot. Three, she did think he was a serious threat, but didn't feel strong enough yet to pick him up. Four, she thought he was so serious that she needed to lay off him now and go over to his side when the moment came.

'Forgive me, Mr Ser-wiff. This is a very busy time.'

She smiled; something I'd only seen her do once before.

I told her pretty much everything, especially about the computerised lists which Danny had let me see. She listened carefully, and made a note about it.

Then I showed her the photo. It rocked her back a bit.

'And this is definitely Mr Lin's daughter?'

'He said he thought it could be.'

'And you know it was taken in Huzhang?'

'Well, if it's his daughter, then yes. But anyway there's a notice on the wall that has a Huzhang Institute of Molecular Biology heading.'

'Can I keep this?'

''Fraid not. It's the only one I've got,' I lied.

'You could let me copy it?'

I shook my head and put it away. It felt good to be in the driving seat for once.

'So level with me, Madame Wu. What are you planning to do about Lin?'

'We are consulting. He told you three weeks?'

'He did.'

'So we have a little more time.'

'But you will take action against him?'

'As I say, we're consulting.'

Hmm. That didn't sound terribly assertive. I began to wonder whether possibility number four might, after all, be the right one.

'If you take action against him, will you let me be there to film it?'

She laughed: a bit creakily, because I don't suppose it was something she did very often.

'You are very persistent, Mr Ser-wiff. I suppose that is why you are good at your job.'

'Yes, well, thanks. Will you?'

Then she surprised me.

'I will certainly consider it. It is a possibility.'

I found a cab and went back to see Alyssa. Gary was with her, and she was up and about, which was an improvement, looking fragile but even more beautiful.

And while I was giving the two of them the details about what had happened at the two rival centres, I found myself coming out with a conclusion I hadn't been aware I was building up to.

'I think it's going to happen soon. That's why Lin wanted me to see the support he's getting. He's going to take the risk and catch the government on the hop. They think they've got three weeks, and can carry on trying to rally support. And he's going to jump.'

'But that doesn't really make sense,' Alyssa said. 'It's much too much of a risk, before Lin has got the amount of support he needs.'

'But suppose the figures this Hong Kong chap showed me aren't the up-to-date ones? Suppose they've got more support than they're letting on? So it wasn't that they wanted to scare Madame Wu about how well they're doing, but wanted to hide how well they're doing. So she'll hit them too late.'

Alyssa did not say anything.

'I think I'm going to start hanging out at Lin's place tomorrow morning, more or less full time,' I said.

'What about me? What about Gary?'

'You're too fragile,' I said. 'And we need you to hang around in the background, Gary, to give us the necessary protection.'

He nodded, but she didn't.

'You don't go anywhere I don't go. I'm the boss. I'm telling you.'

'If you can eat a decent meal and hold it down, then you can come. Otherwise it's just me.'

'Of course I can hold it down.'

That evening Gary had to go and see a relative of his who worked in Beijing. And since Alyssa seemed to have improved, we sat down to a decent Chinese meal in the hotel restaurant – nice and close to her room if she had to make a sudden exit.

I persuaded her to lay off the more robust dishes and order something fairly bland, mostly chicken and white fish. She did keep them down.

'You see – no problem at all. After this I'll get a decent night's sleep, and then we'll be all ready for the morning.'

'You sound like someone's mum.'

She gave an exasperated snort.

69

Things were changing at Lin's house. The driveway was too full of black Mercs and assorted four-by-fours for our taxi to enter. So we had to pay the driver off and walk up the steep approach to the door.

Inside, the place was as busy as an ants' nest. No one took any notice of the two of us. It was clear that a lot of the people were newcomers who had spotted a bandwagon and wanted to climb aboard. Most were delegates from the distant provinces, but there were also quite a few Chinese journalists hanging around too.

Don't think that because they've grown up in an authoritarian system, all Chinese journalists simply pander to the Party line. Plenty do, some don't. This lot seemed quite sharp. And what I noticed was that they didn't hang out in groups, checking every-thing with each other and making up quotes. They swarmed around like wasps. Some even started questioning Alyssa and me, though I shrugged and said they'd have to speak English; and when one of them did, I said I was from Croatia and couldn't understand what he was saying.

There didn't seem to be much chance of getting in to see Lin Lifang. Even his chief of staff was too busy to see us. We had to queue for twenty minutes to speak to his secretary.

'Is there much point in hanging on here?' Alyssa asked.

'Oh well, if you're not feeling well, we can go back to the hotel.'

'I'm absolutely fine. No problem. I just wondered . . .'

'Methinks the lady doth protest too much.'

'You and your fucking quotations. I've read just as much as you, you know.'

'Yes, but you don't trade on it. That's your big mistake.'

Suddenly there was a lot of pushing and shoving, and the crowd pulled back to allow a large, well-built man through.

'Who's that?' I asked one of the delegates from the outback; I preferred talking to them because they tended to be easy-going. If I talked to a journalist, there was always the danger that they would start asking me who I was.

'Chen Huning,' said the hayseed, in an impressed kind of way.

The name was familiar, but I wasn't sure how. I'd have to ask one of the journalists, after all. Yet even when I did, I couldn't work out who Chen was; and I'd never heard of the committee on which he seemed to be a big noise. Still, there was no doubt that he drew a lot of water. He was ushered in to Lin Lifang's office straight away; no waiting to speak to the secretary for him.

We milled around aimlessly for a long time. Waiting is to journalists what scales are to a pianist or stretching to a runner: boring, the reverse of glamorous, yet inescapable. Alyssa and I talked about office politics, and from time to time I tried to get into conversation with the characters who were milling round us. Like waiting, it's part of the job.

The house was hot and airless – they seemed to feel they had to keep all the doors and windows closed, and there was a definite smell of people who hadn't got round to showering that morning. Over the heads of the crowd smoke erupted occasionally, where someone was using an e-cigarette. I was getting desperate for a beer and a chance to sit down. Plus I needed to use the loo, though by this time it would be getting pretty rank.

After a long time a young, self-important gopher pushed his way through the crowd.

'Mr Lin would like to see you,' he said to me.

He led the way back through the suits. I apologised as I pushed past them: you never know under what circumstances you'll see people like this again, after all. The gopher knocked reverentially on the door.

'Ah, welcome. I'm sorry to have kept you waiting so long.'

Lin was at his most effusive; it looked as though things must be going well for him. 'May I introduce Chen Huning, chairman of the ways and means committee?'

Or something; to be honest I find Chinese bureaucratic titles hard to get a grip on.

'This is Mr Jon Swift – one of the world's most famous journalists.'

Lin always played up my value to other Chinese people, I noticed, while retaining a kind of mocking note for my private benefit.

'And his producer, Ms Alyssa.'

She shook Chen's hand warmly.

Chen was the opposite of Lin Lifang. He ignored me and focused all his attention on Alyssa. He probably hadn't met a black woman before, and certainly not one in any position of authority. And of course I could see why he was interested in her: the crisp white shirt she was wearing, her long, clever, mobile face, eyes as dark as obsidian.

'To be frank, everything is going rather well here,' Lin said, addressing me.

'So why not record a quick interview with us now?' Alyssa asked.

He hummed and hawed at first, but that gave me the impression that he'd been waiting to be asked and was happy to agree – yet didn't want to seem too eager.

I won't go through the interview word for word, but directly he opened his mouth I could see he wasn't going to be boring and platitudinous, in the way most Chinese politicians are. They're so anxious not to make a mistake they stick rigidly to the script.

Lin didn't have a script. He just had a great deal of ambition, and a certain amount of probably ersatz passion. The combination made for interesting listening. Most communist Chinese leaders hint vaguely at things, and you have to examine their speeches with immense care for several days afterwards to find out what they really mean.

Not so Lin.

The current Party leadership had failed the country in various ways, he said. It had attracted large amounts of criticism abroad for its repressive approach, particularly towards Hong Kong; and there was too much corruption at the very top of the Party. As a result, he'd obtained enough support to call for an emergency meeting of the Central Committee to be held in a week's time. Chen Huning – Alyssa did a classy pan from Lin to Chen, who nodded; then she panned back again to Lin – had just received notification from the committee that the meeting would take place.

I tried to get Lin to say that he and his friends would be tabling a motion of no confidence in the leadership, but he was far too slippery for that.

'Measures appropriate to the situation will be taken at the meeting,' was the most I could get out of him. He stonewalled everything else.

Even so, it was good stuff, but when I rang London to see if they might be interested in a quick news piece about it, there were no takers.

'To be honest, it sounds a bit too "Inside Cricket" for us,' said the editor I spoke to. He meant it was too boringly detailed. I shrugged. If you're a foreign correspondent, this kind of response is something you get used to.

70

As the days went by, though, the programme editors became more interested in what was happening in China. I suppose they'd read something in the *Guardian*. Now there were slightly tetchy calls asking when I was going to file a story. Sometimes they'd forget Beijing was eight hours ahead of them, so they'd call me during the early hours of the morning. Two different people suggested it might be a good idea to get an interview with the person who was challenging the leadership.

When the interview was broadcast, it caused a sensation. Detachments of foreign journalists appeared at Lin's headquarters demanding to be given interviews. Lin's people told them it was impossible, so they turned on me, implying that I was behaving in an unprofessional fashion. Alyssa got into regular shouting matches, particularly with the French and Italian journalists.

The members of the Central Committee flooded into town, and we filmed them arriving at the airport and at the big railway stations, and going to the big tailors to be fitted for their free suits. There weren't many women members of the committee, but those who turned up looked good in their local costumes. The one topic of conversation everywhere was Lin's chance of success. As a sign that things were hotting up, he beefed up his security detail at least five-fold. We had real problems getting in now, and Lin was so busy he often couldn't see us. The pack of journalists hanging round enjoyed that.

Lin refused to say publicly that he was getting the support he'd need for victory. His officials wouldn't speak to the press either – not even to confirm that he was pushing for a vote of no confidence. The meeting was, they said, merely for the members of the Central Committee to be able to express their concerns about the worsening situation in the country.

Newspapers slavishly loyal to the government were going crazy. As far as I could see, none of them actually mentioned Lin Lifang by name or used the expression 'vote of no confidence'; but there were allegations about foreign influence and dark doings. The *Global Times* went as far as suggesting that teams of Western officials based themselves at Lin Lifang's headquarters and were in hourly contact with their masters at home; something I particularly tried not to be.

The evenings were more difficult than the days, because small groups of Western journalists would hang out at our hotel in the hope of pumping me about what was going on. I'm a moderately sociable sort, so I'd go and sit down with them – until Alyssa took charge. I suppose she thought I was too gabby, especially if I'd had a few Tsingtaos too many. She'd remind me that we had to do a phone interview upstairs, and she'd drag me away, leaving my glass unfinished on the bar. It was like being married.

As the special session of the Central Committee got closer, the interest in London grew exponentially. Two days before the session was due to take place, the guards at the outer gate to Lin's house wouldn't even let me in; and I could see that the crowds of hangers-on had entirely evaporated.

I'd only seen Madame Wu once after my interview with Lin. She asked me some searching questions, though it was obvious that she didn't really understand anything about Lin's campaign. She seemed to think his opposition to the government was in some way ideological; maybe because he'd flirted with those Mao-era songs and slogans, back in Huzhang. But I'd seen him go through some radical changes in the thirty years since Tiananmen Square, and it didn't seem ideological to me: just the reactions of someone who thinks he's spotted a horse that might carry him to ultimate power, and has jumped on its back.

'But of course he has political responses,' Madame Wu replied crossly, looking more like Rosa Klebb than ever. 'His father was a close companion of the Chairman, and Comrade Lin was strongly influenced by him. And now we have grounds for thinking that Comrade Lin is in touch with Western intelligence.'

'Any particular bit of it?'

She said nothing for a while; then she said, as though she was letting loose an insult, 'The British.'

'Oh come on, I don't think that's at all likely.'

'We have reasons for thinking so.'

I'd actually managed to tell Lin about this exchange in person, a day or two before the lock-down at his headquarters.

He laughed. 'Why the British? Because I have my suits made in Savile Row?'

'Or maybe because you passed them a message through me.'

He half-lifted himself out of his seat. 'You told her?'

'No, no, no, I give you my word that I haven't spoken to anyone about it. Not even my colleague, Alyssa.'

'Your word as a gentleman?'

It seemed ludicrous, in an era when a gentleman is mostly just thought of as someone with a posh accent who'll sell anything to anyone. But of course I gave him my word. And it happened to be one hundred per cent true.

He sat back in his chair with a smile. 'I believe you, Jon. You've always been a friend to me. And now, if you don't mind . . .'

That was the last time I ever saw him face to face.

71

The big morning came. At six o'clock, with the city dark and empty, Alyssa, Gary and I met up in the hotel lobby and were driven down to the south side of Tiananmen Square. There we got out and joined the queue of staff members and journalists who would be heading into the Great Hall of the People. For twenty minutes we shuffled forward slowly in the cold, until we reached the head of the queue and were searched. Alyssa had her handbag and phone; I just had a notebook, fountain pen and phone. Gary's small camera took a bit longer, but we were through within five minutes, and started walking across the vastness of Tiananmen Square.

This was where I'd spent all my days, and some of my nights, back in May and early June of 1989. And I'd had Lin Lifang by my side to translate and explain. Now, three decades later, I was going to see whether he might become the next leader of China.

By Christ, I'm nervous, I thought. Alyssa said nothing but I was certain she felt the same. Not so Gary. I'd been with him in gun battles, bomb explosions, mass arrests and artillery barrages, and he always looked the same: earnest, perhaps, but never nervous.

The cold cut through my coat, and the sharp wind froze my ears. In 1989, it had been too hot for me to wear a jacket. How active I'd been then. And now? I might not even live through the day, I thought, if things turn really nasty. But that was no way to approach a moment of history.

We strode up the wide steps to the main entrance. The delegates were starting to arrive, but they were channelled into the right-hand side of the entrance by a cordon. They looked straight ahead, not talking, frowning with the seriousness of deciding their nation's future.

I wanted to talk to one or two of them as Gary filmed them, but Alyssa warned me brusquely that it was too risky: if we got thrown out, we'd miss the whole thing.

Now I wish I'd taken no notice of her and we'd been thrown out like she said. But you never know what's waiting for you, just around the corner.

There are, I suppose, hundreds of meeting-rooms and offices in the Great Hall of the People. Somewhere among them is the room where Chairman Mao used to sleep all day long, while groups of young girls were kept ready for when he woke up and wanted them. His teeth were greenish black and he never used to wash. 'I bathe myself in my women,' he used to say.

Essentially the Great Hall is a huge theatre. There's room on the stage for thousands of delegates, with the top leaders sitting at the front, looking out over the audience. The audience sit in the stalls and the dress circle; and above them are the official journalists, whose job it is to regurgitate everything that's said onstage, and not, of course, to deviate from it, if they know what's good for them.

Except when the people on the stage disagreed among themselves. Today, it seemed, we were going to see that happen.

Most of the Chinese journalists had got there early and now sat in their dozens in the steep rows above us, chatting or reading or dozing. It wasn't easy to find three seats together, but finally we saw some in the row that in a Western theatre would be 'G'.

There'd be no need for Gary to film the action on stage, because the whole thing was going to be broadcast live to the nation and the world by Chinese Central TV, and we would just use their pictures. Instead he got loads of cutaway shots of journalists and officials, and even of me scribbling away in my notebook.

Several television monitors showed us what was being pumped out: essentially, just the stage with a growing number of formal-looking characters in dark suits and red ties, and the occasional woman. The Chinese Communist Party is pretty much stuck in the 1970s.

Usually, there would be a set programme for the meetings, and everything including the speeches was timed with the greatest precision; which is helpful if you want to go to the gents and still get back for the big moment. Today, though, no one knew what the big moment was, or when it would be. There was loud chatter from everyone around us and in the stalls below, and a lot of excitement. It was like listening to kids settling down in their seats at a panto, before the curtain goes up.

On the stage, the delegates were all assembled. Like the journalists in the press gallery, they'd started off by greeting each other and talking, but now the seriousness of the situation was starting to get to them. They went quiet.

There was no sign of the president. Could he conceivably stay away, when the session that challenged his hold on power was just about to start? All round us, the journalists were starting to discuss it in low voices.

Then they went silent again. Yet another dark-suited figure was coming onto the stage from the wings: Lin Lifang.

There was total silence at first, and then applause and cheering from some parts of the hall. Lin walked along the line of senior officials, not looking at any of them, and went straight to the empty seat near the far end reserved for him. In the press gallery people started talking animatedly, and there was even applause from some of the journalists.

Still no sign of the president.

At that point, the live television feed was cut. All round us in the gallery the monitors went blank. Madame Wu, in a severe black trouser suit, walked onto the stage with five large men in suits.

They walked fast in a phalanx to where Lin was sitting, and she leant over him. There was the briefest exchange between them. Lin stood up with a faint half-smile on his face. No one laid a hand on him, but they surrounded him as he walked off stage left. There was shouting and whistling from his supporters on the steep rows of seats.

Then there was silence.

We'd just witnessed the collapse of a coup d'état, and a counter-coup by the leadership. There would be no vote on the pro-Lin motion. No wonder the president hadn't shown up; he'd wanted to keep clear of the whole business.

For want of anything better to do, the delegates started to get up and wander out of the theatre. What they, and we, didn't know was that every delegate had to pass through a narrow gateway set up outside the various exits into the grand lobby; and their electronic passes were checked there. Those who supported the leadership were allowed to leave through the main entrance and head out into Tiananmen Square; those who were known to have supported Lin Lifang and his motion of no confidence in the leadership were ushered quickly to the side exits to the square, where a fleet of buses was waiting for them. No force was used.

The delegates obediently climbed onto the buses and waited to be driven off to be interrogated by the Ministry of State Security.

The three of us found it hard to work out what to do. We were still sitting in our seats when Gary spotted a group of four security agents in identical coats and scarves erupting into the press gallery, just as the first bewildered hacks were starting to make their way out. The pushing and shoving attracted Gary's attention, and he saw one of the spooks pointing up at us.

'We've got to get out,' I said.

We could of course simply have sat there and waited to be arrested. Maybe that would have been the sensible thing to do. But it goes against the grain, if you know you're being hunted. We just followed our instinct, and got out of there.

A look round showed that no other State Security goons were arriving, so we pushed our way against the flow to the exit at the top right of the press gallery. It was a long way away, and there were loads of offended hacks who had to make way for us, but the goons had far more ground to cover – twenty or so more rows of seats, steeply arranged, with dozens of journalists trying to push their way out. I reckoned we had about a minute's lead.

Funny how we all seem to have enough mental capacity to carry out calculations like this, even though my chest was heaving with exertion and I was getting heartily sick of saying '*bào qiàn*' to everyone I bumped into. At one stage my coat got caught on an armrest – these things never happen to people in movies – and something ripped as I pulled it free. By then Alyssa was in the gangway and stretching her long legs to get to the exit at the top, and Gary was following close behind.

I chased after them, puffing a bit. The goons were still some way back, ensnared in departing journalists. Their faces were looking up at us, and they didn't seem happy.

We reached the exit at last. By chance a cleaner had left a bucket and broom outside on the landing, so Gary was able to jam the broomstick through the handles of the doors. It wouldn't hold them more than a few seconds, but every little bit mattered. While I was watching Gary working away with the broomstick, I went back over my memory of being behind the scenes here before. Thirty years before.

Actually, I'd been telling Alyssa something about it when we were crossing Tiananmen Square, but she had that 'Is this another one of your stories?' look on her face, and I gave up before the key bit. A couple of days after I'd arrived in Beijing in May 1989, Mikhail Gorbachev, the President of the Soviet Union, had come here to kiss and make up with the Chinese Communist Party at a big ceremony in the Great Hall of the People. The only problem was that thousands upon thousands of Chinese students were swarming all over the square. Poor kids – they thought old Gorby could help China turn democratic with a few words in Deng Xiaoping's ear, when he was finding it impossible to do it at home.

It was hard enough to get the Gorbachevs in their Russian ZIL through the crowds and into the Great Hall of the People; and by the time the big occasion was over, the crowd had quadrupled in size. They weren't in any way hostile, but there were just too many of them to get through. And to add to the fact that they'd already lost, the Chinese security people decided they'd have to take Gorby down into the bowels of the building and slip him out of a side door, right round the back. From there the ZIL whisked him to the safety of the leadership zone at Zhongnanhai, Gorbachev muttering irritably the whole way, and Mrs G trying to hush him up and stop him giving offence.

How do I know all this? Because my cameraman and I were with the Gorbachevs and their officials on the long dark cobwebby trek through the basement. We'd been filming the meeting with Deng, and when Gorby was whisked out no one liked to stop us from going with him. Maybe they thought we were from Soviet TV. Anyway, the best thing was, even after thirty years I could still remember how to get down there.

'I've been down this way,' I said, pressing the button on a little side-lift and hoping to God it was the right one. 'When I was here with Gorbachev.'

'I don't think . . .'

But the lift arrived. What was more, we could hear the goons banging their shoulders against the door we'd come through. Soon there'd be a splintering sound from the broomstick.

I pushed the bottom button.

At that point Gary dropped his bombshell.

'I'm staying.'

I knew that look on his face. When Gary has decided something, there's no changing his mind.

'I'll hold the door, and that'll give you a chance to get away. Look – I'm Chinese, and I've got full accreditation. There's nothing they can do to me.'

It wasn't true, but at that moment the lift arrived, and the goons seemed to be yelling and pushing harder than ever. The broomstick began to give way.

I grabbed Alyssa and pushed her into the lift, and followed her in. I saw Gary's shoulder holding back the door. It couldn't last more than a few seconds.

Moments later we were in the basement. I didn't know whether we were in the right part of it, but at least no one was shouting and screaming at us.

When we got out and found ourselves in a corridor, I was going to turn the overhead lights on, but Alyssa shook her head. She was

343

right, of course. Our phones would give us enough light to see our way.

We didn't run, but walked fast, side by side, past miles of cupboards and filing cabinets, and stuff that people had dumped here in the past. I saw at least one poster with Mao's big face on it, and there were even some pictures of Lin Biao – Mao's eternally faithful sidekick, who eventually abandoned China and tried to fly to Russia, for whom he'd been working secretly for years; he died in the resulting crash. By God, I thought as we hurried along, there must be some interesting stuff here, if you only had the time.

I made the mistake of saying this out loud. Alyssa just looked at me.

The thing about corridors is that they always go somewhere. And eventually – God knows how long it took us – we came to an exit.

It was padlocked.

By now, though, I was getting into a Jason Bourne frame of mind. A little way back I'd spotted an iron rod, leaning against a cupboard. I ran back and got it, then jammed it into the chain which belonged to the padlock, and turned it a couple of times. Nothing happened.

'Oh, for Christ's sake,' Alyssa snorted.

She grabbed the iron rod from me, twisted it another turn, pulled it in a different direction from the one I'd tried, and even caught the padlock before it fell so as not to draw even more attention to us.

It wasn't an outer door, just an internal one that led to another corridor. But I could see a door at the end of that, with daylight shafting through underneath it.

'Not fucking bad,' I said.

She was still holding the iron rod, but there wasn't any need for it now. The door was one of those you get in cinemas, with a bar you have to push. I did so. And there we were in God's bright light, side by side, Alyssa still wielding the iron rod like Boadicea in her chariot.

Nobody was around. It was hard for a moment to work out where we were, but it looked as though we were somewhere on the far side of the main entrance to the building, with the Great Hall lying between us and Tiananmen Square. Perfect.

72

'Where on earth do we go from here?'

We had to find some way of getting back to our base so that we could edit our pictures and satellite them to London.

'Let's head for the avenue,' I told Alyssa.

It was close by, and almost empty. All the action was still going on inside the building or in Tiananmen Square, and no one was taking any notice of the back of the building. We walked down to the avenue as quickly as we could. There are lines of metal railings down the sides and middle to stop jaywalkers, so we had to walk a hundred yards or so away from the square to the nearest pedestrian crossing. Still nobody was following us.

'But I don't see where you want us to go after we've crossed over.'

There was a tetchiness in her voice.

'Down there.'

I pointed to a tree-lined road that ran northwards alongside the edge of the Forbidden City.

It took us a bit longer to get to it, but by now I was starting to relax. No sirens, no police cars, no signs of pursuit. We slowed down a bit. That was a mistake.

Then we began to hear a siren. In China, you're never alone. One of the many unattractive sides of Marxism–Leninism is that everyone is a snooper, and someone must have spotted a tall Westerner and a black woman and decided that we might be interlopers.

We hurried down a side street where there weren't any shops, just a little network of *hutongs* of the kind that are mostly being pulled down. That was good and bad. Good, because it gave us the possibility of places to duck into. Bad, because if we took a wrong turn into a dead end we'd be caught like rats.

'I don't understand why we've got to run. Why don't we just hand ourselves in.'

'Look, if we get picked up now there's a good chance the State Security will take us away and interrogate us at their leisure, and might try to make us give evidence against Lin. We wouldn't be able to see a lawyer, or anyone from the embassy. But if we can just keep out of their hands and get to the bureau, they'll never bust in there and arrest us without a proper warrant. We'll have the time to get on to London and the embassy and a lawyer or two, and there's a good chance that State Security will decide to lay off us. It'd be bad PR otherwise.'

'Good thinking, Batman.'

The prospect of action always seemed to bring out the best in her.

By now we were halfway down a long, narrow street with entries to *siheyuans*, traditional courtyard houses, on either side of us. Alyssa had put a scarf over her head, so she was a bit less noticeable. There wasn't much I could do about my appearance.

Some of the *siheyuans* were still being used as family houses; others had been converted into workshops or garages. My plan, inasmuch as I had one, was to find someone who seemed likely to be sympathetic, and tell them I wasn't feeling well. That would give us a chance to get off the street, and Alyssa would be able to call the bureau and get them to send a car for us. Everything would depend on the person we came across.

Alyssa thought it was a good idea. Given what happened next, that's a weight off my conscience.

We found a particularly attractive place, with an entrance gate that had once been painted the traditional vermilion, though that had faded years ago; it still had a copper door-knocker, now green with verdigris. Outside was a single bashed-about stone lion; the other one had disappeared. The gate was open, and the traditional screen wall, which gives the family privacy from the street, had obviously been knocked down. There were piles of junk dotted around the courtyard.

'What do you reckon about this one?'

Alyssa shrugged and nodded. There was no telling.

We went in and looked round. The place seemed quiet. A little brown dog walked over and sniffed at my shoes, and then a girl of around seven poked her head out of one of the doors and yelled for her mother. A woman who looked to be in her late fifties came out; surely not the mother? She looked us up and down suspiciously, and I rolled out my inadequate Chinese.

'I'm feeling ill. Can my wife and I sit down here for a bit while we call a taxi back to our hotel?'

I didn't tell Alyssa what I'd called her.

The woman seemed reluctant, so I did something which, with hindsight, was probably a mistake: I pulled out a roll of hundred-yuan notes and gave her a couple.

'Maybe you could make us some tea and give us somewhere to sit?'

Two hundred yuan was an absurdly large amount of money to give her; maybe I was thinking of the tax I paid to Mr Chang at the hotel whenever I saw him. Anyway, she grabbed the notes and stuffed them into her bosom so deep you'd need equipment to get them out. And without smiling or even saying anything she pushed a couple of plastic stools in our direction. Then she went back into her den. The kid stayed looking at us, and the dog curled up and went to sleep.

'Seems OK,' I said cautiously to Alyssa; but that's not what I felt.

I didn't like the look of the woman, and the heaps around us stank. I saw now that they were piles of old rags.

Nothing happened.

'I'd better get us a taxi,' Alyssa said after a while. 'But I'll need the address here.'

I walked over to the doorway where the woman had vanished, and pushed a grubby curtain aside.

She was on the phone. And the moment she saw me, she dropped it.

'Well, I didn't know who you were,' she said defensively. At least I think that's what she said.

I ducked out again and called to Alyssa, 'She's called the police.'

And at that moment we heard a siren at the far end of the street.

No good running out there. Alyssa jumped up and grabbed my hand, and we dashed across the courtyard and through a gateway opposite. There was no way out, but the wall was only about seven feet high and made of those grey *hutong* bricks.

'Over here.'

I made a stirrup of my hands, and Alyssa hoisted herself up onto the top of the wall and dropped down on the other side. I took a lot longer and was a good deal less graceful, and landed painfully on my side and shoulder. By now there was shouting in the courtyard, but we picked ourselves up and ran down a narrow passageway between two walls. At the far end was a wooden gate, which was open.

We found ourselves in another open area with a building on one side of it. An empty building, apparently. You don't have the luxury, at a time like that, of checking it out. We made a dash for it.

Bad choice.

Inside, five men of different ages were lying on the floor, mostly asleep. I said I was sorry, but going back outside seemed a bad idea. They were completely bemused, mostly by Alyssa, and we hopped over their prone bodies and pushed through the door at the back. It was a toilet, one of those porcelain holes in the ground, and it really stank.

This was no time to be delicate, though. There was a window with no glass in it, and I forced the upper part of my body through it and came down hard on the outside, head downwards. Then I reached in and pulled Alyssa through.

'Ugh!' she said – and again that grin, as though this was the kind of thing she was happiest doing.

Another courtyard opened up in front of us, with a grand house at the far end of it: two storeys, with one of those long, sloping hipped roofs you get on traditional Chinese houses. You know, the sort with little glazed figures in a line down them.

By now we could hear the police after us, shouting loudly and not sure where to go.

'We'll have to hide in that house,' Alyssa said in my ear, and we ran across to the main door.

Thank God, the place was empty. There wasn't even any furniture. We crashed up the dusty stairs into the upper room, and flattened ourselves against the wall behind the doorway.

Policemen's boots sounded loud in the courtyard.

'Try there!' one of them shouted.

We were caught.

Then I saw the skylight which someone had untraditionally cut into the roof.

'We can get out there,' I said in a whisper. Alyssa nodded.

We tiptoed over to the skylight, while the sound of baffled men below rose up through the floorboards. It opened. I made a back for Alyssa, and she clambered onto it and out onto the roof on the far side, so no one in the courtyard could see her. She reached down and gave me a hand up. It wasn't easy, at my age and in my physical condition, but you can do amazing things if you're scared; and I was fucking terrified. I hauled myself up, got a knee on the outside edge of the skylight and got myself through.

So there we were, hunched down on the roof so we weren't visible from below, and I closed the skylight as quietly as I could. With luck, the police chasing us would take a look round the room and go away.

Luck wasn't with us that day, though.

I heard them charge into the room we had just left, and then there was shouting: they'd spotted the skylight, and guessed we might have climbed through it. Not really surprising, I suppose. One of the cops climbed out, rather as we had, and looked me right in the eyes. I saw his mouth open in surprise, and he started yelling.

'Let's get down that way,' Alyssa said, gesturing at the eave that pointed elegantly towards the ground. She was scared, I'm sure, just like me; but unlike me she was excited too.

There didn't seem to be anyone down there, on that side of the house. I nodded. It didn't look too difficult. Chinese eaves have loads of traditional terracotta figures on them – dragons, phoenixes, lions, that kind of thing, all lined up one after the other.

They're supposed to protect the house from fire and drive away demons.

Alyssa went first, crawling down the roof on all fours, and reached the eave she'd pointed to. It was only about fifteen feet off the ground. She grabbed on to one of the figures and looked back at me with an encouraging grin.

'It's easy,' she said, and let herself down further, using one of the figures.

It just snapped off – weakened by time and weather, I suppose – and she slipped over the edge. I can still hear the sound she made, landing.

I scrabbled down the eave and looked over. She was lying on the ground, sprawled out.

'Don't worry, I'm coming down,' I said, and swung off the eave close to its lowest point, and let myself drop. It can't have been more than six feet. She'll be all right, I told myself: it's such a short way down. I rolled over, picked myself up and ran over to her all in one movement. It's all right. It must be all right.

But she wasn't moving. I couldn't see anything wrong, except that dreadful stillness. It must be all right. It must be.

I threw myself down beside her, and put my arm over her as if I could ward off what had already happened. But it was too late. A lifetime too late.

Angry, frightened, a bit crazy, I put my face close to hers. She just had a faint expression of surprise.

It took a couple of the police to pull me off her. One of them put a couple of fingers on her carotid artery, then turned to look at his mate. And he did that thing they always do in films: he shook his head.

'For Christ's sake, don't be so fucking stupid. She's all right. I know she's all right. It's just a short drop.'

The woman who'd called the police came up to gawp.

'You fucking, fucking bitch,' I screamed at her.

But she didn't understand or react, any more than Alyssa did.

They called an ambulance. I refused to go with them in their car, and when the ambulance came I told them that whatever they did to me I was going with her. They looked at each other. But Chinese police are human like the rest of us, and they didn't stop me when the ambulance crew came and picked her up very gently and put her on a stretcher. And all the way to the hospital they let me hold her hand.

As though that could do any good.

73

I don't really know much about what happened after that. Everything seemed to merge together – lights, and a bit of shouting, and someone putting a blanket over me, and taking me somewhere and trying to talk to me and giving it up as a bad job because I didn't answer. I mean, what was there to say?

And after that I must have had some kind of fit or something, because as far as I could tell there was an entire day I couldn't account for: like being on a bender, only without the headache when I woke up.

I was in an institutional bed, which I assumed was in a hospital, and a faintly familiar face was leaning over me and asking if I was all right.

'Of course I'm not fucking all right,' I said; and then the reason for it came rushing back to me, as bad as a kick in the guts, and I suppose I started crying. Me, at my age.

'I'm really sorry,' Gary said gently.

I gripped his hand as a wave of self-pity came over me.

'Gary,' I said, to fix the name in my own mind.

'Don't worry about anything. We've got it sorted. You'll be out of here when you're able to move.'

'And go where?'

There wasn't anywhere I wanted to go, now that this had happened. And I found I wasn't prepared to put into words what 'this' was.

'London. No one's going to press charges, or anything like that.'

I started to remember what had happened when I'd seen him last.

'Are you OK?'

'Oh sure. I told them I was trying to stop you.'

'They believed that?'

'Not really. But they were so angry with each other for not catching you, they eventually let me go.'

But I hardly registered what he was saying. I was thinking about other things ... and that I'd never get over what had happened.

Gary seemed to understand this, and he stayed quietly in the corner, making sure that I had everything I needed. Then someone came and gave me a couple of little blue pills to take. Quite soon after that, everything faded out and I didn't have any more thinking to do.

I was feeling woozy when I came to; that was the pills. There wasn't anything wrong with me physically, except for a few bumps and scrapes, which someone had painted with yellow stuff and bound up with bandages. The trouble was all in my head, and no amount of bandages could sort that out.

I stared at the ceiling for a while. The girls at the bureau had sent me a big bunch of flowers, which someone had stuffed into an inadequate jug. The smell of roses filled the room and, in my bemused state, started to fill my thoughts, a bit like the young Proust.

I detest those awful formulaic detective stories where the entire cast of characters minus the one who's snuffed it gather in the library and the detective explains to them who the murderer is. But I had the time now to think things over, and it was a relief not thinking about anything else.

Someone had betrayed Lin Lifang, and someone else had betrayed me, and that had led directly to the death of Alyssa. I had to fight the effects of the pills and the smell of the roses: lovely big red and yellow roses, with long thorny stems, whose influence I had to ignore if I was to think properly. I shifted my position so I couldn't see them.

I had helped Lin to keep Raj's lot informed, all those weeks ago in Oxford. They had known everything he was planning to do, and the poor sap had thought they would help him. Well, who knows? If he'd won I'm certain they would have lucked out. But they must also have been keeping in touch with Madame Wu's lot. Just as I was. The difference was, I'd told Lin what I was doing, and the spooks hadn't. I wondered how long they'd kept up the pretence of being on his side; right up to the end, I suppose.

And Alyssa? And me? We were just collateral damage. If that bit of roof furniture hadn't broken when she grabbed it, we'd have been fine. In gaol, maybe, but probably not for long. What had we done, after all? Been eyewitnesses at a coup, that was all. Or rather, at the prevention of a coup. An entirely peaceful affair, and bloodless except – but I didn't want to go there. I wasn't strong enough to deal with that spreading pool the colour of the red roses.

Now, somehow, Raj was sitting beside me.

'Have you been here long?'

'Not really. Just popped in to see how you were.'

I couldn't see the point of beating about the bush.

'You were playing poor old Lin off against the government, weren't you?'

A pained expression came across his rather kid-like face, and he made a little twiddly gesture with his finger that I'd seen in so many rooms in so many dictatorships over the years. It meant that there were mikes in the room, and people might be listening.

Then, to do the lad credit, he gave me the faintest of nods, and turned down the corners of his mouth in a way that seemed to say, 'I'm sorry about that.'

Item two on the agenda: 'Why aren't I in gaol?'

'Part of the arrangement we've made with the authorities here. You're free to leave the country whenever you like.'

'Gary Sung as well?'

'Absolutely.'

Item three: 'And what about Alyssa?'

'We've been on to her next of kin – or at least your people in London have. No close relatives. She used to have a boyfriend but he faded out. They want her ashes brought back and scattered somewhere there.'

'So when's the . . . cremation going to be?'

I found it hard to get the word out.

'Yesterday.'

They don't mess around. Dictatorships, I mean. Or spies, for that matter.

'I went. I thought you'd want me to. Your colleague Gary went too.'

I didn't know what to say or do. Raj could see that, so he muttered some excuse and left the room.

I just lay there. How could all this have happened? How could a woman so brilliant and full of life be smiling at me and climbing on a roof with the grace and agility of a mountaineer one instant, and be dead and turned to ashes the next? And then, inevitably, what was going to happen to me, alone and a prisoner, with my job about to be taken away from me?

I promised you, didn't I, that I'd be completely honest with you? Well, I am being. I mean, I know that whining about myself at a time like this is pretty low, but it's what I felt.

I couldn't even bear to stay in bed, so I managed to get into a sitting position, my head feeling as big and as tender as an overinflated balloon, then got my legs over the edge of the bed, and stood up. It was like being on a fairground ride, with the room careering round me, but even so I made it over to the window. The room came to a halt. There was a car park outside, with half-a-dozen police cars in it and policemen standing round talking and, yes, looking up at me. I went back to bed.

'Can I come in?' Raj put his head round the door.

'Sure.'

The fairground ride came to an end.

'Richard's himself again,' I said.

'Sorry? Who's Richard?'

'It's a quote. Laurence Olivier stuck it into his film about Richard III. Shakespeare didn't write it.'

'I honestly don't know what you're talking about. Can I get you anything?'

But there wasn't anything I needed or wanted or would know how to use, so I asked, 'Am I a prisoner here?'

'I thought I'd explained it, only you were probably a bit too woozy,' Raj said patiently. 'Under the terms of the arrangement you can fly back to London whenever you want. They'll even pay for your ticket.'

I thought about that for a moment. My bosses would go crazy if they knew that the Chinese Ministry of State Security was paying for anything, let alone my trip home. Suppose the *Daily Mail* found out?

I explained the problem.

'Well, we'll pay then.'

'Same difference, I'm afraid. We can't take money from spooks. I'll just call the office in London and they'll book me on a flight.'

'I'm afraid they've impounded your phone. Hers too.'

He obviously didn't feel that saying 'Alyssa' would help.

'You gave our phones to those bastards.'

Anger seemed to do me some good.

'I didn't give them to them. By the time I got here, both phones had gone.'

'And you didn't ask for them back.'

He had such a comical, hangdog look on his face, I couldn't yell at him any more.

'I think you'd better explain the entire deal to me.'

I won't quote him word for word. For a start, it took ages to worm it out of him, and anyway I'm sure there were lots of things he didn't tell me. But it was crystal clear that SIS had been working side by side with State Security, and I was a very small part of a much bigger story. Our spooks had clearly got an agreement with their spooks that I should be shunted off as quickly as possible, with no action taken against me for the various crimes and misdemeanours I'd committed. Which was fine for me. But . . .

'What about Terry Ho?'

'Yes, well, we asked them to let him go as part of the arrangement. They said they would, but I'm waiting for final confirmation that they're keeping to the agreement.'

'Well, you have been a little Father Christmas, haven't you?'

'Not him, really, just one of his elves.'

It was a good line, and I chuckled over it.

How, you may ask, could I laugh when that superb, vibrant woman was dead and her ashes scarcely cold? I don't know. I suppose our minds are compartmentalised sufficiently to be able to hold different emotions at the same time. Maybe, I thought, I'll take it up with the shrink I will undoubtedly need to consult when I get back to Blighty.

'I could do with a bit of kip,' I said.

Terry Ho surfaced before I left, and I was able to go and see him. His girlfriend still watched over him with the kind of pity and forgiveness I don't think I've managed to elicit from any of the women I've spent time with. He didn't look too bad, actually. I suppose as part of letting him loose on society they felt they'd better do him up a bit, like a dodgy second-hand car dealer getting an old VW ready for the showroom. A dentist had done some actually not too bad work on his teeth, thank God.

He started saying sorry the moment I set foot in the door, but I managed to shut him up.

'Look, I would have done it to you if those bastards had caught me. There's nothing I wouldn't have told them. And my teeth are in better shape than yours.'

That made him grin, and when he told his girlfriend what was so funny she smiled too, and shot me a grateful look over his head.

Gary came and took me back to the hotel.

Mr Chang was waiting to open the door to me. He must have known the whole story. When I held out the usual couple of hundred-yuan notes he actually refused to accept them.

74

Back in London I had to consult an awful lot more than a shrink, it turned out. Police, diplomats, lawyers, uncounted bureaucrats from my own outfit, and a trauma counsellor who was wished upon me. Years before I'd covered a war with him and he'd mostly stayed in the hotel. 'I need to keep in contact with the office,' he explained.

'Look,' I said to him the moment he appeared, older, more smarmy and wrinkly browed. 'If you insist on trying to counsel me I shall tell the head of whatever crap department you've emanated from that you know as much about PTSD as I know about . . .'

Only at that point my imagination let me down and I couldn't think of a subject I didn't know anything about; there are so many of them, I suppose. He gave a grin, which raised him in my estimation, and suggested that he should sit in the corner of the room for half an hour and then leave.

As for me, I lay in bed (they were putting me up in a rubbish hotel near the office, with a beautiful lobby and tiny, ill-furnished rooms) and for his benefit I sang the old Aaron Copland song.

> Yes, we're all dodgin', a dodgin', dodgin', dodgin'
> Yes, we're all dodgin' out away through the world

Well, the poor chap had a living to earn, you see, and messing about with a few heads that had already been comprehensively scrambled was by no means the worst thing he could have done. He left eventually, with another rueful smile, and I never heard any more about the possibility that I might have PTSD.

One of the first things I had to do was see Alyssa's boyfriend, the muscular, wealthy hedge-fund manager. I knew his name, Steven Mortimer, and the company he worked for, so I rang him.

I stumbled through the basics, pretty awkwardly. There was a silence at the other end. Then: 'I'm really sorry to hear all this, but I don't think there's anything more I can say. We didn't break up on very happy terms, I'm afraid.'

I stayed sitting down for a while after that. She'd given me the impression that their relationship was still active. Was that to keep me at bay? No, I don't think so. I think Alyssa simply didn't want to admit that her relationship with Mortimer was over. And she didn't see what business it was of mine, which was entirely correct, of course.

With the help of a couple of other people I managed to assemble all the materials Alyssa and I had sent back to London, including the letter to myself I'd sent while I was pretending to be Sir David Attenborough, and Lin's famous manifesto.

That was great, by the way, and it was a pity we couldn't use more than ten or fifteen seconds of it. 'I'm afraid it doesn't work,' the producer said. Producers always say that about stuff they think is boring or gets in the way.

Lin's manifesto wasn't really boring, though it was full of jargon and very wordy; what statement by the Chinese Communist Party isn't? The bit we used in our documentary was this:

We must see to it that all our cadres and all our people constantly bear in mind that ours is a big socialist country but an economically backward one, and that this is a very great contradiction. To make China strong and rich will take at least two more decades of intense effort.

But the joke was on us – on me, really. Someone pointed out that Lin had cribbed most of his manifesto from Mao Zedong's 'Little Red Book', and just smoothed the edges and brought it up to date. So the producer was right to keep it short, after all.

Altogether, though, we made a cracking documentary. Explosive stuff. It's not often you get to see the inside workings of a major coup, after all. Everything was there: Lin Lifang's challenge to the leadership, the murder of Martin Prinsett, the photo of Lin's daughter Lily taking the bottles out of the laboratory fridge and the rest of it. Lily refused to be interviewed, but her lawyer put out a statement that agreed, basically, that the person in the photo was her, but that she had no idea what the bottles were, and what had happened to them after that. It occurred to me that Lin had done his best to keep Lily out of it all.

I made it clear in the script that SIS had been playing Lin off against the leadership. There was a lot of fuss about that, and afterwards the head of SIS wrote a really nasty letter to the *capo di tutti capi*, my ultimate boss, which contained words like 'irresponsible' and 'borderline treasonous'. But I didn't mention Raj, either by name or function. I reckoned that he deserved better of me than to have his cover blown.

At the end I had to put in the business of Alyssa's death, which was really painful. Every time I tried to record the script for that bit, I choked up. But I could see everyone was getting sick of the time I was taking, so I forced myself to think about something entirely different as I read through my words; and that time I managed to get it right.

The documentary got a big audience, and loads of people sent me sympathetic emails. It won some awards, too, if that's what anyone cares about.

I reluctantly went in to work the morning after it went out, and people actually stood up and clapped, as though I'd done something worthwhile like saving the life of a friend and colleague.

After a bit, the boss sent a message to say he wanted to see me: Charles, the one who was getting rid of me, that is. The documentary had been good, he said. Well, yes, but a bit more praise wouldn't have gone amiss. He didn't seem particularly interested, though; he kept looking out of the window at the smokers standing on the pavement.

Shall I tell him now that he's the worst wanker I've ever had as a boss? I thought. Then I decided I wouldn't. Good decision, as it turned out.

'Must be good to be back,' said a familiar voice as I wandered back across the newsroom, trying not to make eye contact with anyone.

It was one of my oldest friends in this benighted place. We'd once shared the last of a bottle of Scotch while sheltering from several hours of shelling in a big empty sewage pipe somewhere north of Kabul, years before. That creates a bond between you, believe me. For a start, it means you can trust him not to glug the whole lot down before it's your turn.

'Sort of.'

He laughed. 'I saw you sitting with Laughing Boy in his office just now.'

'I was trying to see if I could chisel a few more weeks here before he chucked me out.'

'Did it work?'

'No. He was too preoccupied.'

'That's not altogether surprising. He'll be out of here before you are.'

A feeling I hadn't had for quite a long time started to come over me like a hot flush.

'Seems some top-level back-stabbing went on, and the word is, he's going. Spending more time with his family, apparently. You can only feel sorry for the family.'

Weirdly, I did. Not for the family, but for him. I knew what it was like to be eased out, to find that everything you've hoped for and planned has blown up in your face because no one gave you or your interests a single thought. Don't worry – I'm not turning mawkish. I just had a moment's empathy for him, which is a great deal more than he ever had for me, or for the other poor eejits whose careers he'd destroyed.

'When's he going?'

'End of next week, I'm told.'

I felt a bit like that character in *A Man for All Seasons* who betrayed Thomas More: the Duke of Norfolk. Later, Henry VIII sentenced him to death for treason, then died the night before the duke was to have his head chopped off. So he survived.

I might too.

I said goodbye, and drifted away in a daze. Across the room sat Brian, Charles's chief executioner. If anyone would know whether I was still for the chop, it'd be him.

'Hi, Brian – how goes it?'

But Brian had his head down, emptying out his desk and putting stuff into boxes. That meant I didn't really need an answer.

Yorick, my tomcat, remembered me. He broke out of Mrs Gomulka's arms and launched himself at me like an orange missile. His bony little head struck me on the upper thigh.

Various people had come looking for me, she said. Chinese people.

'Recently?'

No, not recently.

I pulled the urn out of my suitcase and arranged it on the mantelpiece. I suppose that proved, finally, that I was Irish at heart.

'That looks nice,' said Mrs Gomulka.

'Up to a point,' I said, and told her what it was.

She gave her notice soon after that.

75

Are there rules about where you can scatter someone's ashes? I expect so: on this side of the Irish Sea there's nothing but bloody rules about everything. Back in Dublin you could scatter all that was left of yer Da on the bar-top in Finnegan's in Dalkey, the world's finest pub, and no one would object. In fact they'd probably stand you another pint on the strength of it.

Alyssa deserved better, though. I carried the gunmetal urn around for days, trying to think where to take her. Her distant relatives were just that – distant. They didn't seem particularly interested, though they were happy to take over her flat and sell off the contents. Brockwell Park was the nearest open area to where she lived, but that didn't seem quite right, with kids kicking footballs all over the place, and some Gauleiter likely to show up during the proceedings, asking what I thought I was doing. Greenwich Park? I knew she liked it, but I was sentimental and wanted to put her where I could come and visit her often. Greenwich was much too far away for me to drop by regularly. Oxford, where I lived, wouldn't be right at all: she thought it was far too snooty.

And then I remembered sitting opposite her in the restaurant in Beijing and listening to her quote Edward Thomas:

. . . and round him, mistier,
Farther and farther, all the birds
Of Oxfordshire and Gloucestershire.

I knew now where I was going to take her. The motorway to Oxford crosses the Chilterns, and as you drive west you suddenly come through a cutting and get the whole landscape of Oxfordshire lying there ahead of you. And maybe, for all I know, Gloucestershire as well.

And so, not many days after our documentary on the fall of Lin Lifang had gone out, with Alyssa's name on the credits, I drove to the spot and opened the lid and held it high above my head; and a wonderful line of fine grey dust flew out of the urn on the wind and hung in the air for a moment like a flag in the breeze. And then it settled on the hillside. Now I could come back here to talk to her any time I chose.

76

That's not quite the end of the story. More than a year afterwards, after I'd been reinstated in my job by Charles's successor, I was taking a day off at home; and, as usual, I blocked another bid for freedom by Yorick and wandered along to the hotel where I'd bumped into Lin Lifang, all that time before. There, sitting all on her own, was Lin's daughter Lily.

'I thought I might find you here,' she said.

'Well, you have. How's Brasenose?'

'Yeah, good, thanks.'

'Molecular biology?'

'Yeah. Your documentary turned me into a bit of a target, though.'

'I'm sorry to hear that.'

'Well, now I've got political asylum and the right to remain here, so maybe it was OK in the end.'

Awkwardly, I asked her, 'Are you all right for money – the fees and all that?'

'Yes, yes, my parents set up a trust fund for me. Before, you know . . .'

I did know: before Lin's coup attempt.

I asked her how her mother, Madame Jade, was getting on in prison. She'd been sentenced to life for ordering Martin Prinsett's murder.

'I never hear from her.'

She didn't sound particularly upset.

Silence for a bit; then, 'The reason I hoped I'd bump into you was that I've just had a letter from my dad. He seems to be running everything in prison. He does a lot of reading and gardening, and he's studying calligraphy. Oh yes, and they let him wear his own clothes.'

An image of him, sitting right here at this very table in his beautiful suit, came forcefully into my mind.

'He added a bit at the end of his letter that he wanted me to show you.'

She folded it so I couldn't see the part that he'd written to her, and handed it over. His spiky writing, when I deciphered it, made him sound as jaunty as ever.

My dear Jonathan,

I just wanted you to know that I bear you not the slightest ill will for what happened to me. We have always been friends, you and I, ever since those extraordinary days in 1989. And in case it is necessary, after that session we had in my house, I would just like to confirm to you that I was not in any way responsible for the unpleasant things that happened to you and my dear friend Wei Jingyi in the place where you were both imprisoned. Please accept my word of honour on this.

I wonder, though, if you could do me a favour? I've finally persuaded the prison authorities to let me wear my own shoes, but all the shoes I had were confiscated when I was arrested and I have had to wear these grey plastic abominations which the prison gave me. Could you ask Lobb's whether they could make me a couple of pairs in oxblood? They have my lasts.

Thank you, dear friend, and please keep a friendly eye out for Lily's welfare.

Your affectionate

Lifang.

'Your dad wants me to look out for your welfare.'

'Yes, well, I can do that for myself, thank you very much. But it'd be nice if you could get him the shoes.'

Lobb's is an extraordinary place in St James's, London, where the cheapest pair of shoes they knock up for you would cut a big hole in my monthly income. When I went in there, a few days later, a man who looked like the French ambassador to the Court of St James looked down at the things I was wearing on my feet, then asked in a frosty voice how he could help me.

I told him.

Dubiously, the grandee checked through their records. Then his voice defrosted several degrees.

'Ah yes. We do indeed have the lasts for Mr Lin Lifang, and can certainly make up a couple of pairs for him. Oxblood, I think you said?'

I nodded grandly.

'We don't seem to have an address for him.'

I pulled out the piece of paper Lily had written out for me.

'Prisoner number 829476, Qincheng Facility, North Beijing.'

There were some extra postal details, which I won't trouble you with.

I thought the grandee might baulk at this. But no.

'Mr Lin is far from being the only customer we have who is experiencing temporary difficulties of this kind, sir.'

He gave my shoes one last look as I went out.

Strange, the direction life takes you, I thought as I sank a double Jameson's in a pub nearby. Not exactly an original notion, I accept, but suitable enough when I thought about my skinny translator in Tiananmen Square, and my tall, elegant pharaonic queen of a producer. I'd never see either of them again. Lin was in Qincheng for the rest of his natural life, and Alyssa was – well, I tried to brush away that last mental picture of her, and replaced it with the elegant line of grey dust curling away over the Oxfordshire hillside.

Catching the barman's eye, I put a fiver down on the bar counter and left. And, because I've always got dozens of quotations swilling around in my brain, a stray line from something else Edward Thomas wrote came floating into it:

. . . and I rose up, and knew that I was tired, and continued my journey.